BOOTLEGGER'S COVE

by

Rob Tillitz

ISBN: 1-4392-2455-2
ISBN-13: 9781439224557

Visit www.booksurge.com to order additional copies, or
www.Amazon.com.

Autographed copies from author at http://shop.robtillitz.com/main.sc

Dedicated to my Children:

Jasmer, Alison,
and Andriana

And the best deckhand <u>ever</u>:

Jeffery Jasmer Lindberg

ACKNOWLEDGEMENTS

First and foremost, I must give credit to my good friend and editor, John Timothy Miller: Thank you JT, you not only smoothed this story out, but got me, personally, on a fine pathway. You're *the best of the best*, and deserve much more credit than I am giving you here.

Kirk Charlton, my illustrator, is the finest artist I know, and I'm lucky to have his talent on pages that bear my name. He did three interior illustrations plus the two boats on the cover passing weed in a skiff.

Christina Olsen painted the lighthouse that haunts the pages that separate the Parts. She's a first rate talent, and a dear and longtime friend.

And finally, Kindra Dean did endless typing and research and has been the glue that binds this novel together. She also came up with the reverse imaging idea that made the cover look so intriguing.

There were many others who contributed to this tale, both in the organizing, and by helping mold the actual story. You know who you are, and I thank you for your participation and support.

Too, I must concede that this is a work of fiction. There are parts, places and people that resemble reality, but that is all coincidence, and a testament to my inability to make up anything more clever.

PROLOGUE

SPRING, 1992

KARACHI, PAKISTAN

"SO YOUR NAVY will bring the hash out to my boat?" Bubba asked Mohammed Shamir Jang, somewhat incredulously. He'd heard that the Pakistani Navy participated in the loading of hashish, but was nonetheless surprised when Mohammed told him that this was how it would go.

"Yes, Mr. Lee. We are a poor nation. The beautiful green and white uniforms you see our sailors wear cost more than we pay them for their first year of wages. So we allow them to supplement their incomes. Actually, we encourage it. It will cost one thousand U.S. dollars for them to bring the load out to your boat. They will also stand by your ship until your skipper is safely underway; an added bonus in an area infamous for pirates."

The *Mr. Lee* he referred to was actually Lee Rothman, more commonly known as Bubba. Bubba was buying a load of hashish for shipment to the United States. He had other associates, stateside, who would have the load picked up when it reached the other end. His long-time friend and confederate, Jay, would take care of all that. That wasn't his job. His job was to send the drugs safely on their way from the port of Karachi. Bubba's ocean-going tug was anchored in Sonmiani Bay, but would motor nearer to the area of the Karachi wharfs when it was time to load up. The Aussie skipper of the ***Strident*** was a punctilious man, anxious to get underway.

"Very good, my old friend, I will give Captain Alistair the fee and instruct him to give it to the Captain of your Navy boat as soon as the cargo is transferred. Or half, then half, if that is preferred," Bubba said.

"Half, then half, sounds too fair for anyone to argue." Mohammed smiled.

They agreed on the timing, made further arrangements as to how and when Bubba would pay Mohammed for the load, shook hands, and parted feeling confident each had made a clean deal. Bubba, however, was already having thoughts of the next part of this endeavor – moving the hashish halfway across the world. He'd let Jay worry about getting it into the United States. That was something else entirely. The important part was that this was Operation Rehash, and it was time to roll. The fix was in. And he was now working both sides of the street.

THE ***STRIDENT*** HAD been underway for a week when it approached the Strait of Malacca between Sumatra and Malaysia. As they left the Indian Ocean, passing through the Great Channel into the Andaman Sea, Captain Alistair had all hands armed and ready on deck. The Malacca Strait is 400 miles long and fraught with pirates. At the speed they were making, it would take about twenty hours to clear the strait. Half of that time would be in the dark.

Al had timed it so that they would traverse the first half of this dangerous passage at night. He felt his odds were better at night, where the Strait was not so narrow. That way, as they approached the narrow southwest end of the Strait, he would have daylight on his side. Al hollered at his first mate, a burly Australian named Chapman.

"Keep a sharp eye. I can see small blips on the radar. They show just a mile or so ahead. It's likely to be fishing boats, but keep sharp."

"Aye aye, Cap'n."

As time passed, tension seeped further into the already jittery nervous systems of the crew. All of these men knew how dangerous these waters were. They'd been on edge preceding this leg of their journey. Once they hit the Great Channel entrance to the pirate zone, though, the danger was magnified exponentially. They all knew this. There was no coast guard to turn to when you were hauling drugs.

"Cap'n," Chapman spoke loud and clear, so everyone could hear him. "I see one boat now. It's a fishing boat. I can see the guys working nets in the deck lights."

"Okay, Chap. Rest easier, but don't get too comfortable. We've got a long night ahead of us."

THE STRIDENT MADE it completely through the Malacca Strait without incident. It was only after they'd left the Singapore Strait, setting a course that would thread them through the Kepulaua Islands, that the trouble they had so assiduously avoided finally found them. All hands were focused ahead on the South China Sea, and the Luzon Strait beyond that, and no one noticed the pirates speeding up on their stern. Indeed, the pirates must have known this would be so. The small craft of the pirates blended in with other commercial vessels in the dark of night, and were upon the tug before anyone was the wiser. The smugglers were too busy watching the busy hand of the magician, and did not notice the deft hand.

It wasn't until a grappling hook clinked over the stern rail that someone noticed them. And by then it was almost too late. The Filipino crew were all bedded down except their foreman, Fernando, who was the only one able to communicate with the two white men. It was Fernando who spotted the three-pronged hook as it took its bite into the inside of the stern bulwark.

"We got 'um some company!" Fernando got very excited, very quickly.

This was the reason Alistair was picked for this job. He was fast and aggressive. His large, athletic frame moved like a panther. He grabbed the AK-47 and was out the back door of the wheelhouse as the first pirate came over the stern.

"Tat, tat, tat, tat!" The pirate was blasted backwards and into the tug's foaming wake. This man's appearance was a ruse and a diversion, and it almost worked. For two other pirates had come up over the bow bulwark as Alistair and Chapman were concentrating on the stern. The Malaysians were on Alistair's back with knives before he was aware they had boarded. Fernando was on *them* in an instant. His flashing knives, Chinese butterfly knives, slashed and pierced them before they could do any damage to Alistair. A pristine deck was instantly awash with blood. Chapman wasted no time tossing the corpses of the intruders over the rail.

AS SUDDENLY AS it had begun, it was over. By the time the Filipino crew boiled up from the lower decks and the fo'c'sle and stood bristling with arms, there was nothing under the deck lights except a smeared pool of blood and the steady low throbbing of the engines.

The pirates had come with only two boats, and two men per boat. The boat in the stern could by seen motoring away with a single frantic man handling the outboard tiller. The other boat was adrift.

"Better walk the rails with flashlights and AK's," Alistair instructed.

"Aye, yi, yi, Captain!" Fernando said, and the others started to laugh. Fernando's English wasn't as good as it could have been.

BUT ALL OF this was in the future. All of this was yet to come. The timelessness of life on the sea eventually made every sailor upon it wonder about the difference between what had already happened and what was yet to come. But this was yet to come.

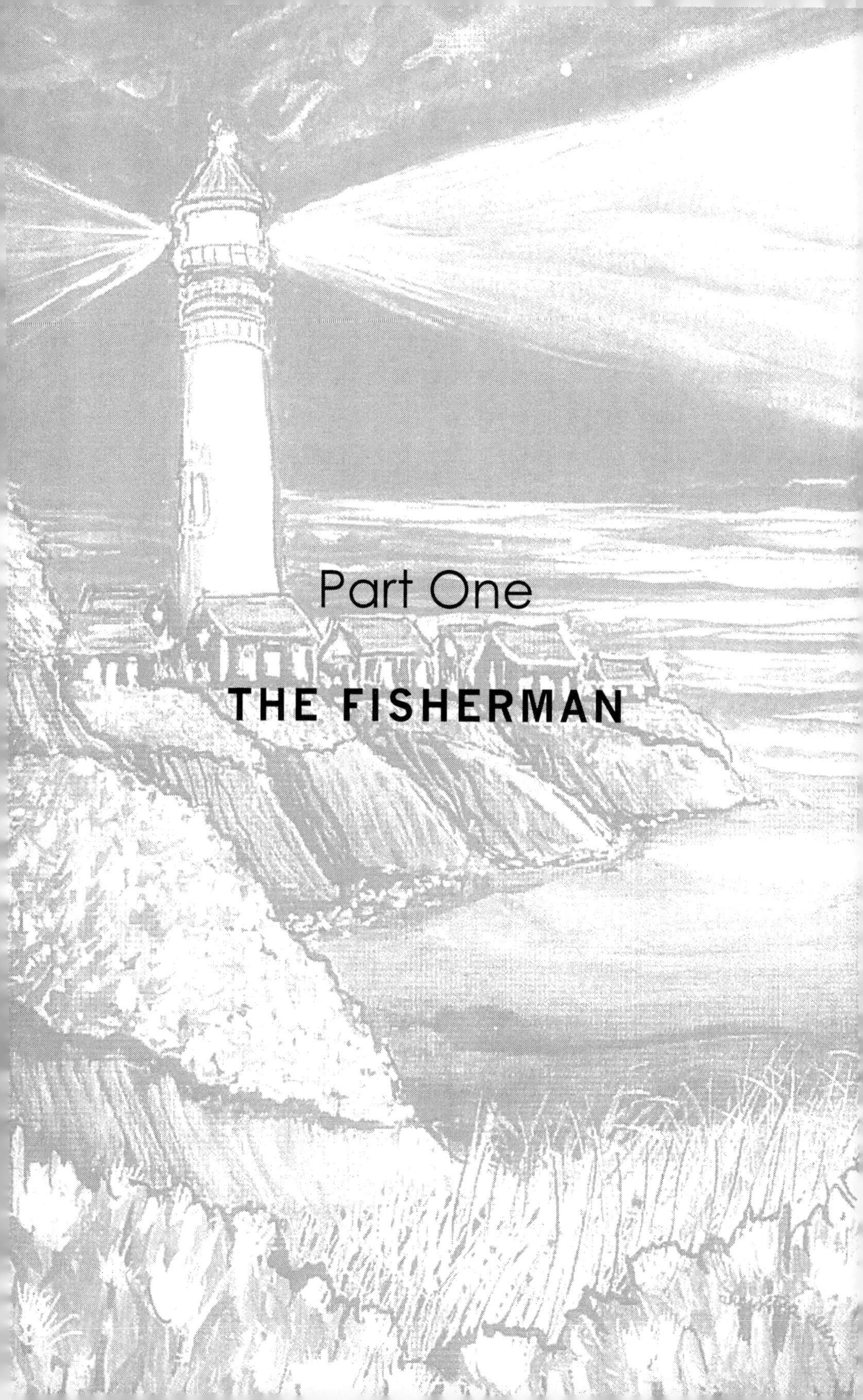

Part One

THE FISHERMAN

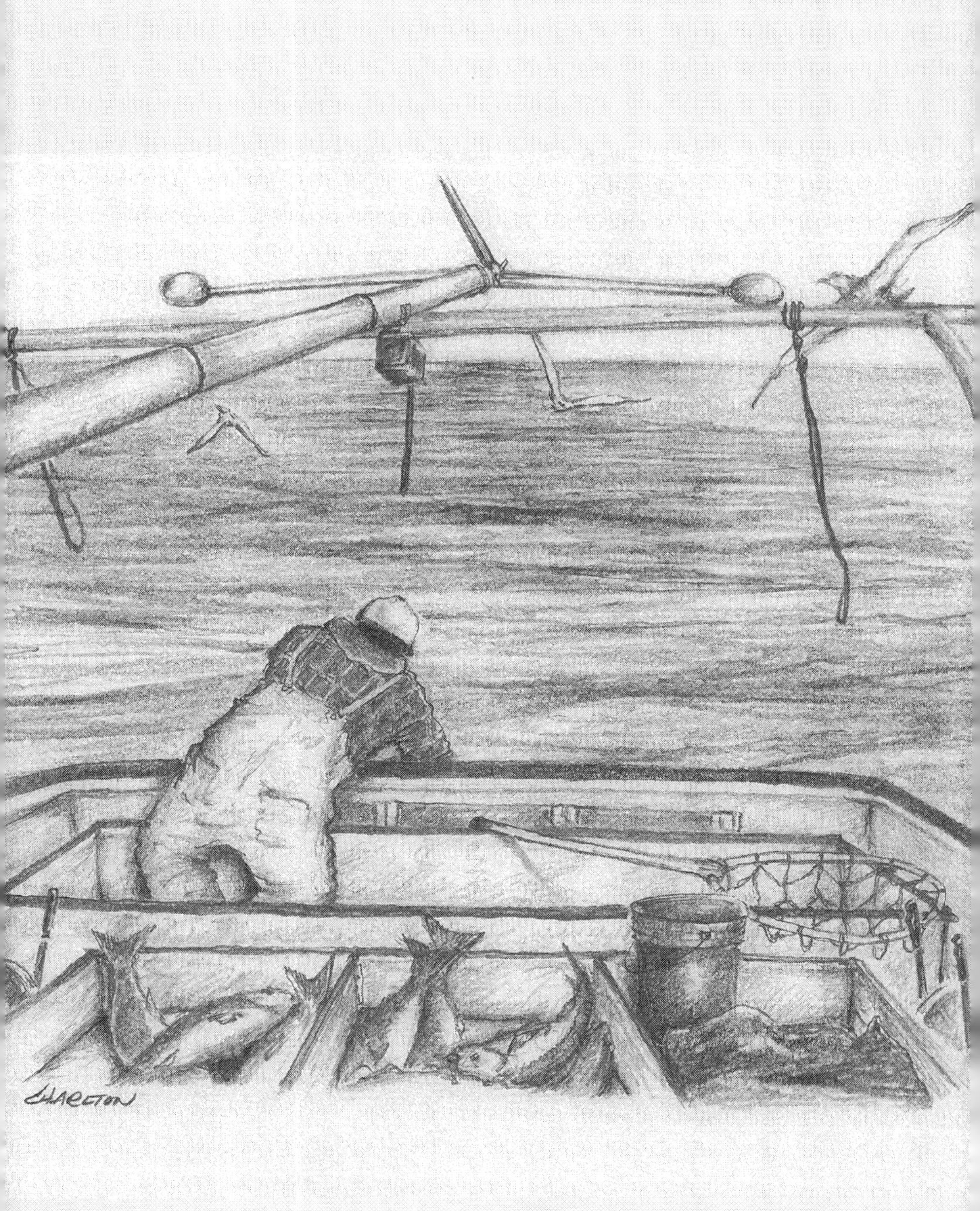

In the trolling pit.

CHAPTER 1

MAY 1, 1980.

26 MILES OFF the coast of San Francisco.
12 years earlier.

"NET! COME HERE and get the fucking net ready."

Gar the fishboat captain was energized. The diesel engine pounded slowly at trolling speed. The yell was to the other man on the boat, Jeff.

Gar was hunched over the stern rail about as far as one could go outside of the trolling pit without falling into the ocean. It was a glorious spring day, the ocean was flat and that cloudy-green color that salmon love. Seabirds chattered and shrieked at one another, and the smell of coffee and bacon drifted out of the wheelhouse. It was sixty-one degrees in the early morning air.

The gurdy was still winding up as Gar reached over, unsnapping linesnaps from the trolling wire then straightening to coil the monofilament leaders into the leader box. He carefully inspected the split-tailed herring baits, changing the bad ones. He had watched the fish hit and seen the porcelain insulator, out of the corner of one eye, on the first big jump. It was certainly a splitter, and likely a giant one. Gar's experienced eye guessed the unseen fish to be over thirty pounds as it struggled on the hundred-pound-test leader.

Gar yelled, "Hurry up," just as Jeff burst out on deck, excited when he saw the fish running in different directions.

Jeff ran back to the stern and jumped into the pit while reaching for the net in the same motion. He laid the hoop net across the stern rail, with the scoop end hanging out over the water.

"Are we in 'em, Garaloney?" Jeff rippled with energy. Gar had been given the handle "Garaloney" some years earlier, by his skipper at the time: it was because of his expertise at abalone diving.

"You know it, Jeffer." Then, to the uncaught fish: "Pump, you mother-fucker! Pump your heart out," he hollered at the trolling wire that was being wrenched hard.

Now bent all the way over the stern rail again, Gar had the auspicious linesnap, which was jerking madly, in sight. But he did not want to bring it up too high while the fish was thrashing its head from side to side. Not yet. He would not take a chance of losing this beauty.

"Are there any boats coming on your side?" Gar's stomach was flooded with bile, as if a swarm of butterflies were circling inside. He took a moment for caution, knowing the Chinook would require his full attention for the next ten minutes, which was plenty of time for another boat in the small fleet to get close enough to lock outriggers with them.

"Clear into the middle of next week," Jeff sang out in his exhilaration. There was nothing like a hundred-dollar fish to spike the adrenaline.

IT WAS OPENING morning, and they had come out of the anchorage at the Southeast Farallon Island at daylight, snooping their way down toward the rest of the Half Moon Bay, California, boats, looking for a spot to fish. They set their gear into the water about nine miles south of the Farallon anchorage at *Pa's Canyon*, named after Carl Burlesque. Carl, or *Pa*, had caught tons upon tons of rock cod dragging *Old Pa Rock*, located deep, and on one side of the canyon. But there were more than rock cod here. There were salmon, and it was opening day of the season. Gar and his crewman Jeff were trailing their gear across this canyon head in near-perfect salmon fishing conditions.

There were spring murres squabbling raucously all around the boat. The Murre is a streamlined bird, gregarious and social, noted for agile swimming ability, and their presence on the surface of the ocean is usually a sign of fish. Baitfish are driven to the surface by feeding salmon from below. And the murres feed on them when they come up to escape from the salmon. So fishermen watch for these birds.

The whiteness of the famous Pete Seger song's, "Little Boxes on the Hillside" at Daly City, and on up into the Sunset District of San Francisco, were just visible from 22 miles off Pedro Point. Perfect opening-weather presented itself with just an occasional lazy swell rolling through. Clear blue sky with some wispy white clouds, and a hardly noticeable six to eight mile per hour breeze, just sufficient to keep the kelp flies at bay.

Beyond the normal smells of an older wooden boat – deck caulk, fir, bilge water, and always diesel – the ocean offered its salty aroma. It smelled this morning as shrimp taste. *Just exactly like shrimp taste*, Gar observed, while scrutinizing the salmon's latest run, along with the smells of different paints lingering in the air. The topside smelled of lacquer, while the bottom paint reminded him of early school days. It was a smell like crayons or clay, with an underlying reek of tar.

GAR HELD THE kill cord high and over the back of his hand, pinching the line tight to his palm with his right thumb. The linesnap was just six or eight feet away. The fish had mellowed, swimming just behind and slightly away from the boat. The game now was to ease the fish closer, inch by inch.

Gar pulled long and slow on the line, surfacing the silvery prize sufficiently to inspect both its size as well as the position of the hook. The fish was a monster for this time of year. Normally the fish are smaller in the spring, but this one was by no means small.

"I'm bettin' thirty eight," Gar guessed, meaning what the fish would weigh at the dock, which would be after it was dressed, because salmon must be cleaned and gilled as soon after being caught as possible.

"I'm taking *overs*," Jeff countered.

"He's hooked good," Gar said, breathing out.

A suck in, then exhaling, "Come on, baby. Come to papa."

Another in and out: "Atta boy, don't be shy, just get...." Now holding his breath, "Oh, no, don't do that!" The fish was starting to sit on its tail while head thrashing again. The thing fought with an admirable frenzy, tearing up the water and becoming a blur of manic activity. Water splashed into the air for thirty feet around. But it couldn't last. No fish could sustain such mortal activity.

When the fish was again within reach, Jeff had the net ready. The fish's head was within swinging range, accordingly Gar grabbed his gaff, but instead of gaffing it Gar turned the gaff's hook out away from the fish and clubbed the giant perfectly on the soft spot between and above the eyes, knocking the beast into fish incoherency.

"Good Morning!" he breathed reverently.

All over but the hallelujahs now, Gar let the fish drop back in the current to just astern of their position while Jeff simultaneously slipped the dip net behind the fish. Jeff levered the net up over the rail of the stern. It took Gar's help, grabbing low on the handle, then on the far side of the net, to lift the fish over the rail. They flopped it onto the deck where another couple of whacks to the noodle were delivered to insure its capture.

Elated, the two fishermen let go with a jubilant, beginning-of-the-season scream, then turned back to their work. The fish would go thirty-eight pounds, easy.

Gar increased the speed of the boat a little bit, kicked off the autopilot, and spun the wheel thirty degrees for a slow turn. He did this almost automatically, and spoke to Jeff.

"I'll turn your way so you can run your bow line. I better run us back up through that spot before we get too far away. We're in 'em! I can feel it. I love this canyon. It never lets me down. And we found it all by our lonesomes." Gar loved finding his own fish. It was an integral element of his independent nature.

Jeff was busy on *his* side, and then he called for the net. Gar already running his bow line back out, paused the gurdy for fifteen seconds to net Jeff's fish then set the net back in its position hanging slightly out over the stern. Jeff's fish was a keeper, but would only go about eight pounds dressed. It was a nice medium, and he told Jeff that.

Jeff took two more keepers off that wire, and shook two shorts, laughing all the while. This was good fishing, and if it stayed just like this they would break the hundred-for-the-day mark. And with a decent grade of fish to boot. That was always the goal: A hundred fish or better for the day.

WHEN THE BOAT was pointed straight back on their reverse tack, north toward the island, Gar took a moment to run up to the pilothouse and check their position on the Loran and make a mark on the chart. He left Jeff to tend the lines. They fished eight leaders on six lines, for a total of 48 hooks in the water. Gar wanted to insure they were going to pass back over the canyon head again, right at its tip.

It was a simple collection of spring colors out the window of the cabin: green ocean, blue sky, nothing elaborate, a chill in the air, and a sunny glare sparkling on the smooth sea. Gar watched the other boats rising and falling on the green swells, a busy pair of men in every stern, the outriggers rocking as if a pair of knitting needles, giant knitting needles, had been poked into the amidships of each of the shiny-white trollers. Every boat had their pair of men working the stern, the bows plunged meanwhile slowly forward, all in identical directions, no one at the helms. Trails of burnt diesel smudged the otherwise perfect sky. Chatter spilled from Gar's array of radios. He did not hear good fish reports from those boats that were not on this spot.

THAT DONE, HE ran back and jumped into the pit. The float line that he had idling in was just up into position and without slowing the gurdy, Gar pulled the handle on the float board and set the float well out of the way behind the gurdy and wire. He had witnessed floats laid in the deck bin kicked over the side by lively fish not yet knocked out. And this was unacceptable.

The two fishermen ran through the rest of the gear, joking back and forth, thinking life wasn't too bad. And when finished they had thirteen keepers on deck with a solid eight-pound average weight. These were decent-sized fish for spring fishing. With the big splitter, the average was likely over ten pounds for the moment, but that average would be reduced as they continued to catch school fish of the seven-to-eight pound variety.

This is how the fishing went. The gear was run, and the fish were cleaned. All of this with seagulls circling, diving, and screaming harshly behind the stern. The oily smell of the herring baits, and the fresher smell of salmon blood filled the air. Gar ran up to the pilot house, telling Jeff over his shoulder, "I better check in with the boys, real quick."

IN THE WHEEL house, he first tried the radio called the *Mouse*, also known as the Mickey Mouse. This is fisherman-speak for the C.B. radio. Switching to the Half Moon Bay fleet's "secret" channel nine, Gar whistled a "Phweee-phwuuu" (that was a sort of secret whistle).

Michael, Gar's hero, mentor and role model (and, some would say, the best salmon fisherman ever) came back smartly.

"Is that you, Lips?" Gar, in addition to being called "Garaloney", had inherited the handle "Lips" because years before when he had deckhanded with a very serious fisherman named Nardo, he was never allowed to come in out of the summer sun. His lips were burned raw for several summers straight.

"Wall to wall, and tree-top tall. How they bitin' for you? Come back?" Gar replied.

"We're just out front of home, moving steadily up and out. And we have three little rags for the morning. Not much doing." Michael responded. A *Rag* is a barely-legal sized salmon.

"Oh boy, doesn't sound too awfully shiny. We're on that favorite canyon of mine and Pa's, and we've got an unlucky number, with one monster for the morning, over." Gar tried to downplay his excitement.

"You got green or brown water?" Mike asked.

"Well, it was all green – the good green – but now I see an occasional puddle of brown. I don't know yet if it's the good brown or the bad brown. We'll see. But I have lines going, and things look plenty fishy. I gotta go. Lotta rips, too," he added as he threw down the mike and ran out the door.

"Keep gettin' 'em, Lipaloney. We'll see you soon." Mike clicked off, in a hurry to get to his gear.

Mike was grateful to Gar for the report, and wanted to get to Gar's location as quickly as possible. Although he was the mentor and role model to an entire generation of Half Moon Bay salmon fishermen, Michael McHenry was not too proud to listen to good advice when he found it. Fishing is an utterly pragmatic endeavor. You go where the fish are if you want to catch them.

CHAPTER 2

SUSAN STARED AT Gar with glittery, gold-flecked brown eyes, then her eyes narrowed dangerously. This was always the sign that she was about to unload, and Gar tried to prepare himself. She slammed her hairbrush onto her make-up table, rattling the mirror and punctuating the explosiveness of her words.

"Damn it, I'm tired," she said to Gar, her voice just under a shout. "I was on my feet for twelve hours yesterday at the restaurant. My wrists hurt. My ankles are swollen."

"I know, sweetie." Gar tried to placate her, but it wasn't easy once she got started.

"And then I get home and you aren't there!"

"I've got to get ready for the salmon season. You know that."

"All I know is that you're never home."

Gar thought of this exchange as he raced from the pilothouse back down into the pit. He couldn't get the scene out of his mind, and it troubled him. But he let it go when he reached the activity on the stern of his boat, allowing the reality he faced there to displace Susan's scowling face. Seagulls cried mockingly overhead, as if sent by Susan.

"You okay?" Jeff turned from his work and noticed Gar's blank stare.

"Yeah, I'm fine," Gar replied, turning to his work.

Gar's face almost never scowled. Six feet tall and stoutly built, he was a jovial and handsome twenty-eight year old man with a square jaw and piercing blue eyes. His eyes were the color of the sea, and, like the color of the sea, always changing hues and always a little different every time you saw them. And Susan was his pretty counterpart. At least she used to be. But he couldn't think of that now.

"Yeeehaahh," Gar let go, trying to lighten his brooding mood. He had tremendous financial obligations, and the pumping of the salmon lines was a promise of relief.

IT WAS MAY 1, 1980. The year that the United States Hockey Team upset the Russians at Lake Placid; the U.S. hostage situation in the embassy in Iran continued while President Jimmy Carter sat on his hands in frustration; "ABSCAM", whatever that was, broke in the news; and eight U.S. service members died trying to free the Iranian hostages. The Shah of Iran would die in July, and Ronald Reagan would sweep Jimmy Carter in the November presidential election–489 electoral votes to Carter's paltry 49 electoral votes. The Eagles, Billy Joel, and the Doobie Brothers dominated the pop radio charts.

Ruminations of Susan kept intruding upon his work. How could that have happened? He kept trying to equate the state of the relationship to one of the Eagle's hits: Lyin' Eyes? Or, maybe, Desperado?

"Minkia butana, a freakin' submarine just came up alongside of us," an Italian voice broke over one of the deck speakers. One of *The Yukon Gang,* and Gar and Jeff cocked amused ears.

"Don't worry about them," another Italian voice came back, "they won't eat too much."

"Afundagulu," the first guy, Mario, came back in mock indignation, and Gar and Jeff chuckled.

The year previous, he and his girl friend–no, he and the one and only love of his life–had somehow gone their separate ways. They had lived together for a time in young lover's bliss in Susan's mother's duplex. Sue's brother lived in the other half.

During his initial six months of residence there, Gar bought his first boat, the 44-foot ***Visit***. It was an old yet stout, wood, Tacoma-built halibut boat. He pondered this as he stood on the ***Visit***'s after deck, working to make the boat's payments. He bought it from an older mentor and role model, Geno, and somehow managed to get a floating interest loan for the full purchase price from Production Credit Association. It was very unusual to borrow the full price with nothing down, but Gar had an excellent reputation and his parents cosigned the note, using their home and restaurant as collateral.

Additionally, Geno, who was well into PCA himself with a new and bigger boat under construction, also cosigned the loan. This kept the old ***Visit*** in the family, as Gar grew up in Half Moon Bay and attended the same high school as Geno.

Maybe it was the boat. Was that it? Gar still wasn't sure. It was supposed to have been the living arrangement, but that didn't completely add up. They had been so much in love that Gar had failed to recognize that his living, unmarried, with Susan in her Mother's duplex, was causing dissention between Sue and her parents.

It was only when he came home from a busy month of fishing salmon far away from home, and Sue announced that she was moving a couple of hundred miles south to San Luis Obispo–in the mountains–that Gar figured out something was wrong. Unfortunately, he did not understand what was happening quickly enough to prevent it. He knew only his side of things. That Sue was moving to the mountains and that he, with the weighty financial responsibility of the boat, was relegated to a life on or near the ocean.

Gar had gone from being so in love he could hardly eat, to being frightened, lonely and in pain. Almost overnight his life became an existence of hard work and harder drinking. It was a life that hid, but never fully relieved, the bewildered hurt.

THE DAY WORE on, and as a result of Gar's radio conversation with Michael, the fleet moved into the area. The water continued its change from olive green to coffee *au lait* (which would bring the hake as the sun set), and the murres got so fat feeding on the anchovies that the salmon chased up to the surface that they were unable to fly back to their island roost. Shearwaters, looking like black, long-beaked seagulls, worked the area for bait, along with albatross, cormorants, and the odd pelican–which look like a rocking chair falling out of the sky when they dive for bait.

Jeff sauntered into the cabin and announced: "We had 157 fish for the day; they're all iced down, and the deck is ready to go for the morning."

"Good job, Jeffery, I'm going to cook you a steak dinner so good you'll be wanting to pay me to work on this boat."

"Yeah, right," Jeff went back on deck to smoke.

A SUCCESSFUL OPENING day under their belts, they ran up to anchor at the Southeast Farallon Island. Gar got busy cooking the steak dinner during the hour-long run up to the anchorage.

Jeff, brown-haired with more blond highlights than Gar, was still new at this. This was his second season. He was a quick study, though, and a hard worker. And he was an even harder partier. With Hollywood good looks and shocking silver-blue eyes, women found him irresistible. A few inches shorter than Gar, his aggressive assault on girls gave them little chance to say no. He was a younger, better-looking version of Gar, and he would become a highline salmon fisherman one day.

Jeff was a very simple guy because he only liked two things: women and work. But mostly women.

AFTER SMOKING ON deck, Jeff came in to find Gar talking on the radio–one of many in the pilothouse. He was speaking to Sully.

"Okay, Sully." Gar was boisterous and jovial. "What channel do you want to sleep on?"

Tim Sullivan had the ***Marilyn J***, a 55-foot steel boat, and was a fishing equal to Gar; unlike mentor to both of them, Michael (Mike McHenry), who owned the 61'9" long, 18' wide, ***Merva W***. Being equals, they checked back and forth with each other quite often while Michael, the proverbial "Old Bull," aloofly observed from the perfect space he liked to maintain. There is a hierarchy among men who go to sea. It is everywhere and has always been observed.

"Let's keep it right here with the squelch turned up, or is it down?–I never remember. But, anyway, do you have me squelched now?" Gar asked.

"Got you fine," Tim answered. "You got me?"

"I already had you. Good night, Sully. Chhheeccck you in the morning. What time do you think, about 4:30?"

"Let's see, twenty minutes to get out of here, an hour to where we should be. It gets light at 5:30. I don't think that's enough time, unless we drop the gear in a little early and tack down to the spot?"

"Let's do that. I'm tired. See you in the morning." Gar finished.

"Throw Jeff a cookie." Tim got in the final word.

"Hey, Lips!" Michael asserted his dominance.

"What's up, Mackerel?" Gar came back brightly.

"You haven't sung the song yet," Michael demanded.

"All right. You're right. Here goes." Gar clicked off a moment to take a breath and get ready to sing his signature song. The song, *The Salmon Song*, has several verses, but Gar only sang the chorus tonight. With a sort of even tempo, similar to the tune of "Someone's in The Kitchen with Dinah," Gar keyed the mike and the song boomed out:

"I like salmon fishing,
Salmon fishin's all right;
And I like salmon fishin',
Cause the beach is in sight.
Oh, if I had my wayyyy,
I'd salmon fish ev-e-ry dayyyy;
And go in at night,
And fuck everything in sight!"

This was greeted by a moment of radio silence, during which Gar knew the men in the other boats were chuckling among themselves. After a moment, the sound of Michael's voice came over the bulkhead speaker.

"Good night, Lips. You did good. See you in the morning." Mike closed that day for business.

"What a dumb song." Angus, who was forever contentious, once again tried to dampen the evening's spirits for Gar. Gar had not noticed him in the fleet of boats that arrived on his "Pa's Canyon" fishing hole. Maybe he went another direction, and was just now running up for the hot bite. This seemed likely, as there was definite venom in Angus's voice. He had long been a self-appointed rival of Gar's. And he vied, like another sibling, for Michael's attention. Perhaps because Gar was from Half Moon Bay, and Angus wasn't, it made him jealous. Whatever the case, Gar was constantly plagued by Angus making everything a contest. But this night he did not respond to the taunt.

THE FIRST DAY of the salmon-fishing season finally through, Gar stepped out on the back deck to look at the number of boats that had joined him in the anchorage, and his nose was immediately shocked by the ammonia smell emanating from the many tons of bird shit on the island. There were about a hundred anchor lights twinkling in the night, reflections of the boats' cabins and deck lights distorted by the lapping water made the whole scene magical. And over it all flashed the rhythmic and benevolent beam of the Farallon Island Lighthouse, situated high atop the southeastern most island in the group. The lighthouse's probing, revolving beam lanced the darkness of the night, offering a benign reassurance to the men under its sway.

The boat creaked at anchor, as wooden boats do. It creaked and rocked softly in the surge of the Island, and the wind-driven rotary-turbine ventilator that capped the exhaust stack over the propane stove made a "tick-tick" sound in the cabin at a pace consistent with the wind speed. This night the ticking gyrations were a slow and measured cadence. In thirty knots of wind it could tick wildly, many beats to the second.

It had been a good day. Maybe 1,300 pounds, at an average price of perhaps $2.00 a pound, figured out to around a $2,600 day. Gar needed to make about ten times that before he could start thinking about making the boat and insurance payments for the year. He had his work cut out, all right.

He plugged in an eight-track tape of Hank Williams Sr.'s greatest hits, and hit the bunk while it played itself out. There was no need to take off rain gear before going to bed because he rarely wore it. Levis, the traditional blue or red, plaid cotton shirt, and tennis shoes for running back and forth from cabin to pit, these were all that he normally wore. And the only thing that came off tonight, before getting into bed, were the tennis shoes. Normally he would strip to his boxers and get in between sheets, but tonight he could only kick off his shoes, fall into the bunk, and pull up a sleeping bag he kept folded for quick naps.

His thoughts turned immediately to Susan as he listened to the soulful strains of Hank Senior. They became the jumble of confused uncertainty they always did when he thought about her and what had gone wrong. He had enjoyed a very successful opening day of the season, yet he didn't think of that. He thought of her, and wondered why this should be so.

The lighthouse beam flashed its way faintly and regularly into Gar's cabin, and was the last thing he saw before sleep overtook him. The boat rocked gently at anchor, and the occasional brief flashes from the lighthouse's beam were a peaceful comfort.

CHAPTER 3

MAY 2, 1980.

ANGUS IS ONE of those type of guys who carefully saves his partially used tube of Chap Stick from one season to the next. It is said that he has had the same tube of Chap Stick going for six years. He winces when he looks at a bill in a restaurant, if he looks at it at all. He doesn't buy bananas because they sell them by the pound, and he doesn't like to pay for the weight of the peels. He's a cheap bastard.

As the Z-Squad saying goes: "Nobody likes a cheap bastard." Gar flew a blue stay-sail with a white "Z." Michael was the president of this elite squad. Gar had joined late in the game, but he nonetheless took it seriously. Angus was never a part of the squad at all, though he clearly wanted to be.

THOUGH THE ALARM was set for 4:30 a.m., Gar woke up tossing well before then. He was still angry about Angus' comments. After he made his dig about the Salmon Song, Gar discovered him on another radio frequency telling someone he didn't get *called* to the Pa Canyon spot until late. This thinly veiled criticism implied that Gar had purposely not called Angus to the spot.

The wind was on the increase, and this was already building more swell. Gar reran the radio comments in his mind as he climbed out of his bunk. Tired from the long previous day, the thought was fragmented. "Goose," which was short for *Ang-Goose*, had opted not to run up to the Islands the night before the start of the season as Gar had done. That put Gar at the north end of the traditional opening day fishing grounds. Angus chose to go south, and, as it turned out, that put him out of position. It was simply the spin of fortune's wheel that put the two at their respective fishing sites.

Gar had called after his first run through the gear, and reported his thirteen school fish plus the one big hog. When fishing is good, fishermen don't like to announce that fact more than once, for worry that hundreds of boats will converge on the spot. They want their pals to come share in their good fortune, but not everyone. So advising just their pals is tricky because everyone is listening in.

Goose was once again being an asshole, blaming Gar for his own bad luck and poor judgment. The problem with this was that it would only serve to escalate an already antagonistic relationship. Goose would later screw Gar in a similar manner, and justify this because of his opening day failure.

STIFF AND SORE, Gar climbed out of bed. He first eyeballed their basic situation. Had the anchor slipped? Were there any other boats close? Was there water in the bilge? The Farallon Island's Lighthouse continued to circle its probing beam into the dark vastness of the night. The anchored boats rocked quietly in the swell, and sea birds squawked feebly, not ready to start their days until there was more light.

After taking a leak over the side, Gar washed hands and face and brushed his teeth in the small sink. With Crest on his breath, he climbed down the ladder to the engine room. The fo'c'sle bunks were at the forward end of the engine room compartment. The entire area encompassed about a third of the boat's overall length. The fish hold embodied the middle half of the vessel's linearity, and the rest was comprised of the trolling pit, constructed as a step-into concavity cut through the deck in the stern.

The chores in the engine room–checking the oil, greasing fittings, opening fuel valves, and checking the engine water level–always woke Jeff up.

"You ready for round two, Jefferson?" Gar said happily when Jeff's head popped up.

"Mmmm...I think so," Jeff said, and then he inexplicably and entirely irreverently broke into song:

"Ooohhhh, nothin' could be fina'
Than to be in her vagina
In the moor-oor-nin':
Nothin' could be sweeta'
Than to have her suck my peeta'
In the moor-oor-nin':
Ooohhhh, some people like to wake up to bacon and eggs,
But I like to wake up with my head between her legs;
Oooh, nothin' could be fina' than to be in her vagina
In the moor-oor-nin'."

"You're a dandy," Gar commented, laughing. "A real fucking dandy."

THE ANCHOR PULLED by 4:30, Gar whistled at Sully who already had *his* ground gear spooled on the anchor winch.

"That you, Lips?"

"Mornin', Sull. You sleep all right?"

"Like a baby, what about you? Did you and Jeff go out for a beer or two before beddie-bye?"

"Yeah, right. Out like a light is all we did. What about Merlo? Did you and the little short fat fucker go dancing?"

"Wish we could have, but Merlo didn't want to go." Tim continued the facetiousness. They were 20-some miles and many hours away from any dance halls.

"Oh, well, we'll get this trip in and then have some party time. If you treat me real nice for the next seven days, I'll buy you a vodka-grape," Gar said.

"I always treat you nice, Lips, you know that."

"Yeah? What about that time you were in 'em at the old Crescent City Frontier Bar and didn't call me?" Gar alluded to an ancient event, but he did it with a smile.

Sully licked his lips, rubbed his nose with his knuckles, adjusted his glasses and stood up real straight before replying. Gar could see him do every single one of the things in his mind's eye, for he had seen them in sequence a hundred times.

"I only had three girls," Sully said, "and I didn't need your help. That's why I didn't call."

"Yeah, right. You had about two-and-a-half too many, is what I heard later. The one you did take home kissed and told."

"Nah, na, na, na. The reason I had three girls there was because one was my date, and one of the other ones was the girl you took back to the motel, and she came back to the bar–how shall I say it, unfulfilled? And the last one was another unsatisfied customer of yours that was looking for greener pastures." Sully shot back.

And on it went as they ran to the south. There was a lump to the ocean now, a constant undulating swell that was starting to get choppy yet remained intermittent. But there were no white caps yet. The morning birds were still there, having slept right where they finished *their* fishing the evening before. The flashing beam of the lighthouse became tiny and insignificant in the distance behind them.

ALMOST TO THE spot, Gar steered the ***Visit*** a bit inside of the groove he worked the day before. The California coastal tide book indicated San Francisco Bay was still ebbing out to sea, which meant the current would be pushing hard offshore: Beginning inside the groove with the offshore current made sense.

The sun was just about to make its appearance on the eastern horizon. A riot of colors were reflected from the serried ranks of clouds miles further out to sea, and the dark, foreboding hills of the coastline were emerging, backlit by the glow to the east. Seagulls tagging along with the boats, looking for breakfast, shrieked their joy at the prospect of sunlight and a new day.

"Hey, Lips, you gunna try to get up current of me?" Michael was a mile or two in front of Gar, and they had been running the same course. Mike spoke to him on the radio almost simultaneous with the ***Visit***'s course change: Michael pays attention to everything.

"Yeah, old habit." Gar fired back. "I always try to stay up wind, up current, and one up too."

"Heh, heh, heh, yeah Boy, I noticed the tide was ebbing. I guess we'll just go down here a little further and throw 'em in and see what happens. Skin says we need a good trip because he wants to buy an island." Mike referred to his crewman, Pete. Pete was christened "Peter Skin," and that was most often shortened to just "Skin." Hardly anyone ever called him Pete. At least not anyone who knew him.

"Why does he want to buy an island? So he can stock it with babes, and be his own competition?" Gar asked with a smile.

Mike answered. "No, he says it's a name thing. He wants to buy an island and name it *Can't Say*. And then he'll build his house there, and when he's ashore mingling with mainland folks, and they ask where he's from, he'll be able to answer, *Can't Say*."

"Ha, ha, ha, I like that. Sort of like who's on first. That Peter Skin, he's a thinker, isn't he?"

"He, he, he. Yeah. He comes up with this kind'a shit all day. Like just yesterday. He's back in the stern, busy, and I'm up here doing something. And he gets out of the stern pit, takes off his rain gear, runs all the way up here into the cabin, stands next to me, farts, stays for a minute to make sure there's no more gas in his pants, then runs all the way back to the stern, puts on his rain gear, jumps back in the pit, and starts running a line. That's the kind'a shit I gotta put up with."

"Yeah, I know what you mean. The other day Jeff says to me, 'Hey, Gar. Did you hear the one about the lady that farted in the barrel?' And I said no, and he says, 'Well, you would have if you were in the barrel.'"

"THAT'S NOT THE SAME, Lips," Mike chastised.

"I gotta go set my gear." Gar clicked off.

"Keep getting' 'em, Lipaloney," Mike sang out, then added reflectively, "She's starting to look clear out to the west."

MIKE WAS REFERRING to the phenomenon that precedes the northwest wind, the predominant wind at this time of year. It was already puffing five or ten knots, and a west-northwest swell was building. They would likely have wind before the day was over. The phenomenon was a subtle clearing of the atmospheric haze, which generally envelopes the California coast for many miles offshore. A sudden visual clarity to the west meant that a wind was building out there, and it would soon be upon them.

The ***Visit*** was a deep draft boat built like one of those weighted-bottom tumblers for kids, the kind that when knocked over, right themselves again. The boat was a "roller" as fish boats go. It had been doing this for almost fifty years, and it always came back. Fishing in the wind was not, *per se,* unsafe. It just increased the difficulty level–to do anything–incrementally and, at times, dramatically.

"HEY, GARALONEY," ANGUS hollered on the VHF radio on channel eleven. Thankfully, he'd waited until Gar set his gear.

Gar shuddered, thinking the Mouse radio he had used yesterday did not transmit so far, and could not be caught on a direction finder. The VHF, on the other hand, wasn't a place fishermen liked to pass information if trying to protect the sanctity of a spot. Why was Goose using the V?

"That you, Goose?" Gar came back on the Mouse on their normal working channel, channel nine, which was actually the designated emergency channel. They used it because truckers and other people didn't use it. It had less clutter.

"Yeah, I got you fine," Goose remained defiantly flippant by continuing to speak on the VHF. "When you had your good day yesterday, were you passing right over the canyon? Or more inside, like where you are now?"

Goose persisted in this effort to disclose Gar's spot to the rest of the fleet, as well as let the other partners know that they hadn't been called when Gar had a good day. It was pure back stabbing. Goose knew Gar had not specifically said to anyone that he had had a good opening day. And again, Gar had called on the channel he presumed Goose, as well as other friends, would be listening to. If anything, Angus should be angry with Michael, and Sully, for not telling him they had stacked their gear on the boat, early in the morning, in order to run up to Gar's spot. It made Gar mad.

"Hey, Goose, do I detect animosity in your voice? I reported first thing yesterday morning where I was, and what I was doing."

"Yeah, but I was down below your Mom's restaurant, straight off of Bootlegger's Cove, and evidently out of range," Goose challenged.

"I apologize. I just assumed you got the word," Gar said.

"No. We scratched around in various spots from San Gregorio on south for forty-six fish, of the smallish variety, and I think you guys did much better than that." Goose sounded whiney and self centered. But Gar thought he always sounded like that, so it was no surprise.

"Yeah, we had a decent day; maybe a little better grade of fish, too. Most of our fish came before lunchtime, though, so I don't think you would have made it up here," Gar hedged some more, knowing only abject contrition would placate Angus.

"That's why we have *Big Sets* (a more powerful radio), and codes, and we make up our calling schedules. I listened on my Big Set at 9:00 yesterday morning, and you weren't on schedule."

At least Angus was now talking on the Mouse, rather than broadcasting their business to the entire fleet via the VHF. But, Lord, what a pain in the ass he was being!

"All right. You're right. I'll be more attentive in the future," Gar said trying to appease.

"And your old partner, T.D., was on there for the 9:00 a.m. schedule looking for you. I told him you were probably too busy." Angus, with this admission, let slip that he did know Gar was catching fish at 9:00 a.m., which was not very long after Gar had made his morning report to Michael and the rest of the Half Moon Bay boys.

Gar let it go, saying, "All right, Goose, thanks for that. I'll ccchheeeck you later." The "check" was drawn out like the Italians down on Fisherman's Wharf like to say it. In fact, much of the way the guys talked to each other was influenced by the Italian fishermen that had been fishing this coast for more than a century. And the San Francisco Italians talked the same way as the New York Italians. Sort of like gangsters, Gar guessed.

"All right, Lips, keep gettin' 'em." Angus couldn't quite let it go.

BACK OUT ON deck, the breeze had freshened a bit. The walk to the stern was trickier with the boat wallowing from side to side, and Jeff had several fish already in his kill bin. The lines were pumping.

A trolling operation (Special thanks to Marie De Santis for the illustration).

CHAPTER 4

A SALMON BOAT operation consists of six weighted trolling wires in the water that are wound up and down on hydraulic-powered spools called gurdies (short for *hurdy-gurdy*). Fifty-foot-long wooden poles, sometimes called outriggers, scissor out and are used to add spread to those lines so they won't (in theory) get tangled. The poles, mounted at mid-ship, are lowered to protrude out at about a fifty degree angle oblique to the fishing boat. About 1:30 on a clock dial.

Normally, the first line set is the dog line. This line seems to catch the least number of fish of all the lines, and this may be why it is called the dog line. It is floated back 100 feet behind the slow moving boat.

The next line set by the fishermen is the tip line, so called because its tag line hangs from the very tip of the pole. The tip line has a heavier, thirty-pound lead weight, and doesn't drag back at such an angle as the dog line, and is only floated 50 feet behind and out away from the boat.

The last line set is the bow line (pronounced like the bough of a tree). It must be understood that each of these three lines–the dog line, the tip line and the bow line–are lowered from each side of the boat. So there is a starboard tip line, and a port tip line. And the same for the others. A total of six lines extend from the boat into the water, three from each side, and with guiding lines off the poles these lines are fanned out.

The bow line gets run in and out of the water the most, as it's the closest and quickest to reach. And it seems to catch more fish. Maybe it catches better due to its proximity to the boat, or perhaps the steeper angle at which it sheers down into the depths. The reason why it catches more fish is a good topic for barroom discussion. Gar usually argues that it fishes the best because it is the handiest, thus run the most, and therefore the baits are usually fresher. Not to mention that constantly running the line up and down tends to give the baits more action. Michael would likely say: "I don't know, Lips, I never really thought about it," even though he certainly had. And Angus: "Well, you know, I have all my lines fishing equally, and we don't give any more credence to one over another."

Angus, a surfer, has a socialist mentality and is pedantic in the extreme. Although he is a fine salmon fisherman, and Gar respected that.

Gar voted Republican, himself, because the Democrats wanted to save the environment by stopping all the commercial fishing on all of the oceans in all of the world. Jacques Cousteau, their poster boy, was the worst–even though his documentaries were interesting.

Gar doubted Michael voted, and was certain Sully didn't. Quintessential fishermen are apolitical. The ocean has its own politics.

THE BOW LINE coming up was pumping wildly, and Gar smiled. As always he sang a few bars in his head: "I like salmon fishin'. . . . Salmon fishin's alright, boom, boom, boom," and adrenaline coursed through him in anticipation of catching fish. He could see the first linesnap as it came up, and it was pointed out at an unnatural angle. Any angle other than straight back meant there was a fish on the line.

"Salmon fishin's alright, boom, boom, boom," he was singing out loud now.

A fish on the top spread was good, likely a forerunner to many more. When salmon are active, and on the surface, it is normally because they are stirred up and feeding. It seemed to Gar that this happened more on windy days, and the wind was blowing harder today. The entire sky was clear now, and the west had a wind haze. This was the exact opposite of earlier atmospheric conditions. There was the smell of the Islands present, although they were almost ten miles away from them. They were upwind-miles and the odor of the seabirds trailed all the way to Gar's new fishing hole. Today he was more inside of where he had worked yesterday, closer in towards the shore. The fairly large fleet of perhaps 200 boats was visible working just outside, tiny automatons hard to fully distinguish in the early light. Gar chose to keep working in towards the shore, allowing for the offshore set of the current. Even though the murky tide pouring out the Golden Gate was not ebbing as hard now, there was nonetheless an offshore push that seemed like it would continue to dominate on this day. With the wind coming onshore, and against the current, the sea promised to build quickly and get nasty before the day was over.

As if to lend credence to this theory, the ***Visit*** took a big roll, then corrected back and forth in a series of three compensating after rolls. Gar swore harshly to himself, then shouted at Jeff.

"Net! Just follow it up. He's hooked good."

When a fish is hooked good, and it is not a real big fish, the fisherman simply plays it to the stern and takes a few wraps of leader over and around the back of his hand. Then, while he lifts the fish over the stern, the other fisherman follows it from underneath with the net in case the fish pops off the hook. If the fish does fall off the hook, it falls into the net. And if it doesn't, the fish doesn't lose any scales by entanglement in the net. Sometimes the hook catches in the net, which burns more time unfouling it, so it is better not to actually have to touch the fish with the net.

Back and forth Gar and Jeff followed-up each other's salmon, taking sixteen school fish off the gear. Not quite the same grade as yesterday, but a *very* nice start to the day. They ignored, for the moment, the cooking pot they could hear rolling around up in the cabin. They also ignored the temperature that was down into the forties.

"We're in 'em again!" Gar crowed, as he ran up to check their position and note it on the chart. While there, he stowed the pot and other loose items. He also put in Jimmy Buffet, the A-1-A eight-track tape, and grabbed a pack of pastries to take back to the stern to share with Jeff. He didn't want to turn around yet because the lines they had just put back into the water began pumping again. This meant the salmon were following, and a turn back in the opposite direction might queer the bite. The Michael Henry School of Salmon Fishing (*MHSSF*) taught that the secret to salmon fishing is to get the fish following you. That's why Michael was called a vacuum cleaner. He would tack by you, and get your fish to follow his boat instead of yours.

There was a good reason that Mike McHenry was a role model and mentor to an entire generation of Half Moon Bay fishermen. And reduced to its very barest essence, it was simply because he was brilliant at what he did, and he was a nice guy to boot. He started fishing while still in high school, though he knew long before that that he was going to be a fisherman. All through his high school years he went out fishing as a deckhand with whoever would have him, and he saved every dime of what he earned. Upon graduation, he had enough. And he started to build. He single-handedly built a sixty-one foot, nine-inch, steel-hulled fishing trawler in a field in Princeton Harbor. And when he was finished, he owned the quarter-of-a-million-dollar boat free and clear.

He named her the ***Merva W***, after his mother, who as it happened never saw the boat. His mother had got sick and gone blind. But when he had finished the boat, the strapping young man carried the crippled woman from one end of the boat to the other, so she could run her hand the entire length, touching every square inch of the freshly painted steel, in order to understand what her son had achieved. He was ten years older than Gar and most of the new generation, but they all acknowledged Mike McHenry to be the best fisherman to ever come out of Half Moon Bay, and the best there ever would be. The man lived to fish.

Gar interrupted his thoughts of Mike McHenry, and switched them to the other single most important person in his life: *What is Susan doing right now?* Gar wondered, as he checked his code sheet. But there was no time to think of Susan, so he dismissed her from his mind. The fishermen used codes to talk, and though the rest of the guys were working right outside him, Gar thought he'd better satisfy Angus and make a report.

Small groups of fishermen use these codes amongst themselves, and their use is universal. And the codes are closely guarded secrets from season to season. The radios in Gar's pilothouse, with nearly 200 fishing boats in the vicinity all sharing information with their various codes, were positively alive with chatter as one boat's crew reported to another. Information crackled from a number of the radios, but Gar leaped right in with his information, knowing his fellow Z-Squaders would be able to tease his voice out from amongst the prattle. Though not a Z-Squader, Angus was nonetheless privy to the codes.

Gar multiplied the sixteen fish times an estimated eight-pound average, and figured out 130 pounds was just better than the word "scratchy" on his code sheet. So he called Angus and told him, "Goose, my first time through the gear is just a little better than what I would call scratchy."

"Keep gettin' 'em, Lips," Goose came back after a few minutes, but with no report of his own.

SUSAN SAT IN her old bedroom at Mom's house, and while Gar was wondering what she was doing, she wondered what Gar was doing. It was early, and she brushed out her shoulder-length blond hair, thinking Gar was certainly fishing right now. Her hair was very fine. Brushing took only a moment. She checked her petite figure in the vanity mirror. At twenty-four she still had the figure of a teenager. In fact, she still looked like a teenager. A diminutive golden-eyed blonde with a Katie Couric cuteness, and an engaging smile, she invariably had to show identification when ordering wine in a restaurant. And the person inspecting the identification still didn't believe she was over eighteen. She was the quintessential California beauty, not unaware of her charms, and when she batted her eyelashes at unsuspecting shop clerks, she left a trail of devastation in her wake. She wore baby-doll pajamas covered with little red hearts, and couldn't pass a kitten in the street without petting and cooing over it.

Gar. Did he still think about her? He would put his salmon trip in, regardless of the weather. She had learned that much about him. He was very serious about his profession, and fishing came first. He reminded her of her Dad. There was no one as stubborn as Bud, and she knew that if her Dad had ever seriously pursued fishing, he would have been a stick-and-stay-and-make-it-pay type of fisherman too.

Thinking of Dad brought thoughts of her mother, Grace. She and Grace had had a fight recently. Susan blamed Grace for the break up with Gar the year before. It was still an open wound. She thought it might never heal.

This was how it always ended up with thoughts like these. She couldn't manage to hold a track or find a solution. She and Gar could never pick up where they left off. In her heart, she knew this. She wished there was a way to try, to find again what they once had shared, but she didn't know how to do it. She was dating another fisherman now, and felt sure Gar was too proud to take that in stride. An unfortunate series of events had occurred that could not be corrected; like humpty-dumpty and all his pieces once he had fallen.

Preparing to put on her shoes, she looked at her toes. Gar loved her toes and had joked about them. Her toes were ovaled on the ends like little smiley faces. She had several times painted smiley faces on them, thinking about Gar when doing so.

On the radio, Bob Seger's "Against the Wind" song played. At her folk's house in El Granada, she was only a few blocks from the ocean, and she could tell the wind was already blowing. Knowing Gar had run up to the Farallon Islands the night before last, she guessed he was still there and was, accordingly, "running against the wind." Sometimes all the popular songs reminded her of Gar: Blondie's (which could be her) "Call Me;" Christopher Cross's "Sailing;" and, Michael Jackson's "Rock With You." She wished she could rock with him one more time.

Susan had gone to see the new *Star Wars* episode–*The Empire Strikes Back*–and remembered when she and Gar had watched the first *Star Wars* episode together. Had that much time really passed?

On her way out the door she kissed an old photograph she kept on her vanity. A picture depicting Gar and herself with another couple in some field in Oregon, picking (or at least looking) for mushrooms. He was a handsome guy. She had been a cheerleader and the captain of the color guard on a popular marching team, and as such, she had had her pick of suitors. Nonetheless, she had picked him. And she missed him.

"THE WIND WAS blowing harder now, fifty knots or thereabouts..." Jimmy Buffett sang in his title "A-1-A" song, while Gar turned the boat back up into the wind. They had done well on their first long tack down the hill, catching 37 fish. Now, heading back up, the white caps resembled a rolling green field densely populated with thousands of white sheep; it was blowing a steady twenty knots, maybe twenty-five. He goosed the throttle, thinking they would likely anchor early today. It was Friday, and the *Dukes of Hazard* came on at nine o'clock. That Daisy Duke was Gar's favorite TV girl. His loins tingled at the mere thought of watching her strut around in her skimpy shorts.

The nice thing about fishing the Gulf of the Farallons, and one of the several reasons Gar favored doing so, was that the TV reception was very good (being right out in front of the City). This made anchoring during windy afternoons a much more attractive prospect than continuing to muck about in the chop. The Islands were a rockpile on the edge of the continental shelf, yet still within the sphere of influence of the tides produced inside the Golden Gate Bridge, and there was a wide diversity of fishing options. Like an investor's portfolio, when fishing the Farallon Island area, if one spot didn't work there were a number of others that one could try, and surely one of them would produce fish. But if it got real nasty, there was still the Dukes of Hazard. Hemingway would have been appalled, but there you go. Civilization evolves.

"HEY LIPS, ARE you gettin' 'em?" Mike hollered on the Mouse.

"Yeah, we're pickin' the occasional straggler." Gar responded after having run up from the stern.

"We ended up way outside you, and we got, well, let me see. I'm going to try to put it into code. You know how far it is from my house to Annabel's house; well, we got that and a little more," Mike said. Annabel is Gar's Mom.

Gar's Mom and Dad owned a restaurant and bar called the "Gazos Creek Beach House." It was located on Highway One, midway between Half Moon Bay and Santa Cruz, and had been there as "Pinky's" for many years before his parents bought it and renamed it. The distance from Mike's house in El Granada to the Beach House was probably about 35 actual miles, so Gar guessed Mike had around fifty fish, which was similar to what he and Jeff had caught.

"Yeah, right. I think, if I'm reading your code, we have about the same. But then again, if I don't get your code, you either have more than me, or less. I guess it doesn't matter, because it's getting too windy to leave my groove anyway. As a matter of fact, I think we're going to anchor up early and get ready to watch Daisy Duke tonight," Gar said.

"Breaker, breaker, breaker! Can a poor working postman get in on this channel? Come back." Red Rathborne, the Half Moon Bay Postmaster who also had a small salmon boat, asked to jump in on the conversation.

"Is that you, Lick 'em and Stick 'em?" Michael asked.

"You bet, Michael. I got a new code myself, it's called, appropriately, the *Zip Code*. You see, you take the last two numbers of the Half Moon Bay Zip Code (19), and you subtract 10, and you get what I got for the morning drilling away back and forth out here in front of home (Pillar Point)." Red joked over the radio, but he was clearly aware of the importance of codes.

He had a small boat, and fished more for fun than profit. So nine fish for the morning was a good catch for him.

"Oh, all right. You're gettin' 'em, Red. How's your wind down there?" Mike asked.

"It's just starting to come up. I hear you guys talking like you have more, so I expect we will soon enough. I don't think I'll be here too much longer. So I'll let you guys go, and check you tomorrow. You staying out tonight, Michael?" Red asked.

"Yeah. I don't know. We'll see what the day brings. All right, Lick 'em and Stick 'em, we'll give you a check, either way, tomorrow morning. Throw your deckhand a cookie," Mike joked, as he knew Red didn't have a deckhand.

GARALONEY AND JEFF made a very long tack on a course against the surging swell of the ocean, "up the hill" in the parlance of fishermen, and this took about four hours. Then a short 45 minute tack back along the same course in reverse with the wind, and they had covered the same distance. Now almost back at the top end of their tack, they had 127 fish for the day, and Gar decided it was time to go anchor. It was six o'clock, and they were beat.

ANCHORED AND FED by eight o'clock, the boys did a few last-minute chores before retiring to their bunks. The Dukes of Hazard would be on in a little while, though Jeff wouldn't stay up for that.

Tomorrow was another day. The wind-driven rotary-turbine spun insanely, the tick-ticking echoing about the cabin at a rate consistent with gale-force winds. Gar laid back and activated the TV on the shelf over the end of his bunk. They were laying like ducks here behind the Island, and with many of the boats having run back into town he did not worry about slipping his anchor and drifting into another boat.

The wind had a way of wrapping Gar up like a warm and fuzzy security blanket. And the Farallon Island Lighthouse flashed its rhythmic and benevolent beam over the gently bobbing boats. Gar was fast asleep before Daisy Duke even appeared.

CHAPTER 5

MAY 3–6, 1980.

AT THREE O'CLOCK in the morning, Michael called over the radio: "Hey, Lips, wake up. You're draggin' your anchor. YO, LIPS, WAKE UP!!!"

Gar swam up into a state of consciousness only reluctantly, but was instantly alert and panicked when consciousness was realized.

"Oh, shit! I'm right on top of this guy! Jeff, get up here, quick!" Gar shouted.

Gar leaped from his bunk and realized that his boat was in imminent danger of colliding with another boat. The wind was smoking. Perhaps its speed was that "Fifty knots, or thereabouts" that Jimmy Buffett sang about the day before. The wind was a thing alive, tearing the tops off the swells and sending them hurling into the blackness of the night.

OUT THE BACK door, Gar discovered he had drug his anchor so that his stern was right on top of Jimmy on the ***Osprey***'s bow, and he was right on top of his anchor cable. The situation was such that Jimmy's anchor line was leading at an angle right under the ***Visit***'s fantail in the proximity of the propeller. Gar already had the engine fired, but he feared that putting the boat in gear might wrap Jimmy's anchor line in his propeller. He prayed Jeff would hurry up out of the fo'c'sle. An engine started in the middle of the night without first checking the oil was a risky proposition, and done only in the case of an emergency. That he had started the engine would warn Jeff.

JEFF WAS UPSTAIRS now, and none too soon. Gar shouted at him. "Go up on the bow and start winding up the anchor so we can get away from this guy. Damn, we're close!"

Jeff looked out the back door and saw how dangerously close they were, but still had time to offer a quip. "Oh, fuck! We got an *osprey* about to have us for breakfast."

There was no need to explain to Jeff, despite his joking, how dangerous it is when two boats come together on the ocean, especially two wood boats. They can tear each other's hulls up in no time at all. And it would be even worse for *these* two boats, with their outrigger poles distended and locked into the fishing positions.

When two boats collide and entangle outrigger poles, it not only results in broken poles. It generates additional problems. With all their rigging lines, the boats will likely end up actually tangled together, making separation difficult. And while these tangled lines hold the boats together, the swells of the sea cause the hulls to continue to collide and smash. Untangling is futile. Sharp knives and bolt-cutters to sever rigging quickly is the only answer. Once the boats free themselves, an immediate trip to town for several days of costly repairs is a given.

JEFF STARTED WINDING up the anchor cable. Jimmy had finally awakened and was out on his bow, letting some of his cable out, which allowed his boat to drift back. Quickly the two boats started distancing themselves from one another, and Gar put the ***Visit*** in gear, idling ahead, easing tension on his anchor line, and Jeff continued spooling the ground gear onto the winch.

These operations were conducted in silence, accompanied only by the shrieking sounds of the wind. Each of these veteran fishermen knew what needed to be done, and they did it in silence. The Farallon Island Lighthouse flashed its beam over this scene with an increased urgency, illuminating the tensely-worked boat maneuvers and wind-torn spray.

AFTER THY WERE clear, Michael came on and dispelled the tension. "Hey, Lips, looks like you're okay," he said. "We're going to get the fuck out of here. If you're staying out, why don't you come over here and take my spot? We're going to bunch it. It's pretty good right here. There are bottom ridges here that run northeast-southwest, and in a northwest wind like this it seems like your anchor catches in those. Even if you slip out of one, you'll catch the next one."

"All right. Yeah, we're staying out and finishing our trip. Well, we'll at least give it a day and see what happens. Thanks for that. I'll idle over and hang tight off your starboard stern until you get clear, then sneak right in there where you were," Gar said.

"Yeah, slide up in here and tell Jeff to throw it over when your meter says nine fathoms. That's always been the best for me," Mike instructed.

"Roger. Okay, I see you're clear, so I'm slipping in. Hope it was as coital for you as it's going to be for me." Gar allowed himself a small joke. The danger was past. He watched as Mike's boat motored away from the anchorage.

"Yeah, I've tried all over this fuckin' rockpile, and this seems like the best. I've never lost an anchor either, like you will over by the Coast Guard buoy," Mike said.

"Roger that. I left one there last year. Tom Monahan (an abalone diver) was going to keep his eyes open and maybe buoy it off, so we could come on a flat day and try to get it. We busted it off on a morning just like this one. I couldn't ever get around upwind to try backing up on it that way. It was another one of those nightmares. I actually had it buoyed off before we broke it, but the buoy chaffed off later on. I finished my trip though. I quit a little bit early every night and came in and tied off on the Coast Guard buoy," Gar said. The danger just past had made Gar garrulous. He knew this, but he couldn't stop chattering. Besides, this was Michael he was talking to.

"Thatta boy, Lips. That's how you put in a trip," Mike said, then his voice changed. "Holy shit! We're just getting out here into the wind and swell, and it's sloppy as fuck. You are not going to make it down to Pa's Canyon today, Lips. It's too fucking shitty. You got leaders to tie, or something like that, you better do it, cause that's the kind of day it is." He paused for a moment. "You might get a short tack up the inside to maybe the North Island or the *Pimple* for a few hours until you can't stand it, then a really short one back down to the anchorage. That's all I'm bettin' you'll get today."

"Alright. Yeah, we'll find something to do. Okay, I'll check you in a bit. I want to make sure I get this hook set right. We might be here a few days," Gar said.

"Good luck, Lips. We'll see you in town, or maybe we'll be back out in a few days before you finish your trip. Keep your powder dry." Mike clicked off.

"Yeah, all right, good mornin' to ya, Mackerel. Thanks for the heads up. I almost got my lunch served early there with Jimmy. Good lookin' out," Gar said into the microphone, then hollered at Jeff to throw the anchor over the side while he backed the boat up, playing out cable. When almost all the cable was out, Gar pounded on the window and hollered, "Dog it off," which Jeff did. He had the maximum amount of scope out so that they would ride better and be less likely to drag the anchor. The boat tossed from side to side before the cable became taut. Then it bucked a bit.

"PHWEEEE-PHWUUUU, WE'RE coming by your stern, Gar." Sully's voice floated through the speakers a few minutes after Gar and Jeff got their anchor set. There was a perceptible lightening of the sky on the eastern horizon, though dawn was still a ways off. It was more a feeling than anything visibly tangible. But a new day was impending.

"Roger," Gar acknowledged. He looked out the back door to see Sully idling slothfully into the wind just astern of the ***Visit***. Sully was up on his flying bridge and Merlo was out on the bow, grinning from ear to ear as only Merlo can do. Gar liked Merlo. Everybody liked Merlo, for that matter. He was a good kid, and a hard worker. And he was a very polite young man as well.

OUT ON THE ***Visit***'s stern, Gar and Sully had to speak up to hear each other, but they didn't have to shout. "What's up, Sully? Did you do any business here the last couple of days?" Gar asked. He and Timmy Sullivan were always good competition, and though they liked to compete with one another, neither begrudged the other good fishing.

"Yeah, we cracked a hundred both days." Timmy sort of eased into it, not wanting to outright admit that Gar probably had him beat. "How did you guys do? I know you must have done real good."

"We had a hundred fifty seven the first day–with one hog–and a hundred twenty seven yesterday, whatever that adds up to. Somewhere around two hundred and eighty four for the trip so far, I'd guess." Gar reported this with a Merlo-sized grin.

"Yeah, I knew it. You got us, Lips."

Then Merlo chimed in. "It must be that new paint job that's doing it for you."

"Yeah, I don't know. We just set our gear into the right spot for a change," Gar replied.

Then Sully cut to the chase. "Hey, Lips, we're going to batter our way over to the point this morning and anchor. Angus came by my stern last night and said they had some pretty good fishing up on the north side of the point in the shallows, just outside the crab pots. He told me not to tell you, but you know how that goes. You're my partner, Lips. Just don't let on that I told you. He ran over there last night. I don't know if they will get to fish there today, but I'm sure they'll have much better weather on the inside than out here on these fucking islands."

"Yeah, I know. We're halfway to China out here on this fuckin' rockpile. I'm sure it's gonna' be better in there. Okay, we'll hang out here today, and then see what happens in the morning. I'll try to come by your stern when I do get over there. Goose, he's got too many radios and channels, so I won't let on about this on any radios. What a prick, though!

He's getting even because he thinks I sandbagged him the day before yesterday. I made my report...."

"Yes, I know," Tim broke in. "You two will never quit."

"Sully, tell me the truth. Do I start these things, or is it him?" Gar asked.

"No. I think Angus likes to get it going with you. I don't know what it is with him. Are you sure you're not brothers? Because you fight just like me and my brother," Tim answered seriously.

Then Merlo added, "I think Goose is jealous 'cause you have too much fun in town, and he doesn't know how." Which was probably the closest thing to the truth as anything else.

"Yeah, Mer, I think you're right. Okay, you guys better get going if you're going to do it. I'll see you tomorrow. Good luck." Gar waved as Timmy backed away.

Jeff, who had been standing silent the whole time, yelled, "Don't get your balls wet on the way over there!"

Timmy yelled faintly back, almost too far away to be heard. "Throw Jeff a cookie, Lips."

BACK IN THE cabin, and now wide awake at 4:30 a.m., Gar told Jeff that they would just do some chores this morning, and to catch another hour or two of sleep if he wanted it. Jeff enthusiastically agreed to this and disappeared into his cubbyhole after shutting off the engine.

Gar gazed for a while at the rhythmic circular sweep of the lighthouse beam and felt himself becoming mesmerized. He shook his head, and grabbed the microphone to call Michael before he got too far away.

"You pick me up, Michael?" he inquired. "You still in range?"

"That you, Gar? Mike's sleeping." Peterskin's voice floated faintly through the ether.

"Hey, Skin, what's going on? You a little stiff after laying around all spring then jumping back into it?" Gar asked.

"Yeah, not bad. I'll live. Hey, did I tell you what happened up in the City the other night? Come Back." Pete's signal strength improved and his voice became less faint. Pete loved to tell jokes. He had gone to college up in Oregon and was a preppy type of guy. A lot of fun, he was probably Gar's favorite drinking buddy. He was a handsome guy and wore intelligent-looking glasses. And he was a good running partner when picking up chicks.

"I give up, what happened?" Gar bit.

"Yeah, well, I ran into this midget hooker, and I paid her thirty-seven dollars to go up on me!"

"Ha, Ha, ha. Now that's funny. Hey, did I tell you about this gal I seen in the hardware store the other day? She comes in and asks the guy behind the counter for a three-inch strap hinge. She's got it written on this piece of paper, so you know her husband had sent her. So, anyway, this guy behind the counter says, 'Hey lady, do you want'a screw for that?' And she says, 'No, but I'll blow you for that little clock radio up there on the third shelf.'"

"All right. I can't take it anymore. Next you'll be trying to ask me about the lady that farted in the barrel. What else is new?" Pete asked.

"Nothing. I thought I'd spend the day catching up on chores, but it's only five o'clock in the morning, and I'm already bored. So I don't know what we're going to do yet. Maybe we'll go try a tack up the inside, like Michael suggested. It's only about three minutes from here to where it's deep enough for me to throw in my gear. So I could still make the sunup bite, if I hurry," Gar said.

"Yeah, I'll tell you what. You're lucky you're not here. We're not that far below where we fished yesterday. And it's plain shitty. But we're going with it. I'd hate to be going the other direction right now. Relax, Gar, you'll get plenty of fishing time. The season's young. Come back."

"All right, Skin. I gotta' go decide what I'm going to do. I'll see you subsequently. Good luck with your island, *Can't Say*. What a beauty. Cchhheeeck you later. And, oh yeah, I just called to tell Michael I like this spot. No more over by the Coast Guard buoy for me." Gar clicked off.

"Good bye, Lips. Don't let your meat loaf." Pete signed off.

GAR LEANED BACK in his running chair to think. On the ***Visit*** the running seat was a bar stool. Geno had never built a comfortable, bolted down running chair, because he did not want anyone to fall asleep on wheel watch. Gar decided that was wise when he bought the boat, and had never changed it. The stool would get tossed around in rough weather, though, and you had to hang on just to sit on it.

Processing information often took time and quiet. And there was no better time than right now for that. It was early. After he and Pete had exchanged pleasantries, there was no one talking on the radios. Everyone was gone to town, or sleeping late. There was just a steady whirring noise coming from the wind-driven rotary-turbine ventilator. The thing was spinning too fast to make a tick-ticking noise. There was just that and the mesmerizing sweep of the lighthouse beam, endlessly circling.

Gar thought about what the weather might be like at Point Reyes, which was twenty-two miles inside of his position out here at the Island. The weather can change dramatically between a mile or two off the beach, and twenty-two miles out. It would certainly be much better on the inside, and since Gar was considering fishing out here, today, why shouldn't he consider fishing in there? There was a very real possibility that Goose, and now Sully, were in there catching fish, while he wasn't. That thought was the genesis of a shift in plans.

The idea of simply sitting here all day was working on Gar. As a deckhand with a man named Fache Martin a number of years earlier, he had wasted many days, although he had had a lot of fun doing it. Fache was called this because a San Francisco Chronicle reporter had once gone out with them to look at Russian trawlers and had printed: "Martin, who hides his baby face behind an elaborate set of whiskers and mustache...." So *Baby Face* came first. He didn't much care for the name, but nobody gave a damn about that.

He was a very aggressive Z-Squad member. Called *Babyface* after the news article, then the Italian's shortened it to simply *Fache,* which is face in Italian. Fache liked to chase women, which was the primary pursuit and raison d'être of the entire Squad. And low crawling was an accepted activity within the Squad. Low crawling was when you took a girl from another Squad member. It was a basic proposition that if a nonmember low crawled the president, he could become a member. That was the loophole Gar had used when he approached Michael and asked if he could buy a blue sail and put on the coveted white "Z." True, the girl he used had been one of your garden-variety throw-aways, but he had nonetheless stolen her from Michael. When he pointed that out, Mike acquiesced.

"You know, Lips," he told him. "I think with your heritage we gotta let you in, not to mention you earned it."

Gar had also asked Johnny T, who was considered the co-president of the Z-Squad, and Johnny T had said, "Hell, yeah. I thought it was automatic when you bought the boat that you would get a sail. I don't know why you waited so long to ask."

Gar figured he had confirmation and reconfirmation, and he bought the sail. The day he rigged it on the boat was a memorable day, and he reminisced about that now.

The wild and crazy times the Squad spent in Eureka at the notorious waterfront bar, the *Vista del Mar*, were prominent in those memories. Gar had actually won money on the *Vista* (for short) before ever setting foot inside the place. He was working for Fache, and neither he nor Fache had ever been to the Eureka waterfront, or to the *Vista* (also called the VD Club). They worked their way north with the more experienced Squad members that year, from Bodega Bay to Fort Bragg, and finally the fish set in at the Light Ship below Eureka. They ended their trip following the other boats into town looking for the *Vista del Mar*. They wound their way up the lengthy channel into the Eureka waterfront area, sometimes called "Two Street," to get there.

They were behind John Dooley, who had the ***Hazel Lorraine***. The sulfuric stench from the pulp mills was powerful. Gar spotted a small, single-story, run-down building painted a faded burnt-orange color. The building was settling on several of its corners, making the roofline hog's-back crooked. It had a small beer sign, four-inch black letters on a lighted white background, that said simply: **VISTA DEL MAR**. There was also a small martini-shaped neon sign flashing off and on in the window, signifying cocktails were served there.

Gar pointed this place out, as they were meandering up the channel, and said that it must be the *Vista*. Fache immediately disagreed. He hypothesized that a place with a reputation like the VD Club would certainly be much bigger and fancier. Gar tried to use logic, insisting that the bar had the right name and was in the right area, and John Dooley was swinging in to tie up right there. But Fache was adamant. So they bet five bucks. And of course, Gar ultimately won.

The *Vista del Mar*, though, lived up to its reputation and was certainly a remarkable dive. It was even less to look at on the inside. Paneled with the same faux-walnut surfacing as the ***Visit***'s cabin interior, it had an L-shaped bar in a room with just enough space at one end of the "L" for a pool table. An eight-person, round hatch table was squeezed into the corner opposite of the right angle of the bar's L. There were, perhaps, a half dozen other small tables, with maybe twenty chairs scattered around those. The bar itself was outfitted with a number of bar stools. Packed, the place couldn't hold more than 125 people, and that would be too many, with the drinkers jammed down the hallway to the restaurant, as well as outside into the small parking lot.

But, howdy, did they know how to make a drink! The drinks were at least doubles, and they were sold cheap. One could get drunk on the five dollars Gar had won from Fache, and blot-o'ed on ten. It made buying drinks for girls very affordable...And there was no shortage of girls.

"A HUGE PENIS makes for a life of disquietude," Gar remembered telling the girl at the *Vista* bar one morning, when she asked why he was drunk before noon.

She said something like, "Oh, you poor baby. What happens? Do you trip on it getting in and out of the shower, or what?"

"No, it's just that girls, once they've slept with me, become amative to the point that I've actually started working at doing a bad job in the hope that they won't be satiated. But you know how that goes. Love making is like war. It's easy to begin, but hard to stop."

Gar's voice had doubtless been slurred. She had bit, though, and shortly thereafter she took him home and fucked his brains out. She was one of those waterfront women who prey on drunken fishermen like Gar. And you couldn't blame her for that.

She was "squad material," in that she liked their panache. The guys of the Z-Squad always maintained a class act. They normally did well fishing, and on their way to town they tried to clean and dress more thoughtfully than the average fisherman. This, in and of itself, provided a substantial edge in the singles pick-up scene.

There were plenty of activities on the waterfront singles outlook–boat barbeques, volley-ball games, swimming parties up one of the rivers, pie fights, and, of course, sexual intrigues. Gar had learned two basic secrets to picking up women from the Squad: you've got to make them laugh, and they don't want to sleep with just anybody. They want to sleep with a "somebody." And this is what made the invention of the Z-Squad so ingenious. Overnight, a random assortment of average guys became *somebodies*, and it therefore became *dernier cri* for waterfront women (and others, too) to sleep with a Z-Squader "somebody."

One year the Squad pooled all the money they made from an incidental catch of rock fish they snared while on a salmon trip. This amounted to several hundred dollars. Peterskin and John Dooley took the money to a local supermarket and bought a couple hundred frozen cream pies, then they stopped at a pizza parlor and convinced them to thaw the pies in their pizza ovens.

Peterskin and Dooley returned to the *Vista* with the pies, walking in with a shopping cart they had stolen from the supermarket stocked completely full, and immediately started handing out the pies. It was mid-afternoon and most of the customers, already aglow, didn't understand why they were being treated to so much sugar, until, with the last pie handed out, John Dooley stuck a chocolate cream in someone's face. Roberta Flack's, "The First Time Ever I Saw Your Face" was playing sentimentally on the jukebox when this happened. Someone else did it to someone else, and the frenzy began. With extra pies sitting on all the tables, patrons were able to quickly reload. It turned into a free-for-all.

One classic moment was when Jimmy Dawn took a pie down to the boat to Sully, who at the time was too young to drink, and told him he was missing the pie fight and he should go up there and throw some pies. Timmy responded, saying, "Okay, yeah, gimme a pie." And at that Jimmy Dawn unhesitatingly crammed the pie in Timmy's face. The story lives in infamy as a Squad legend.

One of the lessons learned was that a man should never say, "gimme a pie" in the middle of a pie fight. For years afterwards, the sound of a Roberta Flack record caused instant and inexplicable hilarity in coastal California waterfront bars. The stories spread and the legends grew.

HAPPY SQUAD RECOLLECTIONS triggered, conversely, unhappier childhood musings for Gar. He had grown up in the very small community of Pescadero. Not only that, but he was from out in the boondocks of that small town.

They lived a mile or so up a dirt road that was muddy a fair percentage of the school year. Walking to school in the mud meant muddy clothes, and because of this Gar and his siblings were dubbed "The Oakies."

The fact that Gar's abusive stepfather drank habitually on an otherwise tight budget meant that there was little money for school supplies and clothing. And this further supported the other kid's justification for calling Gar an Oakie.

But there were good Pescadero memories, too. Wintertime there and the steelhead fishing, and when the occasional salmon came up Pescadero Creek to spawn. It was terrific fun to chase those salmon. And there were also plenty of trout and crawdads to fish for in the summertime.

He had come a long ways since his "Oakie" days in Pescadero, he reminisced now, and successfully paying for this boat was incredibly important to defining who and what he had become. He had truly come a long way. And he had done it with sheer determination, and all alone. The guys in the Squad, and even Susan for that matter, didn't really know about the Oakie days. They only knew Gar's folks now had a fairly successful bar and restaurant business south of Pescadero on Cabrillo highway One. Gar's Mom had eventually divorced the abusive stepfather of the early Pescadero growing up period, and remarried a plumber from up the coast in Half Moon Bay. And even though Jack was a hard partier, he was nonetheless a good provider, and never abusive.

Jack was a long-time marcher in the local drill team, named the *Caballeros*. This was the same team for which Susan had captained the color guard. It was a fun group that consisted of dozens of successful Half Moon Bay respectables.

The past, for Gar was indeed troubling, but he had since worked very hard to overcome it. At Pescadero elementary school he had been the class clown, working little at his lessons. But he'd passed tests like a Rhode's Scholar. In seventh grade they gave him an IQ test that determined that Gar was genius with an IQ of 150.

The genius thing never meant much to Gar, other than giving him confidence in times, such as now, of indecision. He always felt he had the ability to think things through to the most logical conclusion.

SETTING OLD MEMORIES aside, Gar thought about the situation at hand and decided to go set the gear just outside the anchorage, and point the boat up and in toward Point Reyes. This was a variation of the up-the-inside-of-the-islands-until-the-wind-became-too-much tack, that he had been contemplating. He went down to the engine room to check the oil and grease the fittings, meanwhile singing the "Nothin' could be finna" song.

"You changed your mind, didn't you?" Jeff poked his head up from his cubbyhole.

"Yeah, let's go set 'em," Gar replied. "And make a long one up to the Point and see what those guys are doing. I'm already bored."

"Yeah, I was just laying here thinking about what Sully said, that Goose probably heard something good. And that he likely won't call us for a few days if he does find something. Let's go do it." Jeff jumped enthusiastically out of bed.

Mike McHenry and the ***Merva W.***

CHAPTER 6

THE WIND WAS blowing at forty knots, and the ***Visit*** rolled hard at trolling speed. But they were quartering into the wind, just east of north on the compass, and with the staysail raised they laid over to starboard and didn't ride too bad. The sail took the snap out of the roll. As long as they weren't taking green water over the bow, at the risk of breaking out the front windows, the trip would be a harmless one.

They only had two tiny salmon at twelve o'clock, and Gar decided they would eat lunch, stack the gear aboard, then kick the throttle up a few notches to just a little bit short of running speed so they could get to where they were going. Gar wanted to go to the Point Reyes area, about 15 miles northeast of their present location. So after a lunch of bologna sandwiches, they did just that. They took one more little fish off the gear while checking and changing bad leaders, and put on shiny new baits in anticipation of setting the gear no later than tomorrow morning. Gar had once caught fish right on the outside edge coming into the Point Reyes anchorage (which is on the southeast side of the long protrusion that comprises the point bluff), and thought with as much daylight as there was, they might yet find a place to make a day of it.

APPROCHING THE ANCHORAGE, though, they saw immediately that there were no birds working, or any other sign that made Gar want to set his gear. Because of this, he ran up and into the bight of the Point, which is a long cruise paralleling the majestic red-bluff cliffs on the south side of the promontory that makes up the cape. The promontory is a long neck of high, solid rock that's as ominous as it is large. The 75-foot-tall lighthouse on its tip is a tiny little toy, insignificant looking in the light of day, in contrast to the towering point which rises four times as high.

The Point Reyes Lighthouse has the distinction of being the westernmost lighthouse in the State of California, and sitting atop a 300-foot promontory as it does, it is indisputably the tallest lighthouse in the state. But it is so high up one can hardly see it. It is like an erect and admonitory finger pointing into the sky. It is a very old lighthouse, but sitting as high up as it does, its bright beacon can be seen for countless miles out to sea. An infinite number of vessels have avoided the dangerous rocks at the base of the Point Reyes promontory as a result of this lighthouse, and generations of sailors have regarded its warning beam. But in the daytime, of course, it is nothing. Just a slender white spire perched high up on the bluff.

The weather had changed. The once brutal sea was tender now, and flat: the wind had abated, and the sun was warm. The boat, traveling once again at full speed, was once again a pleasure to live on. The stench of cow manure came to the boat as it approached the promontory. The wind, no matter what direction it is blowing, always seems to swirl around to the east side of the anchorage, where high atop the cliffs dairy cows roam in the fields. Anyone who has ever been to the Point knows they are there when they smell the fecund aroma of Mendoza's cows.

TODAY THEY TOOK the extra time to run all the way into the anchorage. The Point itself is about five miles long, and so is the anchorage. Of course, the further into the bight one ventures, the nicer it gets. There's less swell, more sun, and diminished wind. Nevertheless the smell of the cows.

All the way into the furthest reaches of the bight was a dock where the Yukon Gang hung out. The dock was so far back in the loop that it was barely visible, remaining unseen until one was almost all the way into the natural crook behind the huge cape.

Gar ran up amongst the identically-painted, Monterey-style salmon trollers that belonged to the Yukon Gang. This was a group of vintage Italians, led by Mario on the ***Barbara Ann,*** who had been around for many years. When he found a suitable spot, he hollered at Jeff to toss the anchor over the side.

Beat from a long, tough day making the crossing from the Islands, and now with the sun settling down on top of the huge promontory that stood hundreds of feet above the bay, Gar started dinner. He reminded Jeff to throw some more ice on the fish, and make sure there was plenty of bait ready for the morning.

THE LOVE BOAT was showing on television, but the reception wasn't very good. So Gar's attention was only minimally devoted to the program when Timmy whistled on the Mouse. Gar answered immediately.

"Where are you at, Lips?" Timmy said. "I heard you earlier saying you were afraid you'd bust your anchor off, so you ran over here. Blink your deck lights so I can come find you and sleep by your side." He was obviously very close, judging by the strength of his radio signal.

"I'm right here, Sull. I'm blinking them ... On ... Off ... On ... Off ... You see me?"

"Okay, I see you. You're way the fuck up in there. We're coming, though. I'll see you in a few minutes. I want to get up next to you." Sully was repeating himself and was obviously tired.

TEN MINUTES LATER Timmy was once again bobbing at Gar's stern. He had good news. From the flying bridge he said, "You'll have to follow me out to this tremendous spot in the morning. We're going to get up at 3:45, and leave by four o'clock. It's a long ways out and around. But we ended up with a good day. It's pretty shallow, and you have to look out for crab pots. Maybe like 21, and into 19 fathoms. Much nicer grade of fish. I might have one to bet with now, too."

"Yeah, so, we use four-fathom stops." Gar did the math in his head. "So how much wire do you let out, and what do you use, like six leaders?" Gar was excited, but at the same time mildly disconcerted. This was shallower than he was used to fishing.

"We just put out seven spreads. I've got three-fathom stops. Then I just try to make sure I don't bump bottom with my leads. It'll take you a couple of passes and you'll get the hang of it. You have to kind of keep turning the boat in order to bend around the fathom curve," Tim added.

"All right. How far above the Point do you put in?" Gar asked.

"Just be up and follow me in the morning, Lips. Trust me. It's one of those deals that I can't explain with simple readings. You'll see what I mean when you get there." Timmy was rather apocryphal sounding, almost as though he was teasing his friend, and he seemed to enjoy sounding this way.

"Okay. Are you going to tell me how many fish you had, or is that part of the suspense?" Gar couldn't stand it.

"Well, we didn't break a hundred, but if we'd of had one more we would have had triple digits," Tim said. He was trying to stand up real tall. He was somewhat challenged longitudinally.

"Holy Geesus fucking Christ! You don't have to be secretive here. We're not on the radio," Gar said, laughing. "Besides, that's a pretty fucking good day, and one worth crowing about."

"Yeah, we're happy. And the grade is excellent. Lotta splitters. I think I got one I'll bet on, too. What's the bet?" Tim asked.

"Well, a round of drinks for the four of us seems fair, doesn't it?"

"You're on, Lips. All Right. I'm going to go to bed now. Still smells like cow shit in here, doesn't it? Wish that Mendoza would quit feeding them so much. Oh yeah, the wind wasn't too bad up there. But there's a lump, and you'll see about the current." Then in an aside, "Hey, Jeff, has Lips been throwing you those cookies I told him about?" Tim asked.

"The only cookie I want is that Cookie McClure," Jeff grinned. "The new cocktail waitress at the Princeton Inn."

"If anybody can get her, It's you partner. All right, see you guys in the morning. I'm outta here at four sharp." Tim started backing away.

"Thanks, Sully. We'll be ready. Good night, Merlo. Keep smilin', it makes people wonder what you're up to." Gar waved goodbye to both of the fishermen.

Merlo gave a familiar holler as they were almost out of range. "Keep gettin' 'em, Lips."

Everybody talked like Michael.

WHAT GOES AROUND, comes around, Gar thought as he laid back in the bunk. He was thinking that if Goose had told him the night before about this new spot, he too would have had another good day. Instead he had three small rags to show for a very long day on the water.

Don't get mad, just get even, and *what goes around, comes around* were two famous Z-Squad mantras. Gar wondered, however, if Goose had now gotten even, or if he should try to retaliate in light of the fact that Angus had backstabbed him again.

The prospect was wearying. Retaliation was not really a part of Gar's disposition. It wasn't worth the effort, he decided, then focused his attention on the Fantasy Island television program. There was a girl on the show, a new guest on the Island that looked a lot like Susan.

God, he missed her. He considered the fact that he was bobbing in an anchorage at Point Reyes, and she was only about fifty miles away from him. But it might as well be the outer reaches of Mongolia.

AT FOUR SHARP, Gar was drifting off Sully's stern. He hadn't bothered calling on the radio, as he could see Tim and Merlo were awake and busy.

Tim pulled his anchor and Gar followed him out of the anchorage.

THEY ROUNDED THE west-southwest tip of the Point at daybreak, and a few miles further north Timmy slowed down while hollering on the Mouse for Gar to set his gear into the water anywhere he felt like, just not too close.

Gar looked at Jeff standing up on the bow of the boat, blowing steam off a cup of coffee and smoking a cigarette, and felt a premonition of good fishing to come. It was nothing he could put his finger on. Just a feeling. But there was something about the brightening pink sky of dawn, and the cormorants calling overhead, that was utterly entrancing. There were fish here. And they would get them. Gar yelled at Jeff and the two men shared a grin before getting to work. The sky overhead was a riot of dawn color and the grins of the men broke into spontaneous laughter. There was no need for explanations. This was a good place to be.

Gar ran a few minutes outside of Tim, and slightly ahead of him, which put him in a position where he could watch Timmy by simply looking up from his starboard stern work post.

IN THE PIT, Gar and Jeff put out just one flasher and four baits on each line, a total of only five hooks per line. It was indeed shallow here. The insulators and springs looked dead, though, after all the gear was set. But they could see Sully, every other minute, throwing yet another shiny salmon onto his boat. Sully was also much further astern after only twenty or so minutes of fishing, and Gar figured they were going too fast. But the throttle was as low as it would go.

They watched Sully continue to put fish on his boat. And they noted that he continued to fall further and further behind, and it was almost too far to see just exactly how much business he was doing. Frustrated, Gar got out some of Geno's old tire drags that he had never used, and started rigging those.

He put them over the side, and could see by the angle at which the bow lines hung back that the boat had slowed some, but they were still flying in the current. It was that early morning tide coming out of the Golden Gate. Though they were forty miles from San Francisco, the water coming out of the Bay was almost as swift as it was in the narrows under the bridge. Well, maybe not that bad, but it was amazing how strong the current was. He now understood what Timmy had talked about the night before.

THE FLOPPER STOPPERS were weighted, bird-shaped stabilizers that hung from a chain midway out on the poles, and they had several holes to pin the shackle in. Gar always used the center hole, but thought now if he hung them from the back hole they would tip forward and provide more drag. So he did that. Half an hour later he could see by the new angle on the bow lines that they had slowed considerably.

They also had several lines pumping.

BACK IN THE stern and running through the gear, the boys started putting fish on the boat. Nice, fat, ten-pound Sacramento River fish. Sacramento River fish have distinctive brown backs, are wide and deep, and have large black spots speckling the dorsal area.

Jeff couldn't help himself. "Yahoo," he shouted into the air. "I think I like this spot."

"Yeah, but they keep stripping the baits." Gar liked the spot too, but he was more pragmatic. The problem with bait fishing is that when the fish bite, then get off the hook, you not only end up losing the fish. You thereafter tow around an empty, unbaited hook until it is finally changed out with a baited hook. It is enough to make a fisherman mad.

"Maybe we should use spoons," Jeff suggested.

"I thought of that, but I don't want to take the scent out of the water. You know, I've got an idea that will partially solve our problem. Remember those short leaders up in the gear cabinet, the ones with the spoons tied on? I used to use those on my bow poles. I'm thinking we also have those crimp-on stops we could put halfway in between our regular stops. Maybe we could use just one of those in between the four-fathom stops. Then we'll have, every two fathoms, an alternating bait arrangement. You get me?" Gar said.

"Yeah, piece of cake," Jeff said, clambering out of the pit. "I'll get them, and the crimping pliers."

THEY WENT THROUGH the gear, working in the changes, including adding leaders with spoons. As they did this, they took six-or-eight nice, fat fish off the gear. When the work was done, Gar turned around as Sully had done thirty minutes earlier.

HEADING BACK TOWARD the Point they were bucking into the current and it required considerable throttle to make headway through the water. Gar pulled the drags, but left the floppers in. It was still quite rolly here, although with much less wind than at the Island. And there was a long, lazy swell. The shoreline was close enough they could see the waves breaking on a ten-mile-long sandy beach. Beyond the beach there was tuled marshland, and the tang of marsh mud wafted upon the air.

The fish at first didn't want to bite with the boat going this direction, but after adjusting the speed some more the lines jumped into action.

They passed Angus going up his tack, and he was too busy to wave. Jeff offered an observation. "He can be real friendly at the bar, but he sure is stuck-up out here."

"Unless you have something he wants," Gar finished the thought. "I'm going to holler at him."

UP IN THE wheelhouse, Gar called Angus on the Mouse. "Hey, Goose, how's life treating you?"

Angus got out of his stern, ran up to his radio and said, "Why are you calling me, Gar?"

"Just bored, and thought I'd say good morning to you. Is everything all right?" Gar smiled.

"Yeah, just fine, Lips. I gotta' go. I've got a line hanging." Angus was not very friendly.

"All right, Goose, cchheeck you later." Gar clicked off.

AFTER HALF A day of fishing, they had the spot pretty well figured out. It had taken much trial and error to correct for a powerful current that never seemed to abate. But they had around fifty fish so far, and things looked promising for a good day. Or maybe, with luck, several good days.

Although the groove here was narrow, and more boats were showing up by the hour, not all of them were able to figure out how to fish the current. They were passing at least a dozen boats going the opposite direction every tack, and every hour that number increased.

GOOSE CAME BY that night in the anchorage, and Gar was shocked when Jeff said he was at their stern wanting to talk. Gar went back to the stern and Goose was up on his bow–his deckhand was keeping the nose of the boat up close to Gar's stern. Angus' boat, like Gar's, didn't have a flying bridge. So the deckhand had to drive in these situations.

"Hey, Goose, what's up? Fancy meeting you here," Gar spoke as cheerfully as possible.

"Gar, how many people did you tell, today, about our fishing?" Goose asked accusingly.

"I didn't actually tell anyone. I was so busy trying to keep my boat in the groove, I didn't talk to anyone but you in the morning. And I think Sully a couple of times, but always on the Mouse." Gar replied equably.

"You know why I get so pissed at you? You're always trying to help those nobody assholes who don't mean anything. Are you sure you didn't call some of those guys today? Because there's sure a lot of these assholes that have shown up." Goose had his territorial-surfer attitude set on high. He stood on the bow of his boat like Admiral Nelson at Trafalgar, arrogantly impervious, and disdainfully dealing with underlings only because it had to be done. Angus was not an easy guy to like.

"No. As I said, I didn't call anyone. Although I would have, had the situation come up. I don't know who, exactly, you're talking about, but there are other guys with boat payments to make." Gar allowed a little steel into his voice.

"Fuck those other guys, Lips. You worry too much about other people." With that, he turned to walk back around his cabin, and his deckhand started backing away.

"WHAT A BEAUTY," Jeff observed. Then, after a moment's pause, he asked, "Did you call anyone today, like he said?"

"Hell no! Not a single soul."

"He's sure an asshole," Jeff said thoughtfully. Then he added, "But I bet he did real good today."

"Yeah, probably." Gar spoke distractedly, and went back up to the pilot house to finish preparing dinner. They had 118 nice fish, and he wasn't going to let Goose spoil it. Plus, they had to get up early. Gar was beat after having made scores of trips back and forth across a pitching deck to the cabin, trying to stay on the spot and at the right speed. At this rate he'd wear his tennis shoes out before the trip was over.

Tomorrow was day four. The trip would be at least half over. They tried for eight-day trips, but sometimes only got in six or seven days before running out of something. Patience being one of the things that would run short first.

TWO DAYS LATER Jeff knocked Gar's favorite fishing hat off while swinging the net overhead to scoop a fish. It angered Gar. The webbing of the net only lightly brushed the hat, however this was sufficient to sweep it off Gar's head and over the stern where it quickly sank.

GAR NOW SAT up in his running chair, thinking. This had been the toughest fishing he'd ever encountered. The wild current and more than a hundred boats in a skinny groove were only a part of it. The running back and forth to the cabin, and all the infected leader cuts on their hands, were wearing both men to a frazzle.

And the fishing had dropped off.

They were having to work into eighteen fathoms now, where there were crab pots that threatened to tear off the lines. And they had moved their basic groove south to where the Point was right in the middle of their tack, instead of at the lower end.

The tide at the Point's tip was from several directions at once. They actually moved sideways, crabbing their way up and back. And it took intense attention to stay in the groove. But it got worse than that. There was a twelve-fathom pinnacle that came up on the shallow side of eighteen fathoms, and this would rip their gear, and perhaps poles, completely off if Gar failed to avoid it.

The weather had flattened out. This spot was only *scratch fishing* now at best, and Gar wanted to spend their last few days near the Islands at a place called the *Piggy Patch*. He'd never fished the Piggy Patch, and since they were now rigged perfectly for it, and more importantly acquainted in the applied expertise of fishing in relatively shallow water, this was the time to try it.

Fishing the Piggy Patch required keeping the boat on a fathom curve that would allow the gear to stretch clear down to just off the bottom without hanging it all up on the rocky seabed. He felt in his bones there was no better time to go "drag his balls" through the Piggy Patch.

He was tired, but besides being an intelligent thinker, Gar had been a *very* good boxer during his younger days when he'd first been able to do the Half Moon Bay bar hopping and fighting scene. He was tough as old boots, and the thought of a couple of days at the Piggy Patch invigorated his fighting spirit.

Under his bunk, Gar found an old ball cap and snapped it on. His temper had now cooled.

RUNNING OUT THE back door, Gar said, "Let's stack 'em."

Jeff was surprised. "You all right?"

"Yeah. Let's go pig hunting," Gar said.

"We going to town?" Jeff thought Gar meant to say 'hog hunting,' which was what they called chasing fat girls.

"No. Check all your leaders and put on good baits. Check everything and change anything bad. We're going back to the Islands, and goin' to the Piggy Patch."

Jeff whooped. It was a sound Gar liked to hear.

CHAPTER 7

MAY 7–8. 1980.

THE PIGGY PATCH. West by southwest of the main Farallon Island, there is a twenty-one fathom curve that's shaped like a distorted horseshoe. That is, it is shaped like a horseshoe if one leg of the shoe were bent outward about forty degrees.

To start the Piggy Patch tack, one must begin one half mile, more or less, outside of Indian Head, on the backside of the main island, and point the boat dead center at the front steps of the island's main house. Whoever built that house decided to face it west toward the setting sun. But they likely didn't realize at the time they built it that it looked right at the Piggy Patch. The builders had inadvertently erected a perfect monument on which salmon fishermen could fix relative bearings and positions. The thinking was probably to situate the back stairway facing east toward the anchorage, because that's where the crane sits that lifts provisions off supply boats. Whatever. It is one of those things that worked out well.

The colloquialism, "dragging your balls through the Piggy Patch," of course, refers to the round lead balls that weight the trolling wire.

Thus, on this horseshoe arc, one tacks along the 21-fathom curve that is smack on the edge of where the rocky bottom starts its sharp ascent to the surface, and it follows the island shoreline. It's a good hard edge where fish tend to pile up, and sometimes salmon make up the mix. The M.H.S.S.F. (Michael Henry School of Salmon Fishing) teaches that one should always search for the hard edges where sea creatures tend to concentrate.

"I LOVE CHRISSY," Jeff said. The boys had watched Suzanne Somers in *Three's Company* the night before after coming back across from the point to anchor in Michael's favorite anchorage.

"Yeah, she sure is a hottie," Gar said absently, as they pulled out of the anchorage and rounded Saddle Rock. I'm going to make a dry run up through here and see how hard it is to hold the fathom curve."

"All right," Jeff said. "But I wouldn't mind fuckin' Janet, either. I'm going out to smoke. Let me know when you're ready. We sure are close to the rocks here. I can hear the lions barking. Do you hear them?"

"No, not from inside here." Gar was in the cabin trying to concentrate, and Jeff was outside the back door smoking. Gar didn't smoke, so smoking was only allowed on the deck. Besides, he was concentrating. "I'm holding pretty easily to the 21-fathom curve, but I've got to keep turning the boat. This is going to be just like up there at Goose's spot. I'll be doing a lot more running, though, I think."

"You'll be fine, Lips. Just let me know what I can do." And Jeff meant that. He was the best deckhand Gar had ever had, and he would jump over the side and swim to the Island for some seagull shit if he thought it would catch them more fish. He liked the money, all right, but he liked the glory associated with productivity just as much.

"Okay, we're passing the Indian Head now." Gar hollered fifteen minutes later, "which is like the upper end of our tack, and I've had no problem holding twenty-one fathoms. It only gets deeper from here. Have you got everything ready to go?"

"I just have to get out the bait container. I'll do that now," Jeff said.

"All right. I'm going to run out a ways further, then turn around and get lined up on the house. I'll try to go far enough out so we have time to get the gear set before we get back in to the sweet spot," Gar explained.

"Okay, Cap, I'll be back in my place ... I knows my place, you know, so I'll be back *dere* in de back of de bus," Jeff jived. He was getting excited. Gar knew this because of the increase in his foolishness.

YEARS EARLIER, MICHAEL, Geno, Johnny T, Gar's old boss Fache, all of these accomplished fishermen had one time weighed anchor then sectored out from the island anchorage on a reconnaissance mission in search of a productive salmon hole. They fanned in different directions out into the ocean, and Michael chose the Piggy Patch. On his first pass he reported that he had indeed loaded the gear, however the fish were all brown–which meant all rock cod. After the next pass, though, he called the other guys and reported the fish were all silver. This, of course, meant all salmon.

Gar had viewed an old picture of the ***Visit***–the very boat he was on now–with the deck heaped with a substantial deckload of salmon. Geno had caught something like 500 big salmon that day (which meant Michael probably had a thousand). He had so many fish he had to run in to Half

Moon Bay, because he didn't have enough ice. He and his crew fished until dark, then simply put the boat on autopilot, pointed it toward Pillar Point, and gutted fish all the way in. Evidently they were still cleaning fish after they tied up at the dock. Or so the legend goes.

Michael, Johnny T, and Fache stayed another day and came in the next night with so many salmon they caused a temporary flood on the Bay Area markets.

"OKAY, JEFFERY, LET'S do it," Gar said as he hopped into the trolling pit. They were aimed back at the Piggy Patch, and throttled down to trolling speed.

"Why do they call this place the Piggy Patch?" Jeff asked.

"Well, I'm thinking it's because there are fish here in this spot only occasionally, but when they're here, they're always big. You know, like hogs. Pigs. Hogs. Same sorta deal. Piggy Patch has a nicer ring than Hog Patch." Gar tried to clarify what after so many years could only be surmise. "I guess we'll just have to find out for ourselves. Just put everything out like we had it up at the Point. It should be the same program, except I'm going to have to run back and forth to the cabin even more here." Gar was thinking aloud. "We'll just play it by ear. There might not even be any fish here. I'm told that it's just when there's a good hatch of baby rock cod that the splitters come in here to feed on the little fry."

"Me thinks there was a good hatch!" Jeff said, excited. "Look at this!" He stood aside so Gar could see the line that he'd only put half the leaders on, a line that was still on the way down. It was pumping uncontrollably. The fish were biting on the submerged hooks before the entire string of hooks could be put into the water.

"Ooohhh, baby. Look at that!" Gar found himself singing the Salmon Song to himself: 'I like salmon fishin', Salmon fishin's all right!' He often repeated this refrain in his mind, Zen like, to keep himself from getting too excited. There was no need to try to get motivated when lines started pumping. Especially big pump jobs, like this. The instant one's brain perceived there was a nice fish somewhere down one of the lines, it registered in the medulla oblongata where primordial fluid was then released to pass rousingly through the system.

"Keep puttin' all the gear in, Jefferson, but I think we'll leave the dog lines on the boat the first time we run them. I have a feeling they're just going to be too much. I want to be able to maneuver, and run gear while doing so, and the dogs will tangle. I don't think we'll have as much trouble with just the four lines."

"Okay, boss, but as you can see, my dog line has caught at least one fish, and I'm thinking *more*, judging by how far it's dragging back." Jeff was dubious, as there were many things happening all at once. Of no small concern was the fact that they were pointed straight at the rocky shoreline of the Island, less than half a mile ahead. Stress was mounting for both of them...

"Let's just get them set. I have fish on my lines, too. We're in 'em here, Jeffery... we're draggin' our balls through the Piggy Patch! I'm going to get my lines out and then call Sully, right now, before we have a score. I have a feeling I won't really want to put that info on the radio before too long. I'll tell Goose, too, and then we're covered."

"Where's Sully now? Did he head over here yesterday, or stay at the Point?"

"No, he stayed over at the Point. Said he wanted to finish his last couple of days there, then go home," Gar answered. "Angus' probably still there, too, although I haven't heard him since yesterday morning. Sure wish the northwest wind would come up just a little bit. With no wind there's no gaining any altitude on the fucking bird shit." Gar made a wry grin to accompany this observation. The reek of the birds on the adjacent island was intense.

THE GEAR SET, Gar ran to the cabin to check the fathometer and found they were just shallowing, so he altered course more to the east.

Gar cranked the wheel a little more south of east, and called Sully and gave a very quick report that things looked real good, and they already had lines going, and *please alert Goose*. Then he ran back to the stern to go through his side of the gear.

THE FIRST LEADER had a fish, and Gar was ecstatic. "Holy Fuckin' Balls!" he yelled. "I get really pumped when the first leader, on the first line, of the first day, of my first time in a new spot, has a fish. And it's a dandy, too! Would you look at that?" Gar was speaking as though he had an audience watching, and he was performing for the spectators. "Can you help a poor, broke-down salmon fisherman with the net please, Jeffery?"

"You got it," Jeff said, and he scooped a nice twelve pounder. Twelve pounders were a little too big to do the follow-up-with-the-net routine, so he did it the old-fashioned way.

BACK IN THE STERN, he started the tip line in, and made a couple of baits while doing so. He also covered the fish in the kill bin with gunnysacks, and made a mental note to start cleaning them while the dog line was winding its way in. It was a fair day, slightly overcast but bright, with no wind and maybe sixty-some degrees in the ambient air. The fish would belly burn quickly in this kind of weather and had to be wet-sacked.

He finished running the tip line, and moved next to the dog line. The first spread had a fish, but the trolling wire was at such a steep angle–almost horizontal–that the leader was wrapped around the trolling wire in a tangle. Gar turned to Jeff and said, "I don't want to be an 'I told you so,' but I told you these dogs were going to be a pain in the ass."

"Yeah, yeah, yeah. But you've got fish on there, is your problem, and that's my point." Jeff noted archly.

"I know," Gar said with a high, laughing voice. "We're in 'em!"

He ran the dog line, untangling several snarls, however along with the snarls came five nice fish off that line. This was for a total of ten for his three lines. Not bad fishing. He nevertheless hoisted the dog line weight aboard, put it in its holder, and stowed that float for another day. Today they would concentrate on running just the four lines.

BACK IN THE cabin, south of Saddle Rock and the anchorage, Gar could see they were getting deeper. He watched the meter and wrote down their Loran readings, then started to plot them on the chart just as Jeff yelled. When Gar instinctively looked out the front, because the sound seemed like a "look out for another boat" yell, he noticed the bottom had come sharply up on the fathometer. He cranked the wheel seaward while punching the red throttle button for more speed. With more speed the leads would drag back and, thus, come up off the bottom. Hopefully they would rise up far enough to clear this unexpected rock pinnacle they were passing over.

"BA-BAM! SPUR-UNG!! TWA-ANG!!!" Lines were snapping and there wasn't much that could be done about it. Gar yelled to Jeff to get down in the pit and out of the way, which he did, though it was pretty much over by the time Gar yelled.

The two bow leads had both popped off and those lines, un-weighted, were now stretched back trailing merrily behind. The lines snaked and writhed along on the surface of the water with all sorts of colors gaily mixed in with the tangle. The colors were a nice assortment of various species of rockfish they had incidentally caught off the pinnacle, and these fish were now wound around the trolling wire. Ironically, Clark on the ***San Pablo***, a long-time Island fisherman who came out from Sausalito, hollered on the radio at almost this exact same time.

"Hey, Gar," he said. "I think you're getting too close to that pinnacle."

"Yeah, I figured that out," Gar responded wryly. He instantly recognized the other man's voice. "We just tore our bow leads off and have a mess to clean up. I didn't see that on the chart. It doesn't show very well, or at least it doesn't show as a pinnacle. It's just sort of a fathom difference."

This was the first time he had ever actually talked to Clark, though he had heard him over the radio on a number of occasions, and Gar wondered briefly that Clark would even know who he was. Clark was a real lobo, and didn't talk much to anybody. Perhaps he identified with Gar's apparent tendency to fish reclusively and even independently, away from the politics of who caught what and failed to report it to whom when fishing with the group.

Maybe Clark thought Gar, like himself, did not want to be part of pack politics. If so, he was right.

"Yeah, it's not marked very well. I found out about it the hard way, too. You'll remember it next time, though I'll bet," Clark said, chuckling a bit.

"All right, Clark. Thanks for that. Good talking to you. I guess you've figured out this is where I'm standing by. I've got to go straighten up my mess now. We had a pretty good tack coming down. Ccchheeck you after while."

"Good luck to you guys." Clark clicked off.

GAR GRABBED SIDECUTTER pliers and the new leader box, and hauled them back to the stern. He looked at the two weightless bow lines still following, fishtailing behind them. They stretched back certainly as far as the dog line floats would have, and would likely have tangled with them were the dog lines still out. He mentioned this to Jeff. "I don't want to continue to harp on it, but if we'd left out the dogs, we'd have a bigger tangle than we already have."

"Yeah, yeah, yeah." Jeff wasn't really hearing it. He was busy, getting out new fifty-pound cannon balls to replace the ones they'd left back on the pinnacle.

First tack, and already they'd left their balls in the Piggy Patch. And that's why very few liked to fish there. It definitely had its perils.

"Okay, here's the box of leaders." Gar began his instructions. "Here's the albacore line to tie on your new lead. Take your sidecutters and cut off all those leaders as you wind your bow line in, and throw the linesnaps and hooks and stuff in that plastic catch-all. We actually didn't do too bad. Except it looks like we bent our davits down, and now our pulleys probably won't line up. You'll have to kind of help spool the wire on the gurdy as you're coming in with your line, until I can get everything adjusted. I need to run a stay from the davit up to the mast cross-tree so we don't pull those davits down when we hang up."

Gar paused a moment, looking out to the horizon then around quickly at nearby waters, and then he continued to speak. "I've got a feeling we'll be back here in this Piggy Patch more often now. I like it here. No competition, and the rocks keep a guy on his toes. Plus, I remember Michael saying that there are some years when the fish set into the rocks, and when they do, they do it all year, and all up and down the coast. You know, like next trip we might end up fishing the reef at the Mendocino Light Ship, or at Point Saint George Reef."

Gar said all this as he was clipping off tangled leaders and tossing them in the middle of their wake. He did this so they didn't sink down out where their tip-line floats were still trailing, apparently without any problems after the fiasco.

"At least we can have filleted rock cod for lunch," Jeff offered. "Maybe you'll feel like whipping up a batch of your famous Teriyaki marinade, too."

"Yeah, I'll do that if you fillet them," Gar said.

"No problem." Jeff was his usual cheery self in spite of it all.

THE BOW LINES now fishing again, and the boat turned and headed back up toward the Piggy Patch, they ran the tip lines that had been soaking for much too long. The good news was the several nice fish that hadn't been pulled off in the mishap.

CLARK, MEANWHILE, TACKED up the outside edge of the Piggy patch. He didn't do the horseshoe in toward the house business. He had a bigger boat, similar to Michael's, and fished more conservatively. The bigger boats made up for a lack of maneuverability by being able to fish in tougher weather. Clark started a dialogue with his deckhand as they worked:

"I don't think we'll go in as close as Garaloney. He might be a little crazier than I am. But he's turning out to be a pretty fair salmon fisherman."

"Yeah. They're talking about him."

"I think he's going to be all right. He seems to like fishing the Islands. So I think we'll see him around more. You know how it is. Just like when the salmon set in the rocks some years, a guy gets hooked on this fucking rockpile. It gets to be a habit to just point the boat this way every trip."

"Like you!"

"Yes, exactly like me."

"What about this year? Will this be our year to go north?"

"Don't count on it."

"I didn't think so."

"Did you notice we have lines pumping?"

"As a matter of fact I did. That's another thing about Gar. He's found fish for us more than once. And I think he just did it again. The kid is lucky."

"Yeah, I told you I've had my eye on him for a while. He's got the intuition. You know how some guys can spend half their lives, and hundreds of thousands on a fancy boat, and never figure it out? Well, I think the kid's got it figured out. I just hope he keeps it together, and doesn't get too cocky."

"Naww, I don't think.... Hey! Can you net this fish for me?"

"You bet."

AT NOON GAR still had not breaded and fried the rock cod fillets. He had, however, put them in a marinade of olive oil, soy sauce, garlic powder, ginger spice, and some brown sugar. It was a perfect fish marinade. They had a good start on the day, with somewhere close to half a hump. A hump was a hundred.

And they hadn't hung up in the rocks again. That was because Gar came up to check their depth more often. And Jeff had gotten used to not only running gear while the boat was making sudden turns (a line trailing a good distance away from the boat would instantly be right next to it as the stern swung in a turn), but running Gar's side of the gear too.

Their teamwork was what was making this day successful.

All of that in mind, Gar put a frying pan of oil on the propane stove, locked it in with a semi-elaborate set of raised guide rods built onto the stove, got out the zip-lock baggie of premade breading, and started cooking a mess of fillets. He would fill a nine-inch by fourteen-inch Tupperware container full by the time he was done, and set it on the table. They would then help themselves, mostly as they ran by, eating a fillet more or less like a cookie. Jeff liked to sprinkle Tabasco Sauce on his, and if he had time maybe a smear of mayonnaise.

"OUR POUND AVERAGE is going up at a nice rate with these bigger fish," Gar said to Jeff as he started his bow line up. They were passing by Indian Head on their leg of the tack away from The Patch. The house on the Island was dead off their stern. "Have you been checking their stomachs to see what they're feeding on when you're cleaning them?"

"I knew you were going to ask that. Yes, I have checked them. They're full of little baby rock cod. Mostly orange ones, like those bolina cod we sometimes get," Jeff said.

"Yeah, I figured so. You notice how with all those birds just half a mile or so away over there on the Island, there are no birds working here like when we were down at Pa's Canyon? Or even up at Goose's spot, for that matter?" Gar observed and questioned.

"You know, I was trippin' on that earlier, and the fact that you haven't been trying to imitate the murres," Jeff said.

"The murres don't much like baby rock cod," Gar replied. "Plus, unlike the anchovies that the murres were after the other day, the baby rock cods are down deep where the birds can't feed on them, but the salmon can." Still bringing up the bow line, Gar reached over to grab the next linesnap, which was extended out at an odd fishy angle. He fought the fish in quickly as it was small, then hoisted it right aboard and measured it. "Little bit short," he observed. "Not too many shorties here, though. Have you had to measure many?"

"No. I doubt if I've had a dozen questionable fish since we got to this Pig Patch."

"YOU PICK ME up here, Gar?" Clark hollered on the secret radio (this one was fairly secret–it was a two meter ham radio), and Gar heard it on one of the deck speakers. Of his eight radios, he had two or three, at any given time, hooked up to a deck speaker so he could hear them while working on deck.

"Yeah, Clark, I get you fine," Gar answered, once he got to the wheelhouse.

"Sorry to get you out of your stern. I just talked to a friend on another frequency, and he said there's a pile of boats headed this way with the flat weather. Said all the Oakland guys are coming out. They all blew ice and will come right here looking first. I know those guys, and if they see you working there, they'll crowd you right out of your spot. That's why I didn't come in there. I thought I'd try to establish a tack with a little more breathin' space before the flat-weather fleet gets here."

"All right, Clark, I appreciate that. I don't know those Oakland guys at all. Although, you know, I was born there. We moved over to Pescadero when I was about five." Gar answered, then wondered why he was telling Clark his life history. He was nervous, and wanted to get along with Clark, because he knew Clark was a true Farallon Island fisherman. There was something about the man that he admired, and he wanted to be like him. "I guess I'll try to make a report later on a channel that I know they're listening on, and cuss a blue streak about the rotten luck we're having with too many rock cod, and a poor grade of salmon."

"Okay," Clark laughed. "Let me know if you need a straight man. They know my voice, and where I'm at. They always check me out as soon as they get out here. Sometimes they call, and sometimes they just follow off my stern, shamelessly watching me run my gear. I never let them know when I'm doing any business, though."

And with that, Gar felt a conspiracy, of sorts, had been forged between them.

"Okay. Thank you. Are you guys doing any good out there? I see you going back and forth outside of us."

"Yeah, I think we probably have the same as you do, around fifty, but not as good a grade." Clark spoke matter of factly, and Gar was amazed. How could he know the number and size of fish Gar was catching? Was he that in tune with this rock pile, the "fucking rockpile," as everyone liked to call it?

"You been talkin' to my deckhand? Because I've been real quiet this morning," Gar said, astounded.

"No, I'm just a good guesser. Maybe it comes from too many winters of sittin' around the bar playing Liar's Dice," Clark said.

"Well, you called my hand, alright. Okay, Jeff's hollering something. I gotta' go. Cchheeck you later." Gar clicked off.

THEY FINISHED THE day with over a hundred nice fish, then went to anchor. Gar looked at his log book:

May 1st – 157 fish
May 2nd – 127 fish
May 3rd – 3 fish
May 4th – 118 fish
May 5th – 94 fish
May 6th – 82 fish
May 7th – 106 fish
687 @ 8 lbs = 5,496 lbs

He noted they now had 687 fish and guessed at an eight-pound average, though he thought it might be a tad higher than this. At $2.00 a pound average price, they had over $11,000.00 going into their last day.

Not a bad trip. Not a bad trip at all. Although they had earned every penny of it. He thought it was likely he was underestimating the weight, and with what they would catch tomorrow–their last day–they might actually approach $15,000.00. Now that would be nice.

JEFF WENT TO bed. The wind-driven rotary-turbine ventilator was silent, and conspicuous because it wasn't making noise for a change. With the familiar stench of sea gull waste permeating the air, Gar watched *Taxi*, the show with that sawed-off midget who was pretty funny.

Then he went to sleep thinking about the size of his bunk in relation to the size of the bed he and Susan had shared. It was only a tiny bit narrower. He never did ask her where she found that bed, though he wondered about it now. It was small, like a kid's bottom bunk bed. It was perfect for the two of them, though. They spooned incredibly well together right from the very first moment they had called it their own, and snuggled down into their nest.

The Farallon Lighthouse observed and didn't observe, punctuating the night with pursuits and concerns of its own. Its beam stabbed rhythmically round and round, marking the slow turn of the Earth toward a new day.

CHAPTER 8

THE NEXT MORNING Jeff came upstairs at daylight, wondering what was up (there was a deck-mounted porthole over his bunk area allowing him to see that the sun was shining outside). Why weren't they on their way? Gar explained that because it was only five minutes to their fishing hole, he was waiting for the anchorage to clear out. Mainly, so the Oakland guys didn't see where he was going. "There goes the last one, now," Jeff observed.

"All right. Let's hit it. I've been ready for a while," Gar said, already on his way down the engine-room ladder.

OIL CHECKED AND engine fired, they pulled the anchor and headed out around Saddle Rock. They had put fresh new baits on the leaders the previous night, and it only took ten minutes to set two lines apiece, on either side of the boat. That quickly, they were in business.

And all four lines began the familiar throbbing almost instantly. They were in 'em again!

ANOTHER GOOD DAY was imminent, when at 10:00 a.m. they heard an old-sounding woman on one of the deck speakers, hailing frantically to anyone. Gar ran, forthwith, to the cabin and found her on his VHF.

"Hello, Hello, Hello to the boat with problems" he shouted. "Can you hear me, Ma'am?"

"Oh, yes. I hear you. Please hurry. My husband's in the water, and I can't reach him. Please. I need help. Please hurry!" She was talking and forgetting that she had to let go of the microphone button so Gar could talk. "Please! I tried to reach him, but I can't." She was panicked, and Gar's heart was pounding, but she finally let go of the button.

"Where are you, Ma'am? And listen to me before you speak! Say it fast, then let go of the microphone button so I can speak to you," Gar instructed.

"We were just anchoring at the Farallon Islands, and when my husband came down from the bridge, the ladder broke and he fell overboard." She was obviously rattled, and on the verge of breaking down. "He's in the water now and I can't get him out. He hit his head."

"Okay, Ma'am, I'm not very far away. I have the fishing vessel ***Visit***. Go out and start throwing anything that might possibly float overboard near your husband. I'll be right there." Gar gave the standard Coast Guard instruction to try to get something in the water that the person might grab onto to stay alive.

He headed for the door, and paid no attention as she kept talking and thanking him.

OUT ON DECK Gar yelled, "Do we still have those sidecutters back there?"

"Right here."

"Give me one pair, and you take the other and cut your lines off on the other side of the insulator. Watch me. Just put the two spools in gear and wind them in ten feet and snip."

"Are you crazy?" Jeff demanded, indignant. "We don't have any more lead. We've got fish...."

Gar interrupted, his voice rising to a shriek as he lunged to cut the lines on his side of the boat. "Cut 'em off, NOW!"

LINES CUT AND abandoned–yet more balls left in the Piggy Patch–they steamed around Saddle Rock. The lighthouse brooded in the distance, dark and tiny atop its perch on the main island. Gar headed for the anchorage they had only this morning left, knowing this was the likeliest place to find the ill-fated boat. There were dark clouds on the horizon before them now, and a wind had picked up. The clouds were ominous looking, roiling and spreading much too quickly across the sky.

Gar had his own boat, *in the smokehole*, a dark black exhaust cloud trailing a half mile behind them. There was one oversized cabin cruiser floating in the anchorage, just as he thought there might be. ***Gone Fishin'*** was the name of the boat. The woman was out on deck, fixed intently on their approach. Gar stripped down to his Jockey shorts and yelled at Jeff.

"You drive!" he hurriedly instructed. "Just get me close, and don't hit her. Remember our poles are out."

When they were close, Gar dove off the rail closest to the ***Gone Fishin'*** and swam over to the other boat. The woman was standing at the rail as he climbed aboard. She was sixtyish and dressed in Levis and a peasant's blouse, and she had eyeglasses hanging on a gold chain around her neck. She looked at him, the whites of her eyes blood red from crying, and her soft blue irises reminded Gar, instantly, of cornflowers.

"Did you get him?" Gar asked as he walked to the other side of the boat where a cheap aluminum ladder lay crumpled, pulled away from the back of the cabin and bent over onto the rail.

"No. I can't see him. I threw everything over, like you said. Oh, thank you for coming. You're a hero, diving in the water like that. There are sharks here."

"But, Ma'am, I haven't done anything. Where? Aww, shit. What, how long has he been under?" Gar was frustrated. He gazed out across the empty surface of the anchorage. "Have you called the Coast Guard?"

"No, not yet," she said.

"Okay. You do that right now. VHF Channel Sixteen. Holler Mayday! and give your position as the Farallon Island Anchorage. Is this where you last saw him?" Gar was pointing at the obvious spot.

"Yes, right there," she pointed.

Gar dove into the water where she had pointed, and he noticed the cold more this time. He wasn't quite so wound up as before. And he was certain he was only looking for a body at this point. It had been much too long.

He swam down as far as he could, maybe thirty feet, and raced back up, lungs on fire. He took half a dozen good breaths and tried it again, not able to descend nearly as deep this time. The frigid water already had the man, whoever he was. He wished he had taken the time to put on all his gear, and decided to take the time now and do this right despite the hopelessness of the situation. He had a full set of diving gear, including SCUBA bottle, on the boat.

DIVE GEAR ON, Gar tied off a generous length of crab line (3/8 inch polypropylene rope) to the ***Gone Fishin'*** and sat on the rail with his back to the ocean. Then he laid back and dropped into the water.

All sound ceased, save the gentle suspiration of his regulator, and he peered into the cold, murky and uncertain distance. There was a huge, endless ocean surrounding him.

They were anchored in approximately fifty feet of water, and Gar put two sixty-foot pieces of crab line together. He figured he would swim out away from the *Gone Fishin'* until a little more than half the line had played out, then descend to the bottom until the line came tight, and after this make a circle of the boat above while maintaining the tension on the line. That would describe a circle of about seventy feet in all directions from the boat. He'd then take up ten feet of slack, six times, doing another circle every time he took up slack. In theory, he would cover the entire 140-foot diameter circle around the boat. Such coverage should be sufficient to spot the body in the cloudy water, if it was still there. The more likely scenario was that it had drifted off with the current. But this was a human being. An attempt had to be made.

It was a seriously arduous workout, and it was exhausting. It took him forty minutes and his entire bottle of air to do this, and he had no luck. His head broke the surface where he found the woman, Mable he had learned was her name, staring at him. She had obviously been following the progress of Gar's bubbles. But her eyes were dulled and vacant now.

He was surprised when he climbed aboard to find Jeff standing next to Mable, with his arm around her. Jeff had anchored the ***Visit*** close by, by himself, and swam over to her boat. He was wet, and Gar could see the plastic bag laying there that he had put his own clothes in to keep them dry on the swim over.

"You didn't find Russell, did you?" The woman was defeated; it sounded in her voice. Her shoulders slumped with loss.

"No, Ma'am. I'm sorry. And I'm out of air, now. I'm really sorry." He walked over and took her hand.

"Oh, my," she said. "Your hands are freezing." Then she started sobbing, when she realized how cold the water her husband had fallen into really was. And it had been more than an hour. Russell was gone.

THE COAST GUARD helicopter arrived first and started doing grids. Then the cutter came. They sent over a Zodiac with a crew who seemed incredibly young but capable.

They asked questions and took notes. Mabel praised Gar and Jeff for their heroic efforts, and scolded Russell almost as though he were present. It was heart wrenching to watch this performance. She scolded him for weighing too much, for buying such a boat with an aluminum ladder; and she questioned the reasoning behind retiring just to go salmon fishing.

After a time, Gar asked if they had someone to pilot the boat back to Oakland. Mable and Russell had come out with the indifferent Oakland Gang, who were still nowhere to be seen. The Coasties assured Gar that they would handle everything that needed to be done.

SPIRITS VERY LOW, Gar and Jeff caught a ride back to the ***Visit*** with the Zodiac, after giving Mable a final hug.

They pulled their anchor, took their three tons of salmon, and headed for Half Moon Bay. "Wah-Fum-Mha-Bay," as the Italians called it. En route, they did their best to put the old woman and her loss from their minds.

Gar knew of the abundant munificence of the sea. Indeed, he made his living from its bounty. But he intuitively realized on another level that the sea takes back some of its own. And, in the end, the sea takes it all. Every fisherman knows this, whether he can articulate it or not, and every fisherman has made a wary but separate peace with the final inevitability of this idea.

Gar called Captain John on the VHF radio, his fish buyer in Princeton Harbor, and said that he'd be there by five or six o'clock and would like to unload. When the sweet young girl who worked in the bait shop came back and asked how long it would take to unload their catch, Gar said, "Tell John....Wait a minute, will you? Then to Jeff, "How many fish did we end up with today?"

"We had thirty-nine fairly nice fish," he said.

Then back to the sweetheart on shore, "Tell Captain John we have 687 plus 39, let me see, I'm figuring 726 fish. Course my Mom might put a small bite into that, so tell him somewhere just over 700. I think the grade is pretty good for this time of year, too. So tell him we want a six-and-ten split." Gar was too tired to beat around the bush. Normally he would have hedged with something like, "we did okay." But after this day's ordeal, he was too shocked to play it any way but straight.

The bait shop girl responded with a seductive voice. "That sounds like the best trip so far this season. Where are you going tonight?"

"Some place where you're probably too young to get in." Gar cut her off, as he knew she was likely an after-school worker. A high-school girl.

"Oh, you're no fun. I'll call John right now," she finished in a feigned snit.

Then Gar switched the VHF radio to channel 21 and got a marine operator. He put through a call to Mom, and told her she better bring the big ice chest and get down to the wharf if she wanted to put fresh salmon on the Beach House menu.

THEN HE SAT back in his running chair, watching as the *Little Boxes on the Hillside* started fading from view. He was certain now it was Pete Seger who sang that song back in the early sixties. It was originally about somewhere outside New York City, Gar remembered, probably New Jersey, but everyone in the Bay Area was sure it was about the Daly City track homes that fit the song's description so perfectly.

He reviewed the day's happenings with the ***Gone Fishin'*** again and again, and tried to find that mental corridor that would allow him to escape the thought, and move on to better things. The sea was like a woman, he thought. A beautiful and giving woman. Yet she was also a deadly bitch.

His own mortality, and the pressure to do well, rose to the top of these thoughts. But the mood of celebration that should have been his, coming in with his catch, was just not there.

When he could see the radar towers on Pillar Point, Gar knew they were halfway home. About fourteen miles were remaining, which at seven knots meant they would be there in two hours. He and Jeff spent that time scrubbing the boat and themselves, unusually subdued.

But their mood perceptibly lightened as they approached the shore.

The sea had taken a man today. But it hadn't taken them. And it is only human to realize this at some point when dealing with a death, and this is the point at which it can be let go.

Unloading at Captain John's.

CHAPTER 9

MAY 8, 1980.

ANNABEL AND CAPTAIN John stood on Johnston's Pier, talking and peering to the west-southwest. It was six in the evening. The sun just dipping to eye level, they shaded their eyes as they talked. Then Captain John pointed and spoke.

"There he is now. He's just passing the P.P. Buoy. He'll be here in twenty minutes or so."

"Oh, good. Yeah, I can see the blue sail and the white Z now," Annabel said to John. "Oh, I can't wait!"

Mom loved being a part of it all. When Gar telephoned her via the marine operator, she was thrilled and happily diligent about saying, "Over!" every time she made her reply to what Gar had just said. Since Gar always called the Beach House phone number, and most of the time Mom would talk on the phone located at the end of the bar where all her customers could listen to her talk, she was on stage during these marine calls and loved every minute of it. Not only was she talking to her personal fisherman, but ordering fresh fish from a boat that was right now on the ocean. It was an excellent promotion for her Steak & Seafood Restaurant, and she made the most of it.

"PHEEEE-PHWUUU. YOU picking me up, Lips?" Timmy called.

"Yeah, Sull. Got you fine. Where you at?" Gar answered.

"Well, judging by what you told Elaine at the bait shop, I'm guessing I'm about two hours behind you. We're just down below B Buoy somewhere. Where are you, like maybe coming up on the Green Can at home?"

"You got it. We're one-point-two miles from the Green Buoy, according to my radar," Gar said.

"All right. Goose's not too far behind me. I called my Dad earlier, after I heard you call in, and he called Captain John and told him we would all deliver to him if we could get a better deal. I didn't figure you'd mind since you were going there anyway, and John said he'd give us a six/ten split, plus a nickel. Merry Christmas, Lips." Timmy was proud of himself, as well he should be.

"Sully, I love you. Did I ever tell you that before? If I didn't, I'm telling you now. And I love your father, too. And Captain John, and–did you say Goose is coming? I love Goose, too." Inclusion of this last individual may have been a bit of an exaggeration, but Gar had just made a fair chunk of money with Sully's information and was feeling instantly better. Having lamented Mable's loss all the way in from the Islands, he was now able to put it from his mind and get back to the business at hand.

The nickel was good news. If they had 6,000 pounds, then that nickel translated to an extra $300. But the six/ten split was what Gar was hoping for, because he had many borderline fish.

The price the fishermen had collectively agreed upon for marketing their salmon for this year was: $1.75 a pound for small fish; $2.00 a pound for medium-sized fish; and, $2.25 a pound for large. A medium fish was, normally, eight pounds and over; whereas a large was usually twelve pounds and over. Most buyers were on the loose side, however, and would split at seven and eleven.

The six/ten split, though, was harder to come by and would give the fishermen a substantial raise for their efforts, as a whole bunch more smalls would be mediums, and mediums become large. Basically, they were getting 30¢ more a pound figuring the extra nickel overall, plus 25¢ on most fish because those would go in the bin for the next larger size.

The reason for the increase in price with a commensurate increase in size was twofold. First, the larger fish simply tasted better. The meat was richly marbled and utterly delicious.

And, curiously, the east-coast delicatessens paid top dollar for the larger fish. The big salmon were referred to as "splitters" because they were split in half lengthwise and smoked. Hurried Manhattanites enjoyed it on bagels–with cream cheese–and called the snack bagels and lox. Deli owners and rich urbanites liked to brag about the size of the splitter they had hanging in the pantry.

Of course, Captain John would still do better than anybody else on the dock. He'd likely make $10,000 this evening, and still be home by midnight. Which is more than Gar could say. He knew there was no way, with the other guys coming in right behind him, that he was going to escape closing the Princeton Inn at 2:00 a.m. on this night.

THEY STOPPED JUST inside the jetties and secured their poles up into the mast crosstree.

Mom was bouncing on the dock as she watched her son–her only son–maneuver the ***Visit*** over to the pier. She knew Jeff as a customer at the Beach House, and had actually put Jeff and Gar together as a crew. So when she saw Jeff tossing lines up to Captain John's crew, she called out to him.

"Hello, Jefferson. Welcome back! Did you do any good?"

"Hello, Annabel. Thank you. And, yeah, we had a pretty good trip." He was running around tying lines and his words came out in a labored rush.

GAR CAME OUT of the cabin, scaled the dock ladder, and put his feet on solid ground for the first time in nine days. They had actually left for the anchorage the day before they began their eight-day trip.

He hugged Mom, and shook hands with Captain John, who was John Texiera when he signed his checks. He was quite celebrated in Princeton, owning not only one of the three fish-buying stations but several party boats, as well as the bait and tackle shop.

"Good to see you, John." Gar felt slightly odd calling him John. It hadn't been that long since he had respectfully referred to him as Mr. Texiera. "We've got the results of a pretty good trip on the boat. I'm sure happy to hear about the six/ten split, that will help a lot." Gar wanted to verify this financial factor right from the start, before a single fish came off the boat.

"Yeah, I'm gonna tell my boys to be real nice to you this time," John said. "I want you to keep coming back. And, you know, I appreciate the crab you sell me, too." Gar had sold him crabs during the early season, two Novembers running, before the Crescent City season opened on December first.

"No problem. I'll bring you my crabs next winter, too. How we looking there with the hoist? Is my boat all right where it's at?"

"Yeah, Gar, you're just perfect. Are you guys ready?" John asked.

"You bet," Gar said to John. Then he asked Jeff, "You ready down there?"

"Let's go!" Jeff hollered up from the fish hold where he waited wearing rain gear and gloves. He was two beers into a six pack he had saved on ice just for this occasion.

JEFF FLUNG SALMON into the bucket (a bucket that held about four-hundred pounds, or fifty fish), and the bucket was then hoisted up. The fish were dumped onto a big wood table, with side boards, where they were sorted for size. A small fifty-pound scale sat atop a raised platform on one side of the table, and questionable fish were weighed then pitched into one of the three bins labeled small, medium, and large. The sorter, one of John's workers, had a good eye. But he still hefted one up on the scale from time to time, probably to let everyone else know what a borderline 5.8 or 9.8 pounder looked like.

GAR PULLED FOUR nice nine pounders, and one beautiful twelve pounder, out of the first bucket as these were fish caught that day. He said to Mom, "These four will give you about eighty dinners, which should last you a week, and the big one is for Rudy Rossi."

"Oh, he's going to be so happy!" she said.

"Got to take care of my Godfather." Gar smiled.

RUDY ROSSI, AN artichoke farmer and the conservator of the Cascade Ranch, was crowding eighty years of age. He had been at the Cascade since the day he was born. In the 1920's, and during Prohibition, he got a good start in life by assisting the booze smugglers bringing booze into Bootlegger's Cove. Rudy had regaled Gar with many accounts of those days. He did this over the long, Italian-style lunches Rudy was famous for cooking on the Cascade Ranch. It was a rare honor to be invited to one of these meals. Gar now went to them as a matter of course. Rudy was a good friend.

The Cascade took in all of the beachfront property that stretched along the coast from the Año Nuevo Island to Franklin Point. Franklin Point was the first point of land situated three miles south of Pigeon Point. The Beach House was about halfway between the two points.

On the south side of Franklin Point is a beautiful natural and protected sea inlet called "Bootlegger's Cove." It was named this after those years when Rudy had *borrowed* his father's horse team to pull sleds of booze up off the beach, where it was loaded into electric buses. As strange as it sounded, Rudy said they used buses with a very large bank of batteries to run the electric motors. The electric buses were almost silent, and were perfect for eluding the G-Men who worked in the Prohibition Bureau of the United States Department of Justice. The buses ran the booze up the coast to San Francisco.

The history of this bootlegging through Bootlegger's Cove was of great importance to the early success of Pescadero. Gar began to hear the stories soon after his family moved there, and when he began attending the first grade at Pescadero Elementary School back in 1959.

It was common knowledge that, were it not for smuggling booze, most of the older and successful farmers would not have been able to establish themselves as they did. This history of the area, a history that enshrouded the pillars of the small Pescadero community and had grown into romantic legend with the retelling, was the reality Gar grew up with. He understood this history to be legitimate, important and fundamental. It was a part of his heritage, in a sense helping to define who he was.

The artichokes and the Brussels sprouts of Pescadero grow abundantly and thrive on the gentle slopes that overlook the shoreline. This tiny little belt of land is not only mostly frost free, but the sea spray and fog endow it with a unique micro-climate unduplicated anywhere except small enclaves on the coasts of Southern Italy and Sicily.

And so it was that early in the twentieth century, when farmers were trying to enrich this special land in the Pescadero area, far from the San Francisco vegetable markets and farm supply houses, it took supplemental incomes to survive and grow. Supplementing incomes with activities such as bootlegging liquor helped families through to the time when better roads and transportation were to become available. And it was only with better roads and transportation that agriculture became a sustainable pursuit. Rudy, one of Gar's real-life heroes, knew all about this history. And he was a consummate storyteller once he got to talking about the area. He kept Gar spellbound.

Rudy weighed over three-hundred pounds, was an excellent cook, and he felt he owed someone "the farm" when they unexpectedly brought him something, like a fresh salmon. It was the same in the winter, when Gar brought him live fresh crab. As a matter of fact, Rudy was so pleased with Gar's crab deliveries that he actually broke protocol and allowed Gar to bring Susan to lunch. Women normally weren't invited to Rudy's cookhouse. Gar had only to provide the fresh seafood to be invited to hear the unwritten legends, stories that were told in Pescadero farm cookhouses in such a manner that secrecy was not sworn, but expected.

JEFF SENT THE last bucket up, and this one contained not only six empty cans of Bud Light, but the big splitter they had caught on their first day. The attractive State Fish and Game Warden that had been there checking for undersized fish came over and gawked at its size. This was about the time Jeff topped the ladder onto the dock and, giddy with beer, zeroed in on this unsuspecting civil servant.

"I been out nine days, and I sure am lonely. . ." Jeff said, which prompted the women to take a few steps back. And then: "Do you mind if I touch your gun?" While the woman was thinking of something to say in defense of this verbiage, Jeff pointed to Gar's crotch and said, "You better check him. I think he's got a short in his pants."

The crowd gathered around the big fish roared with laughter, and the game warden stormed off. Jeff beamed good-naturedly at all those about. He was off and running, and Lord help the good citizens of Princeton–and their daughters!

GAR PUT THE big fish up on the splitting scale and had one of the guys help steady it. The scale bounced back and forth between forty and forty-five pounds. It was not an accurate weight, and when Gar explained that he had a bet with Sully, Captain John, who had officiated many such contests, said, "Bring that one inside here and set it on my other scale."

Which Gar did.

John took weights off and put weights back on the beam, then he tapped the sliding weight to balance the beam. "Forty-one and one-quarter pounds is my official weight, and after I weigh all your other large fish, I'll tack exactly that on the tally," he announced. "Including the quarter pound."

Everyone whistled, and discussed what a nice fish it was. Captain John went out and instructed his crew to start fork-lifting totes over to his platform scale so he could get everything weighed and totaled. They did this, and John got busy with his old adding machine, then he handed Gar a Fish and Game receipt that read:

Large King Salmon	—	3,571 pounds @ $2.25
Medium King Salmon	—	2,689 pounds @ $2.00
Small King Salmon	—	616 pounds @ $1.75

"I'll give you your nickel, on the settlement. I just needed to put the market order price on the ticket," John said. "How do you want it? I can cut you a check right now, if that would suit you."

"Well," Gar hesitated. "Can you give me five hundred in cash?"

John answered, "No problem."

"Okay, then, why don't you draft a check for twenty percent of the gross, made out to Jeff Lindburg. Then the balance made out to me, minus the five hundred in cash. And I'll get out of your way so you can unload Timmy, who I think must be real close by now."

"Okay, give me a minute," John instructed.

John was quick with the numbers, and had the checks made out in no time. He handed them across his desk to Gar and said, "Okay, it looks like you guys did real good. Here's your cash." And he pulled out a wad and peeled off five crisp hundreds. "And here's your settlement sheet. I penciled in all the correct totals including the bonus. Have fun. But remember, it's flat calm, and there's still fish out there."

If John had his way, guys would just unload and put supplies on after dark, at the end of the last day of their trip, and then be back on the fishing grounds in time to set the gear at daylight.

"Okay, John, we're going to turn the boat around tomorrow, and then try to get out of here tomorrow night. Although tomorrow is Friday. Or I guess we could just get ready and leave at midnight. Anyway, thanks for everything. We'll see you next time. Wow! I just looked at my check. Not bad! That split sure helped. Oh, and don't forget to tell Timmy how big our monster was." Gar shook hands and smiled his goodbye.

"You bet. I hope you win. Good luck on your next trip." John smiled back, and Gar thought, for some odd reason, that he likely got his smile from his mother. It was a warm and sincere beam.

OUT ON THE wharf, Gar could see Timmy over inside the jetties putting up his poles. He walked over to Annabel and to Jeff and handed Jeff his check.

"Two thousand nine hundred sixty six dollars and ninety-one cents," Jeff yelled excitedly.

"And you still owe me a hundred and fifty for your share of the groceries. Just get it in cash when you go to the bank," Gar instructed. He paid his crewmen twenty percent of the gross, which was at the top of the deckhand scale, but he made them kick back for half the groceries. With a financial stake in the groceries, less food was wasted. And a little undeclared cash always came in handy.

"And do you need a couple hundred spending money?" Gar asked him.

"Well, I probably don't; but I'll take it anyway, since you're offering." And Gar gave him two of the hundreds John had just given him.

"What are you going to do?" Gar asked his mother. "I can meet you at the Princeton Inn in a half hour. I'm planning to come to the Beach House tomorrow some time, if you're trying to make the drive south before it gets too late."

"I think I'll go over to the P.I., and if it feels good, I'll wait. Otherwise, I'll see you tomorrow, honey," Mom replied. She always called him that. Or later on, if she stuck around, it would be *Sam*–her favorite pet name for him after a couple of drinks.

"Okay. Here comes Timmy. We've got to find some place to tie." And with that they headed down the ladder to the boat.

THEY MOVED THE boat down the pier, both Gar and Jeff quite pleased with themselves, and Gar maneuvered the vessel carefully beneath a great, screaming flock of wheeling sea gulls. The birds were excessively raucous in the cooling sea air, appearing in such numbers that they were almost like a cloud overhead, and the reddened sun reflecting off their flashing wings lent a magical air to the beginning of a fresh evening.

"I'm going up to the fish-house (Captain John's) to take a shower," Jeff said.

"I'll wait for you and give you a ride. I see my pickup is still in the parking lot. I'll drop you at your Mom's to get your truck, if you want." Jeff's parents lived only a half mile from the Princeton wharf, across the highway in El Granada.

"That would be great."

GAR GOT OUT his log book and made some rough notes:

TOTAL:	6,876 pounds	$14,834.55
EXPENSES:	Jeff	2,966.91
	Fuel	450.00
	Bait	220.00
	Ice	280.00
	Groceries	150.00
NET (Approximate)		$11,867.64
	Send PCA	(5,000.00)
	Insurance	(5,000.00)

HE BUSIED HIMSELF around the cabin wiping and cleaning, and thinking that minus the $500 draw, he had $1,100 left, which would basically be what it took to re-outfit for the next trip. Billy Joel's "52nd Street" album played on the eight-track while he finished organizing, and straightening up his bunk. Gar sang along to *The Piano Man*, and, *Still Rock and Roll to Me*.

Jeff came back, and they headed up to get Jeff's truck, then over to the Princeton Inn for cocktails. There was still a tiny bit of light in the dusk's gloaming, and the gulls wheeling and crying over the waterfront lent a festive air to the waning day.

CHAPTER 10

AT THE PRINCETON Inn, Mom was sitting at the bar with a local couple who were long-time friends and sometimes Beach House customers. Since the Beach House was twenty-five miles south of Half Moon Bay (about thirty miles from Princeton and El Granada), not everyone could make the drive on a regular basis. Because the Half Moon Bay area was mainly comprised of blue-collar citizens that like to drink, the drive back from the Gazos Creek Beach House could be problematic for some.

"Oh, here's *Sam*." Mom obviously had a good head start. "You remember Bob and Shirley, don't you?"

"Of course. How are you both?" Gar smiled. He bartended for his folks, at times, and he put that cap back on now.

"We hear you had a great big salmon trip," Shirley exclaimed. She had a head start too.

"Yeah. We did pretty good." Gar tried to be modest, but he was all teeth. He couldn't help himself.

"Lemme get you a drink," Bob offered.

"Rum and Coke," Gar said. And thank you."

AN HOUR LATER, Mom said she had to go. Jeff had arrived, and Sully, Merlo, Angus and his crewman were due any minute. Mom was gushing about Sam this, and Sam that, and telling Jeff how he was her little boy, too. She can be very sentimental, Mom can, and indeed is most of the time.

GAR AND JEFF had just snagged a big table when the boys showed up. Gar remembered that Goose's crewman was Brian something, once he saw him. They sat down, and Timmy exclaimed resignedly, "Well, I guess I'm buying the first round, Lips. You got us by about five pounds. It wasn't even close."

"Still, nice fish for this time of year," Gar consoled him.

"You were in 'em, both of you, and you didn't call." Goose said this with his biggest smile, ameliorating the sting of a touchy subject. He looked a lot like Robert Redford, and he could really be charming when he wanted to be. Women went crazy over him, though they usually left him quickly after taking his measure. There was something snide and vicious in his makeup, something bitter and angry inside him.

"Don't start with me, Goose," Gar said.

Angus came over and tousled Gar's hair. He acted as if he was already drunk. He wasn't a real big guy, at 165 pounds, so it was like a kid talking when he said, "Come on, Lips, we're in town now. . . so let's have some fun."

"Okay, I promise I'll have fun if you go sit down." And Gar playfully shoved Angus back to his own chair.

STUPID, LIQUOR-INDUCED grins were smeared on everyone's faces, and the crowd was still thick at midnight. Gar listened to Angus telling this tough and rugged local cowboy, "...my last girlfriend had just turned eighteen when I met her. She wasn't experienced. Matter of fact, I was her first. So, I had her keep her *beaver* shaved, and also made her wear mini-skirts with no panties all the time."

"What the fuck are you talking about?" The cowboy, Gary, was incredulous.

"Well," Angus continued. "With her freshly shaved thing itching all the time, plus her being <u>really</u> self conscious because the mini-skirt barely kept it covered, she spent almost all of her time thinking about *it*–and me–and it didn't take her long to where she was a regular sex maniac."

"You know," the redneck stood up, grabbing Angus by the lapels of his shirt. "That was somebody's sister, and I've had enough of you."

Gar saw what was about to happen and he intervened. "Hold it, Gary! He's with....Just let it go."

"I guess you're into protecting perverts, then," Gary scoffed. The man was spitting mad.

"Just let it go. Let me buy you a drink." Gar tried using one of his bartender tricks.

Gary grabbed the table and tipped it sideways. Drinks went everywhere. As Gary turned toward Goose, Gar vaulted the overturned table and was instantly in Gary's face.

"I said LET IT GO!"

Gary doubled his right fist, turned toward Gar, and let go with a round-house haymaker. But Gar had just completed a nine-day workout and was far faster. He hit Gary with a wicked left-right combination that connected with the chin and solar plexus. It dropped Gary to his knees, where he spent several moments catching his breath. He then stood and walked out of the bar.

Everyone cheered.

Goose said, "I had him handled. You didn't need to step in."

Everyone glared at Goose. The comment was utterly absurd.

TIMMY PICKED UP the table and hollered to the cocktail waitress, "We better have another round!" Then to Gar, "Did I pay you for that splitter bet, Lips? You got us by almost ten pounds."

"Timmy, it was five pounds a little while ago," Gar chastised him gently.

"I lied a little bit, Lips. Our fish was thirty two." Tim admitted this like a twelve-year-old making a confession.

"Ahhh, don't worry about it, Sull. It's only a fish, and only a drink. And, by God, everybody has to believe in something. So I *believe* I'll have another rum and Coke." Gar garbled his words slightly, but he felt that he was speaking very profoundly.

"You're the best, Lips." Timmy was wistful.

"LAST CALL!" SHOUTED the bartender as Gar passed the bar on the way to the men's room.

On the way back, a cute and likely brunette with an intriguing oval face and chestnut eyes (and a tiny bit of baby fat on a slightly plump Half Moon Bay meat-and-potatoes figure) pushed her driver's license in Gar's face and said: "Check it! I'm twenty one."

"What? Wait a minute. Are you Elaine? Oh, yeah. I recognize you now . . . the bait shop . . . sorry . . . I didn't expect to see you here," Gar stuttered, surprised.

"I came here so you could buy me a drink, but now it's last call. I think you better get a six pack and invite me to your boat. Remember, I'm the one that called Captain John for you." She was being very forward, Gar thought. But that's Half Moon Bay for you. The girl had a twinkle in her eyes and the hot, provocative stance of youth. Her entire demeanor was one of sensuality and challenge.

"Okay, you're on." Then to the bartender, "Gimme a couple of six-packs of Budweiser to go, please."

AT THE BOAT, Elaine was saying, "You know, I have never done this before. I don't know why I said that to you. We're just here for a beer anyway, right?"

"You bet," Gar said as he pulled her close. They were standing inside his cabin. The two six packs were on the table situated at the back of the cabin between the bunk and the door. The bunk ran along the cabin wall with the head toward the bow and, of course, feet toward the stern.

He gave her a long, passionate kiss while stroking her temples with his thumbs. "Ummm...." he said. "You taste good."

"So do you." she cooed.

His hands roamed under her shirt and found her bra clasp, and when it was unsnapped, they tumbled back onto the bunk. Undressing, they found, was difficult in the tight space.

Difficult, but not impossible.

"DO YOU LIKE me better than Susan?" Elaine asked, a couple of hours later as she was getting dressed. She dressed slowly, provocatively, her long limbs moving with languid sensuality. This girl was accomplished in the art of seduction, and definitely not new to it.

"How did Susan get into this?" Gar avoided the painful question. He was already feeling guilty as it was.

"I know you're still in love with her," Elaine taunted.

"And I probably always will be," Gar said. Then, changing the subject, "Do you have your car up in the parking lot?"

"Yes, I've got my Dad's pickup." Typical Half Moon Bay girl, Gar mused. Mom makes sure she's dressed nicely before she goes out drinking, and Dad makes sure she's got good a good pickup.

"Okay, I'll walk you up there."

"You trying to get rid of me?" She teased him.

"No. Stay the night, if you want. What's left of it, it's almost five. I've just had a very long day, and I thought your parents might be wondering where you are."

"All right. Yeah, I forgot. We better go." And she stood on her toes and kissed him one more time. She knew this was nothing more than two ships passing in the night. Her young, romantic soul nonetheless needed to make the experience more important than it was.

She was already producing the "movie" she would later play back for her girl friends. She might even call Susan. No, that would be ethically questionable. But she could make sure Sue heard about it....

CHAPTER 11

MAY 9–31, 1980.

"YOU PRICK!" SUSAN yelled angrily. "Elaine is just a baby, and she's my best friend's younger sister. *And* she's got a boy friend."

"I didn't know about any of that. And she's twenty one; I saw her driver's license." Gar squirmed, hating this. After having fueled and restocked the boat, he drove to the Beach House, where a phone message from Susan had been waiting. His heart had soared at once. He dialed her back, hoping against hope that she wanted him for something. Any reason at all would be wonderful.

But wonderful wasn't in the cards. Not today. And, as he had figured out some time ago, it probably never would be.

"You're just a typical fisherman, any port in a storm." She continued to rant and rave. Gar listened for a while, then he got tired of it. He interrupted her.

"You know, since I drive right by Babe's house on my way to Pescadero, I can't help but notice your car there most mornings."

This was the wrong thing to say, even though it was true.

"Fuck you!" she retorted. And slammed the phone down.

VERY DISTURBED AND shaken, Gar poured a stiff shot, gulped it down, then headed for Rudy's. He had called Sue from behind the Beach House bar, so the whiskey was handy. That morning, after the weather-radio predicted gale-force winds, he called Rudy and told him about the salmon Mom had in her cooler, and that he would be happy to deliver it to Rudy's cookhouse around noon.

Rudy chuckled, as only he could do it (from deep within), and said, "Okay, Bobbie, I'ma gunna cooka you something real nice today."

THE BEACH HOUSE sits down in a low spot on Coast Highway One. It is right at the mouth of Gazos Creek, which is why the elevation drops down there.

As Gar topped the quarter-mile rise going south from Gazos, he could see Franklin Point a mile or so down the long beach that extended from the Gazos down to that Point. At the top of the rise is also where Rudy's fence line begins.

The highway, after clearing the grade, meanders away from the ocean, and then proceeds parallel to the coastline as it passes Franklin Point. After that, the road angles slightly farther away, for the next couple of miles, before Rudy's driveway appears.

Gar was enjoying the drive this morning–the view of Rudy's neatly tended artichoke fields–, and despite Susan's harsh comments (where did she come from with all this righteous anger? they had been separated for almost two years), he felt like the master of his universe. Perhaps at this remote end of the county, where there were rarely police, and cows outnumbered people, he was the master.

Rudy's artichoke fields began a quarter mile before the driveway. Gar always smiled here because there was only the green-bitter odor of the artichoke bushes to be smelled. This was different from all the other *choke* fields one passed while traveling along the highway, fields that reeked of the noxious chemicals those farmers dusted with in order to kill bugs.

Rudy, when the *bug dust* was first introduced, decided he wouldn't use it. As the years went by, other growers were forced to steadily increase the toxin level as the bugs built immunity to the stuff used against them. But it seemed that Rudy's plants developed a vitriol of their own that naturally warded off the bugs.

An artichoke plant will live twenty or more years. So it was not difficult for Rudy to take grafts from older plants, plow those under, then replant with grafts that were essentially genetic duplicates of the ancestors.

"CASCADE RANCH," THE old sign, faded and chipped, declared. It hung from a twenty-foot high crossbar mounted atop two posts planted on each side of the driveway entrance. It had been there for probably thirty or forty years, unpainted, and who knows how long it had hung there before that? The letters were carved blocks of wood.

Gar swung up the driveway and five-hundred yards further turned in to the left, next to Rudy's old aquamarine and white Chevy C/K pickup that was parked in front of the cookhouse. Rudy was at the stove, and smiled out the window. Gar waved and smiled back, then looked around as another pickup was coming from the dog-training kennels, another concern on the ranch. Enticing odors of garlic, olive oil, and red wine wafted from the kitchen.

Cook's Kennels had leased ground from the Cascade for a handful of years. There was a big ranch house not too far off to the south (less than a mile) of Rudy's operation. The Cooks lived there, and had built dozens of kennels where bird hunters kept their dogs. Some of the dogs were boarded, others were there to be trained. From what Gar knew about the operation, he had heard that the Cooks had a fine reputation in the dog-training world.

There were three generations of Cooks: Chuck, Sr., Chuck II, and "Chuckie." Chuckie was a few years younger than Gar, and it was him coming down the road now. Gar had known him for years. He was a diving partner, a Beach House customer, and he was currently dating Gar's youngest sister, Lori.

"HEY, CHUCKIE. WHAT'S up?" Gar greeted him at the pickup window.

"Gonna be a good tide at fou r o'clock today," Chuckie, as is his way, cut right to the chase.

"Oh, yeah? You going after abalones?" Gar asked him.

"Well, I was thinking about it, but my lazy brother-in-law, Gregory, doesn't want to go. I don't want to go alone. But if you feel like it, we could probably get some nice ab's. It's a minus-five-foot tide; 5.2 to be exact."

Okay, if I don't get too drunk here. I'm having lunch with Rudy. You know, I just happen to have my dive bag in my truck. I got my gear wet yesterday, and I pulled it off the boat so I could rinse everything in fresh water. Plus, I need to get my air bottle filled. Not that we'll be needing it, snorkling for ab's. But it's nice to have the wet suit, so I guess we can go."

"Yeah, I heard about your *dive*. Dad said you made the San Francisco Chronicle on page seven. A little article about a guy who fell over, and you were a witness or something...."

Chuck was knuckling one eye as he spoke, then he hawked up a lunger and spit. He had allergies and was always expectorating. Doctors, expert in such things, had tested Chuckie and determined he was allergic to dog hair. Gar stepped back a couple of feet.

"Yeah, that's a long story. I didn't see anything. I just dove under the boat looking for the body." Gar made light of it. He was trying to forget about the tragedy.

"Hey!" Chuck interrupted. "I'm going to Santa Cruz tomorrow to the dive shop. I can fill your bottle for you then. Won't even cost you anything, because I've got an air card good for a year's free fills." He was lobbying hard to get Gar to agree to go diving.

Chuckie was a thin, rangy-looking man of medium height and indeterminate appearance. Everything about him seemed average until you got a closer look. Closer inspection revealed a thinning, mousey-brown head of hair and a bad complexion. His lower lip jutted out more than it should, and the intensity to be seen in his hazel eyes bordered maniacal. He was sharp enough, but Gar wasn't entirely convinced of his mental stability. Chuckie spit again into the dirt and looked at Gar with a questioning expectancy.

"Okay." Gar relented. "Looks like we're blown-in any way for a couple of days. We had a good trip, and I had planned to go right back out, but the weather-radio says northwest winds at 25-40 knots per hour. Little too much for me. We generally won't come in because of a gale, but we don't go out in one either. Anything over thirty-nine miles per hour is a gale."

"All right. Where are you going to be at two thirty?" Chuckie asked him.

"I might be right here," Gar grinned. "If not, I'll meet you back here. Have you got a key for the gate, or do you want me to ask Rudy?"

"I don't have one. Rudy's been tight with it lately. I don't know why. We've got keys for all the other gates, but not that one. He says we've plenty of places to train dogs and don't need to go down to Franklin Point." Chuckie spit while complaining.

"Okay. I'm starving. I'll see you at two thirty." Gar tapped the truck door as he turned away to grab the sack with the salmon out of his own truck.

GAR PASSED MIA, Rudy's faithful black lab, wagging her tail. He gave her a scratch behind the ears and smiled. He smiled at the thought of Rudy muttering. Rudy had a mild form of Tourette's Syndrome that, while busy doing something like, say, cooking, he would bark, "Mia, mia," in his gruff, old and gravelly voice. And the dog would invariably look up.

As Gar entered the kitchen, which was certainly seventy-five years old, Rudy spoke to him over his shoulder.

"Sit down, Bobbie . . . have a drink."

"Thank you, Rudy. Where would you like this salmon, in the fridge? I wrapped it in a plastic sack so it wouldn't drip."

"Just put it in that sink, the back one, I'll cut it up in a little while." Gar loved the accent, but never succumbed to the urge to duplicate it. Many times he had been there with Rudy and other Italians while they talked in their "Attsa my meata-boll" accents, but never would he let himself try to imitate them.

"Alright. What's for lunch? You look busy, and it smells good," Gar commented.

"You know what I'm cooking: your favorite! Birds in olive oil, but I didn't have any wild birds, so I'm only cooking chicken today." Rudy spoke apologetically.

"Chicken's perfect today because I'm hungry, and with chicken there's more meat than with the little birds," Gar said.

"Okay, Bobbie, have a drink. It'll be done in a minute."

AT TWO THIRTY, Chuckie came down the driveway, and Gar said goodbye to Rudy, thanking him for lunch. Then he remembered to ask for the key. Rudy took it off his ring, and Gar promised Rudy abalone if the dive was successful.

THEY WENT IN Gar's truck, as it was four-wheel drive. Deep burgundy in color with a buttery-yellow cab top, Gar had bought the rig a couple of years earlier at the Chevy dealer in Gold Beach, Oregon. He still had Oregon plates, which gave him a *worldly* appeal, he thought.

Chuckie opened the gate, Gar drove through, and Chuckie locked it back up. They drove over a rise and dropped back down to the top of the forty-foot cliff overlooking Bootlegger's Cove. Here, they were obscured from the highway.

Chuck said, "We've been doing best right here, lately. It's a little deeper than up by the Point (Franklin Point was a quarter mile north up the rocky shoreline), but there are more ab's here. And they're bigger, too. You know, it's more sandy out in the middle, but there are rocks all around the edges. Just follow me."

"Okay," Gar said, as he started to put on his gear.

AFTER THE DIVE, and back up at the truck with limits of five apiece, Chuck said, "You know, game wardens never look at this place. I've never even seen anybody here, and I've been down here a lot. Sometimes I just come down here with your sister, and we smoke a doobie and watch the ocean. Never see anybody."

"Yeah, we could have probably gotten a couple more ab's?" Gar's eyebrows raised, not knowing where Chuckie was going with this observation.

"Well, yeah, that too," Chuck said. "But I was thinking you could bring that fishing boat of yours in here loaded with weed, and we could bring it in to that little beach right there (pointing) in my Zodiac. Then figure out the best way to pack it up that road right there (pointing again) to a truck parked right about here where we're sitting. That cut down to the beach is the original road Rudy and them used to pull up sleds of booze."

"I'll be damned," Gar said. "I knew this was the cove, or I guess I figured it was, but I didn't know that was the same road. It looks too new to me."

"Well," Chuckie giggled. "I brought my Dad's Cat down through here a while back, and punched it through again. It was still there from before. I mean, you could tell where it had been, but I cleaned it up. It was full of ruts, holes so big I almost lost the Cat in there. I had to push a lot of dirt in ahead of me first."

"Well, I'll be dipped," Gar said. "You know, I know those fishermen on the east coast, and especially in Florida, do a lot of smuggling. But I haven't heard too much about it on this coast. Well, I take that back. I have heard about a couple of different guys bringing pot up from Mexico. But not coke, like over in Florida."

Chuck said, "You probably heard Gregory and I grow weed at the ranch. Well, we sell it to different dealers in Santa Cruz, and they've asked us about bringing weed in, up here, from the ocean, because they know we can get down to these hidden beaches with no problems. Think about it. There's no place from San Francisco to Santa Cruz where anyone has this kind of private access. And you got the answer to all the problems because you have the fishing boat to bring it in on. And, Rudy likes you. He'll give you the key any time you want, and you know it. None of us have that."

"Yeah. Well. I'd never do anything that might hurt Rudy. I love that old bastard, and all the tea in China wouldn't be enough for me to hurt him." Gar was emotional, all of a sudden, and quite emphatic.

"Why don't you ask his permission, first?" Chuckie suggested, "He likes you enough that he would give it to you."

"Which is exactly why I would never ask. Not to mention that I could never face my family and friends." Susan came, at once and unbidden, to mind. Also Michael, Mom, and Geno–the man Gar had bought the boat from. "No, I could never do it. But if you guys ever try, good luck. I guess, then, the history of Pescadero and Bootlegger's Cove would repeat itself. You guys could start the Roaring Eighties, I guess." Gar joked a bit, mildly distressed because he felt like a challenge had been issued and he had chickened out. But how could anyone make less of him for declining to break the law? The fact that the marijuana laws were ridiculous was beside the point.

Growing up in the Bay Area, as a teenager during the sixties, Gar had inherited the liberal view that marijuana laws were created by the same demons that were now putting more restrictions on the commercial salmon season. They had just cut the first fifteen days of his salmon season by delaying opening day, this year, from April 15th to May the first. And there was talk they might chop some off the September ending, too. It was that fucking National Marine Fisheries Service (NMFS) that was responsible. Until just four years earlier, the states controlled all ocean fishing seasons. Now, the feds ran everything out to two hundred miles.

The *200-Mile-Limit* had been a knife in the back, and he had to hand it to the old timers: they had predicted it, and it was sure looking like they were right. What they were seeing now was the end of an era. The long, proud history of salmon fishermen going out to sea on the west coast might be coming to an end.

They said once the feds got involved, you might just as well find another occupation. When at first the NMFS got rid of the Russian factory trawlers, Gar thought it was a good thing. But then President Carter gave them permits to come right back in anyway. And when they did, they made up for lost time, fishing all the favorite salmon holes with legal impunity.

And now, as is the case with bureaucracies, the well-paid employees of NMFS needed to justify their jobs by simply cutting back on salmon season in order to look like they were doing something. It certainly seemed like a racket. The salmon in the ocean certainly weren't an endangered species, and they never would be.

GAR STOPPED BACK at the cookhouse, and took two ab's in along with Rudy's key. Rudy was grinning like a fox while talking with another old Italian *choke* farmer. The bottle of

Seagram's VO, a bottle that Gar had opened earlier, was empty. Gar put the abalones in the same sink, and handed Rudy his key. Not wanting to interrupt, he just smiled and waved. Rudy spoke to him, though.

"Wait a minute, Bobbie, have a drink," he said. "I'll open another bottle for you."

"No. I've got to go to the Beach House and get showered. I've had nothing but salt water baths for ten days, and I need a real shower."

"Okay. Then I'm coming there to buy you one when you get out of the shower. Did little Cook try to tell you to bring in some of his funny weed to the cove?" Rudy stunned Gar with this question.

"Ha, ha, ha," Gar laughed. "Now I know it's time to go. I'll see you down at the restaurant after a while."

Hmmm! Gar thought, behind the laughter. *Where in the hell did that come from?*

Some time later, Gar would figure out that Rudy didn't let the Cooks have the key to the Franklin Point gate because he suspected they might be tempted to use the cove for something illegal. Evidently they had hinted at a desire to do something like this already. And since they showed him little respect, he wasn't about to sanction their unfettered use of what he knew to be, of the ranch's many acres, potentially the Cascade's most remunerative asset. Bootlegger's Cove had paid for the ranch many times over in the past. And it could do so again.

Gar, on the other hand, not only paid constant tribute to the *Godfather*, but his parents' restaurant was almost a second home to Rudy and his wife, Bea. The elderly couple no longer had to drive to Santa Cruz for Saturday night dinner. And Rudy had a bar, just a few miles away from home, where he could drink and shake dice with his neighbors. It was a place where everyone loved and catered to him.

CHAPTER 12

JUNE 1 – AUGUST 10, 1980.

ON THE WAY back to the Farallons, Gar noticed the water was clear blue, rather than the fertile shades of green and brown it had been. There were no birds, and no sign of bait, anywhere to be seen. The only birds Gar saw were high in the sky, obviously going somewhere else. The *shrimpy* smell had disappeared too, replaced by the ozone smell that a hard blow can create.

They had stayed in town almost a week. The wind had blown savagely during that time, as it normally does in the month of May. The sea temperature gauge said the water was 48 degrees. It had been between 51 and 52 degrees on their trip the week before, which was perfect salmon water. All of these indications did not add up to a good thing, but you never know about the ocean.

PASSING OVER PA'S Canyon, the ocean looked so dead that Gar didn't even stop to drop a test line. There were no birds there, nothing appeared on the meter, and the same edgeless, clear-blue water appeared everywhere. The surface of the sea presented a purple-bordering-on-green-and-blue color that suggested mountain ice, rather than the warmer and lighter blue of Caribbean tropics. It was not an auspicious color for fish. And the lack of sea birds was a bad sign.

THE MAIN ISLAND on the south side presented more of the same, and a run through the Piggy Patch showed nothing on the paper machine. They dropped a test line, one bow line, and Gar thought about Mable and Russell while they trolled it for fifteen minutes. It was all to no avail. They didn't even catch a rock cod.

At least the ocean was flat, and that meant it was a good time to gain altitude. Since the wind was always out of the north by northwest at this time of year, and it is always easier to go with the wind than to buck into it, it is prudent to go north during flat weather, as it may not be possible later. Then one can always slide back south–down the hill–if need be.

THEY RAN THROUGH the night, and at daybreak found themselves at Stewart's Point, below Gualala. The water temperature was better, a weak fifty-one degrees, and they had run out of that ugly blue and into some better green-colored water.

Gar noticed good markings on the paper machine as well as more murres diving after bait, and he woke up Jeff. They set the gear, and he told Jeff not to expect much. But they needed to stretch their gear out anyway. Plus, they were close to the rocky coastline here (an edge where sandy bottom met rocky bottom), and on a twenty-fathom curve similar to the conditions they had last experienced at the Piggy Patch. This allowed them to put out the same gear spread.

They made a long tack up, doubling back a couple of times, and then they went to anchor at Fish Rocks. They had a measly thirty-eight fish for the day, and a poor grade of fish at that.

THE NEXT MORNING they set the gear into thirty-some fathoms off Fish Rocks, and took off the short leaders. They returned to their regular gear pattern of a flasher, followed by three baits, repeated and set at the four-fathom stops.

Tacking up in still-flat weather on what was turning into a beautiful morning, they only caught the occasional straggler. Gar manned the radios, most of the time, hoping to hear something about somebody catching fish.

He called up T.D. on the big set, who was south off his home port of Bodega Bay, getting through to him right on the 9:00 a.m. schedule.

"Yeah, phwee-phwee, we got one fish right der offa de point, then my pardner over der got three right der, offa de Fort." The man hesitated for a moment. "Not too much going on right here, right now."

T.D. (Tom Danielson) was Scandinavian. Though grown up on the West Coast, he nevertheless talked like a Minnesotan. Gar sometimes imitated him, but not to his face, as the man was proud and particular. As a matter of fact, his boat was called the ***Sea Pride***. And it surely was, as the boat was never anything less than immaculate. T.D. was comical to listen to with his "right der's" and "right here, right now's." And he kept whistling in his mike to make sure he still had a strong signal.

"Sounds the same all over, Tom. We got what the sea gull left on the rock, for the morning. You know what that is, don't you?" Gar joked.

"Phwee, phwee. Is that the same as the bear left in the woods? Ha, ha, ha . . ." That was another T.D. trait. He would laugh, "ha, ha, ha," when he was done talking, and gradually move the mike further away, so he sort of faded to black as he quit talking.

"Yeah, you got it. The same as the kitty left in the litter box. I can't hear anything anywhere. My partners off Wha-Fumma Bay have nothing. I'm lost. This is another fine deal," Gar said.

"I talked to Calvin a little while ago. They got a little scratch going on up at the cove, you know," T.D. offered.

"Really?" Gar replied. "No, I didn't know that. I'll have to think about that one. I know you're not going anywhere, but we got our traveling shoes on, man. I just might report to you from there tomorrow."

AN HOUR LATER, they pulled their gear and stacked it neatly on the boat, taking the baits off and covering everything real well, in preparation for a long run. Shelter Cove was about fifteen or sixteen hours up the coast, and Gar figured they could be there before daybreak.

However, off of Point Arena they came across nice tide rips, as well as birds working bait balls, so they set the gear in the water with two, bow test lines. They got a couple of hits right away, and dumped in the rest of the gear. And they were very soon glad that they did.

They ended the day with eighty or ninety fish, and on the way in to anchor at Arena Cove, Gar commented to Jeff that though he missed Sully, it was kind of nice to be out of the mix with Goose.

"Other than T.D.," he noted, "and whoever else we bump into, we're on our own."

"I see you're less stressed," Jeff observed.

About that time, though, Hop Sing, an all-American redneck bohemian type of fisherman, called to offer Gar directions into Arena Cove. He explained how to get around the kelp wads inside the cove. And he explained how conveniently the bar, just a hundred yards from the dock, was located. Gar and Jeff were forced to explore that option for a few hours that evening, in search of something warm to take the chill off the night.

The light tower on the point, on the north side of Arena Cove, offered a friendly welcome to ocean-going travelers. The classic-looking black and white lighthouse flashed an auspicious beam over the boat as it motored past that evening. To the two thirsty men, the light might have been flashing the message: "The Bar Is Open–Come On In!"

It took Jeff only an hour to convince a pretty tourist girl to come to see <u>his</u> boat. On their way out, Jeff made a showing of buying Gar a drink, telling the girl his deckhand might be old, but he was nonetheless a good worker!

Indeed, when Gar came down to the boat later, he found the amorous couple upstairs in his Captain's bunk. Jeff was long since through, anyway, and hurried the girl back up the dock. He came back, apologized, and explained he couldn't very well play captain and then sleep in the fo'c'sle.

"What a beauty," Gar said.

THEY ENDED THAT trip in Fort Bragg, selling to Pete at Puccini's Dock. They delivered 400-something mediocre fish for a much smaller payday then their first trip.

The rest of the month continued about the same. The only highlight for Gar was partying with Frank Bender in

Fort Bragg. Frank was an original Half Moon Bay'er, and he owned the ***Susan R***, which was named after Gar's favorite Susan. Her Dad had rebuilt the boat, then sold it to Frank some years earlier.

Partying with Frank was an all out good time. Frank, someone had said years before, had more character than anyone around. And he was indeed a card.

They eventually made a trip to Shelter Cove, after the trip between Albion, Little River, and on up above Noyo at Westport.

THE LIGHT SHIP that June was a big letdown. Maybe a thousand fish were caught during two and a half trips out. Fishing the Blunts Reef Light Ship for eight days straight is just about impossible. Many years earlier there had been an actual ship moored five miles out at the tip of the Mendocino reef. Now it is replaced by a large, well-lit weather buoy. There was usually very good fishing at that spot, but this time it was a disappointment.

Consequently, in between good weather periods, the fishermen tried to make new history at the good ole' V.D. Club. The Vista just wasn't the same, though, without the entire squad.

BY THE FOURTH of July they had made it up to Bandon, Oregon.

Hog country.

And they chased a few of the local Oregon girls, renowned for their robust figures, before Jeff fell in love with Z-duck. "The Duck" was a cute little woman who had first gone out with Peter-Skin, but now just waited for anyone in the squad, and for the last couple of years it had been Gar. She let him down this year, though, when she choose Jeff.

Boats were starting to catch albacore a few hundred miles out, and Gar decided that it was time to pull the plug on salmon and go offshore before he lost Jeff to the passionate throes of the Z-Duck.

Besides, Angus had come north and caught up with them. One night while anchored in Nellie's cove behind Cape Blanco, they all rowed skiffs into the town of Port Orford. Gar got especially drunk there and had some sort of disagreement with Jeff. This was totally out of character and he could hardly remember it because of his intoxication. Goose brought Jeff back the next morning. Little did he know, Goose spent the night trying to convince Jeff to come work for him.

THEY DECIDED TO run up to Charleston, on the Coos Bay in Oregon, in order to re-rig there. Gar built an enclosed pipe-railing shroud around the stern so they could fish albacore off the deck, rather than hopping in and out of the pit. Albacore tuna hit much differently than salmon, and it doesn't take near the time to pull them aboard once they're hooked. An albacore fisherman spends far more time watching and waiting than actually running gear. And with the albacore jigs skipping across the surface, as opposed to the salmon baits submerged many fathoms below, it does not necessitate "pulling a line" in order to see if you have any fish, or still have a good bait. Looking back at the skipping jigs, you see at a glance that you either have a fish on the line or you don't. There is no guess work.

There is a trick to albacore fishing, though, and some fishermen have developed it into an art form. One runs at half speed (three to four knots) when albacore fishing, tacking across water edges or through flocks of birds. Then when a fish hits, the steering wheel is locked so the boat makes a long, wide circle, theoretically over the top of the school that fish came from.

In rougher weather, circling is impossible. Then one simply goes up and back on a course that is not across the wind, yet takes the boat over the spot where the fish hit.

The setup for albacore consists of five jigs, at varying distances behind the boat, trolled off each pole. One long line is extended off the mast center going back about where the salmon dog-line floats would fish. And two short lines are run out right behind each side of the stern. In "hot" fishing, one will hopefully just keep pulling fish off the short lines, as another fish will hit it as soon as that jig is tossed back in the water.

The jigs are six to eight inches long. In days of old they had feather skirts behind a weighted head. But nowadays the skirts are mostly plastic in a wide assortment of colors.

A double, barbless hook is tied on the 300-pound-test monofilament leader's end, after passing the end through the jig head. The double hook makes up for the lack of barbs. One does not want barbs, as the key to albacore fishing is catching and removing fish fast. Barbs slow things down.

THE FIRST TUNA trip they left out of Coos Bay with the refrigeration working well. Of course ice was unnecessary, as the *refer* froze the fish solid. Salmon needed to be kept on ice. With albacore, that wasn't required. The fish were quickly frozen. They outfitted for a fifteen-day trip. They had six drums of fuel on deck and plenty of extra food. Jeff was also well stocked with *Playboy* magazines.

They didn't find the perfect sixty-two degrees albacore water until they were a hundred and fifty miles off of Cape Blanco. It was the right shade of blue, and they recognized it instantly. Not a Caribbean blue, but a nice light blue, perhaps like gin. Or maybe like a clear, wintertime, noon sky. Gradually working to the southwest, they began catching a few fish–maybe fifty to one hundred a day. The goal when albacore fishing is to catch a ton a day. The fish normally average twelve pounds, so it takes around 160-170 fish to make a ton. Fifty to a hundred fish kept them searching.

A WEEK INTO the trip they had maybe three tons, and were working the Mendocino Ridge, which is 200-some miles off Eureka, California. It was a good place for fish, but a bad place in a blow.

On the eighth morning they got up quietly, as they always did, and Gar slipped the boat into gear and jacked the throttle while Jeff simultaneously tossed jigs out. Gar locked the boat into a long, lazy circle, and less than a minute after engaging the gear box he, too, was tossing out jigs.

Lines went down immediately. When albacore hit, they sound, thus a line "down" has a fish on it.

The fishermen in their boats always, of course, drifted at night. And albacore sometimes bunch up under a drifting boat, as feed sometimes does. So it's not uncommon to literally wake up right on top of a school of fish.

And that morning they woke up on top of a dandy. By noon they had put two-hundred fish in the hold, and had at least a hundred on deck. They let the fish flop, bleed, and die on deck. This way they were clean and cool before they were put down into the refrigerated hole. Albacore are quite warm when first caught, and too many put down in the hole at once will shock a refrigeration system.

They finished that day with a circle that brought the day's close to three tons. They had doubled their trip score in a single day.

ON DAY NINE, Nardo, Gar's old boss on the ***Michelle Ann***, and Fred Cefalu on the ***Susan Marie***, showed up. Gar knew then that he and Jeff had a hot hand. Those guys had superlative access to information and almost a sixth sense about fish, not to mention incredible experience, and they were there because it was the foremost spot around.

Gar had a two-ton day to celebrate their arrival.

THE TENTH DAY, the wind came. By seven in the morning they could no longer circle, and had to straight tack directly into or with the wind.

Despite this, they caught fish throughout the day and Gar figured they had another ton on board when a few hours before dark, disaster struck.

A flopper-stopper breached water and flew up on the bow as the boat did a lunge over the top of a steep wave, then a quick drop off the back side. It was a freak occurrence. There was, evidently, slack in that pole's tie down line that the flopper, hanging from mid-pole, had been keeping taut. This must have been the case because, when the flopper landed up on the bow of the boat, that slack now allowed play and the pole did a sharp whip-snap on the next bucking of the plunging boat. About six feet of the tip of the pole suddenly splintered off. Since one of the pole's hold-down lines ran out to the tip, that piece of pole was still dangling. But this allowed yet more play in the pole and Gar feared the way the pole was flopping in and out, that he would lose the whole thing.

That would virtually shut down half of their fishing ability.

He idled down the throttle and set the boat on a heading into the waves, which was a good course for the ***Visit*** as it didn't roll so much that way. He then climbed the mast with sidecutters, knife, stainless crabpot wire (fishermen's bailing wire), rubber wrap (similar to large, two-inch tape, made from inner tubes), and a length of albacore line.

The pole was flying in and out with a throw of at least five feet, and Gar was clinging to the mast with one arm and leg while trying to catch the two-hundred pound pole at the top of its flight. The situation was as dangerous as one could imagine.

And the wind blew yet harder aloft.

GAR GOT AN arm around the pole, and managed to pull it in to the crosstree as Jeff hauled on the pull lines and secured them.

That was the easy part.

Now, with the boat rolling and bucking, motions exaggerated by the increased leverage at the top of the mast, Gar needed to reattach, somehow, the three tag lines to the top of the stump.

It was a hairy operation. It was exceptionally dangerous, and undoubtedly stupid. But it was necessary if Gar and Jeff were to continue fishing.

After an hour, Gar had fashioned a makeshift repair. The pole was let back out, the jigs put back into the water, the flopper pitched back in, the throttle jacked up, and they were fishing again.

They had another half ton for the evening bite, and Gar guessed they had over ten tons on the boat now. They were almost full, as the ***Visit*** held around twelve tons. Albacore fishermen always hope to "Plug" the boat. That's what is called "A Trip." You stayed out until you ran out of fuel, or you finished your trip.

The bad news was that the wind and sea were a tempest now, and with all this extra weight on the boat the ***Visit*** sat a couple of feet lower in the water. This meant there were parts of the boat underwater that had not been underwater in years. And the boat was leaking. Excessively.

The automatic bilge pump ran a steady garden-hose size stream of water, and Gar still had to go down to the engine room every other hour and run the larger inch-and-three-quarters pump that moved a lot of water real fast. Without that, they'd be, quite literally, sunk. It ran off the main engine, so Gar prayed the engine wouldn't quit.

They drifted that night and rode like ducks (the ***Visit***, though a roller under power, performed at her best while adrift). But the bilge alarm still woke Gar to pump out the bilges every half hour or so. It was to be a long night.

He wanted badly to get that last ton, and plug the ***Visit***. He'd never done it before. Not even close. And Geno had only done it once in *his* ten years as owner. But they were taking on entirely too much water. And not only were they straining the limits of their water-pumping capacity, they risked slopping bilge water up into their bins of frozen fish, which would render the splashed-on fish unmarketable.

STRUGGLING THROUGH A long night, Gar prayed that daybreak would cast a more promising light on the situation.

There were no lighthouses out here. There was nothing to offer guidance. There were only the stars, and they seemed to Gar that night to cast a cold and pitiless light on the surging sea below them.

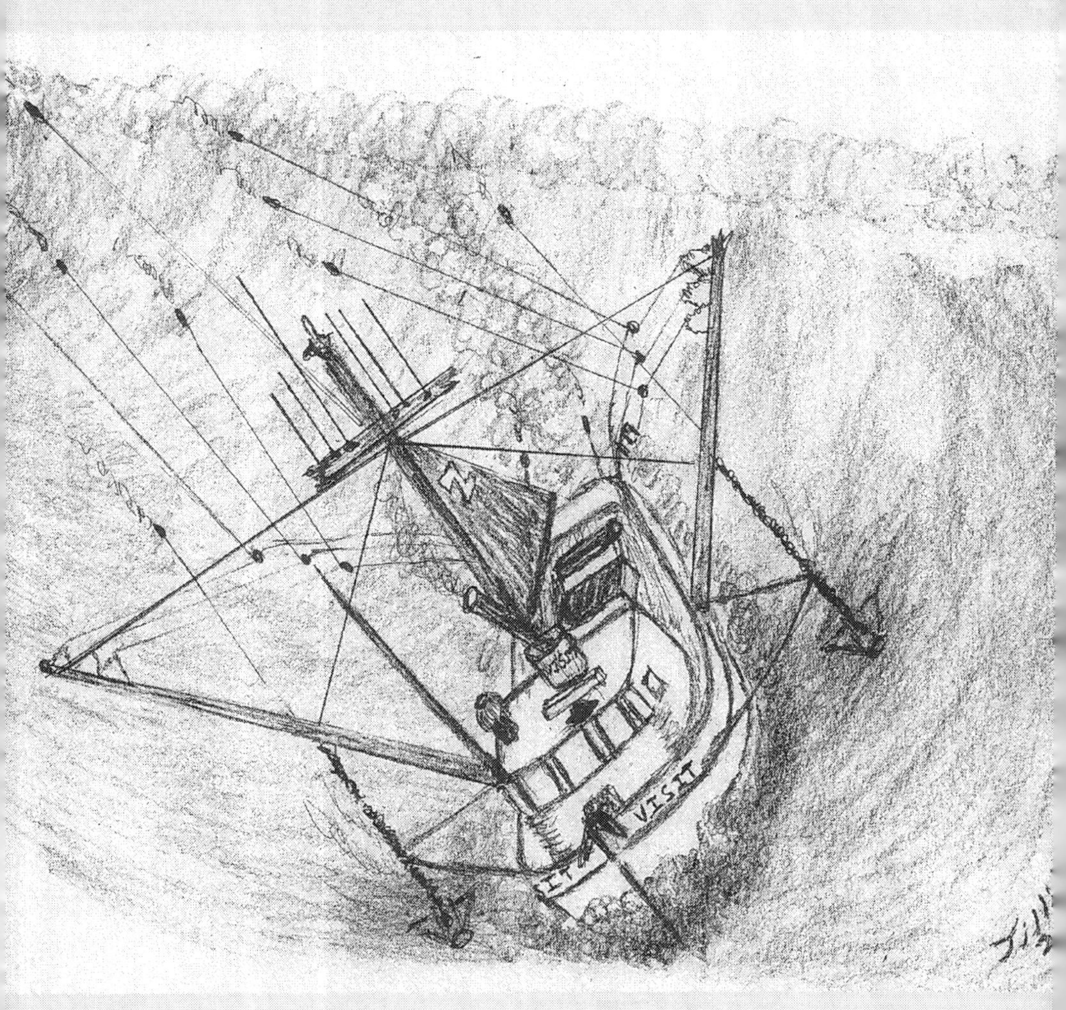

Offshore on the Mendocino Ridge.

CHAPTER 13

EARLY AUGUST, 1980.

NARDO CALLED AT five a.m., and warned that the ocean was becoming much too perilous. He questioned Gar about what he intended to do. Gar thought about it for a moment before replying.

"You know, we're laying here like a duck, hardly rolling. And when I stuck my head out the back door a minute ago, it blew spit right out of my mouth. I come back in, and it's like another world. I just don't even want to put the boat in gear, because I know what will happen."

"Okay, fine, Ravalone (Nardo's version was sort of ravioli and Garaloney mixed), I know how those old halibut boats drift. They were built to fish Alaska and drift out the bad blows, you know. But remember where you're at. This ridge is no place to be right now, and they got more wind coming. You better follow us to town. We're gonna slide with it to Fort Bragg."

"Alright, Narduchi. I *did* lay out my course options while pumping out earlier, and I think the course to Eureka is actually better for me, though," Gar said.

"That's alright, too. You just need to get the fuck out of here. Craig–you know Craig Stoltz–on the ***Summer*** is going that way, too, so you guys can run in together. Just don't take him up to the V.D. Club. His father, Bob–you know Bob–told me to watch out for him." Nardo was being paternal. Gar had been his deckhand not that long before, and it was natural for Nardo to act paternal towards him.

"Okay, Leonardo. I've got some things to do before we put it in gear. We still have half an hour before daylight. I'm hoping to get a few more fish on the way in, you know."

"Ravioli, this is the kind of weather where crew get washed over. Tie down your hatches, and lock the back door. You got enough fish, so go sell them." More fatherly scolding.

"Okay, Dad. Cchheeck you in a while." Gar clicked off.

THE LARGE PUMP ran the entire time Gar talked to Nardo, and now it was pretty much spurting water in a continuous stream. Gar left it engaged. He observed that it never quit pumping. Running a pump dry will burn up the rubber impeller.

There was no danger, with this much water flow, of burning up *this* impeller, so he left the pump to run sempiternally. Although the pump was interrupted momentarily while he shut down the engine in order to check oil and grease fittings. But that didn't take long.

ENGINE FIRED BUT still not in gear, Gar was out on deck with a hammer, and a fist full of sixteen-penny nails. He nailed down all three hatches. He had started to tie them, but didn't like the lay of the lines. He considered that a hatch could slip out from underneath with a deck full of water. The nails were crude, but effective.

The wind was now blowing so hard that when Gar looked into it, it curled back his eyelids. And the westerly swells were towering toward them as high as the mast. But the swells just rolled underneath the ***Visit***, and marched away in their serried ranks. The boat was laid over, slightly, by the wind against the stay sail. The ole' "Z" was good for more than just picking up chicks. And the only movement was up and down as the swells rolled underneath them. It was like being in an elevator, except without the music.

But Gar had music. He had been listening to Al Jolson earlier. The greatest hits collection with, of course, "Swanee." His three other favorites were, "Toot, Toot Tootsie," "My Mammy," and "California, Here I Come." This eight track had become, for barely discernable reasons, Gar's bad-weather tape. Maybe because it reminded him of Mom. And Mom represented security.

WHILE GAR BATTENED hatches, and any other semi-moveable equipment on the boat, Jeff made a Tupperware container of fried egg and mayonnaise sandwiches. This would be their last viable cooking opportunity for at least a day, because the weather promised to worsen before it got better. In good weather, they were more than twenty-four hours, at full throttle, from shore. Today they would be lucky to maintain jig speed (about half speed) with any margin of safety. So it would probably take two days to get back to the coast.

And the wind was blowing so hard it took spray off the tops of waves and flung it like bullets out of a gun. When he was on deck, Gar cursed the spanking gale every time he was struck in the face with another *bullet*. He also noticed that the telltale ozone smell of a hard blow was now in the air.

He would not ask Jeff to go on deck in this weather. Nardo had said, "this is the kind of weather deckhands get washed over." So Gar wasn't going to ask Jeff to go out. He told Jeff to plan on staying inside, to cook, watch the wheel, and monitor the radios.

And the fucking wind-driven rotary-turbine ventilator was emitting a wail like he had never heard before. The rotary turbine was on the roof of the pilothouse and attached to a stovepipe. The bottom of the stovepipe vent was over the stove, and the stove was situated directly behind where Gar sat to watch the wheel. So he could not help but notice the wind-driven noise the turbine made. When Gar fixated on the sound, he thought it sounded like monks praying, or people in hell moaning. Something eerie, like from a ghost movie. Whatever it resembled, it promoted fear, and fear was the moment's buzzword. Fear, Gar thought, is nature's warning signal to get busy. The foundation on which safety is built, he'd once heard.

WITH GAR BRACED in the stern, Jeff put the boat in gear, fed it some throttle, and pointed it on the prearranged course. Gar, meanwhile, tossed jigs over the side and started retying haul-in lines so they wouldn't blow into a tangle. And the fish started biting as if there were no wind and sea at all.

The course they were on was just about sideways to the wind and swell, and Gar left all the port-side jigs, except for those on the short lines, on the boat. Then after a few minutes, he pulled in the longest couple of lines on the starboard side, and left those on the boat too.

They were fishing with only five of their normal thirteen lines. However, the fish kept biting, and Gar kept pulling–even though he was soaked and chilled to the bone.

MID-MORNING WITH seventy-five fish boated since daybreak, a wave three stories tall broke across the stern and Gar held on tight to a davit. His feet were actually out on the wrong side of the rail as the wave roared across the deck of the boat. The power of the wave was stunning.

It had been too close. So he quit and went inside. Jeff was at the wheel, hand steering. He said the autopilot wouldn't hold a course. He looked scared and tired, so Gar took over and told him to take a break.

Jeff went out on the stern to smoke a cigarette, and he pulled several fish. But after an almost identical wave as that which had swamped Gar washed over him, he came back in and sounded shocked when he spoke.

"How the fuck did you stay out there all morning?"

"It's getting steadily worse," Gar mumbled back.

Then he told Jeff to take the wheel back for a few more minutes.

HE WENT BACK to the stern and pulled in the lines, coiling them into an orange-plastic milk-carton crate, then he pulled the nails out of one hatch and threw the fish down into the hold. He nailed that hatch back up and returned to the wheelhouse, bringing a plastic bucket and snap-on lid with him.

Once inside the wheelhouse, he drove nails through the back door, toe-nailing into the jamb, and told Jeff they would have to pee in the bucket for a while.

"Just make sure you snap the lid on tight, when you're done, then stow it back under the sink," he instructed.

In theory, with everything nailed shut, they could roll over, and when they righted themselves the boat would still be floating because no water could get inside. This was an incredible theory, and a disturbing portrait.

JEFF CALLED "LOOK out!" and Gar backed off on the throttle. Jeff stood to the left side of the wheel at the front-side window. He was standing a form of nautical watch, keeping an eye on the swells as they rolled toward them. Every time one got close, he sounded off and Gar pulled the throttle lever back to idle.

After the wave swept under them, he speeded back up, waiting for the moment when Jeff would holler out again.

At increased throttle they were only making a few knots of actual go-ahead ground speed. Gar was hand steering the vessel and their course through the sea was an erratic course, at best.

THROUGH THE TEDIUM of passing hours and the danger of the situation, Gar's mind began to wander. They were headed east toward Eureka and safety. He thought, for some inexplicable reason, of the first two lines of the Rudyard Kipling poem, *Mandalay,* and repeated them to himself, "By the old Moulmein Pagoda, lookin' eastward to the sea ... There's a girl a settin', and I know she thinks of me."

A classic poem that Gar, of course, related to Susan, but what was funny was the well-known fact that the first line of the poem states the wrong direction, as it should be *westward* to the sea. And here *they* were going eastward, and Gar felt that he, too, should be going back westward. They had been drifting so well, not too many hours earlier, and he wished they were still back there doing that.

THE RADIO BROKE that chain of thought. Craig, who had been reporting from time to time on how horribly they were riding, but that they were still okay, was calling again now.

Craig had experienced a shattered side window when a mountain-size sea dumped on top of them. They were a couple of miles ahead of Gar, but had now turned around to head back to sea rather than continue on towards the shore. He was doing this in order to put the broken window to the leeward side of the boat. He had plywood, he reported, and was working on a patch. They had a 110/220 volt electric plant, too, which allowed them to run power tools and a welder.

Craig felt things were in hand, but nonetheless wanted to make his report before going to work. Just in case.

GAR SAW CRAIG coming back toward him and steered a course around him by a safe margin of distance. When Craig passed by, Gar began a slow circle back behind him, reversing his own course so he could escort Craig's vessel while he repaired his window. This was a costly maneuver.

Just as they began the turn, a wave the size of a battleship broke over their entire boat. Poles, mast and everything were submerged. When they came out from under it, the port-side outrigger pole was completely shattered. This outrigger pole had been previously reduced to a stump of its previous length by the accident with the flying flopper stopper, but it had been repaired until it was at least functional. Now it was shattered beyond repair. This was a disaster of the first order.

Now there was rigging in the water, and Gar feared he'd get something in the propeller. He pulled the boat out of gear. This was not the time to wrap a cable or line in the propeller.

He called Craig and reported his predicament. He instructed Craig not to stop what he was doing just to answer the radio call, but to respond when convenient. Craig came right back and said they were okay, still working on their own problem, and he asked if there was anything he could do to help Gar. Gar declined assistance. Craig apologized for initiating the turn of bad luck, then he clicked off. Gar resignedly said it was not anyone's fault, and he signed off too.

The ***Visit***'s situation was more dangerous than the ***Summer***'s situation for a combination of reasons. First, Craig's boat was bigger and therefore more seaworthy amongst these gigantic swells. And a fair percentage of the ***Visit***'s stability was provided by the flopper stoppers that hung off the poles, and now they only had one of those in the water. They were going to have to pull the remaining one out of the water. There was no choice in this because it was on the down-swell side, and would pull the boat too far in that direction: Which would likely roll them over. So they had to put that flopper on board the boat and they had to do it fast. They also had to hoist the other pole into the cross tree, because it caused the vessel to ride out of trim. And all of this added up to the loss of both of their poles, poles which in the "outrigger" position had added greatly to the boat's stability.

In short, they had just lost what little edge they may have had on this situation. And the wind was not moderating at all. The weather, unbelievably, continued to worsen. But the men set to work. While adrift and tempest tossed, they pulled the rigging aboard and lashed everything securely in place. It was very dangerous just being on deck, let alone working with heavy, flying objects aloft, but the work had to be done for their very lives were at stake.

The air was filled with foam and spray and the sea was completely white. Exceptionally high waves tossed the boat crazily, and with the poor visibility there was no chance of spotting small ships, as they would be lost in the towering waves. This much wind on shore would uproot trees, blow the roofs off houses, and be impossible to walk in. It would instantly sweep the feet right out from under you.

And by this time they had lost sight of Craig, which meant they were completely alone. There was no way, after drifting an hour down and away from Craig (as he continued motoring off shore), that the two boats would ever, safely, get back together.

This was a fine example of how critical and tenuous a fisherman's life can be. Fortunes can change in an instant, and the sea can swallow you up.

AFTER MORE THAN an hour of silence, an hour spent in exhausting and perilous labor, Craig came on the radio and said he was all fixed up and headed east again. Their position was twelve miles to the northwest of Gar and Jeff.

Gar did some figuring on his chart table and laid courses out for both of them, courses that would head them in the right direction and maybe put them closer together later that day. His boat was crippled, so loaded with fish that it literally wallowed in the swells, but they were making headway again, and for that Gar breathed a sigh of relief.

AFTER TWENTY-FOUR hours they were halfway in, with about a hundred miles to go. It was early the next morning, and it had been a long night. The weather was better, and they had Craig in sight again. They were running at almost full speed, and Gar figured they could make the Vista del Mar well before last call later that night. He had, in fact, told Craig that. He and Craig then discussed that hopefully for a while. Craig had never been to the Vista, but he had certainly heard the wild stories.

They worked hard at keeping up each other's spirits through radio transmissions, and Gar began to like Craig more and more. Craig's father was the Bandon High School principal, and he had built Craig's boat in his off time–thus the name ***Summer***. Craig, though somewhat young, was pretty well squared away. He had proven himself in a time of trouble and Gar was happy they had made this run together.

Another old Squad expression was calling a drinking buddy a good running partner. The cliché originated with two boats running together like this, but it was bastardized and extended to someone like a drinking or hunting buddy.

Gar and his new "running partner" were keeping each other focused and awake after the long day and night. At one point during the previous night, the engine had sputtered a couple of times, then died. Gar raced to turn off the radar, autopilot, and all other lights and electronics, in order to save the batteries for restarting. His stomach turned to buttermilk as he went down to the engine room to investigate. Thank god it was only a plugged fuel filter, which he changed in a quick ten minutes of wrench twisting. But he had restarted the boat without a problem, and with the light of day he realized that they were through the worst of it.

They would make it. They had beat the sea yet again. They had wrested from her bounty, and they had reclaimed from her their imperiled lives. There can be no greater exhilaration for a young man than this.

CHAPTER 14

MID TO LATE August, 1980.

THE BIZARRE BRIMSTONE emanation from the Eureka Pulp Mill accosted them like a slap in the face when they were just inside twenty miles. Gar had smelled the famous smoke stacks at fifty before.

And the ocean was calming; the wind lessening. Jeff was now out on deck, cleaning and scrubbing. Gar started on the cabin interior with the 409 bottle and a roll of paper towels.

They had plenty of time to really shine up the boat, as well as take much-needed baths, before they got in.

THE V.D. WAS still there, unchanged, and they tied on down the wharf a bit so they were under the Eureka Fisheries hoist. Gar wanted to sell to *Eureka Fish* because he knew and liked Kenny Butler. Kenny was actually up running the Crescent City plant, but would hear that Gar brought his trip in and sold there because of Kenny. It is from such small considerations that loyalties are cemented.

GAR, JEFF AND Craig went up to the Vista. It was just about midnight, and as they entered they noticed how the place resembled the Star War's bar. It smelled like cheap wine and cheaper perfume. Bad company's "Feel Like Making Love" rocked hard out of the juke box: "Ta, Da, Dun...Ta, Da, Dun!" Every sense was assaulted the moment they came through the door.

Several people saw Gar come in and hollered, "Garalone!" as he ushered Craig and Jeff toward the bar. Tina Christiansen, bartender and the owner's daughter, was one of the ones yelling. She started pouring shots of tequila before they even got to the bar. She moved a couple of patrons in both directions, clearing a space while ordering someone else to fetch three stools. The guy she was commanding complained.

"They're all full."

"I don't give a shit" Tina screamed over the music. "Empty them–get some help if you have to."

Turning to Gar and the boys, she became much sweeter. "I heard. I know. You plugged the boat, broke a pole, and refused to leave until Nardo made you come in."

"Holy shit! What do you have, a crystal ball?" Gar exclaimed. "That's pretty much what happened, except we didn't plug it. We needed another hundred fish, or so."

"Well, let's have a shot and pretend you did." Tina was famous for getting guys too *swacked* to find their boats. She would usually pick on one guy until her mission was successful, then find another pigeon. It appeared that Gar was her present target.

"You going to carry me back to my boat and pour me in my bunk?" Gar invited.

"Oh, bullshit. You know I've been trying to get you to take me to your boat for years, and you always tease but never come through. I think you're scared of me." Tina fired back.

She was right. She was physically a big girl. Not necessarily fat, just big. And the way she poured guys right under the table, combined with this wild, crazy laugh she had, was intimidating. Gar always imagined that if he went to bed with her, he might awake later, tied up and with Tina exploring the kitchen cooking-utensil drawer.

"Yeah, yeah, yeah. You're nothing but a big tease," Gar cajoled. "I see your lips moving, but I'm not hearing anything. Let me clean out my ears. Also, let me clean the dust out of my throat. Could you give us a round here? And I'd love to buy you a shot." Gar pulled out his billfold.

Tina reached across the bar and shoved Gar's wallet back, and with a stormy look admonished him strongly. "Put that damned wallet back in your pocket. Your money is no good here. Don't try that any more tonight!" Then she turned to Billy, her brother and the other bartender, and snapped. "If any of these three try to spend money here tonight, get Tiny (the bouncer) and have him make them wash ashtrays."

She appeared to be serious. And Billy twinkled at his sister's craziness. He was a spittin' image of Roy Clark from the Hee Haw Show, and a whole lot mellower than Tina. It was likely she intimidated him, too. She looked back at Billy and raised *just* her left eyebrow. Only people with the right genetics can do that. Billy laughed. Maybe he wasn't cowed by her, after all.

TWO O'CLOCK CAME quickly, and the boys went back to the boats. Tina and Billy tried talking them into going to an after-hours party somewhere in town away from the waterfront, but the fishermen begged off. They did not want to get too far away from their boats. They had a trip to unload early in the morning.

UNLOADING ALBACORE IS a longer process than a salmon delivery. The fish, especially toward the bottom of the pile, tend to stick together and have to be pried apart. And there is much more volume. It's like the difference between silver and gold. It takes numerous large silver bars to equal what one gold coin can put in your pocket.

On the dock there were buckets coming up and going back down, bins of fish everywhere, and forklifts gassing around, moving the bins of fish to the scale and then to waiting trucks.

In the middle of all this, Gar heard his name called out by a female. It was Samantha, the sharp-looking wife of another fisherman Gar had not seen for a few years. She was not with her husband, but rather with another attractive woman.

"What's up, Sam?" he greeted her. "Long time no see."

"Oh, we're just sort of vacationing. Driving up the coast visiting different ports. I saw the Z-sail and couldn't resist coming to see which one of you it was. Where's everyone else?"

She looked better than Gar had remembered her. Something about her was changed. And he realized, in a mental flash, what the sail and the Z-Squad was akin to: They were members of an elite group, like members of a rock band. Otherwise ordinary guys, they were now made famous by a simple title (e.g., Rolling Stones; Grateful Dead; Z-Squad). At least around here. Perhaps this was a product of an Anglo heritage, hearkening back to England in days gone by when there were dukes and earls and the like.

"Well, Michael and Johnny T rarely go north of Point Reyes any more. Geno's moved to Newport, and so has Fache. John Dooley is dragging, now. Nardo and Baby Huey are tuna fishing, but they ran into Fort Bragg. And we're pretty much on our own these days. Timmy comes north with us once in a while, but if he can he stays south of Point Reyes, too. Where's the old man at?" Gar couldn't help asking. He was suspicious that something was amiss.

"We're divorced. I guess you hadn't heard. We separated last winter, and my divorce became final last week. That's why we're on this trip. I'm celebrating." She was very effervescent.

"Really?" Gar drew out the word. This was most interesting.

"Yeah, I'm single now. And very available, too," she added with just as much emphasis. Her friend, meanwhile, who was not as outgoing as Sam, was watching with curiosity how easily Sam was manipulating Gar's interest. The friend was a red head built a little bit low to the ground. Sam was a skinny beachgirl: blond hair, straight and long, with blue eyes and a decent tan.

"Hmmmm," Gar considered. "What are you girls doing for dinner, then?"

"Oh, you don't have to buy us dinner to get lucky. Don't even worry about that. You're going to get laid tonight. Count on it. You just have to decide if you want one of us or both of us." She was looking as foxy and mischievous as it was possible to look.

Gar smiled and said, "I wish you wouldn't beat around the bush the way you do. You need to learn to come more to the point. We're gonna be busy most of the afternoon, but I'm going to get a room at the Harbor Inn..."

"I have one there already," she cut in. "I'm in room three. We can meet you there."

"Perfect. I'll try to get my favorite *Room Two With A View*. How's O.H.'s Townhouse sound for dinner? he asked.

"How's *Room Two With A View* sound?" She countered, all smiles.

THE NEXT DAY, Gar and Jeff woke up at the Harbor Inn. Jeff awoke in room three with what's-her-name, and Gar awoke with Sam in room two. It was all very cozy, and everyone said goodbye feeling that they had done well the night before.

Gar said he'd see them later, if they were going to be around, but these girls were on a mission. They were headed for Crescent City, then up the Oregon coast.

Gar and Jeff headed for the boat, which they had left tied at Davenport's Marine. They had a whole laundry list of repairs to attend to, not to mention actual laundry to do too. Replacing the shattered pole was going to be the number one job.

SEVERAL DAYS LATER, they were repaired and on their way back out. They ran back to the Mendocino Ridge, but the fishing was poor, so they started working south, eventually arriving at a spot off Morro Bay. They delivered half a hold of fish there to Cal-Shell. The Cal-Shell buyer was Fred Cefalu's fishmonger, and Gar thought he'd do what he could to keep in Fred's good graces. Morro Bay was Fred's homeport. You did what you could for your friends.

AFTER WEARING OUT their welcome at The Harbor Hut in Morro Bay (they took a drunken ride on a tour boat and Jeff fell in the bay), and were asked to leave Rose's Landing (another Morro Bay bar), they went back offshore to find only scratch fishing at best.

They spent eight days working toward the City and Half Moon Bay, for just over two tons of Albacore. This, at $1,200 a ton (60¢ a pound), hardly covered expenses. Indeed, after just barely paying his boat payment and insurance premium, Gar was broke. And Jeff was doing only slightly better. With all the old, new and potential girlfriends Jeff had going, he easily spent whatever amount he made.

And then it was September, and the albacore had migrated south to Mexico. Worse, the government's new National Marine Fisheries Service announced that they felt the Klamath River stock were perhaps going to get caught in their entirety during the last two weeks of September. So they were shutting down salmon season–on the whole West Coast of the United States–effective immediately.

Gar figured some bureaucrat must have really pleased himself signing that memo. Maybe it was time to go to work making drinks for Mom and Jack. Maybe this really was the end of an era, and he had chosen the wrong profession for himself. Time would tell, of course, but it wasn't looking good. He turned the boat south with a heavy heart.

Visit, heavy with albacore, flying the **Z**.

CHAPTER 15

FALL, 1980–EARLY 1981.

THE FOLLOWING SATURDAY as Gar tended bar, trying not to notice out the Beach House windows how flat the ocean was, Jeff called to see if any fishing prospects were in the air. Gar explained all the calls he had made, only to hear bad news. There would be no fishing right away. But he invited Jeff down to the Beach House for an afternoon of free drinks and Jeff said he was on his way. He was at his parent's house in El Granada and would be there in 45 minutes.

GAR HAD THIRTEEN people sidetracked at the bar, locked into a Liar's Dice game. Dice was big at the Beach House, and they had enough cups for twenty players if that many wanted to play. Because the view from the bar looked across the parking lot and highway out to the ocean, Gar noticed Jeff drive up in his big yellow four-wheeler Ford. So he had a drink on the bar waiting for him when Jeff came in. But Jeff surprised Gar when he came in with a pleasingly attractive girl.

The girl was nicely browned by the sun and very well curved, especially in the upper torso area. She had shoulder-length fawn-brown hair, hazel eyes, the cutest button nose in an oval face with a slightly squared jaw, and a smile full of gleaming teeth. Gar was instantly envious of Jeff. Especially when they sat down and she pulled out a thick stack of wadded up twenties, ordered a rum and Coke (his favorite drink, too), and said she would be paying for everything.

When Jeff got involved with the Liar's Dice game, ignoring the girl, that really tore it for Gar. So, though he was playing in the dice game too, he played only perfunctorily, concentrating most of his attention on the girl. Cindy, her name was. As soon as he discovered what her name was, it became emblazoned upon his mind. Gar was only nominally participating in the dice game, and his bartending duties began to back up on him.

Gar watched the girl closely out of the corner of his eye, and noted that she threw back her head and laughed openly and naturally, her teeth flashing and the notes of her laughter peeling forth like bright silver notes upon the air. She laughed often and well, and Gar was infected with her mirth. This was a girl who liked the world. This was a girl who found the world amusing.

The attraction Gar felt for Cindy was strong and immediate. So strong that, for the first time in a very long while, he didn't think of Sue at all. And Cindy seemed to be every bit as interested in Gar. Curiously, Jeff seemed to care less.

IT WAS A crazy first hour, or so. Then when Jeff lost the by now fourteen-way Liar's Dice game, he insisted on playing Gar double or nothing for the whole round and he won.

Gar teased Cindy about it. "Don't you think you should at least give Jeff a sloppy kiss for that? He saved you about fifty dollars by beating me, you know."

Cindy scrunched up her button nose, looking like a bunny chewing a daisy, and with the same tone as an indignant young girl demanded, "Why would I do that? He's my brother!"

This was one of the biggest turning points Gar had reached in life. It was like he won the Megabucks Lottery. Those three words, "He's my brother!" changed everything. In a flash, he was around the bar, pawing and fawning like a love-sick young buck in the fall rut. Gar's stepfather, Jack, saw what was going on and left the stool he was relaxed upon. He went resignedly behind the bar to finish Gar's shift.

THE VERY FIRST thing Gar did, when he came out from behind the bar and approached Cindy, was pull his shirt up, exposing his chest. It was muscled and hairy, and he knew girls liked it. And, taking the girl's measure, he actually said to her, "I'll show you mine if you show me yours."

Cindy laughed at this brazen display, the sound spilling out like silver coins across the bar, and told him to slow down. But her body language said, 'not too slow.' It was a classic case of first-sight infatuation. The chemistry between the two of them was intense. They could not leave one another alone.

When Cindy and Jeff announced that they were driving back to El Granada, because Cindy had to go on standby for her job as a flight attendant, Gar said he would follow them. He had to go check the boat. The boat, of course, was fine. But it *was* just a few blocks from Cindy's parents' house.

He never did check the boat. The only thing he did was hang out with Cindy, asking her a thousand questions about her job and her life. She told him about all the exotic places the airline had taken her.

But none of Cindy's job business really mattered. He hardly heard the words she spoke to him. Gar was just dangling on every syllable she had to say so he could watch her scrunch that nose, and gaze speculatively on her amazingly well-rounded bosom.

GAR FELT LIKE he had been struck by the same thunderbolt that got Michael Corleone in the Godfather. And, he thought, the whole thing would be very convenient. There would be little need for taking Cindy on dozens of dates in an effort to win her over with the mutual attraction as strong as it was. They were already like a pair of shears, joined inseparably, and they would be able to get right to a steady engagement. As it would turn out, they only actually went on one real 'date' that fall. Cindy bought Gar a western-wear outfit of cowboy hat and boots, and they went to the *Lanai* in San Mateo. The *Lanai* was a bar and restaurant with a Polynesian theme, featuring high-backed rattan love seats and exotic rum-infused cocktails. Gar and Cindy were to find out that they had no time for dates. The other's company was simply enough for each of them. And they were happiest when they were alone with one another.

THAT FIRST NIGHT spent talking with Cindy, Gar began to feel like he had embarked on a new ocean, an ocean for which no compass had been invented. For the first time he perceived the essence of love, which is a soaring liberty.

He had no thoughts of obedience, jealousy, or fear. It was much the same feeling as he felt for this fishing life, and this amazed him. Perfection and balance and an unlimited confidence could be found on land and encapsulated in a woman, just as they were to be found on a vessel at sea. It was a liberating and exhilarating experience.

They laughed and talked long into the night. Cindy, too, had many questions. She wanted to know why a fisherman wanted to wear cowboy boots and a western hat. And Gar said, "because it makes me look so damned good." She agreed with him.

Cindy's work finally called to tell her she had to catch a flight to New York, early the next morning, and that she would leave from there on an eight-day trip. They hugged for a long time and shared a quick kiss, then Gar left her so she could sleep. It was a night that was to change Gar's life.

WHEN CINDY RETURNED from her eight days of flying, she drove straight to the Beach House. She did not even bother stopping at her Mom's. When she called from the airport and learned Gar was working at the bar, she had only one plan.

As it turned out, when she arrived at the Gazos, Gar was sleeping off a long day of playing dice for shots, and Mom wouldn't let Cindy go out to the behind-the-bar trailer and wake him up. So Cindy learned how to tend bar while she waited. And she asked Annabel every fifteen minutes if it was time to wake Gar up yet.

Eventually, of course, Mom gave the okay. Cindy went out to the trailer, got Gar out of bed, and took him back inside to the bar.

The two of them talked, almost non-stop and without sleep, for two days. It took that long to get everything said. When they finally became lovers, it was like they had always been lovers. They connected perfectly. And so began a compatible sensuality they would share for a number of years.

CINDY WENT OUT on another trip, shorter this time, and when she came back Gar and Jeff had taken up crawdad fishing at the Cascade Ranch.

Rudy gave Gar an old ring net one day at lunch, and the master key to all the Cascade gates, including the one to Bootlegger's Cove. The key, Rudy said, was Gar's. "Keep it safe, and don't do anything I wouldn't ever do." Rudy said this with a fatherly smile. The big man explained that the large upper reservoir offered the best fishing, but the two smaller ones below it would also have crawdads.

GAR CALLED JEFF and told him that he was going crawdad fishing the next day. Jeff said he had to come help; after all, he *was* Gar's deckhand. But they quickly got bored utilizing only one trap. Gar suggested they go back to the Beach House and scrounge material to build more of them. He had the netting on the front of Mom's salad bar in mind when he suggested this.

They returned with that netting, some twine, a bunch of plastic milk-carton crates, and a number of coat hangers. And they had pounds of chicken necks and bacon to use as bait. Rounding out their supplies were several medicinal cases of San Francisco Anchor Steam Beer. The lake water was simply too insipid to drink. But Anchor Steam certainly is not.

They made hoops of the coat hangers, attached webbing from the salad bar net, and tied a bridle with haul-in line out of twine. Then they baited these contraptions and threw them in.

The plastic milk crates were more inventive, yet simple. Those they simply tipped onto their sides, tied a good wad of bait to the "floor," or lowest inside panel, then set them into water that was deep enough to almost, but not quite, cover them. The crates were situated with the *actual* bottom facing shore, and the open top facing out into the middle of the lake.

The theory was that the crawdads would smell the bait and come scurrying up into the wide open, on-its-side crate, and after a little bit of time to "soak," the boys would sneak up on the crate as quietly as possible and tip the thing back real quick, while scooping it up and out of the water. Then the top of the crate would be pointing up at the sky, and the hapless crawdads within would be caught.

These crates worked remarkably well. When Rudy drove up that afternoon and noticed his old ring net sitting up on the bank, and his lake encircled with blue and orange milk crates, he chuckled and said, "Bobbie, Bobbie, Bobbie... only you could think of such a thing. How many did you get so far?" When Gar lifted a gunny sack out of the water where he was keeping the critters alive, and it showed to be at least half full, Rudy was impressed.

CINDY JOINED THE fishing operation on the second day, and was at once a very active participant. Because it involved wading, she stripped right down to her bra and panties. These garments were pearl white, and absolutely stunning against her rich brown tan.

She made Gar swoon, and when she waded in and got the thick black lake mud caked in streaks on her white delicates, Gar fell so hard in lust that it would be years before he would be able to pick himself up. Her metallic laughter peeled into the autumn air, and her long legs flashed in the sunlight. She was an uninhibited and carefree naiad, and Gar was utterly enchanted by her.

It took a couple more days to fish out the three lakes. The original plan was to spend an afternoon at the big lake. That plan was modified, however, after Cindy modeled her "fishing attire."

When they were finished, they had three full sacks of crawdads, hundreds of pounds of them, and Mom put on a special feed at the Beach House, inviting everyone.

Rudy and his wife Bea made a grand entrance as the guests of honor. Gar gave a short speech explaining to everyone that these were Rudy's crawdads, and what a privilege it was to have been appointed as the ranch's official *Crawdad Harvester*.

He did not mention that once the traps were assembled, all he did was follow Cindy around in her endless exuberance (and pristine underwear) like the proverbial donkey after a carrot on a stick.

THE NEXT MONTH they began to work in earnest on the crab gear, and Cindy was there to help paint crab buoys. She did not, this time, strip to her underwear (likely because it was October and now cold outside). However, she did get paint on her face and cheeks. This, too, Gar thought was every bit as sexy and provocative as the mud. Well, almost. Or maybe it was her laughter. It was infectious.

THEY FISHED THE early San Francisco crab opening beginning on the second Tuesday of November, delivering their catch to Captain John. After a couple of weeks, they stacked the gear and moved their operation three hundred miles north to Crescent City, California. This was an ordeal because there were just too many heavy, bulky crab pots to put them all on the boat at one time. This meant several trips in and out of Half Moon Bay, and hiring a big truck to transport a large portion of the gear to Crescent City. There was a two-day run to get the boat up there, and the weather wasn't all that cooperative this time of year.

THE CRESCENT CITY season was only mediocre, and Gar did not get any money put ahead. He did, however, propose to Cindy.

She was making regular trips up to Crescent City and they were now very much a couple. And one night, while lying in bed after an evening of passion, Gar spoke his thoughts aloud.

"You know, a lot of my friends are getting married," he said. "I've wondered what you might say if I asked you?"

"What are you trying to say?" Cindy sweated him a little bit.

"Oh, I was just wondering if you've ever thought much about marriage."

"Of course I have. I'm a romantic young woman. But what are you trying to say?" She looked at him levelly. "You have to say it."

"Okay, ummm." This was not as easy as Gar thought it would be. Finally, he just blurted it out. "Will you marry me?"

Her laughter chimed like silvery notes from heaven and she smiled prettily at him. "I thought you would never ask," she said. "Of course I will!"

THEY SPENT THE rest of the night making plans, deciding they should probably first get a place together there in Crescent City, which they did that winter, and that they would get married in June.

It was a wonderful time for both of them. He was 28 and she was 24, and the world was theirs for the taking. He went out to the sea and she flew off in the sky, but they always came back to each other and the other one was always there waiting.

CHAPTER 16

EARLY 1981.

ANGUS MOVED TO Crescent City that winter too, and was expectedly resentful about Gar's new love affair and engagement to be married. He would go on about how marriage is, "the way a man finds out what kind of husband his wife would have preferred." And, "it is a mistake of youth." Or, worst of all, "it has no relation to love; it belongs to society and is but a social contract."

He was green-eyed with jealousy, and when Gar and Cindy got their house, Angus constantly came by early in the mornings hoping to steal a glimpse of Cindy in her bathrobe. Cindy was the first to catch on to this development, and after telling Gar they made jokes every morning about when Angus would arrive today.

"Wow, it's nine o'clock and no Angus." Cindy might typically say.

"Yeah, he must have partied last night," Gar would answer. "But we'll see him by ten, I'll bet."

"I'm going to change out of my robe so he won't stay long. All he ever wants to talk about is fishing, anyway. And I know you get just as tired of it as I do."

And so on.

Angus, did, however, become unexpectedly congenial for a change. The vitriol from the salmon grounds had disappeared. He now resembled nothing so much as a puppy dog wagging his tail. This, of course, was only while Cindy was around. When she was gone on her flying tips, Angus forced himself to be nice only because he knew she was coming back.

Sure, Angus had girlfriends. His Robert Redford looks stood him well in that regard. But, for some reason, he always wanted what Gar had. He had hired a couple of Gar's deckhands in the past, without first asking if Gar minded him doing so, and even now was promising Jeff more money to come work for him.

The truth of the matter was something that Angus himself didn't completely understand. He wanted so badly to join the Squad–to be accepted as part of the Half Moon Bay fleet–that he saw Jeff and Cindy as an opportunity. His intuition told him that if he had Jeff for a deckhand, and Cindy for a wife, all his other hopes would necessarily follow. So he coveted all that Gar had, all he was able to achieve.

Yet Angus did not have much in the way of scruples, and was more an enemy than a friend. Gar eventually came to consider him a poster boy for *Back Stabbers of America*. But all of that was yet to come.

SUSAN HAD BEEN reading a Steven King novel when Carol called. When she got off the phone, she yawned, tossed the book on the coffee table, and headed for the bedroom.

She was sleeping and functioning almost normal again. Her problem had been no less difficult than Gar's had been. But for her, it was not about longing. It was about guilt.

Yes, she had drifted away from Gar because of the pressure from her family. But it also had a lot to do with her trepidation over the possibility of being married to a fisherman. Fishermen drank too much, they were notoriously unfaithful (a girl in every port), and they lived a life fraught with danger. And she did not want to spend her life sitting home worried sick about the man she really, really loved.

Because of this she felt a sense of dereliction. She had always been the strong one in relationships, the one in control. Her love affair with Gar had gone well beyond any prior experience and it had scared her with its intensity. Her father had taught her to be tough, and she had certainly become so, but Bud had never told her about love. Running away from it, and all of its pitfalls, made her feel weak.

And now Carol had reported that Gar was engaged to be married to Cindy Lindberg. Cindy had been a classmate of Sue's. She wondered if Gar was really in love with Cindy.

Susan had never really been in love with anyone before Gar. But she'd been in love with him, all right. She had recognized all the symptoms. He had bought the new boat, gone north fishing, and called one day on the marine operator, saying he was way out and in bad weather, and had just hit a log. Then the radio transmission had inexplicably broken off. And she waited, worried sick for the next 48 hours, until he got in and managed a phone call. And he was in for a whole day before he got around to that.

There had always been something in Gar that was wild, free and remote. She'd been sure she could reach it, smooth it out. He needed that as much as she did. He didn't know it but his taste for the wild freedom of a dangerous ocean was probably going to kill him one day. This wasn't at all obvious to him, though. And she'd found out she'd been wrong about reaching him. The danger was essential for him, she now believed.

The variety of dangerous scenarios, she learned, about a life at sea all spoke to the danger of the pursuit. He would risk his own life, and it might be possible that one day he'd risk hers. And even if he did *not* risk hers, the fact still remained that he discounted the value of her life every time he risked his own. Despite the fact that he had always returned home safely up to now, her state of emotional uncertainty remained.

Something in her had turned, during that 48 hours after he had called and said he'd hit a log. Something that couldn't be turned back.

SHE HAD GOTTEN past much of the heartache. She was still talking to a couple of her girlfriends, who all urged her to take him back. So Susan had stopped talking to them. She realized that, however deeply she had loved him before, that feeling was now dead. The occasional flashes she used to have of being a grieving wife, perhaps with children, had become intolerable to her. Gar brought those on: The sight of his face, the sound of his voice.

So she had learned that she could live without him. She had started a good job, with potential, which gave her independence. And she was even starting to enjoy herself again. Gar was now getting on with his life, and she would certainly do that with hers. Susan had never been the type to rely on others for her own happiness, and wasn't about to start that now.

"Fuck men!" she thought decisively. Then she chuckled to herself and said, "Now that sounds like fun, right there."

GAR, NOW ENGAGED to Cindy, still occasionally thought of Susan. And each time a touch of sadness came over him. He had wanted to marry *her*. And he knew that if something changed and she called him, telling him not to go through with it but come back to her, he'd go to her in an instant.

There was a reason why he had not tried harder when they'd broken up. He likely could have, at least for a time, forgotten about his boat and put all his effort into her and their relationship. But he did not try this because he knew they would break up someday anyway. Fishing was his life. It was smarter to get the heartache over with sooner, rather than later. And in the end they were both too stubborn to change.

She was falling away from him now. Her influence was fading. He didn't think of her as much. There was a time, for at least a year, when he had thought of her every few waking minutes. Things she'd said, images of her face, moments of their time together. That was all still there in his head, and the images came back from time to time, but not quite as much as they used to do. Marrying Cindy would help to dispel thoughts of Susan. But he didn't know if it would cure him forever.

Cindy was a cheerful companion. When moving to Crescent City, and ever after, they'd drive the long Crescent City to Half Moon Bay drive, Cindy chattering away about the landscape, various road signs and small towns, river crossings, animals dead on the road, and always deer in the nearby fields. They'd play a game that she had played when young, where the first to spot a deer got a candy bar. And every time she won, her laughter rang out like bright silver in the car.

During this time, Gar was in a period of transition, still feeling ties to Susan even as new ties to Cindy were forming.

But the simple fact of the matter was that the ties back to Susan were not simple ties. She had been something different. She had been the love of his life, and the one he'd never be able to completely forget. The new-found happiness Gar was blessed with now was faintly shadowed by an empty feeling of loss.

CHAPTER 17

MARCH–JUNE, 1981.

CHUCKIE MET WITH Vince, his weed buyer in Santa Cruz, at Vince's request. "I wanted to get together with you again on this Bootlegger's Cove plan," Vince said to him.

"Well, so far it is basically your plan," Chuckie replied. "I've talked once to my wife's brother (Chuckie had recently married Gar's sister, Lori), but he wasn't too excited about it. And he's the only fisherman I know. Don't you know any Santa Cruz fishermen?"

"I have one guy in mind, but his boat's not big enough. And he's not the best guy anyway," Vince said. "He's sort of a drunk."

"Well, you know my brother-in-law, Gar, is a partier too," Chuckie warned.

"Yeah, but he's got a bigger boat, and Don, my guy, says he's a hot-shit fisherman. He is likely a much better guy to manage the ocean-end of things."

"Okay. He's sort of busy, right now. He's getting married," Chuck said. "But I'll work on him some more. He and my wife are close–he always says she's his favorite sister–so I'll get her to work on him, too."

"Do it," Vince demanded. "I've got these guys, right now, loading a sixty-foot sailboat with Thai-weed. It's the middle of winter here, but just north of the equator it's beautiful weather. Since we don't have an offload set up yet, they're going to sail over to a safe spot in the Philippines. One of the sailboat guys has his own dock, in his own little bay, on his own beach. So they'll tie up there and wait for me to give the go ahead. They're something like 9,000 miles away. Figuring two hundred miles a day they are, at the very least and in perfect conditions, 45 days from here. And then when I call them, it will probably take them a month to get going. So, we've got to figure around three months from when I give my first 'GO.'"

"Three months. Yeah, I guess they're way down there." Chuckie spit a few times, eyed Vince, wondering if he was on speed or something the way he was rambling along. This guy was organized, but he was a little weird. Vince continued.

"Of course, whatever fishing boat we get to go out and pick up the load will cut some of that time off. But I'm thinking the fisherman would look strange if they go more than a couple hundred miles out, so that's only a day less. And the idea of the fisherman bringing the load in to shore is to <u>not</u> look strange. Everything has got to appear as normal as possible. I've got this mental picture of the fishing boat taking the load aboard, then fishing his way back in–perhaps throwing some fish on top of the dope so it looks like his hold is full of fish, in case of a boarding–so he doesn't look at all out of place."

"Gar can catch fish...."

"My sailboat guys say the Coast Guard really watches sailboats that come in from other countries." Vince rudely cut Chuckie off. "They pick them up on back-scatter radar when they're thousands of miles out. And when they come from another country, they have to check in with U.S. Customs, right away, or Customs will come down to the boat. And I guess sometimes Customs is waiting there on the dock anyway. But if our sailboat guys were to sail right into Bootlegger's Cove and unload, and *then* go into port, in theory we'd have nothing to worry about."

Chuckie nodded and spit again, not sure if he was expected to comment.

"But there are technical mechanics associated with that, too. First, they'd look strange anchored in a cove that even fishermen rarely anchor in, and a fishing boat would not. Second, if there's no wind, or too much wind, maneuvering a sixty-foot sailing rig into a little cove and setting the anchor would be difficult and dangerous. And third, once again, that last hundred miles. Approaching the coast is when the Coast Guard loves to board sailboats coming in from offshore. But fishing boats are running all over the place all the time, and they are not targeted."

"Ahhh. I get it now," Chuck said. "I was thinking what you really needed from me was access to the cove. But you need a fishing boat just as bad. Okay, I'll try again with Gar. Maybe he will suggest someone else if he's not interested."

"HEY, HON." GAR pulled Cindy out of her daydream. They were driving south from Crescent City to Half Moon Bay. "Did I tell you that the Feds are going to close salmon season the last fifteen days of June? It would actually be better if we got married on the 21st, instead of the 14th. That way I'd be off a week each side of the 21st."

"Oh, shit. Why didn't you tell me sooner? No, wait a minute, I think that might be better anyway. I'll call about the park and the reception hall again. Maybe we should pull in to the next pay phone. No, never mind, I'll wait 'till we get to Mom's. I think the 21st would be better." Cindy was already completely frazzled by the wedding plans, and it was still several months away.

"Okay, Hon. You know I'm there whenever you want me. I just found out this morning and thought I'd better tell you about it. You know I need to get as much fishing time in as the weather, and now the Feds, will allow." Gar soothed her.

"I know, sweetie. Did I tell you today how much I love you?" Cindy was as loving as she could be.

"Maybe a dozen times, but I never get tired of hearing it. And I love you too."

IT WAS MARCH of 1981, and Gar still had crab gear in the shallow waters off of Split Rock, just south of the Klamath River mouth. He would bring that in some time in April, then switch the boat over in preparation for salmon trolling. Although his good friend and long-time Crescent City fisherman, David Evanow, kept telling him he better watch out for the March 21st equinox. This would be a week of big swells that would stick those shallow pots, Dave cautioned. The Evanow's were a large family originally from the Great Lakes. They spoke with a Wisconsin accent, saying the O's soft–like boot for boat.

Bringing in the crab gear and tucking it safely away in the shade (sun is hard on crab pots) for next season, was a big job. But switching over the boat, as well as cleaning and painting everything from top to bottom, was a larger project yet.

Nonetheless, Gar, Jeff, and a third man they had hired for the crabbing season, Buster, got the gear all tucked away and ready for next year. And then, though it wasn't Buster's responsibility any longer, he pitched in and helped Gar and Jeff get the boat cleaned up for salmon season.

Gar appreciated the help, and kept Buster in Budweisers during that whole spring cleaning. Gar also made note of the man's good nature and willingness to pitch in and get the job done. He'd hire Buster again. Just as soon as he had an opening. And with the way Angus was constantly working on Jeff, that might be sooner rather than later.

SWITCHING FROM CRABS to salmon, Gar reflected on what the summer might bring. The crab season had been slow, and he needed to put together boat and insurance money in order to make his nut.

He then mused about his career. Gar was a much better crab fisherman than salmon troller. This was an odd thing. All Gar had ever hoped to be in life was the best salmon fisherman he could be, or at least as good as Michael McHenry. But if the National Marine Fisheries kept shortening the salmon season, there would soon be no point to this aspiration. For some reason, he had this odd knack for catching crabs. Maybe it was an organizational thing, as it takes a constant effort to keep hundreds of crab traps, which are scattered over dozens of miles of ocean, situated on top of the crabs.

He vowed to do better this salmon season. That's all he could do. If the NMFS would only let him fish.

THEY OPENED THE season on the deep reef just in front but slightly south of Half Moon Bay. They had decent fishing when the weather allowed. It was another May first opener, and the spring nor'westers were true to their historical patterns. This limited the fishing.

In between trips, Gar and Cindy made wedding plans. Or, rather, Cindy made plans and explained them to Gar, and Gar tried to be helpful.

There was a borderline catastrophe when Gar told Cindy that his mother, and all of her Beach House girlfriends, were planning on doing a spectacular food thing for the reception. Cindy's Mother, Arlene, flipped at this thought. But she later relented on the condition that Gar's family not meddle any further. As weddings go, it seemed like the planning of this one was as normal, yet fraught with problems, as any other large wedding.

At least Gar was able to choose his own guys. Jack, his stepfather, was to be best man. Then Michael, Jeff, Peter-Skin, Oogah-Don (named because he could perfectly imitate an oohgah horn), and Angus, were to be the ushers. Gar asked Angus because in spite of it all, he liked Angus. And he hoped that it might improve their relationship; but it wouldn't, as it turned out.

And since he was allowed to pick his own guys, he decided, over Arlene's objections, that he would also choose tuxedos for the boys. This rattled the bride's family, but they had doubtless allowed for some dissent by the groom's people in their planning.

BY JUNE FIRST, the fish were getting scarce. The water was much warmer than usual, and weathermen were talking about an "El Nino" condition that was never supposed to come north of Mexico.

And Michael was organizing, on the VHF radio so all could hear, a sit-in type of protest under the Golden Gate Bridge. The season closure began June 16th, and the plan was to group so many fishing boats under the bridge on that day that shipping traffic would be stopped.

ON THE FIFTEENTH, the last day before the close of the season, Gar and Jeff went in to Sausalito to deliver a very humble catch of salmon. With the warmer waters, the salmon were very deep and hard to catch. They had maybe a couple of thousand dollars worth. Not much, after expenses, for Gar to honeymoon on.

It made Gar feel uneasy, this shortened season combined with *El Nino* conditions. This wasn't like it used to be. It wasn't like it used to be at all. A man could make an honest living and raise a family fishing for salmon in the past. But it didn't seem to be true anymore. Maybe this *was* the end of an era, the end of a way of life. A change would have to be made to accommodate this, if it were true. It was troubling to think about it. It was troubling for every single salmon troller on the California coast to think about it. Yet they could hardly think of anything else.

CHAPTER 18

MID-JUNE, 1981.

ON THE SIXTEENTH day of June, Gar fired up his engine at daybreak, as did every salmon troller in Sausalito, and he headed for the bridge. It's about a half-hour run from the docks of Sausalito to the Golden Gate Bridge.

As the ***Visit*** approached the steepled towers of the famous red-gold span, the lines of boats coming from the City, Oakland, Richmond, and other directions became visible. Gar couldn't immediately calculate their number, but it was an astonishing sight. There were hundreds and hundreds of fishing boats.

UNDER THE BRIDGE, Gar counted 240 boats, and more were still streaming out from their docks.

The idea to stop shipping traffic in order to protest the Feds' closure of the salmon season was looking like it just might work. There certainly was not enough room, amongst this clutter of bobbing boats, for a ship to squeeze through. Certainly none of them would try it.

When the Bay Area news helicopters started circling the area, Gar got out a roll of black electrician's tape and lettered

"LET US FISH" on both sides of the ***Visit***'s white cabin. The newsies appeared to like it for the simple message it conveyed. It became a focal point for the circling helicopters.

BY MIDMORNING, SEVERAL large ships were lingering just outside the bay's entrance. They were maybe two miles off, between Point Bonita and Point Lobos. Then one ship slowly began its entrance. The tide had just shifted–the water was now ebbing out of the bay–and the pilot obviously figured he could idle slowly into the current in such a way that he would not smash over the top of a fishing boat, yet still retain steerage.

There has to be water flowing by the ship's rudder for it to be able to steer though. And this was only accomplished with the ship's huge spinning propeller to drive it forward. It was actually a very dangerous maneuver.

WHEN THE SHIP was almost directly under the bridge, Gar took the ***Visit***'s bow right up to the ship's bow and *kissed*.

It was ballsy, but with much easing forward, then backing down hard, he touched the ship lightly. The fact that the ship was only making about a knot of go-ahead speed helped.

And the news helicopters loved it. This maneuver presented a shot of the tiny ***Visit*** and the huge ship, nose to nose, that made the front page of the *San Francisco Chronicle*. "David and Goliath" was the headline, and "A Day Under the Bridge" is what the protest was entitled. Some years earlier, there had been a string of rock concerts at the Oakland Coliseum called, "A Day on the Green." This was obviously a takeoff on that.

BACK IN SAUSALITO that evening, the newsies swarmed the docks like locusts. This was the first time anyone had tried such a thing, and the public wanted to hear more about it.

Gar was interviewed by a beautiful and exotic looking African-American newscaster from one of the Bay Area TV stations, who he would always tell everyone afterwards was trying to get a date with him. But Gar was about to get married, so she was out of luck.

The date part was, of course, pure fantasy. But she did put Gar on the air for a couple of moments. He managed to get his two cents in, saying that the solution was all real simple: Instead of paying all those National Marine Fisheries bureaucrats all that money to make regulations, they should spend the money on hatchery programs that would put salmon in the oceans, streams and rivers of the West Coast.

Gar had not yet learned that the federal government doesn't ever do anything that will decrease personnel. But he sounded logical and he looked good on TV.

THE NEXT MORNING, actually just past midnight, Gar and Jeff untied in accordance with that night's ebb tide. They wanted to slide out *with* the powerful under-the-bridge current. Bucking a flood tide can add an hour or more to the egress from San Francisco Bay.

As they were sliding out, Gar noticed another boat, a trawler coming from Oakland or maybe the City. He commented to Jeff that this was unusual as there was a small craft wind advisory of 15-30 knots predicted. Gar had thought that he would be making this run alone, as everyone was tied up due to season closure and the wind.

He would have kept the ***Visit*** tied up too, but he had to get it home and tucked safely in his berth in Crescent City so he could drive back down to Half moon Bay and get married. He was actually cutting it extremely close, as the wedding was four days away and they had a two-day run in order to reach Crescent City.

And the sea conditions were shitty.

They toughed it up the coast, though, and Gar couldn't help noticing the old trawler was still running parallel with them. It was maintaining a distance just on the edge of visibility, perhaps five miles away.

JEFF WOKE GAR from a nap, shortly after dawn, just as they reached Stewart's Point. Jeff said, "You got it." Then he went down to his bunk in the fo'c'sle.

Ten minutes later Gar spotted a two-foot square by three-foot long metal container, an odd sight because it was metal nonetheless floating in the water. The minute he saw it he thought it looked perfect for a salmon washbox. They could put it back in the stern, between the bin boards, and let the deck hose run into it. Then toss salmon in it to wash around before storage in the hold. They actually already had one similar to it, but that was beside the point. Fishermen always watch for complimentary stuff floating in the ocean, waiting to be salvaged.

WITH JEFF NOW up on deck, Gar maneuvered the ***Visit*** alongside the metal container while Jeff tried to capture it with the salmon net. Close in, Gar could see that the thing was constructed of sheet metal, and that there were axe-like gouges in the sides. It was otherwise completely enclosed.

Having no luck getting it into the net, let alone over the rail, Gar grabbed a salmon gaff and stuck the object when it surged close enough to the boat. Jeff grabbed another gaff and did the same. Together they waited for the boat to roll, and then they heaved the container aboard using the momentum of the boat's roll.

The thing was completely sealed all the way around. But liquid ran out of the two hatchet holes which had been chopped into it. Gar touched the liquid lightly, worried that because of its slightly orange color it may be toxic. But he found that his fingers didn't sting or burn upon contact with the liquid.

He grabbed a salmon cleaning knife from the stern and stuck it in the top of the can. It was like sticking a can of soup. The razor-sharp salmon knife opened the sheet metal top like a child cutting through construction paper with a pair of shears.

As they both somehow expected it would be, the container was stuffed full with long plaits of marijuana buds. They were more an orange-red color than green, and when Gar pulled one out it was half as long as his forearm and bigger around than his thumb. Although he had not fooled with pot for a number of years, he knew this was a decent grade of weed because it was all buds. It had a pungent odor and a sticky feel.

Gar noted with alarm that they were drifting close to the beach, close enough so that they could see a pickup truck had parked at the edge of the cliff. A guy was outside of the truck, looking at them through binoculars.

Gar hot-footed it to the cabin and put the ***Visit*** on a course offshore but slightly to the north, as that was their original, intended direction. There was something about that guy staring at them so intently through binoculars that made Gar distinctly uneasy. It could have been a tourist traveling innocuously up the coast. But Gar didn't think so.

MEANWHILE, ON THE unidentified trawler that had shadowed Gar up the coast, the skipper radioed his "contact" boat. "We're here on the coordinates. Where are you?"

"Uhh, we're hauling ass away from there," a voice hissed in response over the secret channel. "We had to abort. We tossed all our *fish* over the side. We chopped them all a couple of times first so they would sink." The contact radio voice was hurried and nervous.

"WHY THE FUCK DID YOU DO THAT?" The trawler skipper yelled into his microphone.

Contact-boat came back defensively: "Didn't you see that cutter there in the area?"

"That's a fucking research boat! You know, like a Jacques Cousteau type of boat? They've been here for months taking bottom samples. Oh no, please tell me this is a joke?" Trawler pleaded, but then saw one of the metal containers floating by and asked, "Hey! Were your *fish* silver colored, and squar'ish?"

"Yeah, sheet metal," Contact-boat divulged quickly, as though afraid of broadcasting incriminating information.

"Oh, God. I see a couple here now. Oh, fuck me royal!" Trawler-skipper groaned, but then, thinking on his feet, he ordered: "Listen, you tell your people what happened. And tell them we had nothing to do with it, and that we are out of it. We're getting the fuck out of here, and pronto. I'm out!"

Contact-boat finished: "Okay, will do. Sorry, and good luck."

Contact-boat likely knew what trawler-skipper was thinking: *Salvage*!

THE TRAWLER SKIPPER turned to his crew and explained that things had changed. They were going to pick up what they could. The good news, though, was the mother boat would report a total loss, and whatever the trawlers picked up would be theirs to sell.

They had contracted to take the entire load from the mother boat, bring it to a dock in Richmond, then collect their $200,000. They would salvage an easy $200,000 picking up containers–likely much more–and still wind up with less risk, only having to haul a small fraction of the load to town. The less you haul, the less you are exposed.

"Damn," Trawler thought to himself with a smile. "I'm sure a lucky sum' bitch."

AS GAR AND Jeff angled offshore, Tom on the ***Armadillo*** called on the radio saying he'd noticed Gar pull out of Sausalito ahead of him, and figured Gar was somewhere within radio range.

"Got you fine, Tom," Gar came back. "Yeah, I didn't notice you, although I did see a faint blip behind us on the radar now and then. I don't think you make a very good target."

"No. I know I don't," Tom offered slyly. "I've always kept it that way on purpose, because I sometimes like to be sneaky."

"Ahh, like when you're slinging splitters over both shoulders," Gar challenged.

"Well, yeah, something like that. But we haven't done that this year, for sure. It's been real slow for us," Tom said in his careful, modulated way of speaking. "What are you doing, going to Crescent City? I assume that. I know you're getting married. Congratulations on that, by the way. And I wanted to tell you that you guys did a good job organizing that protest. I know it was Michael's idea, but you are the one who talked it up, and were the one that sold it. Good job!" Tom was honestly thankful. He was an original highliner salmon fisherman out of Washington State, and Gar had deep respect for the man. It was Tom's nature to be frank and honest. Gar liked that, too.

"Well, thanks for that, Tom. Yes, we're headed home so I can put the boat in the slip, then go back to Half Moon Bay and get married. I guess you'll be standing by here on this channel. I'll do the same. Say good afternoon to Teri. I'm sure she's as cute as ever. I've got to go do something right now, so I'll talk to you later."

Gar signed off in a hurry. He had spotted more containers, and at the very least needed to decide what he was going to do about them. He already had the fisherman's ingrained inclination to "put as much product on board as it is possible to do, today, as tomorrow may not offer a damned thing."

THEY PICKED UP four more containers, and took a pass on a bunch of others. The containers weighed well over a hundred pounds apiece, but Gar figured they probably only held fifty pounds of dried weed. Jeff estimated they could wholesale the pot for around two thousand a pound, which meant each container was worth an easy hundred-thousand dollars. Times five, they had a half million on the boat. At least, in theory.

They were rich. And for the first time since Gar had signed the ***Visit***'s loan papers, he felt relaxed.

He could pay off the boat, and buy Cindy a house. New cars all the way around.

Wow!

Jeff grew excited too. He noted that the quality, as well as quantity, of his women was about to improve dramatically. He didn't balk for a second when Gar said that he felt a fair split was a three-way split. One share each, plus one share for the boat. In other words, Gar would get two thirds, and Jeff would get one third. After all, Gar was risking both his self, *and* the boat. Jeff was only risking himself.

After the initial excitement wore off, however, Gar mulled over the question: was this right? This was the first of many salmon season closures made by the National Marine Fisheries Service. One could bet on that. And Gar doubted there was any reason for this, or any future closures, other than to justify NMFS paychecks. Defiantly, Gar decided, "Fuck the Feds," and he vowed to keep this windfall as a dower. It was an unintended and fortuitous benefaction from the dubious new acronymous government agency, "NMFS."

He was fairly sure that had this happened a year earlier, when they were in the middle of a salmon trip in the same area, with a boat payment already in the hold, he would not have kept the first container aboard, nor would he have picked up the four additional bales.

All considerations of his wedding aside, the Feds and this new *El Nino* had changed the prospects for fishermen completely. With yesterday's protest still fresh in his mind, the moral question of whether or not this was "right" was a simple one. It was not only right, it was necessary. Never before had the duration of the salmon season been dictated by man instead of the salmon themselves. Previous generations of West Coast salmon fishermen had not faced these obstacles to earning a living.

THEY WERE RUNNING north and home, all right, but Gar kept angling more offshore. The normal and straighter course would keep them within ten miles, at the farthest, from shore. But by Fort Bragg they were thirty miles offshore, and by Eureka they were fifty.

SOUTH OF EUREKA Tom came on the radio, cursing, saying that a helicopter just passed over them with a bullhorn, ordering they go to Channel Sixteen, the Coast Guard VHF frequency.

Gar listened in as the Coast Guard instructed Tom to come into Eureka for an inspection of his fish hold. Word was obviously out that there were marijuana bales floating all over the ocean just south of Point Arena.

Gar was nervous and scared. But, strangely, the adrenaline surges he was experiencing caused him to smile. That, and perhaps the fact that he might have become wealthy. Two-thirds figured out to $333,333. He decided three was his new lucky number. He called Tom back after the Coast Guard conversation, on a much shorter-range radio, and asked him what was up.

"Oh, these sons-a-bitches got me on some sort of hot list. They think I was into smuggling, some years ago, and every time they get a chance they hassle me," Tom explained.

"Well, were you?" Gar couldn't help asking.

"I'll never tell," Tom giggled. But he just did.

"Well, better you than me," Gar said in a way that he thought he might be telling Tom that he was packing. But he thought afterwards that it probably just sounded flippant. And he felt bad about that, because he liked Tom. Not only that, but Tom was likely taking the heat off the ***Visit***. Any further thoughts about making himself more clear to Tom were instantly stifled, as he worried he might then have to share his good fortune. Greed was already setting in.

"Yeah, okay, fine. I'll go do this. Good luck again to you and your fiancée. Hope I get to meet her sometime. We'll see you when you get done with the honeymoon. I'm out." Tom clicked off.

"Okay, Tom. Same to you and Teri." Teri was Tom's wife and deckhand. And Gar clicked off, too. His gaze, directed at the horizon, was thoughtful and worried.

PART WAY BETWEEN Eureka and Crescent City, maybe a little north of Trinidad Head, the fog settled down over the ***Visit*** like a welcome comforter. Gar figured this was a good thing, as he deduced that the Coast Guard had spotted Tom while doing random fly overs. They would not be able to spot Gar in this fog.

The five containers were right out the back door, on deck, and ready to be tossed over should anyone come close. Of course, they were well covered from view with good-old, deck-colored gunny sacks. The tops of the canisters were cut open so they'd go straight down, should scuttling them become necessary.

And the timing was beautiful, as Gar estimated they'd arrive in Crescent City Harbor at 2:30 a.m. The slackest period of the night would be just beginning as they tied in the slip.

AND INDEED THIS was so. The buoy light on Round Rock to the south of the jetties at Crescent City greeted them with its silent strobe. They ghosted quietly past, eyed suspiciously by a pair of vigilant brown pelicans. The old Battery Point Lighthouse to the north of the harbor continued to flash its additional warning into the night, though it was removed from the harbor entrance and made redundant by the newer light on Round Rock. The old light appeared dimmed, as though by distance and age and a lowering fog, and its warning went largely unheeded by modern mariners.

They tied up in the foggy slip at 2:45, and had the five well-bundled bales in Gar's truck by three. Both men were running on the energized effect that secretions from the adrenal gland produce.

GAR WORKED THE rest of the night at the house alone. Cindy was down in Half Moon Bay at her parent's house. He washed the first container of pot in fresh water, but noticed when doing so that much of the orange-red color was leaching out. He thought this might be the THC that is the primary intoxicant of cannabis. So he did not rinse the other four containers in fresh water. Instead, he hung their contents in gunnysacks out in his tool shed. Before heading south the next afternoon for the wedding, he added a small space heater to the tool shed drying operation.

THE POT IN the house was the main focus, and Gar called a friend to borrow a dehumidifier to add to the large room where he had spread all the buds out on newspaper. It was amazing how quickly the dehumidifier, a deluxe model from Sears, sucked all the water out of the air. The super-arid air then drew the excess water right out of the weed, desiccating it perfectly.

At first, Gar was emptying the dehumidifier's water catcher, which held more than a gallon, about every hour. Then after that started to slow down, he began foraging for dry buds amongst the jumble on the family-room floor.

All told, in the limited hours Gar had to work before heading south to Half Moon Bay, he salvaged maybe twenty good pounds of perfectly dried weed, and another twenty pounds that was mostly dry. He took all this with him, packaged in garbage bags, arranged in assorted suitcases, and covered with clothing.

He would get it distributed, the next day, to two old schoolmates who he knew did that sort of thing. One of the mates even ponied up ten-thousand dollars–in advance–so Gar could take Cindy on a decent honeymoon. This was the best part of all.

With ten-thousand dollars in his pocket, the $1,200 he had netted from his salmon trip was much less important. Gar went to a travel agent and bought a first-class Hawaiian honeymoon package for the two of them. They had planned on Lake Tahoe, for a two-day, three night stay, but now they would enjoy an entire week in Hawaii on the island of Maui. When Gar told Cindy this, she squealed with glee and leaped into his arms she was so excited. And Gar was thrilled that he could make her feel like that.

THE *DAY-UNDER-THE-BRIDGE* HEADLINES were quickly replaced with news stories of all the marijuana bales, packaged in sheet metal, that were coming ashore. They were littering the coast north of Bodega Bay.

Gar noticed these stories with interest, amidst all the wedding excitement, but he did not get distracted. He continued to occasionally wonder if he was doing the right thing. But when they went to Memorial Park, in Pescadero, for the ceremony, he recalled his *Oakie* days there, and he became convinced that he'd come a long way since those years. How he had gotten to where he was didn't matter. He believed that he was locked on a course that he could not change. Like when a series of boating circumstances force a skipper to proceed one way, and one way only, otherwise suffer a total loss.

He was in it now. One way or another, he was in it.

Part Two

THE SMUGLER

CHAPTER 19

JUNE, 1981–MAY, 1982

"SEA-WEED" THEY'RE calling it." Gar's old school mate said. "I still haven't sold the batch I advanced you the ten-thousand for yet, though."

"Oh, shit, and I was hoping to come back from Maui to another pay day," Gar spoke plaintively. He was still decked out in Hawaiian shirt, shorts, and sandals. And he was sporting the first suntan on his legs that he had had in many years.

"Naw, there's a lot of this stuff around. You're not the only one to pick some up. You might be the only fishing boat, but I'm not even sure about that. I just know that a shitload washed up on the beaches somewhere north of the City." The friend who had advanced Gar the money for the weed, a man named Chris, explained it all very casually.

"Hey, how'd the wedding and honeymoon go?" Chris changed the subject with facile alacrity as he jumped up to flip the cassette over. They were listening to some sort of cool-jazz tape with a song that Gar recognized. It was *The Girl From Ipanema*, with Stan Getz blowing the tenor sax.

"Oh, it was nice," Gar mused. "Really nice. I guess my Mom summed it up best when she said one of her girlfriends told her there was more love going on at our wedding than any she remembered. Maybe that was because of the three-minute kiss–with three feet of tongue!–that I gave Cindy after the preacher said to kiss the bride. And Maui, what can I say about Maui? I got my butt burned sunbathing on our private balcony. I was only out there for a half hour. I couldn't sit right for a couple of days. But Cindy rubbed me down frequently with Noxzema. That was a lot of fun, right there. And then there was the 'Mile-High Club' on the way home." Gar was all grins as he related these memories to Chris.

"That's cool. And you sound good. Relaxed, I guess. I'll try to move the rest of this weed for you. Check with me next week." Chris had a good, honest voice as he assured Gar everything would be all right.

This was when Gar had the first inkling of the damnable casualness of the drug business. He wondered if, in the end, they'd wind up calling it even on the twenty pounds of marijuana he'd left with Chris, and the ten-thousand dollars Chris had advanced Gar for the twenty pounds.

Hmmm. This drug business, he began to suspect, was not the straightforward proposition that fishing was. It contained an entirely different brand of people

AS IT WAS to turn out, Gar learned a lot about selling pot from the Sea-Weed pick up that introduced him to the drug game. He did not get much more than that first well-dried twenty pounds properly marketed. He sold that for only a thousand a pound. Well under the two-thousand dollars a pound they'd originally estimated. Then the second twenty pounds, the one that had been mostly dry when Gar bagged it and headed south for the wedding, that became a cursed batch. One guy claimed there was a shoot-out over it where a friend was shot and all the weed was stolen. Another said that when he sold it he was paid in counterfeit bills, and was damn near busted when he went to the bank to deposit the cash so he could mail a check up to Gar in Crescent City. All Gar's contacts were in the Bay Area, and he still lived up north. So the stories never did sound coherent at such a remove. All told, Gar received, at first, what he normally might have made salmon fishing. But because he didn't fish much the rest of that season, he spent money at a much faster rate. Mostly, of course, Gar spent his money on his new bride. Later, when the amount of money became vastly increased, he began to spend it on senseless stuff.

Jimmy Buffett sings about money made smuggling in *A Pirate Looks at Forty*, crooning: "I made enough money to buy Miami, but I pissed it away so fast...never meant to last...never meant to last."

And, howdy, was Jimmy Buffett ever right. Having cash in hand all the time, and wads of cash coming in spurts from the various distributors Gar had turned up, served to loosen the purse strings. Many a round for the house was bought in Gar's ebullient new existence that did not include, for the first time in his life, worries about money. The money flew in, and it flew out just as fast.

Some of it was spent wisely, though. He bought new crab pots, increasing his Dungeness crabbing operations by double. That made his 1981-82 crabbing season at least profitable.

And this was a good thing, because the summer of 1982 was the first season which saw the *El Nino* arrive in full force, and there were no salmon. The Sea Weed–only the real moldy stuff that didn't get dried well was left–still paid small and sporadic dividends. But once again it was Gar's crab traps that put the bacon on the table that season.

Well, that, and, as Gar was to discover, Chuckie's up and coming new scheme.

AT THE BEACH House after the first salmon trip in May, 1982, Gar was drunk and despondent. He sat next to his brother-in-law and lamented, as only the intoxicated and truly sorrowful can do. And he gazed at a painting of a lighthouse behind the bar. It was a white one with a large black stripe circling up its length, kind of like the famous coastal beacon in Brittany, France, though it may have been a painting of one of the New England lighthouses. The sight of the thing made him morose.

"We had sixteen fish for six days. And they were small fish, at that. Do you get the math? That's about two and a half fish a day." Gar stopped for a moment and stared sightlessly at a rack of pork rinds. "And we caught some sort of fish I've never seen before. They're called lizardfish, and they look just like a fucking lizard. I'm so sick I could just spit. As a matter of fact, I think I will." And he spit on the floor, then laughed at how drunk he was. "And now I think I'll just shit."

Gar headed off for the men's room, leaving Chuckie sort of opening and closing his mouth, looking for something to say. Chuckie wasn't much of a talker, and he didn't do well at all around the crazy, off-the-wall drunkenness that Gar was displaying. Chuck was a weed smoker and preferred solitude and quiet thought.

BACK FROM THE restroom Gar grabbed his rum and Coke, took a good slug, wiped his mouth with the back of his shirtsleeve, and managed, "I couldn't even shit. That's how bad it's got."

Like that explained anything.

"You know, I've got someone you should meet," Chuck offered, pumping his eyebrows a couple of times.

"Oh shit, not now, not here," Gar sobered, knowing where Chuck was going with this. "But we could talk about that tomorrow. How's the tides? Is it time for a dive? I know I'll need a good dive to sober up tomorrow."

"Yeah, we could probably get a few ab's. It's not that good of a tide, but I think we'll be all right. Just have to go down a little deeper. Maybe an extra couple of feet. It's not a minus tide. Maybe just about even. And, you know I think I could get my friend up here, the one that I want you to meet. How's ten o'clock sound?"

Gar nodded mutely, and Chuck continued. "I'll have Vince come up. He's an early bird. We'll be in here by nine-thirty for coffee, and leave as soon as you're ready. Have you still got the key?"

Chuckie was talking faster than Gar ever remembered him doing. And then Gar flashed on why he'd spit on the floor earlier. It was because Chuckie was always spitting. But then the man's question sank in.

"Yes, I've still got the key," Gar had a calculating grin now. "It's real important, isn't it?"

"Yes," Chuck said simply. "It is."

HUNG OVER AND perhaps still a little bit drunk, Gar awakened in the behind-the-restaurant trailer. It was eight'ish. He could sense this by the amount of light and the pressure on his bladder.

Time to meet this Vince," he thought, lucid despite the previous night's debauchery. He laid still in his bed for a time, trying to sort his thoughts, and decided to reserve judgment about the entire endeavor until the parameters of the thing were made clear to him. A feeling of lassitude imbued him, and a growing sense of moral impassivity.

And so it began. Not with a decisive flouting of the social contract, but with a curious sense of indifference.

CHAPTER 20

EARLY MAY, 1982.

CHUCK, GAR AND Vince went to Bootlegger's Cove, as planned, and Vince watched while Chuckie and Gar each surfaced a number of times, eventually returning to the shore with a gunnysack full of abalones. Wearing tasseled loafers and carefully creased slacks, the older Vince did not appear to be in his element. His balding hair and the studied nonchalance behind aviator sunglasses were perhaps better suited to a cocktail lounge than a sun-drenched beach.

Vince lived in the housing tract behind the Wrigley's Gum Factory in Santa Cruz, and he had a perpetual odor of Juicy Fruit Gum clinging to him like an odiferous persona. Everybody in the neighborhood smelled like this. And this was a fine and pleasant odor to be found surrounding a child, but it just didn't work for a grown man with a lupine cast to his countenance, and one who was wearing tasseled loafers on a beach.

"THIS PLACE REALLY is perfect." Vince commented after the guys came up the bank from the dive. The midday sun shone through a mild upper haze of clouds that had all but burned off. It was already seventy degrees outside. Beads of sweat dotted Vince's pale forehead. "It's here in the middle of nowhere, yet a relatively short drive to Santa Cruz once the trucks are loaded."

Chuckie sniggered and said, "I told you." And Gar gazed at the small inlet, conceptualizing the ***Visit*** anchored there, unloading bundles of Thai-weed into a Zodiac. The dive had cured the hangover, but not that other feeling in the pit of his stomach.

Gar felt uneasy. He gazed at the Pigeon Point Lighthouse two miles north. Wheeling and crying gulls surrounded the soaring candlestick, just as they surrounded him here, though he could not see them at such a distance. The lighthouse appeared as a stern, admonitory finger being held aloft. Suddenly, Gar didn't want to see it. He shifted his gaze away, and invited the other men to leave with him.

DRIVING BACK DOWN to the Cascade Ranch, Vince turned to Gar. "I'm going to pay you seventy-five thousand as soon as I get the stuff to Santa Cruz," he said. "And you come down to pick up your money. And when everything's all done, if I do as well as I hope, I'll bonus you another twenty-five."

"Okay. That sounds good to me. But I need to know a few things, like how much space it will take, and...."

"Oh, don't worry. A couple of guys are going to come and inspect your boat. As a matter of fact, they want to come down here and anchor for a half an hour or so. Sort of a dry run, to get the feel of things."

"That's plenty doable," Gar said. "But you know it's about a three and a half hour run from Princeton Harbor down here. It will be an all day thing–coming down, anchoring, then running back."

"They know." Vince assured him. "They're sailors, and have a good idea of what's involved."

"All right. When do they want to do this?" Gar asked.

"I think, sometime real soon." Vince thought about it for a minute before he spoke. Then he said, "I'll tell Chuckie, and he'll tell you, but you better be on standby this coming week."

LATER ON, AFTER Vince had gone back to Santa Cruz, Chuck told Gar that Vince was the offload manager, but these other guys would be the actual owners of the load. "They're the money guys," Chuck stressed. "Vince will try to make you think he's the big cheese, but he's just working for these other guys."

They sat on the front porch of the old ranch house at the Cascade Ranch. Rudy's smaller, neater, yellow cottage nestled in the trees on up Cascade Creek.

"Well, if they're the money guys, will they understand that I can't standby for too long, because I have to go fishing to make money?" Gar was disconcerted with both his poor outlook for the salmon season, and the fact he was being told to standby without any recompense for doing this. At least if he fished he might make some money. He watched as a hundred dragon flies darted in the afternoon sun.

"I'll talk to them," Chuck picked up Gar's reluctance. "And maybe I can get you some compensation for your down time. We'll call it Workmen's Comp." He laughed at his own witticism.

"All right, that sounds good. Maybe I won't have to fish as much during this planning phase, if they can help me out.

Remember, I have a wife and a house to take care of now, too." Gar was more upbeat at the prospect of receiving compensation for his time.

"Oh, these guys have got lots of money. The one guy I know that's coming, Wallace, is sort of tight though. But I think he'll pay. Whatever, if it means keeping the project going." Chuck said.

"Okay, I'm going back up to the Beach House. Let me know something tomorrow. If you talk to Wallace, tell him I'm losing a thousand a day."

"You think you're losing that much?" Chuck was surprised.

"No." Gar said. "We have our thousand-dollar days, all right. But right now it's not even thousand dollar weeks because of *El Nino*."

"Okay. I'll do the best I can for you. And don't worry too much. These guys are real easy to deal with, and they're mostly honest. They're not trying to fuck anyone. They know better." Chuck always liked it when he could talk tough. Though Gar thought it was usually unnecessary. All of a sudden the dogs in the kennels began an insane chorus of barking.

Gar remembered hearing once that when Chuckie's best friend didn't pay up for an ounce of weed, Chuck went to the friend's house and sliced open the guy's waterbed and took his change jar. This seemed like harsh justice, but it said something about the kind of chap that Chuckie could be.

CHAPTER 21

MID MAY, 1982.

WALLACE WAS NOT very tall and he had neatly-cut blond hair. He dressed in shorts, was mouse featured, and he had a weak hand shake. He smoked nasty little black Toscanelli cigars that stank to high heaven. His friend Bob was only a little bit taller, but in all other ways he was the opposite of Wallace. Bob had a dark complexion with coarse black curly hair, and he was an obvious weight lifter. He nearly broke Gar's hand when they shook on the back deck of the ***Visit***.

Wallace and Bobbie had insisted they meet at the boat. Gar later figured this was because they did not want Gar to see the make of their car, nor the license-plate number. Though different in appearance, these two shared the elusiveness that drug smugglers acquire after years of clandestine schemes.

IN THE STRANGE year of 1982, the British were fighting the Argentineans in the Falkland's War. *Gandhi* was showing in the theaters. John Lennon and Yoko Ono did the *Double Fantasy* album. And Toto sang *Rosana* for a Grammy. But most remarkable and strange of all to Gar, and to all the fishermen on the West Coast of the United States, it was the year that *El Nino* came.

The *El Nino* is a climatically significant disruption of the ocean-atmosphere system, characterized by a widespread weakening of the trade winds and the warming of surface layers in the central and east equatorial Pacific Ocean. The term *El Nino*, Spanish for "the Christ Child," was originally used by fishermen to refer to a warm ocean current appearing around Christmas off the west coasts of Ecuador and Peru and lasting for several months. The term has come to be reserved for exceptionally strong, warm currents that bring heavy winter rains to the United States.

The 1982-83 *El Nino*, climatologists would later observe, was the strongest to ever find its way to the Pacific Northwest. Aside from the extremely abnormal weather it brought, the 1982-83 *El Nino* flipped the California, Oregon and Washington fishing industry upside down. Normal fish, such as salmon, completely disappeared. And warm-water fish, such as mackerel, moved in.

And fish that no one had even heard of, like *Lizardfish*, were caught with increasing regularity. The salmon fishermen had to make up their own names for some of the different species they took off their salmon trolling gear, fish that had never been seen by them before. It was weird. The fishermen never knew what was going to come up from the deep on their hooks. It was also a nightmare, as what did come up was unmarketable. The U.S. Government declared these two seasons an official disaster.

THE FIRST THING Wallace said, after introductions, was, "I'm going to have a VHF radio, with direction finder capability, delivered and installed tomorrow. That is, if you are agreeable?"

"Oh, yeah. Are you talking about a *Polaris* VHF?" Gar asked. "I've wanted to get one of those."

"That's the one." Wallace smiled, seemingly satisfied. He puffed his cigar and gazed off into the distance. It made Gar feel like this was question number one on the test, and he'd gotten the answer right. The cigar was sure smelly though.

THEY TALKED WHILE running south from Princeton to Franklin Point; heading for the little bay on the leeward side of the point–Bootlegger's, soon to be Smuggler's, Cove. Wallace and Bobbie climbed in and around the boat, tape measure and calculator in hand, jotting figures down on a note pad. After an hour or so, they told Gar the boat would be sufficient to handle their load.

The weather was decent, not much wind, which was abnormal for May. It was sunny, with a low westerly swell, and the ambient air was warm due to the sixty-degree sea temperature. A sea temperature of fifty degrees was the average for this time of year. Just south of Pescadero they began to smell the chemical odor of the bug powder on the Brussels' sprouts. Then they came up on Pigeon Point, on past the Beach House, and finally to Franklin Point, where they cut inside to the cove. Gulls wheeled around the Pigeon Point Lighthouse screaming senselessly and endlessly, and the men watched this as they passed.

Other than this, they saw very little bird life as they cruised along the familiar coastal landmarks, indicating a lack of baitfishes in the too-warm *El Nino* water. But there was a bounty of kelp flies, which kept everyone huddled in the cabin. They were close enough to the beachside cliffs that they could see that the burgeoning ice plant that thrived along this stretch of coast (and had ever since someone had planted it fifty years earlier), was in full bloom, presenting a riot of purple flowers on emerald green. This was an exotically beautiful ground cover. The low, rolling slopes of the coastline beyond were a morose and desolate prairie-brown.

GAR TOOK THE ***Visit*** right up into the small bight that was Bootlegger's Cove. There were rocks all around them, dangerously close off the stern, after Jeff had tossed over the anchor. As fishermen go, Gar considered himself an expert at shallow-water anchoring. He'd performed this operation numerous times in many different coves up and down the coast. He was doubtless more adventurous at this procedure than other sailors due to his knowledge of shallow waters, gained from years spent diving for abalones.

Wallace commented on their anchorage. "You got us right up in here, didn't you?"

"Yes. I wanted to take some readings and line up some landmarks. I'm figuring I'll be anchoring in here as close as possible, and at night. See there?" He pointed towards the north. "I'll be able to just see the Pigeon Point Lighthouse blinking over the top of that rock. That will be my guide. I'll probably come back here again before the big night. When might that be, by the way, have you decided?"

"If you tell us today that you are committed for sure, then I think we're talking about forty-five days. Maybe somewhere around the fourth of July. Hey," Wallace brightened," "that would be perfect. I've always had good luck with holidays. The Coast Guard, and other police, are all too busy with drunks and what not." Wallace was enthusiastic now, with the thought of July fourth being a target date for the off loading.

Gar took advantage of this. "Did Chuckie mention to you that this down time, while I make plans with you guys, is creating problems for me at home? I have a new wife to support, and I can't afford not to fish. At the same time, I feel obligated to you and the plan."

"Oh yes," Wallace said as he dug into a backpack that had never been far from his reach. "Here's thirty-five hundred. That's out of my money. I don't know what you have going with Vince, he's the one paying the offload crew. But I wanted to do something to help you along. I'll be getting you that radio, too, that I think you will need. There will likely be some other things, like a double-hulled skiff, that I'll be getting. All that stuff will be yours when we're done. Except the skiff, which I think you should probably sink."

"Wait a minute," Gar interjected. "Why would I take a skiff? I thought we were going to try a side tie. Although I don't know that that will be possible."

"We were often able to do side ties in the Caribbean, but not always. Different times we were glad to have a skiff, and then we'd sink them once we were done, so any fly-overs wouldn't see them on deck." Gar listened to Wallace say this and was impressed that they could afford to sink a more-than-five-thousand-dollar piece of equipment. This was a league that he had only heard stories about, and he was now a part of it. Bobby and Jeff looked on, smiling and listening.

"Okay. Thank you for the loot. Just let us know what you think we should do. I've got a lot of experience at a lot of different things, but not this." Gar was happy with some actual cash in his hands, though he knew it wouldn't make the boat payment. That was over $20,000 this year. PCA's floating interest rate had sharply increased with inflation.

He immediately peeled a thousand off and gave it to Jeff, who had been relatively quiet. He had answered Wallace and Bob's questions, but not said much more than that. Gar, besides wanting to give Jeff money before it disappeared into his own pocket, also wanted these guys to know there were other mouths to feed.

Handing Jeff the money, Gar said, "Why don't' we wind up the anchor, and get out of here?"

Jeff said, smiling, "You mean, make like sheep herders, and get the *flock* out of here?"

"You better stay out on the ocean. Anybody who would say something like that doesn't know anything about *flocking* sheep." Wallace finally said something that wasn't serious.

All of the men laughed. Gar put the boat into gear once the anchor was raised, and spun the wheel. He noticed a soaring albatross off his port bow, a good luck bird to fishermen and sailors everywhere, and he smiled. Albatrosses were said to be the returned souls of dead fishermen, and Gar had seen them fly for hours without ever flapping their wings. The birds were said to be able to sleep while floating aloft, and could travel for thousands of miles. But sighting one this close to the shoreline was rare. Seeing one now gave Gar a good feeling. It was a sign of good luck. Maybe this thing was going to work out.

CHAPTER 22

EARLY JUNE, 1982.

GAR HAD CONCERNS. Who wouldn't? But he needed to touch base with Rudy. And more importantly, Cindy.

When he did talk to Cindy–she already knew all about the Sea Weed–she was anxious but expressed her support for the venture. Gar was left with the feeling that she was trying to be an agreeable spouse, as much as anything.

AT LUNCH ONE day, Gar spoke to Rudy. "I anchored in Bootlegger's Cove the other day with some friends of young Chuckie."

Rudy smiled, and said, "What took you so long?"

"Oh, I was just feeling things out."

"Bobbie," Rudy spoke almost tenderly. "That cove was good for me, and I hope it's just as good for you. God bless you."

And that was all that was ever said again about the cove. And the master key Gar had in his possession was never mentioned again.

Gar felt like he was covered. He wanted to ask Mom for her opinion, but thought better of it. She would be fine with it, he felt certain, as long as it was successful. To tell her beforehand would only cause her to worry.

So with success as his goal, Gar decided it was a go. And he considered, during moments of quiet contemplation, that this was what men did when faced with adversity and change. They rose to the challenge. Legal considerations aside, if the National Marine Fisheries Service was going to abridge the salmon-fishing season until a man could no longer make a living at it, something else must be attempted in order to make ends meet. Just as the early Pescadero farmers needed to supplement their livelihoods with bootlegging before establishing agriculture in the area, and developing a market for their goods, so too would Gar supplement his own livelihood. His was just a more contemporary manner of doing so. He would do this thing. And he would do it well.

CHAPTER 23

LATE JUNE, 1982.

BY GAR'S JUNE 21st wedding anniversary, the foreign sailboat was well on its way from the Philippines. Everything was going along as planned. The sailboat would be at a spot approximately eighty miles off Franklin Point on the afternoon of Saturday, the third of July. The goal was to get a sighting of the boat, at least, on that Saturday during daylight hours. Then a tie-up next to each other and a transfer of the load would be made that night. The ***Visit*** and the ***Ima*** (This was the boat owned by Vince's Santa Cruz friend, Don), would then haul ass through the remaining darkness toward shore and the salmon-boat fleet. The fleet was scattered ten miles from the shore and in. They rarely ventured further from the shore during this part of the season. So they would need ten hours of running time to get to where they could throw out their salmon gear and look inconspicuous amongst the other fishing boats.

The numbers weren't quite adding up. It didn't get dark until nine at night. Even if it all went smoothly, it was not likely that they would have finished transferring the load before midnight. And the sun would come up some time before six in the morning. So they would likely need to run at full throttle until mid-morning on Sunday the fourth.

Then there was the fact that it is an ingrained part of a fisherman's superstitious nature never to start a trip on a Friday. It is considered bad luck to do this. Gar knew better than to tempt fate by leaving on Friday the second. So he would have to leave town, at the latest, on Thursday, the first of July.

Which meant there were ten days and counting until it was time to go.

CHAPTER 24

THURSDAY, JULY 1, 1982.

IN ORDER TO avert suspicion, Gar and Jeff ran the boat down to Santa Cruz the last week of June. Along the way, Gar took down his Z-sail out of respect for the squad. They took on the necessary provisions at the Santa Cruz boat basin. And they departed for the rendezvous on July first. They were given a whole laundry list of last-minute instructions. So many that Gar grew impatient and spoke sharply to Vince, Wallace, and Bob.

"I've got this," he snapped. Then, to Jeff, "Untie us."

And they were off to "bring in the goodies," as Jimmy Buffett would say. The weather was balmy and the sun was beaming down and the adventure had begun.

JUST OUT OF Santa Cruz Harbor, Gar's shadow, ***Ima*** Don, called on their prearranged channel. He said he hoped the sailboat would be on time. An innocent enough thing to say, really–for a neophyte.

Gar flipped out. He turned the ***Visit*** around, headed straight back for Don, and had him heave to. He yelled across the distance between the two boats.

"Let's get something straight. Do not talk on the radio unless you have to, and if you do, speak only about fishing. Okay?"

Gar was nervous enough about the appearance of this endeavor as it was. But he figured he could placate his Half Moon Bay friends with a story that he was doing one of Mom's Santa Cruz friends a favor by running with Don for a salmon trip. He could never explain, though, why they might be meeting a sailboat.

THE WEATHER THE next morning was calm, but by three in the afternoon they had twenty-five knots of wind. They had anchored at the *Ano Nuevo* anchorage on Thursday afternoon. Friday morning they went out to thirty fathoms and put in their salmon gear. From there they trolled west, toward the distant horizon, and they kept going west all day. They didn't catch a fish between them. But they looked quite normal should the Coast Guard be checking. And that was the thing about this endeavor. It seemed to be about appearances.

AT SUNSET THAT night, they were thirty or forty miles offshore and well outside the shipping lanes. So they spread the boats a couple of miles apart, disengaged the gearboxes, and drifted for the night. Each boat turned on plenty of lights. And they left the engines running to keep the batteries up.

It was still windy, but the ***Visit*** laid nicely while drifting. The type of stars visible were the kind that you could almost reach out and grab. And outside the pool of light cocooning the ***Visit***, the ocean was an inky black, with occasional silver chevrons of pale moonlight reflected from the waves. The thin sliver of a new moon began its ascent above the eastern horizon, signifying a fresh start. Gar felt in his marrow that this beacon was a portentous sign of hope.

THE NEXT MORNING, Gar was awake well before daybreak. He found Don on the radar. The two boats were now five miles from one another. He motored over to Don's stern, and gave him a few blasts from the air horn. Don came out on the back deck birthday suit naked, which didn't surprise Gar. Then Don's deckhand appeared, equally exposed. This caused Gar to snicker. And Jeff, in the cabin, was laughing outright.

Don didn't even notice the derisive laughter. He and his crewman stood talking unconcernedly on deck. Gar warned him again about the use of the radio.

Gar cautioned that two small boats are like needles in a haystack in this much ocean–*until someone keys the button on a mike*. All that has to be done is the press of a button, and a direction finder will instantly reveal one's direction, and if there are two D.F.'s working together, they can triangulate a position. Instantly. And apart from this, Gar was concerned because so many people knew his voice, and if they D.F.'d him way offshore, they might become suspicious.

THE TWO BOATS continued offshore toward the designated point of rendezvous. It was actually a location on one particular chart where a combination of bottom-characteristic markings appeared in the shape of a perfect Christian cross. Of course, the cross had Loran coordinates that Gar had plotted.

The fishermen-turned-smugglers took it slow that morning, bucking the twenty-knot wind chop toward *The Cross*. Thankfully, some cloud cover had moved in. This would thwart random fly overs by Coast Guard planes.

SEVERAL HOURS BEFORE sunset, Gar spotted the high-masted sloop. She rode easy in a gentle swell. When he spotted her, the sailboat lay dead ahead off the ***Visit***'s bow. Gar had plotted a perfect course. The sailboat sat exactly at the intersection of the cross. The high mast was back lighted nicely against the horizon and the lowering sun. Stationary seagulls floating on a breeze gave the nautical scene a picturesque peacefulness.

It was Saturday, July third, late in the afternoon.

OF THE VERITIBLE encyclopedia of instructions Wallace had given them before leaving the dock, Gar chose exactly none. He simply keyed the mike on the agreed VHF frequency, on low power, and said: "Wee'rree Heerre."

The sailors replied somewhat skeptically. "Is this who I think it is?"

"I understand you've run out of propane," Gar stated. "I'll be by in a few minutes. Stand by for further instructions."

"Roger. Ten-four." The man in the sailboat responded with much more conviction.

Smuggling weed on the high seas!

CHAPTER 25

SATURDAY EVENING, JULY 3, 1982.

UP CLOSE TO the sailboat, it took a while to convince them to just lay there out of gear. They had their sails down, all right. And there were three men on deck. But it was as though the men on the sailboat spoke a different language. Gar kept yelling at them to take their boat out of gear so he could maneuver close enough to talk to them, and they steered evasively under the power of their tiny propeller as though afraid of getting too close. Gar found out later that these men had been at sea for a long time, and were initially afraid that Gar was going to ram their craft. Long periods at sea make men leery and suspicious. Finally, Gar was able to convince them to simply heave to and drift.

The procedure fishermen have established over the years for transferring materials, or talking, at sea is for the lead boat to drift while the trailing boat noses ahead, slipping the shifter in and out of gear, keeping the boats close but not too close. It is best to keep the vessels separated by maybe twenty-five feet or so. Whatever is necessary for a conversation. Sometimes things, including people, are passed this way. Passing things means easing forward bit by bit, then at the last second backing down hard just as the item is tossed (or if a person, he or she jumps) at the final second. It's not foolproof. But it's safer than it sounds.

The wind was blowing a steady twenty knots, with an easy six-foot swell. As the men on the two boats worked out an understanding, Gar looked more closely at the three men on the sailboat. They were all dressed in tropical clothing, despite the wind. And they all had deep-water tans. One man, bigger than the other two, appeared to be the leader.

"Did you bring us supplies?" Was the first question they asked.

"Yes," Gar shouted. "I have cases of beer, ice chests of food, a bottle of propane, and a little plastic baggie with some kind of white powder that Wallace said you'd be very happy to get. He said you'd need the propane worst. If you want me to send that over right now, throw me a line and I'll tie the bottle on."

Almost in unison, the three sailors shouted back. "Fuck the propane, send the cocaine!"

Until that moment things had been tense, but everyone now began to laugh. Such are the ways of strange men when they meet in dangerous situations. The laughter was a relief to them all.

"Okay, look." Gar took command. "Here's what I suggest we do. First, side-tying is out of the question." They murmured amongst themselves and Gar continued. "We have a long, stout tow line. Do you have one?"

"Yeah," the biggest guy said. "We have to get it out of the anchor locker."

"Okay." Gar continued, speaking carefully. "We'll pass you one end of our tow line and we'll secure that line from our bow to your bow. It's about two-hundred feet, if I remember right. Then you pass us one end of your tow line, and that one we'll tie from stern to stern. We will both lay sideways to the swell, adrift and out of gear, but I'll lock my steering hard over to the left, and you lock yours hard to the right. I will drift faster than you anyway–I can see that by how we're drifting now–but by locking our wheels I will tend to tow you sideways, down wind and down swell." The sailors were listening intently, and Gar figured he had done the right thing by not passing the bag of cocaine over right away. He had their attention. And this was important. Not an easy thing to do either as the sailboat drifted very poorly. Several times Gar thought it was going to roll completely over, but it always came back.

"Okay, I follow you," the big one with a thick black beard replied. "But then what? We slowly take up slack to get alongside, close enough to pitch bales?"

"No. We'll never be able to get that close in this weather. Not without tearing up our boats. We'll use the skiff to shuttle back and forth. They tell me that it can pack four-thousand pounds. We have plenty of lightweight crabbing line we can rig to haul the skiff from you to me. Those lighter lines will go from the skiff–one from the bow and one from the stern–to both of our amidships, and we will have to haul hand over hand. Don't worry, I've done this before, when a friend broke down and I had to go over and show him how to get his boat running again. It was done under conditions exactly like this, and we hauled a skiff back and forth with tools and parts. Then when we got his boat running, it was with food and beer."

Gar added this last as a bit of an incentive, then sat back, arms folded, waiting for skepticism. But Blackbeard just stood there, thinking it over.

"Okay, we throw bales in the skiff, you pull it over, empty it, and then we pull it back..." Blackbeard finally said.

Gar cut him off. "We're only two guys, and you are three, so I think you should put one of your guys in the skiff to pass the stuff up to us. Or I'll go back and forth in the skiff, but you put one of your guys over here to help us load my hold. It will go much faster that way."

"Just a minute," Blackbeard called out. The men on the sailboat conferred amongst one another, then Blackbeard spoke again. "Okay, we've got a volunteer for the skiff, but he says you've got to give him the baggie on the very first trip. He cannot stand the thought of drowning and going to hell without being somewhat medicated."

"Ha, ha, ha," Gar and Jeff got a good laugh out of this. The tension eased some more. Gar was thinking that these guys were going to object to his taking charge, but they were happily amenable to all of his suggestions. "Here comes a haul-line. Catch it and pull over our towline, then tie your towline on to the haul line and we'll pull it back. Let's get this show on the road. I think we can get a lot done while we still have some daylight, and I know we'll be happy for that."

"Okay. I'm Tom, by the way, and I know that you're Gar. It's good to meet you." Tom, with the big black beard, smiled.

"You too, Tom. Maybe we can have a beer in town some day." The each passed the bitter end of their respective tow lines, then Gar grinned over at Tom and spoke to him again. "Okay, I've got your heavy-line and you've got ours. Now take this lighter line and use it to pull the skiff over once we get downwind from you."

Then Gar instructed Jeff to leave the boat out of gear so that it would swing on its own, down current. Which it did with no problem, allowing them to launch the skiff over the side. And the operation got under way.

DOWNWIND A COUPLE of hundred feet, Gar could hear jubilation coming from the sailboat. The sailors were pumped up. As well they should be. They'd been sitting on this load for a long time, and they were finally passing it off into competent hands. It was a relief to be rid of the responsibility involved with such a valuable and illegal cargo.

THE HOOK-UP AND first skiff load went even better than Gar expected. The sailors were whopping when the first load went over, and they were whooping when loading the second. They seemed to get more excited as their boat emptied. After each load they disappeared into their galley to do another line.

The entire load was supposed to be ten tons. When they got to what the sailors said was eight, they stopped. Don was to take the last two tons on the ***Ima***. This was insurance, in case the ***Visit*** sank or was intercepted.

Whatever. It was fine with Gar, as the ***Visit*** was stuffed. Pot is a very bulky commodity. And this Thai-pot must be very potent stuff, for it was robust smelling. Gar was not able to distinguish between the marijuana of different nations, for he was not an aficionado of the stuff, but he could tell by the smell that this Thai-weed was powerful, indeed.

DON GOT HIS load safely aboard the ***Ima***, and they were all done at two in the morning. The sailors threw all the lines in the skiff and told Don to pass the skiff back to Gar, and they told Don to tell Gar that he was a "*bad hombre*." When Don delivered the skiff, effectively concluding the transfer operation, he gave Gar the message from the sailors.

To which Gar responded, "Yeah. They were pretty gnarly their damn selves." Gar, too, could be cool when he wanted to be.

Under the thin crescent of a waxing moon, each of the boats withdrew from the area, embarking on their individual courses. With Don following in the ***Ima***, Gar watched the sloop hoist sails and slip silently away to the west, back to the Orient. There was left on the ocean no trace of their presence.

CHAPTER 26

EARLY MORNING, JULY 4, 1982.

"THAT WAS DAUNTING," Jeff said. The transfer was done. All the bales of grass were tucked into the hold and in various niches throughout the boat. The skiff taken back from Don was now destroyed and tossed away, sunk in 2,000 fathoms, and they were running full throttle toward land.

It was not quite daylight.

"Yes," Gar agreed, and he took a big bite of a peanut-butter sandwich. "It was exciting, actually, loading all the *stuff*.

"Not too much different than a hot-bite of fish, but I'm beat now. It won't be light for another hour, so how about if I take a nap until it gets light? Then you can sleep the rest of the morning. I doubt if we'll put the gear in much before noon. That will give you five or six hours." Gar licked jelly from his fingers.

"All right. Sounds good to me. You go ahead." Suddenly, Jeff started laughing. "Hey, when that goofy Don had his deckhand throw us the line to pull over the skiff, did you notice Don was up in the cabin buck naked, with nothing else on but rubber boots? And he was smoking a big cigar.

I don't think that guy's quite right. Both of them, for sure, are not full bags of groceries."

"Yeah. I was thinking that it must get real hot inside his cabin. His house is right over the engine–like ours–but we've got heat insulation, and I'm thinking he doesn't. Or he's just your average three-dollar bill. I don't know, maybe both." Gar was chuckling too, but yawning as he sat on the bunk and took his boots off. He continued to speak though. "Keep going due east, and watch the radar real close. Probably wouldn't hurt to look up at the sky, too, once in a while. Just let me close my eyes for an hour, but don't be afraid to wake me up if anything looks wrong .... geez, it smells like fucking weed in here."

And with that, Gar swung his legs up and under the sleeping bag. The sleeping bag was spread over the narrow bunk along one wall of the main cabin. He was just two yards away from Jeff. Jeff sat on the barstool running seat over on the opposite side. But his seat was forward, at the console of electronics which included the steering wheel and shift.

"Better not get too far away from the nature boys," Gar mumbled before he fell asleep. He was, of course, referring to the free spirited crew of the ***Ima***.

OVER ON THE ***Ima***, Don, still wearing only boots, reflected aloud while puffing his cigar. It was indeed hot in the wheelhouse. "I bought two cigars when I decided to do this thing. One to smoke after I got the stuff loaded, and the other after I get paid. These are just five-dollar cigars. But the next ones I buy will be Cubans, and I won't care what they cost."

"Well, I won't be buying anything to smoke for awhile," said Don's crewman. He was all dressed up in Levis, with bare feet and no shirt. "I'm taking some of this shit home. I don't care what Vince said about that. But I will be buying a new surfboard–maybe a Weber–and a new guitar, too–maybe a Stratocaster."

"It's your call, Pawdna. I didn't hear you say anything about pussy, though."

"Well, with my new board, and new guitar, and my natural physique, I'll get the pussy. Don't you worry about that."

Don laughed. His crewman was a quintessential 97-pound weakling. "Okay, pard. I'm sure you'll do fine." Then: "Oh shit, there's something on the radar. I better call Gar."

"If you call Gar, he's going to yell at you again."

"Okay," Don said. "You're right. Go look out behind us and to the north. I see a big blip, moving fast, on the radar."

Standing in the doorway, the crewman said, "I see it. It's a container ship."

"All right. I guess I'm a little edgy. Doesn't it figure that the ocean gets flat as a skating rink as soon as the load is transferred?"

"Sure smells like weed in here...."

CHAPTER 27

LATE AFTERNOON, JULY 4, 1982.

THEY FOUND THE small fleet of salmon-fishing boats around noon, easily slipping in with them and trolling along with the flotilla for several hours. Then Gar called Don–which startled him badly–and asked him if he wanted to go in early and anchor behind Pigeon Point. Don, audibly shocked, stuttered out a reply.

"Yeah," he managed.

Gar continued, "I'll anchor and you come tie off my stern and we'll barbeque."

"Okay." Don couldn't believe it. Gar's earlier admonitions about the use of the radio at sea had him gun-shy, and he was flabbergasted at Gar's easy invitation and the suddenness with which it appeared.

THE ***IMA*** TRAILED from the ***Visit***'s stern by a single, 25-foot line tied to its bow. Don and Randy, the crewman on the ***Ima***, were on board the ***Visit*** and listening to Gar speak.

All of the men sat around a Weber grill on lawn chairs, watching steaks sizzle in the late-afternoon light. The men drank beer from cans and Jeff reached out occasionally with a pair of tongs, turning the steaks. The aroma was exquisite, the sizzling sound accompanied by the cries of cormorants and gulls wheeling overhead.

"See, out on the ocean I've seen the Coast Guard come up on a fleet and run around with Zodiacs, boarding everybody," Gar explained. "But I've never seen them do that in an anchorage. I think they're afraid they might wake someone up who will start shooting first and ask questions later. In here, we're safe. Plus, we're only a couple of miles away, now. By staying here on my stern until it's time to go down to the cove, we avoid looking suspicious to the other boats anchored here with us. When we move in the middle of the night, I'll tell my Half Moon Bay buddies on the radio that you and I partied late and decided to go down to *Ano Nuevo* so we can sleep in."

"You think of everything," Don said, draining his can of beer. "But I'm not gonna lie to you. I thought you were sampling the goods when you first suggested we barbeque together. I know Vince and them are driving by on the highway, checkin' us with binoculars right now, wondering what we're doing."

"Yeah, well, let 'em wonder. We'll bring 'em their goodies in a few hours, and they'll be just fine." Gar spoke decisively.

"Okay, paawdner," Don drawled, though he'd probably never been south of Bakersfield. "You've done a good job, and it's been a real pleasure working with you." Don seemed to be relaxed and easy now, instead of tense as he had always appeared to be before. Maybe it was the beer.

And the Jimmy Buffett *A-1-A* eight-track tape was playing "A Pirate Looks At Forty." The men quieted to listen to the words.

"Yes, I am a Pirate,
Two-hundred years too late;
The cannons don't thunder,
There's nothin' to plunder;
I'm an over forty victim of fate.
Arriving too late....
Arriving too late."*

Birds wheeled and the sun was a huge red ball on the horizon and the men thought about what it meant to be a pirate in the modern world. Perhaps that's what they were. The steaks sizzled and the pile of empty beer cans piled up and each of the men secretly smiled to himself. Two hundred years too late for the cannons, but not too late for the plunder. Not too late at all.

* Jimmy Buffett, "A Pirate looks at Forty."

CHAPTER 28

MIDNIGHT, JULY 4, 1982.

BOBBING EXACTLY WHERE they'd anchored with Wallace, the faithful lighthouse lined up perfectly over the top of the rock, Gar was nervous about Don, who was crowding the ***Visit***'s stern. This was understandable. It was dark and rocky, and he did not know the anchorage. And the brilliant stabbing beam of the Pigeon Point Lighthouse occasionally bathing the area with its sweeping illumination seemed to make the darkness even blacker. Gar broke radio silence for about three seconds and murmured, "Just tie off my stern again, Don."

Don was perfect, whispering simply, "Roger."

CHUCK CAME UP alongside the ***Visit*** in a Zodiac big enough to haul twenty or thirty bales at a time. It was powered by a fair-sized Mercury outboard. "Fancy meeting you here," Chuckie tittered his high-pitched giggle. And he was spitting like a llama, too.

"Yeah, everything went fine," Gar said. "Have you got any extra guys to help us get this stuff out of the hole? We've got fifty or so bundles up in the fo'c'sle, too. We're stuffed."

Chuck's brother-in-law, a nimble dark-haired man named Gregory, who made his living scuba diving, spoke up enthusiastically. "I'll come up and help." He and one other guy were wet suited in the Zodiac with Chuckie.

"All right," Gar said casually. "Sure is a beautiful night. Here, catch." He tossed Chuck a ten-pound bale that caught him right in the breadbasket.

THE UNLOADING WENT smoothly and much faster than the at-sea transfer. In a matter of minutes the entire cove was redolent with the rich, bittersweet smell of marijuana buds. The odor clung to the men's hair, to their clothing, and seemed to imbue the very air. They had two Zodiacs, and one of them emptied Don in a couple of trips. With Gregory and Jeff tossing bales out of the hold up on deck, and Gar loading them over the side into Zodiacs, they were finished in less than two hours.

And with the last bale tossed to Chuckie, Gar said, "Okay, now you've got the ball."

"Thanks. When you coming to the Ranch?" Chuck asked.

"I think we'll run back to Santa Cruz right now. That's where my pickup is. Then I'll see you later today. How's that sound?"

"Well, I'll call you at the Beach House. That would probably be best. I'm not sure when we'll be completely done. I want to take a little nap later, too."

"Okay, brother-in-law, we'll wait for your call."

ON THE RUN down to Santa Cruz Gar called Cindy, as they had arranged to do beforehand, via the Marine Operator. The code they had agreed upon was simple. If he called using the boat name, ***Cynthia Ann***, everything was cool. If he used some other name, it wasn't.

When the Marine operator asked Cindy if she would accept a call from the fishing vessel ***Cynthia Ann***, Cindy took the call. She was her usual happy, bubbly self, and right away she started saying "Over" before she was even done talking. The relief they shared was almost palpable. Gar jokingly suggested she come to the Beach House and Cindy surprisingly agreed. She said she'd be there for lunch.

Gar was momentarily flabbergasted, but not really surprised that she would travel over four hundred miles in eight hours. He answered simply, "Okay, Hon. I love you."

"I love you, too. Over and out. Over!" Cindy signed off.

CHAPTER 29

JULY 6, 1982.

IT WASN'T UNTIL Tuesday that Vince had all the "tea" moved around. Chuckie had been calling Gar up until that time at the Beach House and telling him not to worry. Then on Tuesday morning Chuck asked Gar to come on down to the Ranch, saying they would follow each other for the ride into Santa Cruz.

Payday! And Gar was excited. So was Cindy. She was going to be the one to count it all. She'd done that for some company she'd worked for, and was very fast with money. She was anxious to prove this to Gar.

THEY ARRIVED AT Vince's house, a nondescript tract home with a neatly-trimmed lawn in the shadow of the Wrigley's Gum Factory, and Don was already there, smoking a cigar. "What's with all these cigars?" Gar wondered. Don looked better with his clothes on, though. He was dressed in pseudo-western style, with round-toed boots and a pearl-snap shirt. Vince was natty in beige chinos, a light-blue cotton shirt, and cordovan loafers. The loafers had tassels, Gar noticed, and he considered whether he should buy a pair when he got paid.

VINCE GOT RIGHT to business. He started stacking bundles of currency on the low, glass coffee table. He called out a new total as he added each rubber-banded packet of bills to the pile. "This is a five, so that makes fifty-five. And this is a ten, so that's sixty-five, and here's another ten so that's seventy-five...."

"What about?" Gar started to speak, but didn't get to finish.

"And here's another ten, so that's eighty-five. I'm paying you the twenty-five bonus I promised. And there's ninety-five, and five more makes a hundred. And I want to thank you guys for doing such a good job." Vince was beaming as he said this.

All of a sudden the cloying scent of Juicy Fruit Gum that was suffusing the neighborhood smelled outstanding. Gar stared at the banded stacks of currency on the table and smacked his lips. His mouth tasted like it was filled with the gum, but there was nothing there.

Gar shuffled the bundles over to Cindy, who had set up a place for herself on the fireplace hearth, and she began counting. She completed the task in record time, finding only a couple of discrepancies. Vince adjusted these without argument.

AFTER A FEW more *atta boys*, Gar and Cindy left. Chuckie stayed at Vince's house, as he'd brought his own truck.

It was almost party time. They just had a couple of stops to make first. At the top of that list was the taxman.

"NOW PLEASE, BILL me for your time," Gar said to his bookkeeper, who conveniently lived in Santa Cruz. He was also Mom's tax person.

Gar had carefully contrived a cover story for the money. He'd been selling fish for cash, and he was wondering now how to pay his bills with it. The tax guy said not to deposit $10,000 at any one time, or the bank would automatically call the IRS. The deposits had to be slightly less than this amount. And it would be necessary to make up copies of receipts for the fish. The receipts needed to balance with the deposits.

This was basic Money Laundering 101.

It was easy and it was fun. Gar and Cindy went to the two Santa Cruz branches of the Bank of America and deposited $9,500 in each. Then it was on to Well's Fargo, where they deposited $9,500 in Cindy's account.

Next, they drove up to the Half Moon Bay Bank of America and Gar deposited another $9,500 in his account. This was followed by a trip to Production Credit Association, where Gar wrote a check for $24,000, catching up his boat loan. Cindy mailed a $4,500 check, from her account, off to the Marine Insurance Company. Then they swung by Cindy and Jeff's mother's house where Jeff was waiting, and they paid him. He was ecstatic to have $20,000 handed to him in cash at one time. Gar cautioned him to be careful with so much money.

THEY MADE LOVE surrounded by the hundred-dollar bills that rained down upon them, bills tossed by the handful up into the air. They had driven over to the Villa Chartier Hotel in San Mateo, with its adjoining Lanai Bar, where they'd previously spent their wedding night. It seemed like the logical place to go to get drunk and screw. The Lanai provided room service to the hotel and had good champagne on the menu. And the exotic tropical bar was right next door. They could go there and eat and suck down *Sidewinder Fangs* in order to keep up their strength.

Life was good.

CHAPTER 30

NEW YEAR, 1983.

GAR AND CINDY were bummed because the Redskins had beat the Forty-Niners in the playoffs. The Skins had won on a horrible call that instant replay continued to depict on every, single sports report. But the couple was ecstatic when Cindy became *late* for her monthly visitor. Football scores suddenly became irrelevant.

BY THE BEGINNING of March, the doctor confirmed Cindy's pregnancy and Cindy called, that same day, to inform her airline. Once a flight attendant does this, she goes on immediate leave. Gar had never seen Cindy so happy. The prospect of motherhood had her glowing like an angel.

THINGS WERE PERFECT for the newlyweds. They were pregnant; and they'd bought a home with an acre out on Elk Valley road in Crescent City. Cindy had a new van that allowed her to cruise down to the Bay Area and shop at her favorite malls. They had a nice circle of friends, couples their own age, they spent time with. And Gar's fishing was somewhat less demanding, allowing him to spend more time at home with Cindy.

Jeff, however, didn't like sitting around. Angus noticed this and finally succeeded in convincing Jeff to go work on his boat.

THEN THAT APRIL, an event occurred that changed everything. Gar left the harbor with a ton of fish carcasses to hang in his crab traps. His crab gear was situated in shallow waters, stretching from the Klamath River mouth and on south for about five miles. The hanging bait caused a slight list to port on the boat. This was because the crates were tied against the port rail on that left side of the boat.

It was a clear spring morning. Rain and a westerly swell were predicted. This meant Gar would have to move his crab pots out of the shallow water, or the swell might stick them in the muddy bottom, and he would risk losing them. This promised to be a big job, and likely not a productive one as there was fewer crabs in the deeper waters.

Because of this, Gar decided they would start making trips, picking up the pots and taking them home. They had two weeks until salmon season opened. This was just enough time to put away the crab gear, switch the boat over, and make it down to Half moon Bay. Or at least to the Farallon Islands.

WHEN THE BOAT was loaded with crab pots, they headed north, up the coast toward Crescent City. The sea was building out of the west. The boat still listed to port, leaning toward the swell that was spanking the ***Visit***'s left side. Gar thought this was cool, because–with the back deck stacked high with traps–had they been leaning away from the swell, it would have tended to roll the pots off the stack. Rolling off pots is not a good thing at all. They're damned expensive and no one wants to lose them.

THE SEA AS they passed the Klamath River mouth was ever more confused, and on the north side, right in front of Three-Mile Rock, a sharp wave slapped the ***Visit*** especially hard on the left side. This occurred just as the boat took a sharp roll into the sideways swell. The wave filled the back deck with water, and all at once the ***Visit*** was lying over well past the danger point.

Gar sensed trouble even before it was apparent. He reached up, as was mandated, and pulled back the throttle, while at the same time he turned the boat away from the list. And this was the exact, wrong thing to do.

A boat turns by rudder and via the stern. So if you want to go right, this is accomplished by the stern swinging left, which points the bow to the right. Imagine a wheel barrow where *you* swing to the left to steer your load to the right.

So when Gar slowed the ***Visit*** down, the boat squatted and took on yet more water. And when he cranked the wheel to the right–he was doing this while broadcasting a 'Mayday' on the radio–the stern swung out so it was directly exposed to the pounding waves.

It buried the back deck instantly.

With the stern and back deck buried in the ocean, the ***Visit*** took water in through not-completely-sealed hatches, and that water, of course, sought the low side, further inverting the vessel in that direction. In a matter of moments, the boat reached a point of no return. The ***Visit*** began to sink and there was no saving her.

The same second Gar had pulled back the throttle, he'd started the Mayday call, saying only his boat name, the number of men onboard (three), Loran reading, and the depth. From that instant until the water was coming in the cabin back door was mere seconds.

It was very fast. And it was irrevocable. In fact, the entire catastrophe took on a nightmarish slow-motion quality that made the experience rather bizarre. Gulls wheeled and screamed mockingly about the foundering boat, and each rushing wave took on a portentous inevitability.

Buster and Steve, who had replaced Jeff this season, were already preparing themselves to abandon ship. Steve had a wet suit hanging by the back door. Buster was putting on a life jacket Gar threw him from under the bunk. Gar never did get one on himself. He started to answer a radio return call in response to the Mayday, but then he realized that the cabin was filling too fast.

They had to get out. In less than one minute the ***Visit*** was on her side in the pounding waves. They had an inflatable life boat on top of the wheelhouse and Gar scrambled to get to it.

THE LIFE RAFT was in a canister up on the ***Visit***'s cabin top. With the boat on its side, and going down rapidly by the stern, the canister was only partly in the water. It was about three foot square in size, a foot off the cabin roof, and held down by a metal band.

The metal hold-down had a catch that would release automatically when the boat was under five-or-more feet of water. It had a punch button on it, too. Gar slammed the button and the canister floated free.

The life raft had a nylon pull cord that was tied to the cabin roof. The idea was that when the canister floated away, the deadheaded pull cord would come tight and trip the inflation mechanism. The manufacturer had learned that a long pull cord was best, as this would allow the canister to float free of the ship's rigging before the line became taut and tripped the inflation cycle.

Steve, an experienced fisherman, knew this about the pull cord. He started peeling line out of the canister. He pulled out a hundred feet before he got resistance and the raft finally inflated.

With inflation, though, came movement. The raft ended up shooting right out into the middle of the mast stays, and the mast was now laid out across the surface of the sea. This was the worst possible scenario. If the life raft got tangled under a mast stay that was going down, the life raft would get dragged down with it and they would lose their only hope.

And this is what happened. A stay began taking the raft under, and the three fishermen stared at it, aghast. This was tragedy on top of tragedy. This couldn't be happening. One of the men must have uttered a prayer that was heard, for the raft suddenly released. But in doing so, it squirted yet further away.

THE THREE MEN were now sitting up on the bow, on the actual side of the boat. The rest of the boat was under water. Steve, who knew about sinking boats from another experience (that's why he kept his wet suit hanging by the back door), cautioned they should jump in before the boat completely sank if they didn't want to get sucked under—a myth that only happens when the giant propellers of large ships are still spinning when they go down. The problem with jumping was that they had to jump in away from the side containing the tangled rigging, and that meant jumping in away from the life raft. The wind tore at their clothes as they discussed this, and the waves splashed already cold and sodden garments. There was a natural reluctance to jump.

But they did it. The three men leaped into the waves. The choice now was to tread water until the boat completely sank, clearing the way to the life raft, or swim around the wreckage and try to make it to the life-saving device. The men were quickly separated by the crashing waves, and Gar found himself alone.

And he was foundering. He had not had time to take off his heavy rubber boots, and they were dragging him down. Each time Gar struggled to remove one of the boots, he sank down beneath the waves. And he couldn't get it off before he had to scramble back up for air. He kept trying and trying and felt his strength beginning to fail.

And the raft was blowing further and further away.

BUSTER AND STEVE made it to the raft, but Gar continued to struggle without flotation. He simply could not shed his boots. He told himself this was ridiculous, that he was going to drown if he didn't get the damned things off, but try as he might he couldn't get it done. They were literally dragging him down. As he struggled and struggled and felt his strength fail, he was filled with a sense of sadness.

A review of his life was beginning to pass through his mind. This really does happen. Cindy and the thought of their unborn child were Gar's focus, and he fought desperately to remain afloat. Then it began to seem hopeless. His legs weighed a ton, he was chilled almost to the point of unconsciousness, and the raft was still a hundred feet away. He wanted to call out for help but was too weak.

He prayed instead. He prayed and fought with his last remaining strength.

Then a huge swell picked him up and shoved him toward the raft, while at the same time the raft slid off the back side of another swell and back towards Gar. In the twinkling of an eye, Gar was at the opening of the covered raft, and Buster and Steve were hauling him in.

It was truly a miracle, and Gar credited Cindy and their soon-to-be-born child as the reason God answered his prayer.

But the ***Visit*** was lost.

CHAPTER 31

SPRING, 1983.

DISENCHANTED, DEPRESSED AND dour, Cindy and Gar sat in the kitchen of their Crescent City home, out in the woods at the end of Heacock Lane. The enticing smell of oatmeal-raisin cookies filled their little house. Cindy was baking pan after pan of them, trying to seduce Gar into eating. Gar was the one who was dour. When a fisherman loses his boat, he loses a piece of his soul. It was pouring rain outside. The storm that had sunk the ***Visit*** was still upon them. But it was warm and cozy inside their house.

Cindy, at the dining room table, spoke reasonably to Gar, who was across the room at a desk fitted into one corner of the dining area. "You can't quit," she said. "It's who you are." Her hands rested flat on her now prominent tummy.

Gar answered her with the same unenthusiastic monotone he had maintained since losing the boat the day before, "I have always said that I would fish hard and not worry about the risk until I lost a boat. A lot of guys go their whole lives without losing a boat. But I have always maintained that I would fish until that point, then if I ever sink, that will be the end of it. I don't want to do it anymore, now. It's not the same. I guess it's like when your woman goes out on you.

The trust is broken and it will never come back." Gar sniffed. He had an arctic-sized cold since the sinking that he couldn't seem to shake.

"Well!" Cindy considered this remark only briefly. She definitely had something to say about it. "If you want to say that, then when your girl friend–or woman, as you say–cheats on you, you get a new and better woman, one you can trust. That's all."

Gar stared at her. She had a point. Gar was sitting at the desk because that's where the phone was. It rang steadily that entire day. It rang again. Gar talked a minute, hung up, turned back to Cindy.

"That was Jeff," he told her. "He and Kim are coming over."

JEFF AND HIS lovely, vivacious wife Kim arrived and listened to the story of the sinking with rapt attention. They gobbled down cookies as they listened, Kim helping Cindy to take one batch out of the oven and put yet another in. When Gar had completed the tale, it was Jeff who came straight to the point.

"So what are you going to do about a new boat?" he demanded.

"You and your sister been talking?" Gar shot a glance at Cindy.

"No."

"But my brother's right," Cindy interjected.

"You have to get another boat." This time Kim weighed in. She spoke plaintively. "My little boy thinks his uncle Gar is the one that catches all the fish sticks he likes to eat. All those crabs at Safeway, too. You can't not fish anymore." Kim had a five-year old son from a previous marriage.

Gar didn't know what to say. It wasn't fear that kept him wavering with uncertainty so much as disgust. When you lost your boat, you called it quits. Didn't you?

THE PHONE RANG again. "Lips!" Came the response after Gar said hello. It was Michael McHenry. "Tell me what happened," he said.

After listening to the story, Michael adopted a fatherly tone. "This is all about courage, Lips. Are you determined enough to get back on the horse? And I'll tell you what. There's a lot of guys that wish they were in your shoes. You're gonna get insurance money to start all over again, with a newer and better boat. It's a new beginning. I know I get tired of my old tub sometimes, but I'm stuck with her. You figured what you're going to do yet?"

"No. Not exactly. I'm waiting for the boat surveyor now. He's going to come interview me on what happened, then report to the insurance company. My agent says it's just a formality. I guess when I get the check I'll figure it all out."

"Okay, kid. We're pulling for you down here. Let us know if we can do anything. I'll let you go. Sounds like you've got a house full of company." Mike was done.

"Okay, Mackerel, thanks for that." Gar hung up.

"Well?" Cindy knew how much influence Michael had on Gar.

"All right, Honey Bun. I guess we can take a look. You going to feel like driving around boat shopping?" Gar was worried about her now obvious "condition".

"Have you seen me not do anything since I got pregnant?" She challenged him with mock severity, but she was clearly pleased that his outlook had been changed by his old fishing mentor.

"No. No, you've been busier than before, actually."

"Well, if you need to travel around to look at boats, I'm driving." She spoke matter of factly.

"Okay, I guess it wouldn't hurt to look. Geno told me I should come up to Newport. And I know there's a boat broker down in Fort Bragg. We can check those out for starters."

"That's better!" Cindy said, exultant. She rose to her feet, dusted flour briskly from her hands onto an apron, and went to retrieve another batch of cookies from the oven. Gar gazed at her retreating figure, bemused.

LATE THAT SPRING, she drove Gar to Fort Bragg, and there she convinced him they should buy the ***Proudfoot***. She didn't pick it out for him. But when she saw how his eyes lit up when looking the boat over, she knew it was what he wanted.

CHAPTER 32

FALL, 1983.

THE ***PROUDFOOT*** WAS a sister ship to the ***Johnny T***. She was constructed of steel, reached just under fifty feet in length, and had a bottom designed like a duck's underbelly. What made her significantly different from the ***Visit*** was that her bottom had *wings* extending out perpendicular to the keel, five feet under water and flat and parallel to the water's surface. This duck-belly and bat-wing configuration gave the boat a wonderfully easy ride. Unlike her predecessor, the ***Proudfoot*** was not a roller. And the boat was powered by a four-cycle Cummins Diesel that *chugged* rather than *screamed*. This was like the difference between a four-cycle Harley Davidson and a two-cycle dirt bike. It was a most pleasing difference, indeed.

Steel construction made for many more options when trying to rig new or different equipment. With steel, things can be welded on or cut off, and the boat does not lose any of its integrity. Once a hole is drilled in wood, the plank is forever weakened. She wasn't as big a steel boat as the ***Merva W***, which remained Gar's dream boat, but she was a step in that direction.

Gar got the new and better replacement for the old ***Visit***, and he was happy Cindy and Michael had brought him to his senses. She was a beauty. Built right there on the Noyo River, the boat enjoyed a sterling reputation.

He, Buster and Cindy cleaned the ***Proudfoot*** from stem to stern while down in Fort Bragg, and Gar had it salmon fishing at Shelter cove, north of Fort Bragg, by the fourth of July. With *El Nino* still affecting the salmon fishing, Gar's abbreviated salmon season was no more than a shake-down cruise for the new boat. Nonetheless, the mere fact of the vessel indicated a new start, and he was proud to own her. And that fall, Gar, Buster, and Jeff, who couldn't wait to leave Angus, adapted the ***Visit***'s spare crab-pulling equipment (fortunately stored in the gear shed and not lost) to the ***Proudfoot***. And they readied the crab pots for the coming winter season.

THE BIG EVENT that fall was on September second, when their son, Jasmer, was born. After a long, arduous eighteen hours of labor, during which Gar held Cindy through every contraction, Jas came out, but only after Gar pushed on Cindy's tummy. Jasmer came down the chute butt first, and he got stuck. When the obviously frightened doctor said, "Nurse, push <u>hard</u> on her stomach or we're going to lose this one!" Gar moved in, admonishing the nurse.

"I know I can push harder than you," he snapped. And he lined up about where Jasmer's head was, and pushed until the infant popped out from between the pelvic bones.

Then when the doctor was struggling with a tangle of oxygen and other unlabeled tubes, Gars' fishboat instincts were triggered and he jumped right in, unsnarling the mess of hoses and lines so the doctor could go to work on Jasmer. Though Jasmer went blue, the doc eventually got him breathing normally. Ever after that day, Gar felt certain his pushing and untangling had saved his son's life.

It was touch and go from the beginning of the actual birthing, but Cindy was amazing. It was her strength that gave Gar a healthy seven-pound boy. In fisherman's speak, he was a "Nice Medium!"

THE NURSES FINALLY chased Gar out, telling him to go home and sleep. On that early morning drive home, going up the pretty country lane called Elk Valley Road, Gar felt like he had been transported to nirvana. He understood life and smiled at its simplicity. He had a beautiful wife, and now a very handsome son.

He could not imagine his existence being any better than this. He waved at the red robins, as they hopped around through the grassy fields after worms, and shouted into the morning stillness.

"I got a son, and he's gonna be president one day! Or he'll quarterback for the Forty-Niners! Or maybe both!!"

It was a beautiful fall morning. The sun had never shone any brighter than it did on this day.

CHAPTER 33

SPRING, 1984.

GAR SNATCHED UP the phone on the desk in the dining room in time to hear Chuckie expectorating what sounded like a lunger. Hardly a pleasant sound.

"That you, brother-in-law?" Gar said, rather than hello.

"How'd you know it was me?" Chuck was amazed.

"I could hear the dogs barking out in their kennels." Gar lied.

"Oh, yeah. Yeah, we've got about two hundred dogs right now. One gets going and then they all go. Hey, you need to come down here. Wallace wants to talk to you."

"Really. What happened to Vince" There'd been some animosity after their 1982 scam, when Chuckie and Gar realized that they had put the whole operation together and only made a hundred thousand apiece, while Vince made more than a half-million for doing almost nothing. Two years later, they were still upset about it.

"No. Vince is out. Wallace is going to work directly with you and me." Chuck said.

"All right. I can come down this weekend. I'll bring Cindy and my new son, Jasmer. I'm sure my sister would like to see her new nephew," Gar said.

"Yeah, and your boy Jasmer can meet his cousin Jennifer." Chuckie laughed. "Where did you get the name Jasmer, by the way?"

"Well, Cindy's father was killed when she was only, like about two, and his name was Donnie Jasmer. So we named him after her Dad. We kind of decided Donnie was too common, and went with Jasmer instead. Oh yeah, that's right Jennifer is what, four months older? Jasmer was born September second."

Gar reeled off random thoughts aloud, mainly for Cindy's benefit. She was sitting right there in her easy chair, breast feeding their "big boy," as they liked to call him. There had been some disagreement on the name Jasmer, actually, and Gar was trying to smooth that over. And he wanted to give a bit of warning to Cindy that they were about to take a road trip south, possibly for money. Lord knew, they needed it. The crab season had been a poor one and they were broke.

"No, Jennifer was born in March, so she's what? Six months older?" Chuck figured it out.

"We'll have to watch them in about fifteen years. I don't want them to become kissin' cousins." Gar laughed now, and ended the call. "See you this weekend."

"All right," Chuck said. "Call us when you get here, and I'll set up a meeting with Wallace. He's ready to roll."

THAT WEEKEND GAR met Wallace and Chuckie at the Ranch. Wallace appeared to be unchanged. He kept a stinking black cigar screwed into his face and he talked around it. He said he had a similar-sized load coming in early July, a load of Thai-weed from Thailand once again, and he questioned Gar about the size of the ***Proudfoot***'s fish hold. Gar confirmed that it was at least twenty-five percent larger than the ***Visit***'s hold, and so more than adequate. Wallace said he saw no need, then for a second boat. And since Vince was not involved, he could double Gar's payment to $200,000. Gar got him to go $250,000, and the deal was made. But Gar insisted that Wallace advance him $20,000 this time, in order to pay bills until July.

The fourth was on a Wednesday this year, so they were shooting for a Saturday, July seventh pickup. This was to be followed by a July eighth offload at Smuggler's Cove. The name *Smuggler's* had almost permanently replaced *Bootlegger's* among Gar, Chuck and their small group.

It wasn't Prohibition and the 1920's anymore. But, then again, it might just as well have been.

CHAPTER 34

EARLY SUMMER, 1984.

MIKE McCUTCHEON AND his long-time confidant, Ronny, had discovered the truth about the source of Gar's supplemental income. The three fishermen were good friends as well as running partners. Gar had tried explaining away his better-than-it-should-have-been income with stories of monetary gifts from parents and in-laws. Neither Mike nor Ron believed it, however, and they constantly whispered to Gar that they'd like to get involved, and to please keep that in mind. They both had their own boats and were trustworthy seamen, and they had a lot to offer.

So when Wallace offered Gar the new contract, Gar tried to think of a way to include Mike and Ronny. And there was Buster and Jeff to think about. The $250,000 was mentally divided dozens of times before Gar finally had it figured out. He spoke to the men individually, and persuaded everyone to go along with his assigned part of the plan. The smartest way to lock a guy in, Gar discovered, was to lay out what the job entailed, then ask the prospective employee how much it would take to make him happy. Invariably the person would be tentative and ask for much less than Gar would have offered.

The following roles and terms were agreed to. Jeff and Buster would take the ***Proudfoot***, transfer the entire load of Thai-weed from point A to point B, and get paid $50,000 and $25,000 respectively for their work. Mike would maintain his presence in the area as back-up, in case the ***Proudfoot*** broke down. And he would fake a sinking to distract the Coast Guard should they get too close. Ronny would simply haul Gar out there so he could oversee things. This was requested by Wallace because the sailboat crew of two years before had insisted that Gar be on site. Mike and Ronny would receive $25,000 each. And Gar would end up with $125,000.

Gar was pleased that he had arranged to distance himself from ever actually possessing any of the potent Thai-weed, yet was still making six figures on the deal. But he was slightly deflated by the difference between a quarter-million dollars and an eighth-of-a-million dollars.

CHAPTER 35

JULY, 1984.

RONNY HAD THE ***Coho***, and Mike had the ***Carol Ann***. Both of these were forty-some foot older wood boats of the same vintage as the ***Visit***.

Some years earlier, Gar bastardized Mike's name to Mike Minkia-Cutcheon (instead of McCutcheon). Minkia, for short. Minkia is a popular Italian cuss word, and for whatever the reason the name stuck. To most it was meaningless; just another handle fishermen were famous for having. Fishermen talk on many radios, mostly on illegal frequencies, and rarely use real names or call signs. To Italian speakers, however, Minkia always got a laugh. It fit well with Mike's jovial personality.

Gar and Mike had always gotten along well together, as they were very much alike. Both were big men, red-neck type drinkers, happy go lucky in their personal lives, and very serious about fishing. They even looked alike, although Mike was bigger, dark eyed, and maybe a little bit quicker to laugh. Both of them liked to dress up before going out on the town. To those who did not know them, they would never have been mistaken for fishermen.

Ronny, on the other hand, wore an enormous red beard it had taken him ten years to grow, was light in hair color and complexion, and he never wore anything but fishermen's plaid shirts and black Big Ben work pants. And Ronny rarely drank; he was more of a stoner than Mike or Gar. He did, though, have the type of outlook that forever searched for the humor in things. And what was perhaps most important, Ronny had the patience necessary to put up with Minkia and Lips when they were drinking.

IT WORKED OUT well for Ronny. He gave his crewman a paid trip home to Trinidad (the town north of Eureka, not the island). Bus fare to Trinidad was much cheaper than paying a smuggler's wage. And there would be one less person in the know.

Gar became Ronny's crewman, and they had an easy time together while running out of Moss Landing to *The Cross*. Ronny let Gar sleep the first eight hours, then woke him up to a nice bacon and egg breakfast. For the previous smuggling operation, Gar had left a few days early. This time they left at three o'clock on the Saturday morning of the intended rendezvous, and ran twelve hours straight to get to the Cross.

THE SMALL ARMADA arrived on the spot in the middle of the afternoon. The sailboat was there, drifting, and had neatly-coiled lines ready on deck. And they had an inflated Zodiac trailing alongside.

"Mares tails and mackerel scales" were what fishermen called the configuration of clouds in the skies, clouds that presaged wind and possibly rain. But the sun still shined brightly in the west, on its way down to meet with the deep blue sea.

WITH GAR UP on the bow, Ronny maneuvered the ***Coho*** to the stern of the sailboat. The sea conditions were the same as for the previous operation–sloppy. Gar hollered first.

"I didn't bring any propane, or any cocaine, this time," he said. "How have you guys been?"

"Hey, Gar. We're cool. Let's just get this done, and we'll go into port and get it all." It was black beard again, and he sounded tired. He'd aged in the two years since Gar had met him here on these same coordinates in the North Pacific. Maybe he had been through trials such as Gar had experienced. Losing a boat and having a son, for example. The type of things that mature a man but leave him spread a little thinner.

"Okay, Tom." Gar remembered the man's name. That's my boat over there, the ***Proudfoot***, with my same crewman, Jeff, at the wheel. He'll pull over and you guys do the same hook-up. That cool with you? You got enough guys to do it, or do you need me to come over?'

"No, Gar, we're all right. We're much better prepared this time. All the packages are dug out and loose from their hiding places. We did a heavy exercise program this time while crossing over. We're ready to roll on this end.

"All right, Tom. Sounds good. I'm going to back off and let you guys go to work. I'll be standing close by and monitoring channel eighteen on the VHF and channel eight on the C.B. Just whistle if you need anything." Gar signaled Ronny to back away while waving goodbye to the sailors.

"You're still one *bad hombre*!" Tom smiled and waved him off.

JEFF PULLED THE ***Proudfoot*** over while Gar urged Ronny to hang real close. Minkia was keeping his distance. Minkia was not as lucky as Ronny in that he had a crewman, Sonny, who he would have to pay more than bus fare. Sonny was a part time crank dealer and had a bit of a hold on Minkia. He would prove to be very bad news.

Gar was nervous as he watched Jeff and Buster make the hook up with the sailboat. They used the same technique Gar had utilized for the previous operation.

Still, shit happens. Everything about an operation like this is a worrisome matter. Gar could smell the pungent aroma of the Thai-weed from half a football field away. The smell wafted across on the breeze, evoking images of exotic Thailand and golden statues of Buddha. He dispelled these thoughts with an effort. This was serious business and there was work to be done.

CHAPTER 36

SUNDAY MORNING.

ON THE WAY back in, as they had agreed upon earlier, the three boats stopped while the ***Coho*** and ***Carol Ann*** took turns easing up to the ***Proudfoot*** stern so Jeff could throw over a fat bundle. A little extra for Ronny, Mike and Sonny to put in their coffers. Even though they had named their own prices, and gotten what they bargained for, when something of that much value comes into possession, people inevitably want more. Gar instructed Jeff and Buster to pick out three of the fattest packages, pass one each to Ronny and Mike, and secret the last in a hidey-hole they'd made on the ***Proudfoot***. This, he prayed, would satisfy everyone's avarice.

The weed was packaged in a clear, thick cellophane that was meticulously folded around the odd-sized but cubed bundles. There was some sort of seal to the packages. Gar thought they were partially heat-sealed.

Wallace said that the Thailanders had crude presses that would press the pot so tight it took steam to loosen it. His loads, though, were pressed just until they could hear the first seed crack. Tight, but not so tight it couldn't be broken apart with minimal hand strength.

The bundles averaged ten pounds apiece, but the three Jeff selected were maybe closer to fifteen pounds. Handled correctly, the sale of these bundles would net Ronny and Mike as much again as the wage they were to receive. It would make for a nice rainy day fund for Gar, Jeff and Buster, too.

THE BOATS TROLLED salmon gear four or five miles off of Pigeon Point to pass the waning hours of that Sunday afternoon. They didn't catch many fish. When darkness descended, Jeff motored in and anchored right where he needed to be in Smuggler's cove. Ronny took the ***Coho*** to an anchorage a couple of miles north of the cove at the Pigeon Point Anchorage. Everybody was to remain vigilant. Mike and Ronny were ready to fake an accident or sinking in case the Coast Guard should arrive on scene.

They had any possible contingency pretty well covered. They thought they did, anyway, as logistically a Coast Guard vessel had to come from either the north or the south. But they hadn't counted on a helicopter dropping in from above.

AT ELEVEN O'CLOCK, just minutes before the beach guys were to launch their Zodiacs, a Coast Guard helicopter buzzed over Mike in the *Ano Nuevo* anchorage. The second he heard the *whuppity-whup* of the chopper, and a moment before they lit him up with their spotlight, Mike whispered into the C.B. channel, "We got company.... Don't move."

Then he went silent for several minutes, minutes which seemed like an eternity to the rest of them.

"Did you hear that?" Jeff said to Buster.

"Fuck yeah, I heard it." Buster was a big Swedish-looking country boy who didn't scare easily. But he had no control over his adrenaline tonight.

THE BEACH CREW were not monitoring that channel, so they kept going with their preparations. But they had been cautioned not to launch until they got a series of flashlight blinks. It was only a few hundred yards from beach to boat. But no blinking light appeared.

They sensed, then, that something was wrong. They could see the ***Proudfoot*** bobbing peacefully in the pale moonlight. It was a clear evening with about half a moon. After a whispered consultation, they tried flashing. But they stopped when they heard the helicopter approaching.

They froze in their tracks, whispered down the chain of people running from the beach up to the trucks to shut up and look inconspicuous. A preposterous command, since everyone was dressed in black and there was absolutely no cover offering concealment.

THEY COULD SEE the spotlight of the helicopter, now, as it worked its way up the coastline toward them. The chopper guys were working the light methodically, obviously looking for something. They were not buzzing up the coast at speed, intent upon a destination, but rather meandering, as though engaged in a search. When it got to the ***Proudfoot*** floating innocently at anchor, with nothing but an anchor light at the top of the mast indicating any sign of life, the spotlight lingered for just a moment then moved on.

Everyone involved breathed a sigh of relief as they watched the chopper continue up the coast. Gar and

Ronny in the Pigeon Point anchorage were the last to see it pass. And when the chopper passed over the ***Coho***, Gar called out and said, "I think they're looking for someone besides us. Maybe another boat's overdue, or maybe they're just going through the motions. Let's get on with it."

Minkia came on the radio, laughing nervously, and said, "I ain't gonna try to bullshit anybody. I fucking near shit my drawers when those guys came by."

Gar came back and acknowledged Mike with the same high-strung but relieved laughter, then called out to Jeff. "Are you guys all right, Jeffery?"

Jeff, who is all about efficiency, replied calmly. "No problem. We're sending the signal now." He would later admit, under the influence of a lot of tequila, that he and Buster had about peed their pants, too.

"Let's clear the radios, then," Gar said. "And get this done."

THE LIGHT ATOP the *Candle Stick* at Pigeon Point seemed to thrum at a slowed and measured rate as it made its circular rounds, calming the pulse of the pack of smugglers. And halfway between where Gar sat on the **Coho** and Jeff unloaded the weed, customers at the Beach House clinked glasses, commenting on the helicopter that had lit up the surf before them on Gazos Beach.

CHAPTER 37

SUMMER/FALL, 1984.

THEY TOOK THE ***Proudfoot*** some time before dawn. A person who does not make his living from the sea can hardly begin to understand what it feels like to have a boat disappear, but it is like a father standing in a crowd holding the hand of his young child one minute, and the next minute having that little hand slip away. It is simply devastating to lose a boat. And in this instance, a number of things led up to it.

AFTER UNLOADING THE weed, Jeff plucked Gar off the stern of the ***Coho*** and they ran down to Santa Cruz. Jeff and Buster stayed in Santa Cruz to celebrate, while Gar drove up to the Beach House in order to console Mom. She and Jack had had a donnybrook over money. The Beach House was operating in the red. They were fighting over a number of things, but the disagreement was compounded by financial problems. The first $10,000 Gar received went toward resolving the financial problems of the Beach house.

It was a short stay at the restaurant. Gar hurried back down to Santa Cruz to collect, pay everyone, pick up Buster and Jeff, and then return to Crescent City where Cindy and Jasmer anxiously awaited him.

Cindy was four-and-a-half months pregnant with their second child. After the initial hugs with *Big Boy* and Cindy, he spoke decisively to her.

"I'm done," he stated. "Forever. No more smuggling. I'm going to go salmon fishing the rest of the summer, or until the Feds close the season. Then I'm going to fix the boat up real nice for crabs. And buy some more pots, too."

"You mean you're going back to being Garaloney, the fisherman. No more, what did Jeff say those guys on the sailboat called you? *Bad Hombre*. No more *Bad Hombre*? And I kind of liked my *Bad Hombre*." She said this and she cuddled up close. Well, as close as she could with a distended tummy. Cindy's a born cuddler, so she made it work.

"No more, Honey Bun. I'm done. I figure I've got enough to make a highliner out of the ole' ***Proudfoot***. My smuggling days are over." A highliner is a consistent top producer. A boat that always returns with the largest catch is admiringly referred to by fellow fishermen as a highliner. The term actually refers to the waterline on a floating boat. When the hold of the boat is filled with a weighty catch, the boat rides lower in the water. So the water line is higher on the hull. Such a boat is instantly and momentarily transformed into a highliner. And a fisherman who catches a lot of fish is referred to as a highliner. There can be no finer compliment to a fisherman.

THE NEXT DAY, the Feds announced such stringent closures for the rest of the salmon season that it was not worth fishing any more this year. So Gar drove back down to Santa Cruz, and he hauled the boat out of the water at Harbor Marine. There he took the bottom down to bare steel and renewed the paint with the latest epoxies, as well as replacing all the zincs. Just about everything that was built of wood was replaced, too. Ironbark (a very hard wood) chafe guards were attached to the hull below the waterline and aft of midship where the crab pots bump when being pulled from the sea.

Chris, the previous owner of the ***Proudfoot*** who carried the boat loan, was sent a double payment.

After all this, Gar's payoff was much diminished. Not so much so, yet, that Cindy and Gar were worried about it. But they had Cindy's hospital stay with the new baby drawing near. When Jasmer was born, Cindy's insurance cancelled at the last minute. They would have to pay out of pocket this time too.

THE CLOSURES WERE becoming so frequent that most of Gar's running partners were seeking other fisheries. Some began trawling for bottom fish. Others tried shrimping. Anything to make the boat payments and keep fuel in the tanks. For Gar, this was extremely depressing. He was stubborn, and would not consider giving up his vow to become the greatest salmon fisherman ever; or at least as good as Michael.

And that is what made the call from the insurance company so disturbing. Because Gar had a total loss claim on his record from the sinking of the ***Visit***, neither Nashburg nor any other insurance company would insure him. Due to the rash of sinkings that the stringent salmon regulations begat–to make ends meet, fishermen had to fish in tougher weather, and this took its toll in lives and boats–the insurance company underwriters were becoming very particular about who they insured.

Gar was driving the 425 miles each way from Crescent City to Santa Cruz, and it seemed like he was doing it every few days. The Beach House, 35 miles north of Santa Cruz, was where Gar bartended some nights, and staged trips back to Crescent City. The unfortunate thing was their restaurant and bar, that had given them so much over the last decade, was coming apart so fast that no matter how much effort Gar put into it, it was not enough. The business was hemorrhaging money. And nothing they tried seemed to help.

Jack left Gar's mother and moved to Santa Cruz with his new paramour. This was almost the last straw. But Mom, who was as stubborn as Gar, hung on. Until she met Lou. Lou swept her off her feet, and that same summer Mom sold the Beach house and moved to Santa Cruz to be with him.

Lou Alongi, nicknamed "Duke" by his Dirty Dozen pals, was a tough, old, Italian grocer who had bought supermarkets low and sold them high. Then he retired, with eight figures in the bank, to a life of leisure in Santa Cruz. After his wife passed away, he moped around until Annabel (Mom) came into his life. Annabel doesn't allow anyone to mope. She's the type that believes there is too much to do and there is just no time to sit around and pine away.

She quickly put the Beach House behind her. And she went to work keeping Lou busy.

WITH THE BEACH House sold, Gar ran the ***Proudfoot*** back up to Crescent City. He put the boat up on the marine ways at Fashion Blacksmith. Raised deck hatches were cut off and flanged so they could unbolt in winter, when flush hatches would bolt on for crabbing. The fish hold was partitioned off watertight, so it could be flooded in order to live-tank crab.

And steel guards were retrofitted around the bat-wings so they wouldn't snag crab lines or buoys.

Because the shipfitters at Fashion do not allow work to be done by the owner of the boat while it's in their yard, Gar took the time while they worked to make a number of trips back and forth to Bodega Bay and Fortuna, shuffling 35 new crab traps at a time out to the home in Elk Valley. There, Buster and Jeff were put to work full time painting buoys and splicing lines to rig the pots.

Gar was stamping out so many fires that he had to buy a new pickup truck. He wore the old one out driving from project to project. Or was it forest fire to forest fire?

THEN CHRIS, THE man who carried the boat loan, called Gar at his home. He said that Nashburg Insurance Company had notified him that the loan was no longer insured, and he wondered what Gar wanted to do about it. He was a real asshole, with a supercilious attitude. He was a person of Angus's ilk–a surfer. And he was maybe even more arrogant than Angus.

But after careful and repeated explanation, Chris was made to understand that Gar had sufficient collateral, should Chris need to come after the loan balance (in the event of a sinking, for example). Chris finally agreed not to worry about the insurance for six months. Gar said he believed that he could pay off the boat entirely after the crabbing season. There was a good sign of crab, and Gar would fish 500 traps, round the clock, with lights this year. He expected a six-figure season. Chris, vainglorious and greedy, relished the thought of a large chunk of cash in the not-too-distant future. Or so it seemed.

TWO SHIPYARD UNDERTAKINGS later, Gar continued modifying the boat for crab fishing. He had another one of his famous laundry lists of things to do to the boat while it sat in the slip in the Crescent City boat harbor. Welder, torches, and a host of tools hauled down from the house were placed aboard the vessel.

IT WAS THE welder sitting on the float next to his slip that tipped him off. He came walking down the dock after a breakfast of toast, eggs, and coffee, ready to put in a full day. He walked right by his slip. This was easy to do because the ***Proudfoot*** was not in it. Then he turned back, and he noticed the welder and torches sitting on the float. They had been locked in the cabin the evening before. That was when he knew something was terribly wrong. He felt like he had been punched in the heart with a fist.

THE MOST COMMON fisherman's nightmare, by far, is to come down to the slip one morning and find the boat sitting on the bottom with just the mast poking out of the water. Every boater has at least heard, and likely even witnessed such a thing.

When Gar realized that it was <u>his</u> welder sitting next to the empty slip, his first instinct was to peer into the water in the hope of spotting the boat. This was a futile hope, but perhaps better than the thought that this was a harbinger of worse things yet to come. There was always a dread, vanguard in his mind, that the Feds might come to arrest him for his previous transgressions, and this thought manifested a terrifying image now.

A fifteen-foot length of stiff cardboard tube, empty now after the antenna it enclosed had been mounted on the boat, laid on the dock. Gar used it as a prod to fish around in the water, searching for his boat. It was as ridiculous as it was futile.

He went up the dock asking around, and one friend suggested he call out on the local frequency and ask if anyone had seen his boat. Gar did this, and got an immediate response. His boat was seen leaving the harbor just before daylight, and there had been a fisherman-looking guy on the back deck smoking when it went by him. "The smoker waved, too," he was told. The thought of the man waving stunned him.

GAR CALLED CINDY. She said she'd be right down to meet him at the Coast Guard station. The Coasties went into immediate action, dispatching a helicopter to search for the ***Proudfoot***. The boat was now logged as stolen.

Based on the information that the early-morning spotter had given, the chopper plotted a probable course and speed and flew right to the boat, which was headed full throttle to the south. Once positively identified, a cutter was dispatched to intercept the ***Proudfoot***. When the cutter came up on the vessel, with emergency lights radiating, the thieves pulled the boat out of gear and came out on deck.

The Coast Guard boarded and questioned the men. They said they were two Fort Bragg fishermen, acting on behalf of an owner who was enforcing his right to seize the boat due to Gar's inability to maintain insurance. Since the boat was documented in Cindy and Gar's names, and the thieves did not have any paperwork from a federal judge that gave them the right to take the boat, the Coast Guard captain ordered them to follow the cutter into Eureka, where Cindy and Gar would be waiting to take back their boat.

IT WAS A long drive south from Crescent City to Eureka to meet the boat. Gar was angry, and Cindy, more affected by this pregnancy than her last, was disconcerted as well. They were both aware that this was only a temporary fix, as Chris would likely get a court order for seizure at some point because Gar was uninsurable.

The cash they had on hand might pay off the loan and resolve this mess, but they still had several months to go until crab season. A baby was due, there were numerous personal and professional financial commitments to meet, the crab gear was only half rigged, and the boat was not yet ready for the fishing season.

Gar had them spread very thin. It was as if he had one foot on the rail of one rowboat, and the other foot on the rail of a second rowboat, and the two boats were drifting inexorably apart.

Cindy cried all the way on the long drive south from Crescent City to Eureka to retrieve the boat. And Gar drove in furious silence

CHAPTER 38

FALL, 1984.

CHRIS AND HIS attorney, Mitch Murphy, met at the Federal Courthouse at 312 North Spring Street in downtown Los Angeles. Murphy was actually an accident attorney complete with TV advertisements. His favorite pursuit, however, was to sue drug companies in national class-action suits. Today he'd do his wife's brother a favor and file a prayer for an *In Rem* Maritime Lien under the Supplemental Rules for Certain Admiralty and Maritime Claims. It was not a complicated pleading, but Murphy would not let Chris know that.

They'd first get the lien, then move under Rule C for an arrest warrant wherein the ***Proudfoot*** herself would be arrested and then seized. It is under the bailiwick of the U.S. Marshals to execute boat seizures. The Marshals not only charge for this service, they normally hold the property in a contract boatyard for a period of time while the court and litigants sort things out. This will accrue many more expenses.

Murphy explained this to Chris, and added that he was certain he could get the lien as well as intimidate Gar. "I'll scare him so silly he'll likely sign over his first born in order to get us off his back."

"I don't care about his first born," Chris lamented. Chris was a nicely dressed thin man with a balding head and the prominent eyes of a crack smoker. This was unusual in a middle-aged man. His eyes were disproportionately large in a thin face, and he blinked them rapidly when he spoke.

"I just want the rest of my money," he cried, "and I want it now. I don't want to wait six more years. I know he's got it, or can get it. He told me that when I asked him what he wanted to do about the insurance."

The court clerk, a tired older woman with vagrant strands of graying hair dangling about her face, accepted the complaint and filing fee with weary indifference. She stamped it "Filed", after looking through it, and then asked, "Will that be all?"

Murphy asserted, "You didn't assign us a case number."

"Yes, you're right," grouched the woman. "I don't have this month's judge rotation figured out. Wait a minute. Okay, Judge Hatter would be up next, so your number will be C84-9275-TJH. Here, let me stamp that on your copy."

And, BAM!, she hit the front page with her number stamp, and the action had now officially begun.

WALKING OUT, CHRIS spoke to Murphy. "I guess $150 is cheap for a filing fee, considering Gar will cough up $32,000 as soon as you get a hold of him."

"Hell." Murphy spat the word with contempt. He adjusted a Men's Warehouse brown suit on his 300 pound, 6'5" frame. "I might be able to coerce him into more than that, telling him we're going to bring a separate civil suit for ancillary damages. Damn, I wish you both didn't live in California. I could bring a Federal action under diversity of citizenship if you were in two different states."

"Hmmm," Chris agreed uncertainly.

"It doesn't matter," Murphy continued. "I won't be filing a separate suit, anyway. I'm just going to scare the shit out of him, so he throws money at us until we go away."

"Judas Priest!" Chris was excited now. He was caught up in the process and the lawyer's words. "I'm glad you're on my team. You really are a son of a bitch, aren't you?"

"And then some." Murphy laughed out loud.

MOM'S NEW BOYFRIEND, Lou, was as tough as a lion when it came to business. He talked tough to everybody, all the time, but family and friends knew he was a sweetheart when dealing with them. It was just when the business negotiations began that he knuckled up.

When Gar got the boat back to Crescent City, after the fiasco that brought it to Eureka, he called Mom and told her what happened. She told Lou, and Lou said for Gar to come to Santa Cruz immediately and talk the thing out. Lou had already proven his sense of business acumen through his assistance in the resolution of the Beach House matter, and this was a fine opportunity for him to shine for his new fiancée. He knew that Gar was Annabel's one and only son. He might not necessarily be her world, but he was certainly the moon that kept that world in balance.

GAR DROVE BACK down to Santa Cruz again. It occurred to him that he didn't even look at the scenery any more. The road through the lagoons south of Crescent City, the redwood highway below Eureka, crossing the Golden Gate

Bridge, and then the long run down Highway One to Santa Cruz was a breathtaking and evocative route. But Gar was on autopilot from so many trips. Today he was hung over from an evening of too many gin and tonics. And the hammering rain throughout most of the trip didn't help.

Most of the trip down the Pacific Coast Highway was along the coast, but where the highway diverged inland, Gar still knew what he was passing on the coast. He knew where the Point Cabrillo and Point Montara Lighthouses were, even though he did not see them. For he knew this coast better by water than by land, and he knew it by land like the back of his hand.

The trip was especially tedious this time because he had so much on his mind. He owed Chris $32,000, the *shyster* attorney had insisted on the telephone, and he had only half that amount in cash. And he had at least double that amount committed to accounts payable.

It would be interesting to see what his new stepfather had to say.

"OKAY, SO REALLY," Lou was analyzing patiently. "They're putting about four grand interest on the principle. You said the rate was eight points."

"Ahh, yeah. Eight percent interest over seven years was the loan agreement."

"From what you've told me you've paid so far, my lawyer would argue you owe $28,000."

"Uh, huh." Gar nodded while sipping a welcome gin and tonic: *hair of the dog.*

"To my view, this Chris fellow needs money, and he needs it soon. Why else would he go so far out on a limb, stealing the boat like that? That was dumb. I think you've got him in a weak position." Lou was smiling. "Probably stuck somewhere between a rock and another rock."

"Really?" Gar said this with a sense of amazement. Lou and the gin were starting to ease some of his worry.

"Yes. He's got this tough lawyer you said called you, saying that they needed at least 32K. In reality, this is just some schmuck doing his brother-in-law a free favor. I had my lawyer check this Murphy out. He's an ambulance chaser. A successful one, mind you, and he's trying to break into the national drug-liability market. He's after big things...."

"You found all this out?" Gar was captivated.

"Yeah. Your Mom said you brought your house deed and boat document papers. I'll take the deed as collateral. And I'm going to give you a certified check from my bank for $26,000. We'll work the payback out later. For right now, I want you to take the $26,000 to Mr. Murphy and tell him this is our settlement offer. Watch and see. We will neutralize him early. By law he has to present the offer to his client. If he doesn't convince his client to accept it, tell him we're going to court where we will kick his ass. Tell it to him just like that. We'll kick his ass. Then tell him that if he has any more questions, to call your attorney."

"I have an attorney?" Gar was incredulous.

"Oh, yeah. You have my attorney, Bob Goldthwaite. Tell him your stepfather is pissed, and wants to turn Bob Go-To-Hell-And-Wait loose on him. Remember, there's no fee available to this Murphy character, and he will fall like one of those big Redwoods you got up there in Crescent City when he hears Goldthwaite's name. Trust me on this one, kid. He will not take a chance going to court with Goldthwaite. We'll get you out of this for 26 G's. No problem. Well, except that you'll then owe me." He laughed. It was quite a performance. Gar was impressed.

GAR HAD AN appointment to meet Chris at Murphy's office at three in the afternoon. At Lou's instruction, he was armed with a bank draft and the boat document papers for Chris to sign off on. Murphy invited him in, then continued to work, shuffling papers industriously while looking over the top of his half-readers. This was a calculated power move, and the man had perfected it. His desk was down at one end of the long office, while Gar sat at the other end. Gar's chair was low, while Murphy's desk sat on a raised Dias. And the lawyer's desk was huge. All of this was designed to make the visitor to this man's office uncomfortable, and it worked on Gar.

Gar sensed he was being manipulated and he didn't like it. After a few minutes spent getting madder and madder, he blurted out his thoughts. "I've come to offer a settlement. I've got a check for $26,000 here."

Murphy looked over the top of his glasses, clearly amused, and said, "You owe us.... Wait a minute, where is it? Oh, yeah. $32,000, <u>plus</u> expenses. Ha, ha, ha, what did you say? $26,000? No ... no ... no ..." He was shaking his head back and forth, laughing like Gar was a three year old, and pronouncing his "no's" like some cowboy, saying Nah, Nah, Nah. "You're going to have to pay us at least $40,000, or we're going to take your house. We've already got the boat."

Gar cut him off, and now <u>he</u> was smiling, albeit somewhat sinister. "Mr. Murphy, you're a shyster piece of shit. But, then you're probably proud of that. You couldn't cut it for fifteen minutes on the back deck of my boat. As a matter of fact, if it wasn't for the fact that you'd undoubtedly have me arrested and sue me, I'd kick your fat ass right here and right now." He strode the twenty feet over to the desk while saying this, and Murphy threw down his glasses, clearly alarmed, pushed back in his chair and searched frantically for a weapon to pick up.

Gar tossed the check on the desk and said, "My attorney is Robert Goldthwaite out of San Jose. He has an office in Santa Cruz. Here's our offer of settlement, which, by law, you are obligated to take to your client and discuss with him. If you have any further questions you can call Bob. Or should I say, Go-To-Hell-And-Wait if you have questions. Ha, ha, ha...."

Having gotten the last laugh, Gar wheeled out of there, leaving the mighty Murphy visibly shaken.

GAR RAN INTO Chris in front of the building. The man looked disturbed, as well he might. This was their first encounter since Chris had the boat stolen. Gar took advantage of this, and told Chris the deal. "Take the $26,000, sign off on the boat document, and we won't turn loose Bob Goldthwaite, who wants to bring criminal charges, among other things. Have you ever read Title 18, Section 2111 of the U.S. Code?"

Chris shook his head, mumbling, "Not really." His large eyes blinked rapidly when he spoke.

Gar carried on. "It says, whoever, within maritime jurisdiction of the U.S., takes, or attempts to take, something from another person, will do fifteen years in a federal pen."

Chris paled. He quickly excused himself, clearly shaken, and told Gar he would be right back. He was going to get the check.

He came back out, after about ten minutes, and spoke rapidly. "If you've got the document papers, we'll go right now to my bank and get my signature notarized by my banker. At the same time, I'll deposit your check in my account. And what the hell did you say to Murphy? The man is fucked up. He about threw me out of his office."

"Oh, my stepfather said I should tell him to take the offer or we'd go to court and kick his ass. But I got it kind of screwed up and offered to do it myself right there in his office. What a piece of shit...."

"He's been married to my sister for ten years, and I've seen him a lot during all that time, but I've never seen him like this." Chris shook his head; his eyes fluttered rapidly and he pulled on his lower lip.

"Well, it appears he's used to treating fishermen like shit and I wasn't going for it. Anyway, I got the boat document right out in my pickup in the parking lot. How far is your bank?"

"Oh, it's just a block and a half. We can walk, if you want." Chris was very polite.

"Sounds good to me." Gar smiled, thinking of how slick Lou was. He'd engineered this whole thing, including citing the federal criminal statute for Chris. He wondered if he had also counted on Gar losing his temper.

AFTER THE DEAL was done, Chris was in a hurry to get home. For some reason Gar thought he was in a hurry to go buy some blow. Chris had kept a thousand in cash from the check. Gar didn't know this for sure, about the cocaine. It was just a feeling he had. But he was pretty sure he was right.

Shaking hands, Chris nervously threw out a laugh. "Man, I can't believe you did that to Murph. He's, like, always in charge. And you had him fucked up. Unbelievable. Wait'll I tell my wife. She might want to hire you. Ha, ha."

"You know," Gar answered him seriously. "I'll tell you something about fishermen. We don't scare very easy. At least not by someone like that. I think he's used to intimidating people, and I'll tell you what, I've been face to face with guys a lot bigger and a lot tougher, and all drunked up in a waterfront bar somewhere where there's plenty of room to fight, and I have done the same thing that I did to him. It's the big guys that are easiest to back down.

"Davy Crockett," Gar was on a roll now. "Davy Crockett had an inscription on the front of his diary that said, *Be sure you're right, then go ahead*. Well, after I got with my new stepfather and figured out I was right, I just went full throttle ahead."

"Judas Priest. I think the mighty Murphy has finally met his match. Oh, and hey! I'm sorry about that business with your boat. Murphy told me it was legal and that, under the law, we had to do it." Chris's attempt to put the blame on Murphy was not convincing, but Gar accepted it. The man's eyes were blinking so rapidly Gar almost expected to feel a breeze from the lashes.

"That was yesterday, Chris. Let's not worry about it. It's all done now. I got the boat. You've got your money. Now I'm going back to Crescent City to finish getting ready for crab season. We've still got a hell of a lot of work to do."

"All right, Gar. I'll do that. Good luck this winter, and for God's sake, be careful. I know you probably don't believe this, but I like you. I would feel bad if I ever heard something had happened to you."

He seemed genuine, for just a moment, and he left Gar wondering. Just for a moment.

Gar pocketed the deed to the boat and walked away.

CHAPTER 39

THE SECRET TO crab fishing, in a word, is uniformity. Gar had learned this years earlier. Keep your hands moving and busy. Make sure your crewmen stay busy. And make every piece, every aspect of your gear, exactly the same. This is the only way to make the endeavor pay. The season is a short one, and the successful crabber will pay meticulous attention to detail, tweaking every pot so it looks just like all the rest.

Unlike salmon, crab are prisoners of their environment. The area Gar fished at Crescent City had only a certain amount of crab in any given year. Whatever that amount is on the December first opener, is it. That is all there will be. Crab do not migrate like salmon and other fish. Fish have tails, and fish such as salmon traverse the entire length of the west coast every season; here today, gone tomorrow. The crab harvest on the other hand, is akin to a pie. The busier you are, the bigger your piece of the pie. And the pie is not going anywhere. But when it is gone, it's gone.

ON DECEMBER FIRST, 1984, Gar was driving the boat, Jeff was running the power-block puller, and Buster and a temporary hand were working the deck. A normal crab crew is three guys, but Gar planned on expanding the parameters of "Rule Two" and to get <u>real</u> busy this year. He needed two back-deck guys because he did not plan to stop work until Christmas Day. They had lights this time and had adorned their crab buoys with reflective tape. The buoys lit up brilliantly at night when hit with the large quartz lights. They would fish around the clock, moving any pots that were not productive to new grounds.

Crabbing is about money. But it's just as much about the team. The level at which three or four guys can operate together and accomplish more than the other boats. Ask a crabber what he remembers most about seasons past, and he'll likely not mention paychecks. He will remember his fellow crew, their compatibility, and the pounds of crab caught.

The people and the crab.

Sometimes, too, crab are fondly called "Bugs". That's because they're nothing more than bottom-dwelling seawater insects. An entomologist might quibble about it, but one look at one of them will tell you that they are bugs. Large ones, true, but bugs nonetheless.

THE DAYS LEADING up to the opening of the season are electrifying. The boats are stacked high with traps. Guys are driving madly and endlessly up and down the waterfront watching for the first sign someone is about to leave to set pots. The talk of price is on everyone's lips. And the thought that maybe this will be that perfect season–the team, the weather, the price, the bugs–to forever remember hangs thick in the cold winter air.

It's a time equal to those days of eager anticipation before Christmas, that kids everywhere remember. Or Superbowl Sunday morning before kick-off. Maybe it's like the feeling a performer gets when the lights come up, and the curtains part, and the fans begin to cheer. Or the anxiety one feels before that first date with someone very special. You can hardly wait, yet are still afraid of the outcome.

Gar got so excited one year he backed his boat into his berth so he could pull straight out and save about two minutes not having to back out *then* go forward. And he had slipknots on the lines so his crew could just pull the loose end, thus saving them another thirty seconds.

THEN AFTER THE season opens, the gear is set, and they start hauling up the pots, that is when the anticipation reaches an excruciating peak. Waiting for that first trap to break the surface and praying it's full is almost more that a heart can stand.

It's an awesome experience, similar to nothing else. And if the traps come up full, the jubilation is almost too much to bear. Years later, a crabber will remember everything about that day: the smell, the sounds, the smiles on faces, and the condition of Mother Ocean. Even how much and what kind of bait was used, what songs were playing on the stereo and who was bullshitting about what on the VHF.

Enticing crabs with fresh bait to crawl into a trap is the same as luring a fish to bite a hook that is shrouded with bait. It is a challenge of elemental but profound proportions. It sounds simple, but it is not. It comes down to a matter of intelligence and mastery over one facet of the universe. And it is this that had captured Gar. Indeed, the challenge of this seemingly simple task ruled his soul. It is why he smuggled grass, continually risked bad weather, went fishing again after losing a boat and almost drowning, and endured long intervals away from Cindy and Jasmer.

Men who come from the sea will tell you that there is no finer profession than fishing, none more honest. Gar's grandfather, who spent most of his 86 years studying the Bible, said fishing was the oldest profession in the world, and that Jesus fished.

"I thought prostitution was the oldest profession," Gar parried jokingly.

"Where did these men get the money to pay those prostitutes?" Grandpa demanded.

"Uhh, I guess they must have worked at something."

"Exactly," Grandpa had exclaimed with his rheumy eyes gleaming. "They fished. It's the oldest, most virtuous occupation and I'm very proud of you." He told this to Gar with absolute sincerity and conviction.

Gar believed him.

THERE'S A CRACKLING sound a polypropylene crab line makes as it rolls through the sheaves of a crab block. It sounds sort of like one of those "creaky door" effects in a scary movie, where the creak stretches for long seconds. Except when pulling a trap, the creak extends for long moments. Or maybe for some the pulling sound is more similar to very pitchy wood when thrown in a blazing campfire–those thousands of crackle-pops that all run together making one elongated noise.

It's *that* sound that linked Gar to Jeff during crab season. He could understand every move Jeff was making based on nuances of that sound. He and Jeff had become an expert all-around fishing team, all right, but when they crabbed, they truly worked as one. They rarely needed to talk, on the boat anyway, as they intuitively read each other perfectly. For his part of the operation, Jeff simply ran the block, making that creaking-crackling sound. And Gar listened to him, and kept the buoys coming alongside at precisely timed-and-spaced intervals. Jeff listened to the change in engine pitch, as Gar worked the throttle, and thus understood where they were in relation to the next buoy in their string of pots. And when it was time to stack part of a string on the boat, rather than rebaiting it, Jeff knew this without being told and started coiling line instead of trailing it.

A string was normally about sixty pots long, the buoys spaced several hundred yards apart. They ran gear so fast, so well, that they needed to leave only half as much distance between buoys as the other boats. This allowed them to squeeze twice as many pots, or more, onto a small area of crab. Because crab tend to bunch up on edges where good bottom (they like sand) meets bad bottom (they don't like rocks), the ability to squeeze more traps onto an edge can often be very productive.

The ***Proudfoot*** was a small crabber, but they operated her at peak efficiency. And again, for those that would question why a man like Gar who lived to fish would engage in something illegal like smuggling, this was the reason. It was so he could keep doing this. It was so they could afford to salmon fish in the summers between federal closures. The one activity paid to enable a continuation of the other.

THIS YEAR THEY had it all together. They moved gear like spiders weave their webs. They pulled all five hundred traps every twenty-four hours, and in this way they were on top of what the crab were doing. They could watch them migrate over the many miles their traps covered. They could keep up with and even anticipate movement–leapfrogging pots to keep their gear situated amongst the bugs.

They gradually shortened the haul-up lines and moved shallower. Eventually they had all the pots stretched out from Split Rock down to the lower end of Gold Bluff Beach. Every one of their five-hundred traps was situated inside of twelve fathoms. The old timers warn that a crabber should never fish inside of twelve fathoms until after the March equinox. This is because the swells and surf at this time of year will possibly stick the traps in the sand, or simply tear them to pieces with the frenzied action of the waves. But the crab are down there. And trying to get them is a gamble anyway. Still, there was a reason the old timers warn against fishing inside of twelve fathoms before the middle of March. And for Gar and his crew it was only December, and not yet Christmas.

But they decided to fish inside of twelve fathoms. It was reckless, but it paid off if you could get away with it.

A crab operation (Special thanks to Marie De Santis for the illustration).

CHAPTER 40

MARCH, 1985.

CRAB FISHING IS hard work. What makes it harder than salmon fishing is the in and out. A salmon trip keeps a fisherman out on the ocean until it's time to come home. Crabs have to be delivered live, and with a smaller crabber like the ***Proudfoot***, that means coming in for daily deliveries.

Go out. Run the gear. Come back and deliver. Go home and regroup. Then, because the workdays with the use of lights are so long, and the weather is normally so bad, it is often easy to make excuses not to go back out.

Gar and Cindy had a VHF radio at the house that allowed them to communicate while he was out. It also allowed Gar, when in, to listen to the other boats talking, as well as switch to NOAA Weather Radio broadcasts for predictions. Often he would tell his crew to expect a call a little past midnight, because the forecast was updated on the twelve's, and Gar would make his decision on whether to fish based on that midnight forecast update.

When the weatherman predicted inclement weather, it was a tough call. An old fisherman's truism is: "No need to come in a gale, but don't go out in one." It is a matter of honest fact that an old friend, Oogah Don, named his daughter "Gale Warning," as it was certain that these were the only conditions under which the child could have been conceived.

This simple thing is what made crabbing more stressful. If they were salmon or albacore fishing they'd stay out in a gale forecast. But during crab season, Gar agonized over these decisions every night. Or at least every other night, as they'd often take more than twenty-four hours to rebait and situate their gear.

AFTER MOVING ALL five-hundred traps inside of twelve fathoms the previous December, the ***Proudfoot*** continued to harvest crab at a prosperous pace. Other boats moved strings of gear alongside them for short intervals, then moved them back out with the first questionable forecast. When placed in shallow waters, a large swell will bury the pots in the sand, sticking them so deep they have to be pumped out with an elaborate fire hose setup that requires weeks of hard work to get all of them loose.

They stuck maybe a hundred traps this season. This was an insignificant amount, considering the profit they were making. Four-hundred traps were more easily tended, anyway, because they could only fish during daylight hours toward the end of the season. This was because when fishing shallow water, a Skipper must watch for rogue breakers. And he cannot do that with the night-lights setup. The lights serve very well for simply running forward down a string, especially with the reflective taped buoys. But swells that have the potential to break must be spotted when they are hundreds of yards seaward, and this becomes impossible at night.

A swell that has breaking potential sends the crew scrambling. The Skipper must run the boat full throttle toward the swell, hoping to clear the wave before it breaks. A breaker might dump countless tons of water onto a boat, potentially washing the men overboard, smashing out the windows, and even flipping a boat over and sinking it. The raw, unbridled power of a breaker is truly awesome.

Their four-hundred traps produced steady enough to make fishing profitable into the spring. They had scores of close calls, but took no breakers. Gar was thoroughly drained from staying ever alert afore the danger. They surpassed the $100,000 mark for the season and partied like the hooch-hounds they were known to be–buying rounds for the house at Wakefield's, a favorite bar which was owned by close friends. Work hard and play hard was their motto. They went after it with gusto.

MARCH CAME, AND so did Cindy's "due date" for their second child. Because Cindy's labor had to be induced with Jasmer, Doctor Mavris now grew concerned. He scheduled visits once a week as March approached, then switched to every few days by the middle of the month. On the 24th, he said to come in first thing in the morning so they could induce labor.

Alison's birthday would have been March 25th, except it took all that day and into the following morning before she was finally born.

Alison Janine Walton. She was beautiful. *Reeallly beautiful*! Certainly Gar was partial. Many would later say she looked more like Gar than Jasmer did. And it was perhaps for this reason that there was a higher degree of familiarity with this child.

Or maybe it was her instant smile. She didn't cry when the doctor spanked her, she started laughing. And she watched her Daddy from the very first second her eyes were open. This time there was not the confusion with the tubes and hoses, and Gar was right there to watch and help when the nurse cleaned and dressed Alison. Throughout the process, she watched and smiled at her Daddy, and it was spellbinding. It made Gar's heart soar. That day, that feeling, was forever engraved on his soul. Contrary to popular belief, father's can also bond forever with their children. It is not something only a mother can do. And Gar's special bond with this child was to last a lifetime.

WHEN JASMER WAS born, they were a new couple in town. But by the time Alison entered their world, they had acquired a number of friends. Gar had a group of his devotees taking shifts in the hospital waiting room. Rob Wakefield was there, and Jeff of course, with Conrad Evanow, and even Angus. Naturally Angus was more concerned about Cindy than the newborn child.

They say that a boy first, then a girl, is a millionaire's family. Like little John-John and then Caroline in the Kennedy family. Gar, with a six-figure crab season, and now a millionaire's family, had much to celebrate. And celebrate he did.

Much to the dismay of Cindy.

CHAPTER 41

SUMMER, 1985.

JEFF AND A friend working as deckhand took the boat salmon fishing while Gar kept Buster and worked on their new house. He hired a carpenter friend to come over to Crescent City from the Lake Almanor area, and ramrod the project. Their place on Heacock Lane, in Elk Valley, was purchased in part because it had a comfortable, but disposable, trailer house on the front end of the property. Their plan had always been to build their dream house on the back end of the acre. The profitable crab season just past now made that possible.

This summer they wouldn't finish the building, but they'd get a good start on it. By the time they ran out of money the house was framed, roofed, sided, and the plumbing was roughed in. They'd put the windows in, too. The home took shape, revealing itself to be an expensive and elegant building. It was striking. People slowed to look as they drove past in the street.

The 2,800 square-foot palace was weathered in, albeit with plastic-tarp doors, and ready for the one final season of prosperity it would take to finish it.

That season would never come. Not while Cindy was a part of the project.

CHAPTER 42

TWO YEARS LATER: 1987.

THEY SAY WHEN you're young you can live on love and throw away the peels. And there is a degree of truth to this observation. The next two years went by in a flash, and though Gar did not have the single prosperous crab season that would have seen the building of his dream house through to completion, he had love, and plenty of it, with his little family on Heacock Lane.

Alison was two now, an exceptional child, and very mischievous. She, to Gar, was as smart as a Rhoades Scholar. She was walking at nine months, and speaking in sentences at eighteen.

Jasmer was in his fourth year, utterly devoted to his hero: His Dad. Gar was as happy as he had ever been in his life. But a school of sharks swam into his waters, and left a bloody pall on everything.

This was when Cindy's young, attractive, and unfortunately promiscuous cousin, Lorna, moved in and brought her son with. Now back in shape after two childbirths, Cindy began to enjoy an almost-single lifestyle again with Lorna's encouragement. Gar was gone all summer salmon fishing, and by the time he realized the extent of the problem in his home, it was too late to fix. He did not have a deckhand anymore, mainly because he had no insurance. So he was not able to leave the boat unattended in temporary berths at the various out-of-town ports he visited. And this meant that he seldom made it home. When he finally did make it home, the damage was done.

At the end of a very hectic salmon season, after weeks of being away, Gar returned home and his family promptly moved out. It all happened so fast, it stunned him.

He was told that he had become too difficult to live with. Though Lorna would later tell him, "We didn't want you there. So we'd just bitch until you'd go back to your boat and go fishing."

He would blame Lorna. He would blame Cindy. He would blame fishing, while admitting he'd become a stressed-out drunk when he was not fishing. He even blamed licentious soap operas and society's permissiveness with regard to divorce. But neither accusations nor confessions would bring his family back. Cindy did not even want to try counseling. She had the sperm Gar had donated, enough for a boy and a girl, and he was now to be discarded like an old newspaper. In the end, Gar thought, if there were others that were to blame, Cindy's Mother Arlene had to be included. She was a natural-born instigator, a feminist with her own marital shortcomings, and she emphatically encouraged divorce. She had never liked Gar's independent nature, nor the fact that he took two of her children and moved them out of her control. She bided her time, and eventually got even.

Of course, Gar knew that if he had tried harder, it would not have happened. He knew he was to blame.

TO GAR, FAMILY was the dream, the only truly worthwhile goal in life. He'd grown up with several stepfathers, and he vowed that his kids would never know divorce. Or that he, himself, would ever go through it. Cindy had an identical childhood, and had made the same promise. But she took their millionaire's family and moved across town, then down the coast to Santa Rosa. With Cindy's mother and cousin encouraging, Gar's family slipped away like a thief in the night.

This was the toughest pill Gar had ever tried to swallow. It was torment. It was misery. It might have been the end, were it not for Wakefield's Bar.

BUT THERE WAS worse yet to come. Over the next two years, as divorce hearings would come up, Gar's old nemesis, Angus, would be there time after time to testify on Cindy's behalf. Because a determination of the value of boat and gear were necessary in order for the court to divide assets, Angus was there to dispute each and every one of Gar's claims. Of course, he did this always in favor of Cindy. If Gar said a crab pot was worth $50, Angus would argue that it was really worth $100.

It was as sordid and vile a thing as any so-called friend could ever do to destroy things. This was a betrayal of friendship which enraged Gar initially, and then only left him yet more depressed.

Cindy, doubtless, had a right to prove her claims in court. But it was Angus's squalid mendacity, actually inflating costs and lying to the judge, that was so disheartening for Gar. For a period of many months, Gar lost his sense of humor entirely. But what was worse, he lost his belief in the innate goodness and decency of people. The loss of this belief threatened to undo him.

At one point during the two-year divorce, he got involved with another importation of marijuana from the orient. This time the smuggling was done by another boat, and he just oversaw the operation in a supervisory role. This provided the money he needed to pay off Cindy and the lawyers, and it enabled him to complete construction of the dream house they had started building together.

Gar fought hard for primary custody of Jasmer and Alison. Finishing the house was part of this custody plan. He wanted to show the court investigator that he had a nice place for his kids to grow up. The plan failed, however, and he was awarded visitation summers, Easter week, and for a week during the Christmas season.

AT FIRST, THIS seemed like the end of his world, but as the years continued Gar was able to spend a fair amount of quality time with his "babies." He learned what a "Disneyland Daddy" was. He took the kids there, and as many other places as it was possible to go. They loaded the pickup with sleeping bags and spare clothes, and they traveled *fast and light*. They camped in every existing camping spot in the Crescent City mountains, as well as in Oregon and much of the Pacific Northwest coast.

They went to Yellowstone and Yosemite and the Grand Canyon. They drank Shirley Temples on top of the Space Needle in Seattle, and heard the lions roar in the San Diego Zoo. And, of course, there were trips to Grandma Annabel's in Santa Cruz. Gar worried when he had custody of the kids that they would get tired of Dad. And he did everything he could think of to prevent it.

There was a cost associated with this change. It made salmon fishing, or any other summer fishery, virtually impossible. And he never did completely overcome his feelings of heavy-heartedness. Taking family photos without Cindy, and looking at the kid's toys, months on end, laying around the yard exactly where they'd dropped them on their last visit, pulled at the strings of Gar's heart. And the sight of the swing set overgrown with tall grass, bereft of activity, was much too difficult to look at for long. Around the house, plants were dead or dying, and the quiet was deafening.

Gar drank too much and spent most of his time playing "catch-me, fuck-me" with a number of the Crescent City girls that he found down at Wakefield's Bar. In his big new house, with the wooded yard, garage, hot tub, workshop, and assortment of vehicles, plus large piles of fishing gear, *catch-me, fuck-me* was the perfect game to play. There were a lot of places to hide. It was fun. But it was empty fun.

GAR DID, HOWEVER, find one bright spot in the course of this otherwise dismal time. He stumbled onto a unique and lucrative niche during the completion of the house project. He took the construction crew to Wakefield's Bar after work one day, where they discovered everyone arguing over the coming Mike Tyson versus Michael Sphinx fight. At that time, fights were shown on closed-circuit television only, and always in as large a venue as possible.

So Gar, who had become accustomed to working the phone all day organizing contractors and the delivery of building materials, made telephone inquiries about the Tyson-Sphinx fight. His goal, since he had a satellite dish, was to pay the $1,000 he had heard was the price to rent a decoder, and get friends to come over and chip in. It worked out better than he expected.

He contacted the West Coast promoter, who was happy to give him the sole rights to Northern California–north of Ukiah–to show the fight. This was under the condition he make a production out of it (selling seats, in other words) at the fairgrounds. And he would be on the hook to kick back a fair percentage of the gate.

Gar put on the show, successfully selling eight hundred seats at $20 per seat. After expenses and kickback, he netted eight thousand dollars. This was not bad for a few days work, especially considering that his original goal was to have a few friends over to watch the fight.

GAR WALTON PRESENTS was born. Crescent City suddenly had its first promoter, and what was to become a new household name in Northern California made its first appearance.

CHAPTER 43

1988.

A YEAR LATER, life was getting better. The pain was not gone, but it had become manageable. Gar was drinking less, too. And they had a fairly productive spring bite of crab going on.

Jeff was fishing the ***Carol Ann*** for Mike McCutcheon. They had a lease/option thing going on between the two of them, which was a good deal for both. Jeff was buying his own boat, and Mike had himself a hard working and honest man who would make the payments on time. However Mike and Jeff were living on borrowed time. All of them were. But they didn't know it. Disaster was about to strike, and the events of the past were going to catch up with them all. And it all started out with Sonny.

Mike McCutcheon and his deckhand of many years, Sonny, had developed contacts and branched out in the smuggling business. They had taken what they had learned years before from Gar during the smuggling operation he had invited them to be a part of, and they had gone into the business with great vigor. Sonny and Mike scheduled and conducted their own operations now, and for a number of years had been quite successful at it. Mike bought himself a new boat, the ***California Sun***, and kept Sonny as his deckhand and smuggling partner.

It was Mike's purchase of the ***California Sun*** that inadvertently dragged Jeff into it, and this brought Gar into it because he was Jeff's previous employer.

So it is that our plots unravel.

When Jeff bought the ***Carol Ann*** from McCutcheon, he came under scrutiny. And it was not the kind of attention he wanted.

McCutcheon and his partner, Sonny, came to the attention of authorities when their boat, the ***California Sun***, was spotted unloading weed in the anchorage at Sister's Rocks north of Gold Beach, Oregon. Jeff was somehow involved with this, or at least the U.S. Customs agents assumed he was.

Jeff wasn't on the actual scene when the incident occurred that brought everything crashing down, but he was reputed to be nearby. And that was enough. The Coast Guard surprised the ***California Sun*** as the weed was being unloaded, and the ***California Sun*** immediately took off and ran straight away into the rocks. The boat broke up on the rocks and weed was floating everywhere: more "sea-weed" for the beachcombers.

But because the ***Carol Ann*** was in McCutcheon's name, as was the ***California Sun***, plus there was a record that the ***Carol Ann*** was in the general vicinity during the bungled offload, the Coast Guard and Custom's people came and seized the ***Carol Ann*** without delay.

THEY ARRESTED SONNY first. The story that went around following his arrest is that they slapped him once to get him to talk, then had to smack him ten times to shut him up. He gave up everyone he knew. And he made up a few names and incidents for good measure. Sonny spilled his guts.

Wallace and Bob were two of the first implicated. They were sucked into the judicial system, and never heard from by Gar again. They were presumably sent off to prison. They didn't talk, but Sonny was doing enough talking for everyone.

And Sonny had been on the ***Carol Ann*** in 1984 when Mike had assisted Gar with a smuggling operation. This information was all the U.S. Customs agents needed to go to federal court under the criminal code, Title 18, U.S.C. Section 981, with a prayer for a civil forfeiture judgment. The judgment was granted, and on a clear, cold, spring day, when Gar was doing well crabbing, members of the Coast Guard decided to deliver the court's order.

THE OCEAN WAS flat. Their crab gear was right outside the breaker and rock line. They were fishing in fifteen to thirty feet of water. Since the ***Proudfoot*** draws about six feet, there wasn't much water under the keel.

On this particular day, the last day Gar would fish aboard the ***Proudfoot***, he noticed the Coast Guard patrolling up and down outside them. It seemed like they were looking for someone. What they were looking for, of course, was him. They wanted to seize the boat. But they were afraid to come in towards the shallow water where Gar was fishing. The gear was right next to underwater sinker rocks that only showed at low tide. And the beach breaker line was less than a hundred yards inside them. They could watch the white frothing hem of the surf undulating up and down the slope of sand, a couple of hundred yards inside the very small breaks.

It was a hairy place to be, and the Coasties wanted no part of it. So they waited for Gar to come in to port. When he got in, they waited for him to unload his crab. And they waited for him to pull over to the fuel dock and put in a thousand dollar's worth of fuel. Then they let him get tied securely in his slip.

With local news cameras recording the footage, they boarded the ***Proudfoot*** in order to serve their seizure warrant. They said, "Bet you've been expecting us, haven't you?"

To which Gar played it cool and replied, "Why in the world would I be expecting this?"

They took Gar up to the police station and showed him an affidavit which outlined the 1984 smuggling operation. Sonny was the affiant. Gar read it all, then commented, "This sure sounds like a wild, exciting story. But none of the part that talks about me or my boat is true."

"Are you sure, Gar? You can tell us. It will go a lot easier on you if you do. We've got more than enough to take down McCutcheon and your brother-in-law, Jeff. It's only a matter of time, and we will get you, too. You might as well save yourself and talk to us. We'll make sure you get off easy. You might even be able to save your boat, if you talk right now."

Gar held his palms up and told them, "I'm talking, but I don't know anything about this. You guys are scaring me. I want to call my lawyer."

When the word "Lawyer" was mentioned, they picked up their papers and walked out. A few minutes later, a much friendlier Del Norte County Sheriff came in and said, "You can go. Those guys told me they 'had nothing further.' Fucking Feds. I hope you told them to go screw themselves. We got no use for them around here."

"Okay. No. I didn't tell them anything. Guess I better call a cab to take me back to my truck."

"All right, Gar. Good luck to you. You watch out for those Feds, hear?"

AS IT TURNED out, Gar had not only finally paid off Lou's interest in the boat, he'd just filled it with fuel when the customs agents took it. All told, he had enjoyed the "free and clear" feeling of boat ownership for about a month. But now he had no boat. And he was on the federal radar screen. It was time to find a lawyer.

GAR WENT TO San Francisco and talked to a number of lawyers: Melvin Belli, Tony Serra, and Patrick Hallinan, to name but a few. In the end, he hired Patrick Hallinan. Pat told him, after he'd talked to the federal prosecutor, that it looked like they'd probably be happy with the boat. No one else was corroborating Sonny's accusations, and without more they would leave Gar alone.

They could fight the Feds in court to get the boat back, but the legal fees would be as much or more than the boat was worth. And that would anger the Feds, making Gar more conspicuous to them. So the ***Proudfoot*** was lost.

Gar was curiously relieved. It could have been much worse. But the part of him that was relieved was only a very small part. The greater part of Gar was devastated. His wife and kids were gone.

And now, so was his boat.

CHAPTER 44

1989.

"OVER TEN YEARS later, and I am still as in love with Susan as I was on the day we met." Gar and Jeff were filled with beer and feeling melancholy. Jeff had just received the boot from Kim. He moved into one of Gar's spare, upstairs bedrooms.

"I've watched you for a long time. I watched you when you were still with Sue. Then I watched you mope around, trying to get over Sue, and marry Cindy on the rebound. Do you think you married my sister to get over Sue?" Jeff probed artlessly.

"The thing about Sue," Gar paused to consider. "The whole thing is very complicated. And I'll tell you, I've been thinking a lot about both Sue and Cindy these last couple of years. When Susan and I split, the hurt was mortal. It was about her, losing her, not having her, never being with her again. With Cindy, it was more about me. Not being successful as a husband. Not being successful as a father. Failing at holding together a family. You know what I mean?"

Gar took another pull from his beer. They sat in his sophisticated kitchen. It had a high vaulted ceiling with an electric-retractable skylight; beautiful custom myrtlewood cabinets; sub-zero fridge paneled in myrtlewood; green granite countertops and bar; wood encased garden window complete with herb garden; the latest *Gaggenau* cook top with grill and deep fryer; and, of course, Mom's big stand-alone butcher block sitting proudly in the center of it all. The bar sat at the back of the cooktop, which allowed an audience for Gar's kitchen expertise (or, some would say, antics). It was a high-class and expensive arrangement, copied in part from Kenny Butler and cobbled together from portions of architectural magazines.

"I know exactly what you mean," Jeff responded. "I love Kim, and I love our little Jessica even more. And it's hard to imagine not being there with them. But, as you say, I guess I feel like I've failed. I want to blame her, and by God she's done a lot of things lately. Going out with Donnie.... You know what I mean? I got so used to having my future pretty much planned. You know, we would continue raising our kids, working on remodeling the house, maybe one day buying another one, fishing and all that. Maybe retiring some day and buying a farm. Now, it's pain and jealousy and being pissed off, pointing my finger at her and what she's doing. I hate it. I hate her."

And Jeff started crying. This was a rare thing for him. He was an outgoing person, but not an emotional one. Not like this. In fact, Gar had never before seen something like this happen with Jeff.

Gar pretended not to notice, though he was damp eyed too. "We continue to lose those that are closest to us, Jeffrey. It must be our lifestyle. Hell, I was upset when you left me to go to work for Angus."

"I knew you were. But I needed to do something different. I'd only fished on <u>your</u> boat. I had no idea what went on with other operations." Jeff seemed to collect himself, but still wiped his eyes with one shirtsleeve.

"Oh, I more or less figured that out. As a matter of fact, I soothed myself with the thought that you were on a spy mission. After all, Angus is a pretty good salmon fisherman."

"You know, he could be better than you." Jeff's eyes had stopped watering. His mind was again becoming analytical. He smiled as the Bobby McFerrin "Don't Worry, Be Happy" song filtered in over the ubiquitous sound system. They were listening to the *Cocktail* CD on the new and deluxe sound system Gar had recently installed.

"The problem he has," Jeff continued, "is that he's too tight. He won't spend a little extra on groceries, or even bait. And when you really need those things, they're not there. Then he'd try to make do without them, rather than go in and get resupplied. And in town, he'll spend half his paycheck on toot. Now, you know I like toot, too. But what I'm saying is that Angus will snort a hundred-dollar gram in a couple of hours, but won't spend an extra hundred on bait and groceries. *You* always kept the boat well stocked."

"Nobody likes a cheap bastard," Gar smiled, repeating the old squad motto. "Not even the fish. But, you know, I was thinking you were pissed about something. There was something else. Something I must have done.

"Ahh, no. Not really. You don't even remember, anyway. I guess that sort of bothered me."

"What?"

"Oh, well, do you remember that time when we anchored at Port Orford, and I didn't come back to the boat until the next morning? When Goose gave me a ride back out to the anchorage?"

"Yeah. I got fucked up that night."

"Yes you did. You got pissed off, too. I'd never seen you like that. Remember we were playing shuffleboard?"

"Yeah, vaguely."

"Well, you thought we were cheating you. You wanted to fight me, because you thought I was cheating you. You said that if I'd cheat you at shuffleboard, then maybe I'd steal, too."

"Oh, boy." Gar gave him a bleak look. "I said that?"

"Yeah, you scared the shit out of me, out of all of us. Then you made me look stupid. And you hurt my ego. And finally you flat fucking pissed me off. I felt like after you said that, that I was the one that had good reason not to trust you."

"I don't blame you. I can't imagine what I was thinking. You know, every now and then, I drink when I'm tired and stressed, and I go real sideways." Gar was shaking his head.

"I'll say. You know, Cindy and I talked about that night, and she said you've scared her like that a few times, too."

Jeff got up and retrieved a couple more bottles of Miller High Life. Jeff always drank Miller, or sometimes Pacifico, after he had spent time in Mazatlan where Pacifico is made.

"You know, something else I've figured out," Gar scrunched his face up into a considering scowl. "Over these last two years. Is that all relationships depend on two things, trust and communication. And I'm really thinking that it's mainly just trust. Communication is what keeps the trust going. It doesn't matter if it's husband and wife, banker and bankee, or even you and your dog. All relationships have to have trust to survive. And like with Cindy, when she and Lorna started going out every night, partying with guys, I lost trust. And really, what you're telling me now is she didn't trust me, cause she thought I might go sideways on her."

"I think you're right. Kim and I did fine until she started partying. And I think we were both suspicious of each other before that. Remember, I couldn't figure out why she would always buy me those whacked-out boxers with crazy stuff on them, then accuse me of showing them to other girls?"

"Yeah. A paradox, we called it."

Then Jeff was serious. "I don't know if I answered your question about my going with Angus that summer, but let me say this: You've been a good friend, a good boss, and a good brother-in-law. Plus, you were a good teacher. You got me started fishing and I know, at first, you didn't even really like me."

"Well...."

"But life goes on, and I'm sorry if Cindy's hurt you. I have nothing to do with that. I went to work for Angus because I was curious, maybe a little angry about Port Orford, but I also thought I might like it better. He can be a lot of fun, you know."

"Yeah, I've had some laughs with Goose, all right."

"But I didn't like it better. He could probably be a better fisherman, if he'd work just as hard at being a better guy. He won't, though. He's got his way of doing things, and that's that. You always respected my ideas, even when I was brand new. He never really did."

"All right, Jeffrey. And now you've got the ***Lyndie J***. And I've got my ***GAR WALTON PRESENTS*** promotions. We've sure not gone down the same paths we started out on. We've made some radical course changes, I'll tell ya."

"When you're up to your ass in alligators...."

"It's hard to remember which swamp you originally intended to drain," Gar finished, and they both laughed, lightening the mood.

GAR HAD ANOTHER livelihood now, but you would never know it by his home. It was the house of a fisherman, and an extremely successful one. The glass of his front door contained a detailed etching of the Point Saint George Lighthouse, a lighthouse that is built atop a rock, six miles offshore. The silhouette of the lighthouse is very distinct, both because of the bell-shaped rock pedestal upon which it sits, and because of the long boom-crane extending from the lee side of the structure. The crane, of course, hoisted people and supplies safely onto the rock. Only another fisherman would recognize this etching for what it was, but he would recognize it immediately.

This lighthouse also has the distinction of being the most expensive lighthouse ever built in the United States. One person died during construction, and a number of others between the years 1882 and 1975, the period in which it was in operation. It was decommissioned in 1975 and replaced with a large buoy located nearby. But it stands there still, a silent sentinel to the past, and it is a favorite of fishermen.

Gar's glass door, beneath the lighthouse, read:

Like the beacon, the Lord guides us;
From the ocean...danger,
To our home....safety.

And this motif was continued throughout the house. Even the pump house on the lawn was a miniature lighthouse.

THAT SPRING JEFF fished for crab on the ***Lyndie J***. He had a lease option on it and was doing well. He continued to live with Gar. Gar's crab gear, leased to yet another fisherman, paid a small income. That income, and Jeff's rent, Gar reinvested to launch various sorts of shows. ***GAR WALTON PRESENTS*** became fairly successful. It presented closed circuit boxing, female oil wrestling, male strip shows, and even a World Wrestling Federation type of wrestling show.

Jasmer loved the wrestling, and thought his Dad was the bomb for doing that one.

GAR AND THE kids had what amounted to a permanent camp set up at Shelly Creek that summer. Jeff stayed with them there, too. Uncle Jeff was very much a part of their immediate family now. Indeed, Jasmer and Alison were his sister's kids. The whole group kicked around on Shelly Creek that summer fishing and roasting marshmallows. Gar and Jeff bonded on a whole new level.

Marilyn, a gorgeous, blond, Crescent City taxi driver, was now spending fairly regular time with Gar, too. Ever since they'd figured out they had the same birthday, she and Gar had become enthralled with one another. The problem was her husband. Marilyn was still married and living with Dick, the taxi-company owner. That didn't stop her from making regular visits to Shelly Creek, though.

THEY CAME BACK downriver the first of August. Jasmer and Alison were coffee brown from living in the sun. Gar, just as tanned, had a sore liver from so much rum. They needed to rejuvenate in the big house for a few days.

Jeff was coming and going as usual on that day. He had a Jeep, a pickup truck, and a 750cc Honda motorcycle. He'd rotate the vehicles, usually managing to drive all three of them every day.

He took off on the motorcycle that afternoon, and shortly thereafter Gar received a call. It was a neighbor and friend, frantically asking what had happened to Jeff. When Gar expressed confusion, the man's meaning became clear.

"I saw them loading him into an ambulance. He ran into a van by G & G Liquors. He looked bad...."

"Oh, shit. I'll try to find out. Good-bye. Thanks for calling, David.

THE HOSPITAL TOLD Gar he'd better come down, and to hurry, which he did. He first called Kim, and she told him that she had already heard and would meet Gar there.

AT THE HOSPITAL, the counter nurse told them to wait; they had Jeff on the table.

Gar pictured him back there where both Jasmer and Alison had been born. Pictured him unconscious and with blood on his head. They'd been told that Jeff had gone over the handlebars head first into a curb. And Gar had already checked the coat closet in the front foyer at home. Jeff's helmet was still there. He worried, but tried to keep strong for Kim. Even though the two of them were divorcing, she was still visibly distressed by this nightmare.

A NURSE CAME out from the dreaded doors upon which they had been focusing. Gar led Kim to the nurse and said, "We're here for Jeff Lindburg. Is he going to be all right?"

"There was a lot of trauma there," The nurse was shaking her head.

"But he's still alive? He's going to be all right?" Gar pleaded.

"I'm sorry." she was an older, granny-looking woman. "We tried to revive him, but he died when he hit his head. I'm really sorry. If there's...."

"Oh, God," Gar cried out. He put his arm around Kim, and they both burst into tears.

Zombie like, they walked out into the daylight. Outside was just another sunny, slightly overcast August day. Seaside Hospital, right on the beach, bustled as if nothing happened. To Gar, it seemed like time had stopped. This intermittent sunshine was totally incongruous. It was like there was this big bubble around him, and no one could see through it. No one could see him. Like this whole world, or at least Crescent City, was a joke.

A really bad joke.

DRIVING BACK DOWN the same road he'd driven after Jasmer had been born–Gar had never been happier that day he'd drove this country lane—but today he sobbed. And he had never been sadder. He only had a couple of miles to reach the house and did not want to cry in front of Jasmer and Alison. He dreaded telling them. And how would he tell Cindy and her parents, when none of them would even speak to him? How could the world go this wrong, this fast?

CHAPTER 45

1989.

GAR WAS EMPTY and drained when he arrived back at the house. He felt hollow. Jasmer and Alison were busy, running with their own playful pursuits, and did not notice Gar's red eyes.

He called back to the hospital as soon as he got home, and asked if there was someone there that could instruct him on how to tell his ex-wife and in-laws about Jeff's tragic death. They put a psychologist on the phone. The psychologist explained that full disclosure, details, and honesty are imperative.

"They will have many questions," the woman explained to Gar. "And you must have ready, honest answers."

Kim called and said that Bob and Arlene, Jeff's parents, were actually due in Crescent City at any moment. They were on their way back from Idaho, headed home to the Bay Area, and were stopping to see Jessica.

Since Gar had insisted Jeff install his own phone line, he suspected they would be calling on that. He set Jeff's portable telephone within reach and dreaded the inevitable ring.

Gar also called the police department and spoke to an officer he knew. It was then that he got the whole story. Jeff had been headed south on Highway One, which is the main drag through Crescent City, and when he came upon the Third Street crossing a van pulled out in front of him. Jeff swerved, but was unable to avoid a collision. He smacked the driver's front fender, was thrown over the handlebars, flew about fifty feet through the air, and landed head first against the ninety-degree abutment of a street-side curb. He actually broke an eight-inch chunk of concrete out of the curb. He had died instantly.

Armed with this information, Gar called Cindy. She was distraught, but not overwhelmed. She said she would be there the next morning. They would drive through the night. Gar said she should come stay at the house–her parents, too. She said her boyfriend, Bruce, would be coming, and Gar said he was welcome too. Bruce apparently had reservations about coming at all, but Cindy wore the pants in that relationship.

Cindy and Jeff's older sister, Barbara, was coming also, which pleased Gar. Barbara, effervescent and Hollywood glamorous, had always been warm and friendly with Gar. She never cared about the divorce; never took sides. Matter of fact, Gar had dated Barbara once or twice years before meeting Cindy or Jeff, and still had a very special spot in his heart for her. He'd have one ally in this ordeal, and that thought was comforting.

At first, Cindy and her parents did not want to stay there. But when Gar offered to leave, saying they could stay there without him, everyone relented and everything worked out fine.

THEY HEADED OUT of the harbor aboard the ***Zarina***, David Evanow's boat. A very sad crowd of about forty souls. They had to go out of State water, three or more miles out, pursuant to regulations, before the ashes could be dumped. They had decided to idle up into the wind while Arlene tipped the ashes off the bow of the boat. Gar had Jasmer under one arm, and Alison under the other. They kneeled up on the bow, hanging their heads over the side.

As Arlene began dumping ashes, saying good-bye to Jeff, giving her love, some of the ash motes floated back up, catching Gar and the kids in the eyes. Alison looked up at her daddy, knuckling one eye, and she said, "Dad, I've got Jeff in my eyes."

Gar smiled sadly, lovingly and said, "We all do, Ali Baby. We all do...."

On the way in, Barbara came to Gar and hugged him tight. Both were overwhelmed with the burden of losing Jeff. Teary-eyed she said, "Don't worry, we'll get through this. And we'll always remember Jeff .... I know he was your best friend."

Lovely and warm, Barbara looked up into Gar's eyes, and for just an instant a spark jumped. Somehow Barbara was able to provide Gar with optimism. She was that kind of woman. With a simple hug, and a momentary glance, she'd managed to make him feel better about himself.

CHAPTER 46

1991.

NONE OF THEM ever really got over Jeff's early death. It was an occurrence which stayed with one and all, subtly influencing perceptions as life slowly passed. But two years later, the hot August sun beating down on the Northern California coast made the memory of Jeff a faint and faraway thing. And the ringing laughter of children in the house made the memory of Jeff a benign and forgiving happening, like the winds rustling faintly through the pines.

Marilyn and her four wonderful children presently filled the big house on Heacock lane. They'd all been there for about a year. Marilyn a little longer. After Jeff passed away, she began spending nights with Gar, and days at Dick's house. This was a somewhat unorthodox arrangement, but it worked. She and Dick, though no longer espoused, still had kids to raise.

The tricky part had been when Gar would call for a cab, which happened relatively often, and Dick would come in response to the call. In Crescent City there is only one Taxi company, the one owned by Dick and Marilyn. They had only two or three cabs. Dick would drive Gar out to Heacock Lane with the animosity palpable and thick in the cabs too-small front seat; like two dogs standing stiff-legged and bristling over a bone.

One night Gar decided it was time to bridge the impasse. "Dick, listen," He said. "Before I came along, Marilyn had already decided she was moving on. We both know that's true. So the fact is that you could have done worse for a future husband-in-law. She could have picked some asshole who doesn't live around here. At least I'm a decent guy with a good house for her to settle into. And the fact of the matter is that you and I could quite easily be friends."

Dick thought about this for a moment before he replied. "That's all well and good, Gar, but you've got to pay for the tush, you know? And what is this husband-in-law business?"

Gar instantly resented such a reference to a woman he was now in love with. And he was frankly surprised to hear Dick talk like that. The man was a very enthusiastic Christian, constantly using the cab as his pulpit. But the husband-in-law play on words got a slight upturn at the corner of Dick's pencil-thin moustache. A small chink appeared in the ice.

Gar noted this, and quickly offered his hand. "Dick, you're a good man, and I have a lot of respect for you. You work hard. You're principled. I'm not trying to take advantage of you. Marilyn and I wound up falling for each other, and that's the way it is. I'll do my best to continue to respect you and what you have started with this family. If you ever have complaints, I'm here to listen and work with you."

Dick took Gar's hand without hesitation, shook it firmly, and said, "Fair enough. When are you going to move everyone in, so I can get on with my life? I've had it with American girls. I'm going to find me a Mexican, or maybe a Central American girl, or a Filipina."

"Soon, Dick. I'll discuss it with Marilyn tomorrow. I think she's staying with the kids at your house tonight."

It was that night's conversation that set everything into motion. Within the week, Marilyn and her kids were all living at Gars' house. And Marilyn and Dick had officially filed for divorce.

AND GAR WAS truly in love with Marilyn. She was a 5'7" tall, 120 pound, blue-eyed blonde bombshell who looked a little bit like Merrill Streep and had the unending vivacious energy of Goldie Hawn on champagne. She could Rollerblade down the boardwalk with the kids all day, and dance all night. She adored fast foods and steadfastly refused to cook. And she was utterly imperturbable. Nothing bothered her.

Gar had to carefully plan their routes on the numerous trips they took together to avoid going past a casino. She would squeal with delight if she saw one, and wheedle and cajole Gar into going inside. He could refuse her nothing. And she was lucky. Dealers seemed to enjoy paying her, and manipulated the cards and dice to ensure that she won. Everyone had fun around Marilyn. Her laughter was infectious and her joy was that of a child. She would walk out of a casino clinging to Gar and beaming, flushed with victory and excitement, and Gar was utterly smitten. Everyone agreed that Marilyn was a hand full. Gar thought she was just right.

THUS THE NINETIES began reasonably innocent, in a domestic sort of way. Marilyn had her four children: Jason, 19; Jeff, 18; Amanda, 13; and Justin, 5. And Gar, of course, had Jasmer and Alison, now 9 and 7, who were often around too. It seemed like serendipity to have all the boy's names begin with the letter "J," and the girl's with an "A." And it was odder yet that Gar and Marilyn's birthdays were both on November 21st. It all added up to a bustling, busy house full of happiness that seemed somehow fated to be that way.

They were all satisfied with their new living arrangement. To a person, they felt like they'd bettered themselves. And it was the children who seemed to make it all work. It was one big happy family on Heacock lane.

Jason and Jeff, both over six feet tall, were basketball players. Gar and Marilyn went to all their games. Because Jason was recently graduated from high school, the boys played for the "Del Norte Taxi" adult-league team. Of course, all the younger kids went with them to games. Everything they did involved everyone else in the family.

Gar quit drinking entirely when the crew moved in. He still did promotions for his moderately successful ***GAR WALTON PRESENTS*** endeavor. Because the house was paid for, he and Marilyn only needed to keep the gas and power bills up, and feed the kids.

They were very happy, very much in love, and satisfied with their joint venture. Where Dick had been strict and overbearing, Gar was easier going, and he used a diplomatic approach when dealing with the kids. Though Cindy had her good points, she did not have the experience or joviality Marilyn brought to the marriage table. The very moment Gar had asked Cindy to marry him, she had said, "You know, I can be a real bitch some times." And she was right. Marilyn, however, didn't have bad days. All of her days were either good or great. She is an eternally happy person. Perhaps it is her steadfast belief in God that buoys her goodwill.

ONE NIGHT AFTER the kids were settled in, a freshly satisfied Marilyn started giggling, saying, "Remember that night I took you home in the taxi? We were fighting, and you jumped out, then I got out and left the cab and started walking."

"I remember. We'd gone to dinner and you had on high heels. I don't recall what we were bickering about." Gar knew she loved telling this story.

"Okay, so I had a couple of drinks...you know I can't drink...and I walked to the Parkcity Superette, and was calling Dick to come get me, when here comes my cab, flying down Elk Valley Road, doing at least sixty in a thirty-five, and you're hunched over the wheel, and I come out of the booth...."

She had to stop, she was laughing so hard. When Marilyn laughs, it is from deep within. Tears of mirth spring instantly from her eyes.

"Did I ever tell you you're cuter than a bug's ear when you laugh?" Gar kissed her and she laughed some more.

"What's so cute about a bug's ear, anyway?" Marilyn labored to catch her breath.

Gar, now amorous again, moved back to an intimate position and said, "Here, maybe I can show you better. Just hold still and pretend like you're a bug's ear and I'm a Q-Tip...."

NOW TWICE SATISFIED, Marilyn asked, "Who is Gregory? I forgot to tell you that he called. Is he one of the guys that you once did your funny business with?" Gar had shown her several of the suitcases that he'd once had filled with money.

"Yes. Gregory's my main contact in the, what should I call it...import-shipping business?" A picture came, unbidden, into his mind. Gregory wearing a wetsuit, grinning up from the deck of a bobbing Zodiac at midnight, ready to unload that first haul in Smuggler's Cove. "He's also related, sort of. What did he say?"

"He was kind of weird. He was talking about the Republicans not lasting forever; you know, like I care. Then he said to tell you it's not an election year. I didn't get it, but I said I'd tell you."

"That's it. I get it. What else did he say?" Gar, excited, sat up so quickly he almost bounced Marilyn off the bed.

"He said he would call back tomorrow, and you better be here."

"Hmmm." And Gar's fancy quickly turned to thoughts of what boats might be available to him. Gregory had this rule. Never smuggle in an election year. It was kind of a stupid rule as every year has some sort of election going on somewhere. But he evidently meant presidential elections.

Gregory needed someone to bring in the goodies, and Lord knew Gar had a need for cash. Not only did they have six kids between them, their house had become the neighborhood hangout, and there were almost always a few extra hungry teenagers to feed. Not to mention shoes. Six kids, especially when basketball is involved, need an unbelievable amount of shoes.

"So," Marilyn cooed. "Are you going to show me what those suitcases look like when they are full?"

"I'm sure going to try, love bug. I'll try to be like Rumpelstiltskin and spin straw into gold."

"Wasn't there a beautiful princess involved in that story somewhere?"

"There was. And there still is." Gar pulled her back down on the bed to play some more.

CHAPTER 47

EARLY 1992.

LATE THE YEAR before, Gar had gotten together with Gregory, as arranged. And Woody and Jay. And he had been disgusted. *Fuckin' weed smokers!* They were all brain damaged. Nice enough guys, but unfocused. They all talked with that, "Wow, man, far-fucking-out" preceding or following every sentence. And when trying to pin down crucial details, Gar had to struggle through tedious, wandering conversations wherein they'd go from generalizations about how much hashish to expect, to the latest Hunter S. Thompson article in Rolling Stone, and then inexplicably to the confirmation hearings for Clarence "Long Dong" Thomas and his affair with Anita Hill.

When they'd first met in the Summer of 1991, Gar had shaken hands with Jay and Woody and declared as simply and directly as he could, "Look, I'm not a rookie at this–far from it. So I can save us all a lot of time. Here's all we will need to know. The square footage of the load. We have to have that in order to choose an adequate boat. Also the weight, within a ton or so. And we've got to know the distance. From where to where, point "A" to point "B". Also, when is it going to happen? The guys that I work with will ask those questions immediately. Then of course, they'll want to know about money."

Gar paused, looking briefly into the eyes of each of the men and then he continued. "But we really must have all the other figures first, before we can talk money. Every one of my partners has more or less worked out a square footage, weight and distance formula. One guy says he'll do it, usually for a thousand a mile. That is if it's a small enough load that he can hide it under a load of fish. The good news on that is that he only charges one way. In other words, since he goes out empty, he only charges the miles he's got product aboard. Worked out to $300,000 last trip."

"Gar, listen," Jay blurted. He was a big, tall blond with an angular build and very sharp facial features. He seemed to be competent, but his was an overbearing competence borne of arrogance. The man was pushy, in a word, and Gar was immediately leery of him. But, curiously, the man was pushy without having the exactitude to support himself. It didn't add up. But what he had to say was certainly interesting.

"We're looking to get you guys twelve million for the fisherman's end," he said. "And I'm thinking somewhere around 5,000 kilos, ten to twelve thousand pounds, will be the weight of the load. And we can bring the boat in real close. Maybe ten miles offshore. Something like that. Can you work with those numbers?"

"What will the square footage be?"

"Wow, man, I'm not sure. I think, I don't know, maybe about a pickup truck full? If it's got a canopy on it and, like, one of those cab overs, stacked cab high?"

Gar grinned wide enough for crow's-feet to crease his temples, knowing this would be a simple task with those numbers. But it was hard to know if this guy was serious. A pickup truck with a canopy? Either way, the staggering sum of twelve million dollars was making him slightly giddy. Hell, a pickup truck full! They could set that on the deck and chuck it over the side if the Coast Guard came up to them.

"Yeeeaahhh," Gar stretched out his answer. "I think I can probably convince the guys to go for that."

THAT WAS SIX months ago, in August of 1991, shortly after Marilyn had informed Gar that Gregory had called. Now, after a dozen trips to Santa Rosa to meet with one or another of the guys, they were less sure on the numbers rather than more sure. Gar could not get it through their smoked-out heads that they needed to firm up the numbers, especially the square footage of the load. Every time they discussed square footage, Jay would spread his arms wide; pick a spot across the room, and say, "It will be roughly from here wide to yea long."

And to that Gar wanted to say, "Far out, man." But he could never quite get into their mindset.

When working with the limited square footage of a boat, Jay's explanation was wholly inadequate. It was absolutely maddening.

The bright side, though, was that Jay was passing small satchels of money–containing three, four and five thousand dollars at a time–and with this Gar could keep the big house going. And he passed Tom and Grady some of this money so they would stay focused on the project.

Grady, who drove the boat during the previous smuggling operation, and his brother Tom, were ready to take over the entire operation. They had many friends who were zealously eager to participate in the tasks that needed to be done.

Grady was a stocky, bearded fisherman with a no-nonsense attitude and gnarled red fists as big as small hams. He could throw a marlinspike with unerring accuracy and enough force to embed it half its length in a telephone pole. He was definitely not someone to mess with. Gar had known him for years, and knew he could trust him to get the job done. His brother, Tom, was also a worthy man.

THE DOPERS KEPT mentioning the figure of twelve million dollars. It was a wonderful motivator. Gar couldn't help referring to them as dopers, when discussing the operation with Tom and the rest of the guys, as the information he was relaying often sounded quite loopy to the more factual-minded fishermen.

At one point, after much traveling up and down the coast, Gar put together an "Operational Overview" for the dopers, hoping to focus their thinking. This consisted of a small photo album, and pictures and captions explaining the various boats and off-load scenarios Grady and Tom had located, and Gar had photographed. Jay and Woody (though Woody, at this point, was almost out of the thing) took this to someone who, obviously impressed, sent back a slightly larger satchel to grease the gears. That person, besides making choices on which scenario he preferred, also *ordered* they burn the photo album forthwith.

As the plan was forming and job descriptions became clear, Gar realized he was little more than a messenger boy between Tom's crew and the principles: Jay, Woody, and the mystery friends. Gar had nicknamed Jay, "Surfer Dude," and Woody, "The Hippie." Jay was six foot and a couple of inches, with blond hair, and really a surfer. Woody was your average middle-aged long hair, though he wasn't necessarily a burnt-out hippie. As a matter of fact, Woody claimed to have flown cocaine for the Iran contras and the CIA back in the day, and he was such a serious person that this was plausible.

The operation had taken on its own direction. What with so many experienced, strong-willed players involved, it worked more like an assembly line, with everyone operating at his own station. Indeed, Jay and Woody had years of experience, while Tom could make the same claim. This was the same Tom on the boat ***Armadillo*** that years earlier, while running north with Gar after *The Day Under the bridge* (and the *sea-weed* pickup), had been called into Eureka by the Coast Guard because he was on their hot list.

Tom's experience was extensive and chronicled. He began fishing with his Dad about the same time he learned how to walk, and was an original salty dog. He even looked the part of a fisherman of old, wearing a gold hoop earring and collarless red and black-striped shirts, with a generally grizzled and unshaven mien. He leered at women, rather than merely look at them, and he had been known to drink rum out of a bottle. He was almost a pirate, though he was a very, very competent man. He was a man to have on your side, Tom was. That was for damned sure.

Gar was now a go-fer and an errand boy. Which was fine with him, as he was not liking this too much anyway.

Fuckin' dopers.

CHAPTER 48

MAY, 1992.

WHAT GAR DID not know was that this whole scam was part of something much larger than any of them, called *Operation Rehash*, and Jay's boss, Bubba, was working for the CIA or DEA, or both. Woody was also leaking information to a federal contact.

This was a controlled delivery.

The legality of this sort of operation was not just questionable, it was illegal if its presence were ever made known to a federal judge. A reverse-sting of sorts, a controlled delivery motivates people to do things they might not have done otherwise. It is similar to a pretty police girl that dresses provocatively then offers herself for a ridiculously low price–say, ten or twenty dollars–to some poor schmuck who's not had a strange piece of tail since high school. Then when the old guy smiles and agrees, they bust him for soliciting a prostitute.

The fix was in, all right, on this operation from the very beginning. And before it would end, there would be duplicity followed by double duplicity. Bubba would set up the whole operation, then get a free pass to import tons of illicit drugs in exchange for a mountain of information.

This is how the drug war works. It's not at all about stopping drugs. It's about how much of the world can be manipulated via Uncle Sam controlling the drug trade and regional economics. And there are incredible profits to be made by the government agencies involved.

Why else would drugs continue to be illegal? Common sense shows us that they could not be any more available. Anyone can buy drugs. Young children have no problem scoring. Indeed, if the drug business were taken out of the hands of non-taxpaying criminals, and legitimized under the bailiwick of someone responsible, it would certainly slow down or stop kids from buying the stuff if they had to show ID first.

But that would take away an incredibly powerful tool from Uncle Sam and all the many U.S. Black-operation agencies involved with the trade. Taking over the drug business, legally, would actually decrease the government's control of many clandestine organizations, not to mention the control currently being exerted over a number of small countries.

Gar was an unwitting pawn in a much larger scheme. All of them were. But they didn't know it.

They were very soon to discover the truth. The fated load of hashish put on an ocean-going tug in Karachi, Pakistan by sailors in the Pakistani navy was soon to arrive. But even best-laid plans go awry....

CHAPTER 49

JUNE, 1992.

THE WILLIPA BAY Fish Company, in South Bend, Washington, had become Gar's main concern. His long-time school chum, Darryl Jones, had taken charge of the tactical outfitting of the building and dock that comprised the fish company. It was a huge building fronted on the backside with a functional wharf of sufficient size for several large boats to tie up at once. The building was large enough for a diesel tractor-trailer rig to back completely inside. In other words, they could back a truck inside so that its rear loading door was at the dock, and the truck was secured within the confines of the building, completely hidden. Thus, with a boat tied at the dock, bundles only needed to move twenty or so feet through semi-exposed air.

Gar devoted his full attention to the fish company. Jay the surfer had become the overall manager of the operation. Woody the Hippie had taken a back seat, and Gregory, Gar's sort-of brother in law, was on standby for the moment. Gregory had the contract to hire and manage the crew that would unload the boat. The big day for that was to be August second, the weekend of the Seafarer's Festival on Washington's Puget sound. This was a carefully selected midsummer weekend when the Coast Guard would hopefully be much too busy to worry about Willipa Bay. Willipa Bay is 100 miles down the coast from the Straits of San Juan de Fuca. The Straits are at the entrance to the Sound.

Grady had secured a lease on the ***Mahi Mahi***, a seventy-foot schooner style fishing boat that measured out with room to spare for the operation. That is to say, if the dimensions that Jay gave were accurate. And that part was still problematic.

Tom was busy. He'd hired a crew for himself and Grady, and was now keeping them occupied. He would later bring in Donnie to drive the truck that would haul the load away from the dock. Tom had known Donnie since adolescence. Tom also hired Richard, another long-time friend with the fishing boat ***Dauntless***, to represent additional backup.

The original idea that Tom would take the load aboard the ***Armadillo***, should the ***Mahi Mahi*** break down, was not an entirely sound plan, as they would need one boat just to haul fuel so the two backups could make it all the way out to the International Date Line and then back in. If the ***Mahi Mahi*** broke down while Tom was bringing in the load in Grady's stead, Richard would tow the ***Mahi Mahi*** in.

Barring a ***Mahi Mahi*** breakdown, Richard and Tom would hang out at about three-hundred miles off the coast, a long way short of where Grady had to go.

So the sea crew now included Richard on the ***Dauntless***, which had a great side benefit as his wife was a buyer for Starkist.

And, now, so was Gar. The Willipa Bay Fish Company was soon to sport a freshly painted Charlie the Tuna sign.

CHAPTER 50

JULY, 1992.

THE GOOD NEWS was that Jay had finally come up with some of the numbers. The ocean-going tug that was bringing the load from Sonmiani Bay near Karachi, Pakistan, would not come any closer than 2,100 miles off the Washington coast. This position is further away than Hawaii, and closer to Japan than anywhere else. It is just beyond the International Date Line at 180 degrees west longitude. When they got there they would be east of Greenwich, rather than west, and they would suddenly find themselves in tomorrow. The latitude of the meeting was to be at forty degrees north.

The bad news was that the load had maybe grown in size, but Jay could not be sure of that. This fact, combined with Jay's generally lackadaisical doper attitude, made Gar concerned and tired. And it just plain made him mad. So much so that one day he quit.

He told Jay that he did not want to be involved with an operation wherein the numbers were so cryptic and where he was held in such low regard that he was kept mostly uninformed.

Jay was upset, but he convinced Gar to continue putting together the Fish Company. After all, Gar could make a good living buying and wholesaling fish. Indeed, he now had the official *Charlie Tuna* Starkist sign posted up on the front of his building. And he had a lease option, in his name, on the huge old building and wharf. They had put a sizable sum down as earnest money on the lease. So much so that Gar would actually be able to pay for the place within five years.

SINCE THE ***MAHI MAHI*** averaged around ten miles per hour, even in bad conditions it was a nine-day trip out and a nine-day trip back in. Accordingly, Grady had to leave on July 12th, which would allow him a couple of extra days. Tom was figuring low, actually, on the mileage his brother would be able to cover. But this was not a problem because the tugboat was dragging its feet anyway, waiting for Grady. Grady could always hang out in the offshore albacore fleet, should he need to kill a couple of days. They were shooting for the August 2nd Seafarer's Weekend to offload, so Grady might need to do just that. He wouldn't find any fishing boats in the area from inside the Dateline to inside of Hawaii. But a day or two inside of the Hawaiian Islands would provide plenty of boats.

GREGORY HAD A single-sideband radio down in the Bay Area with which he and Jay monitored daily reports between Grady, Tom and Richard. They had worked out an elaborate code where all sorts of casual fishing expressions had clandestine meanings. Not to mention that most of these sorts of conversations can actually be truthful while passing on necessary information: "The weather's fine, the boat's running perfectly, we're in good health, I'm sure I'll be in when I said I would." That type of thing.

Jay would discuss the reports with Gregory, who was in charge of the unloading, and then contact everyone else with instructions. Jay was in contact with the tug via satellite telephone as well, and he was therefore able to keep them coordinated with the ***Mahi Mahi***.

ON THE TWENTY-SECOND of July, at nine in the morning, Grady reported that everything was fine. They were headed home, despite the fact that all of Jay's weights and measurements were all wrong. Gar, who had been listening to these reports, even though he had quit, felt some vindication about his decision to opt out.

"Fuckin' dope smokers," Gar thought. "All I ever asked them for, from the very first minute, was the exact numbers. And they still never got it right. How much? Where at? What the fuck was so hard about that?"

It didn't really matter. He had the fish company that the crew would use for only one night, while Gar slept peacefully somewhere else. He would go about a normal life after that.

The problem was that Grady then went inexplicably silent for the next seven days. And Jay began bugging Gar about it.

CHAPTER 51

AUGUST, 1992.

GRADY GOT BACK in touch a week later, after a harrowing week of worry by everyone on shore. He'd had a number of problems. He was the type of guy that blamed inanimate objects and uninvolved persons for the inevitable glitches presented by life. When various things went wrong with the boat–a boat he had never been at sea with–he blamed the boat and all the guys on shore that were waiting for them.

"Fuck those assholes," he said to his crewman, Don.

"They can suffer along with us. I know they're dying to hear from us. Fuck 'em...."

THE ***MAHI MAHI*** CREPT past the Ledbetter Point Lighthouse on the south spit of the entrance to Willipa Bay just past 12:30 in the morning, and she crept into the bay alone. There was no other boat traffic, no chatter on the radios, just the crackling high-intensity beam of the Point Ledbetter Lighthouse as it described its great circle in the night.

The men on the ship were silent as they stole into the bay, tense with dread about a sudden, lancing ray of illumination from a Coast Guard cutter spotlight, but no spotlight appeared. Grady was never so relieved in his life. He had been watching the lighthouse beam for hours, since far out on the ocean, and beyond sight of land, and the beacon promised safety and sanctuary if only he could reach it. And the lighthouse hadn't lied. They had made it. He danced a quick jig behind the helm and steered the big boat in towards the Willapa Bay Fish Company.

ON THE SECOND day of August, as planned, they unloaded the boat at Gar's fish company while Gar slept soundly at the house he'd rented across town. The next day Gar went down and cleaned up with Clorox bleach. Although things were pretty well in order, he wanted to get rid of any smell that might incriminate him. He did not want to be tied to the thing that he had quit. He'd foregone a large paycheck in order not to risk his freedom. And, by God, he did not want to take a chance that something would go wrong with the doper's operation and he might find himself suddenly inundated with federal agents and drug-sniffing dogs.

While he was cleaning, Grady came by. "I heard you quit," he shouted as he walked into the huge building. It was as big as a Safeway store. Gar was off on one partitioned side. The building featured a long, narrow stall that was wide enough for a semi to back into and still leave room for a forklift to come around one side.

Gar looked at Grady–bearded, stocky, five-seven and two hundred and fifty pounds, with a solid Germanic face–and he couldn't help but smile. He offered his hand and said, "Congratulations. I assume all went well?"

"That's the last thing I would say," Grady spat back. "I've never seen such a fucked-up boat in my life. We had more problems. That fuckin' sum-bitch, Herb, that I leased it from. What a piece of shit!"

"Oh, really? I know you had some problems. But you brought in the load, didn't you?"

"Oh, yeah. They got their shit, all right. At least I figure so, as I could see the boat from the motel and it's setting pretty high out of the water now. I went up to the motel soon's I got in. Well, after I took my deckhand to the hospital. He fucked up his shoulder trying to fix the auxiliary generator in bad weather. We had more fuckin' things go wrong...."

They had meandered through the building toward the dock at the back end. The ***Mahi Mahi*** was still tied to the pilings. It floated down twenty feet or so below them; it was the morning low tide. Gregory's crew had unloaded the boat on the high tide just six hours earlier. Gar looked at the boat, and decided to quit trying to solicit any kind of positive statement from Grady. It wasn't meant to be, he figured.

"Holy shit!" Gar suddenly exclaimed, noticing damage to the boat. "I didn't see that. Your bow is all caved in. What happened there?"

"Oh, yeah. We side tied with the tug. That was a big ass sum-bitchen tug, too. And we came together pretty hard there a few times. It was a piss-flat ocean, but surge. You know. I told those fuckin' gooks they had on there, to tie those spring lines tighter, and put in more rubber-ball fenders. We had a ton of those. But they didn't listen."

"Wow! You hit hard. Look at that. What were the guys on the tug like? What kind of gooks?"

"Well, they were Filipinos. But the guy that was driving and his first mate, they were white, but Australian, maybe. I don't know. They didn't have real strong accents, but they definitely talked like they'd spent some time down under."

Grady was scratching his beard and smiling slightly, for a change. It was a perfect Pacific Northwest, August morning. The sun was bright and the sky was an almost neon blue. The smell of low tide mud, a rich, fecund odor, filled the air. Birds worked the drifting tide in the channel that scuttled past the wharf, and a fair amount of marsh grass trundled by with the tide.

"How long had those guys been packing the load? Did they say?" Gar was suddenly intrigued by the fact that Grady had been one-half of a relay team that brought something from the other side of the world. Maybe it was the beauty of the morning, or the rich, exotic smell of the low-tide mud, but his mind was filled with faraway images and Gar caught a growing sense of excitement.

"No. They didn't say exactly." Grady looked thoughtful now. He kept pulling on his beard, which was not very long, but real bushy. Maybe he was trying to make it longer. The hand that tugged at the beard looked like a boiled hunk of beef brisket. "The guy did say that they had a problem with pirates, a lot of pirates, coming through the Strait of Malacca there between Sumatra and Malaysia. Then they actually got attacked after they rounded through the Singapore Strait."

"Pirates. Really? I've heard of that in the South China Sea, but I didn't know if it was true." Gar felt a growing sense of excitement. This really was an adventure. He had quit the operation. But he loved the romance and intrigue of the venture nonetheless. This was the kind of stuff they wrote books about. Somewhere in the back of his mind he made a note of that.

"Oh, yeah." Grady spoke now like it was actually him that had encountered the pirates. "You've got to carry plenty of heavy artillery, forty millimeter or better. Most guys will mount cannons or machine guns, or both, on their bow.

My brother said he likes to take those *LAWS* rockets. Said you just jerk one of those babies out and start strapping it on your shoulder, and the pirates will haul ass out of there. They usually have fast boats, you know. Yeah, this Aussie Captain on the tug boat, he said they had some AK's, or something, that they'd break out and spray half a clip, or so, toward the pirate boat. He said they got right the fuck out of there, right fuckin' now!"

"I'll be damned. They had plenty of action, it sounds like." Gar was shaking his head. "What are you going to do about the bow of your boat? It looks bad. And it may be incriminating."

"Ahh, fuck. I don't know. I hadn't got that far yet. I guess I'm going to give this piece of shit back to Herb. I thought I might try to buy it, but we had too many problems."

"Hell, they were just mechanical, Grady. And nothing major. You didn't blow an engine, or anything like that. All the rest can be fixed."

"Fuck it. I'm giving this sum-bitch back to Herb. Let him fix it. I did enough work on this thing."

"Be careful. You need to fix that hull damage first. He'll see that and go straight to the law. It's too obvious for anyone not to figure out. Shit, you're going to make a lot of money, you should just buy this thing and keep Herb completely isolated from it."

Gar was convinced that Grady was taking this too lightly, and it concerned him. This was a real wrinkle in their operation. He did not want to see anything happen to these guys. They were all friends. And he had himself to think about. He did not want anything suspicious to get back to him.

"Yeah, I'll see what I can get done when I get up to Seattle. Herb's got insurance. I'll make <u>them</u> pay."

"Don't do that, Grady. Just get it fixed and pay cash for it. I'm sure that Jay will kick down. I know I will. Shit, it won't cost more than a few thousand. That's cheap, and it won't raise any flags. For that matter, you might be better off to run out and sink the boat. Have Tom handy to pick you up after you call MAYDAY."

But Grady did not listen. He rarely did. In his paranoid world, where he thought everyone was out to screw him, he did not trust anyone enough to listen to them. Which was another reason Gar had opted out of the scheme.

DURING THIS HECTIC period, Marilyn had become bored with Gar spending all his time in either Washington or Santa Rosa. He had been mostly away from home going on a year.

Gar would call her every night at nine o'clock. He liked this time because it might thwart her plans to go out. And he suspected her of this. After all, she had done it with him when married to Dick. The thought of her out dancing made Gar very unsettled. He felt sure she was doing this, and that it was being done in protest for all the time he'd spent away. It irked him that Gar's time away was producing the satchels of cash that Marilyn liked a great deal. And he wasn't even there to enjoy it with her.

DURING THE TIME Gar was putting together his office in the new fish company, he got in touch with Susan. She put in regular hours at her wholesale food business, so he called her there. It made communication easier, as she was now married and had several children.

They faxed the occasional cute cartoon to one another, and passed the latest local humor. He shared Washington jokes with her and she told him the latest from California. And since they had a lifetime of shared friends, gossip came easy.

It was yet another time in their lives when they were passing each other like the proverbial two ships going in opposite directions; managing cordial smiles and waves, but without the weather needed to stop and "side-tie."

They could speak openly about how much in love they had been more than a decade earlier. Perhaps the distance between them made this frank honesty possible.

"You should have asked me to marry you," Susan said.

"Aww, we'd probably be divorced by now, anyway."

"I don't think so. I really wanted to be with you.... Forever!"

"Then what happened?"

"I don't know. My family was giving me so much shit for living with you. And then, after we broke up, I fought with my mother for several years afterwards. I blamed her for everything."

"So many things that might have been. It's sad, really."

"I know."

That is why they forever called each other soul mates. They not only thought exactly alike, they could not forget one another. There was something there. There would always be something there.

BEFORE THAT AUGUST came to an end, things would get yet more complicated. Gar's lifelong tie to Susan was one thing, but his affiliation with Jay was about to become a real tangle.

Jay called a week after the offload and said, "Look, I understand why you quit. I couldn't get the numbers right. I was a flake and an asshole. So you got out of harm's way. But the job got done. And that's because you introduced us to good people."

"Well...." Gar didn't know what he was getting at. He obviously wanted something. "Hang on, Jay. Let me switch phones." Gar was at the house in Crescent City and there were kids everywhere.

After acknowledging he was in the bedroom now, Jay came back with, "I want you to come back in, at full pay, and help me get everyone their money."

"Holy shit! Should we be discussing this on this phone?"

"No. But I can meet you at the Crescent City Airport in four hours. It's about ten now, so I'll see you there at two. Look for a dark gray airplane with a Navy insignia on it."

"Okay," Gar said. What else could he say?

THEY MET AT the airport and Jay handed Gar a very large bag of money, saying, "I only need you to deliver this to Tom. He'll get it to his guys. Better keep some for yourself. We'll just keep going like this. I got the plane on permanent charter. It's my lawyer, Mike Metzger's, pilot actually. We'll do like this until we get everyone paid. I don't know everybody. You do."

"How much is here?"

"Eight hundred." He paused. "Thousand, that is. Eight hundred thousand dollars."

"No shit," Gar said.

Part Three

EL FUGITIVO

CHAPTER 52

SEPTEMBER, 1992.

GRADY CALLED TO say that the Coast Guard had drawn a bead on him. He'd taken the boat to a shipyard in Seattle, called the owner saying he had hull damage–that insurance should cover, and the owner had called the law.

The Coast Guard was now tasked with investigating who had hit who. The problem, however, was that they brought drug-sniffing canines aboard the boat and got a hit. The dogs went crazy.

So it was now a drug investigation, as well. The owner of the ***Mahi Mahi***, Herb, told them he knew Grady was doing some sort of business with a dude named Gar down at the Willipa Bay Fish Company....

A PART OF Gar was not surprised. He had warned Grady that this would happen, and it did. The only thing that was surprising was how fast everything unraveled after that.

Gar was down in Crescent City. He had closed up shop in the Willipa Bay Fish Company because there was too much going on, and he got a call from the real estate agent who had handled the Fish Company lease. The agent said U.S. Customs had come around asking questions. They suspected a drug-smuggling operation had gone on at the Fish Company involving the ***Mahi Mahi***, and Gar would probably be hearing from them.

Gar feigned incredulousness, and assured the real estate agent that nothing as sinister as that had gone on. Gar had bailed out because Marilyn was threatening to leave him if he didn't come home. This was mostly the truth, as she was definitely bored sitting home alone. Marilyn's eternal happiness is grounded in her basic social nature. Married, and with a houseful of kids, she has a constant audience. With Gar gone, she had lost half of her fan base.

GAR CALLED MIKE Metzger, the high-priced drug attorney who Jay retained. Mike told Gar he'd see him at the airport in two hours, in a dark gray plane with Navy insignia. It was the same plane, a very impressive aircraft, that Jay used to move money. Gar wasn't sure exactly what kind it was, but it was a restored antique, which was why the pilot was able to fly it with a Navy insignia on the tail. It was an enormous, roaring twin engine, capable of seating eight to ten people. It was armor plated and one of those things that everybody stands back from when it is started up. Great gouts of black smoke jetted from the cowlings when the engines were lit off, and the birds for a quarter mile around fled in terror at the sound.

THE PLANE LANDED with a great roaring sound, and Mike Metzger opened the door and told Gar to get in. He then instructed the pilot to fly to Gold Beach for lunch. Along the way Mike had Dwayne, the pilot, do a "skull buster."

It involved doing a loop-the-loop wherein zero gravity is momentarily achieved. But while upside down, and before righting the plane, gravity returns and heads get bumped on the ceiling. Hard.

It was sophomoric. Gar couldn't believe this legendary litigator had given the order. Maybe that's why he was called *Mad Dog* Metzger. The kid flying the plane seemed even crazier than Mad Dog. It was adventuresome, though, and Gar lived, it seemed, for adventure. He had to keep reminding himself of that. He rubbed his head ruefully and wondered what in the hell he was doing here. All he had ever wanted to do was catch salmon.

GAR AND MIKE had lunch while Dwayne busied himself cleaning and gassing the plane. Mike said, "Look Gar. Can I call you Gar? There's a team of Feds up in Seattle investigating the boat. There's a team, another team, out of Portland, looking at you in Crescent City. And another team is down in the Bay Area, looking at guys there. First off, I think you've got a leak."

"How do you know all this. And I don't know anything about a leak."

"I don't know either." He said either like *etha*. Mike was originally from New York and had a quintessential Brooklyn accent. The kind of accent that seemed to impress West Coasters like Gar. Oddly, he was dressed in camouflage fatigues, with a camouflage coat and a black tee-shirt. He was not your average barrister. "But I'm telling you what, these fucking Feds are like, well, put it this way: It's as if a female dog were locked in a yard, during her period of estrus, then taken out and a bunch of male dogs put in. They're running all around, knowing something was just there. Excited as hell. But can't quite find what they're looking for."

"You think they're that excited?" Gar was becoming frightened. Until this moment, he'd figured he was innocent and had nothing to fear. After all, he had quit. No more. But frightening him was likely Metzger's intention. "What should I do?"

"Well, first, yes, they are that excited. And to answer your second question, you did the right thing calling me. How much money you get from Jay so far?"

"Oh, I don't know. It doesn't matter, though, because I passed it all to the other guys." Gar held up his hands, oblivious to the spectacular view of the Rogue River out the restaurant window. "I kept about eighty thousand, is all, but I'm trying to keep some sort of nest egg. Jay owes me quite a bit more." This was actually a lie, as Gar had rat-holed much more than that.

"Give me fifty when we get back to Crescent City. Can you get to it fairly fast?" Mike could move things right along. "If I'm going to put in a Notice of Appearance on your behalf, I'm going to need some earnest money. Give me fifty so I can officially provide *Notice* to the Feds that you are represented. And I tell you they cannot, and I mean can not, talk to you without me there. They'll leave you alone."

"All right, let's do that," Gar replied. "It will only take twenty minutes to get the money."

THAT WAS EARLY in September. Near the middle of the month, as Marilyn's second son Jeff approached his eighteenth birthday, Marilyn complained that Gar had been gone too much and needed to be home on Jeff's birthday. So Gar headed for home on the eighteenth. He had been in the Bay Area shuttling money from Jay to Tom. It was a thankless job, as Jay never did as he promised. By the time he would get a payment to Tom, Tom would be pissed.

Fuckin' dopers.

GAR LEFT SANTA Rosa around noon, figuring on an early-evening arrival at the big house in Crescent City. Driving up Highway 101, there seemed to be extra police coverage on the coast. Gar had more cops follow him, and then turn off, than he ever remembered seeing before. It was almost enough for him to suspect himself of incipient paranoia.

It was pleasant Indian-Summer weather, though. There were no deer visible in the roadside fields, as the hunting season had already begun and driven them into the nearby hills. It seemed like a millennium ago that he and Cindy had driven this route together, playing the game of whoever saw the first deer got a candy bar.

North of Willits, at Laytonville, he stopped at a small shopping center. He went into a Thrifty Drug and bought a Norelco electric shaver with popup beard trimmer for Jeff. The good-natured girl behind the counter happily gift wrapped his purchase.

Out in the parking lot, the police drove by Gar twice while he walked back to his truck. They seemed to be avoiding looking directly at him.

Hmmm....

SOUTH OF CRESCENT City, coming down Klamath Hill, Gar saw something strange in his rearview mirror. Though it was pitch dark, he could see two highway patrol cars trailing him. They were driving without headlights.

It was ill omened and ominous.

When Gar slowed down, favoring the right side of the road, the CHP's would not pass. They stayed well back. And they did not turn on their headlights.

It was too strange.

ON THE NORTH side of Klamath, the CHPs turned on all their lights. This was just as one got in front of Gar's vehicle and one remained behind him. In this way, they herded Gar into a wide turnout ringed by impassable cliffs rising on three sides of the turnout, with rocky ocean on the opposite side of the highway. And within seconds, there were twenty police cars surrounding him, plus a police helicopter circling overhead.

Ironically, just a few miles straight out from this rocky beach, is where the ***Visit*** still laid on the ocean bottom; undoubtedly mudded-in, barnacled over, and home to hundreds of sea creatures.

When Gar had his vehicle finally stopped and ringed completely by flashing law-enforcement patrol cars, the entire scene lit by the spectral glow of the police-helicopter spotlight overhead, there still remained in Gar's mind enough presence to notice the faraway flash of the Point St. George Lighthouse, winking dimly in the distance. Again a feeling of disassociation came over Gar.

"If only," he thought briefly. If only the ***Visit*** had not gone down. If only he were out there in the darkness of the sea, awaiting first light and a chance to set his lines. He did not belong here, he quickly considered.

He had lost his way.

THEY ASKED IF they could toss the truck, saying they'd searched Gar's house earlier. Gar said no. It was a strange feeling, having dozens of various types of police standing in the cold night air facing him, and he standing alone facing them. It reminded him of his early bar-hopping-looking-for-fights days, when he would climb up on the bar in a rowdy saloon and shout, "Hey! If anyone in here is looking for a fight, that's why I'm here."

A local sheriff named Bill Stevens, who Gar knew as the small boy who had accompanied his dad out to Gar's house to pick up a sack of crab one Christmas, conducted the questioning in the headlights of a CHP car. Gar told him to call Mike Metzger, and after suspending questions for an hour, they said, "Unless you want to waive your lawyer privilege and help us, you can go. But we're keeping your truck. We have reason to believe it was involved with a large drug-smuggling operation. The Feds told us to hold it. They're on the radio-phone now. The said to give you a ride to where ever you want to go."

"I'd like a ride to the office of attorney Mike Metzger in Santa Rosa, then." Gar smiled. Santa Rosa was 250 miles away. Perhaps he'd win this stare down after all.

"No can do, Gar. We'll take you where you need to go in Crescent City. As I said, we searched your house today. But when we left, your stepsons were still there."

"Well, good. I was going home for a birthday party anyway." Gar didn't want to sound like this was at all serious; maybe it was all a big mistake.

But they'd confiscated the $5,000 cash he had in his pants pocket. That was no mistake. He had no money, now. And no transportation, either. He needed to get back down to Mad Dog Metzger's where it might be safer.

THE CHP THAT took Gar home was an acquaintance from the Elk's Lodge. He dropped Gar off, and inexplicably wished him luck.

Neither Marilyn nor the birthday boy, Jeff, were at the house. Jason was there, and he explained what had happened. They had tossed the house, asking a ton of questions. "They even took five-year-old Justin out on the deck for questioning," Jason said.

Jason seemed lonely and scared, despite his great height and youth. Maybe that was it. He looked young and scared. Gar reassured him the best he could. This was all a mistake and he would fix it. Jason was finally convinced, and went off happily to his Game Boy in the living room.

In the morning, Marilyn was still not there. And she was nowhere to be found by phone. Gar called Mike Metzger. Mike said he'd call back in a few minutes.

A half hour later, Mike called and told Gar to go to Western Union. "There's five hundred cash waiting there," he said. Then he instructed Gar to go to the Crescent City Airport and take the eleven a.m. flight to San Francisco. "A limo driver will meet you at the gate and bring you here. He'll have a poster board with your name on it. But your name is going to be Blackstone. I don't want to take any chances the Feds might be looking for you." Mike was thorough, but in Gar's opinion he seemed a bit paranoid.

JASON GAVE GAR a ride to the Western Union, and then on to the airport. There was a finality to all of this that both seemed to understand without speaking about it.

As Gar was boarding the plane, he turned for what he expected would be his last look at Crescent City. And there was Marilyn, running across the tarmac. He hurriedly told the stewardess, "One second, please," and scampered back down the stairs.

"Where are you going?" Marilyn was crying.

"To Mike Metzger's right now. Then, I don't know. Jay said he has friends in Mexico...."

"What about me? And what do I do with the money you've given me? I've saved about $80,000 of it."

"Keep it well hidden. Somewhere far away from Heacock Lane. Call me from a pay phone later. I'll be at Metzger's in a few hours."

"I love you."

"I love you, too...."

AS THE PLANE began to taxi away, Gar felt like he was in a movie: *Casa Blanca*, or something. Marilyn stood waving sadly with tears running down her face, and Gar's mental gears spun wildly. He was leaving something on the tarmac here, something it would be impossible to regain.

He knew he'd never see her, or Crescent City, again.

As the plane circled south, heading down the coastline, Gar identified all the familiar landmarks; the many rocks and coastal anomalies. Floods of memories, good times and bad, clicked through his brain. At this altitude he could see fishing boats, but not enough detail to identify them. Yet because he was so well acquainted with everyone's fishing habits, he knew which boats they were simply by their location and direction of travel.

THE NEXT DAY Mad Dog had Marilyn fly down. When she got there, Mike suggested they get married. "Things are going to get much worse," he informed them brusquely. "Married, you won't have to testify against each other."

So they did. Dwayne flew them to Lake Tahoe, where they spent their honeymoon night at the Sunshine Motel. On that night they conceived a child. She would be born in Mexico. Gar thought that the flood of emotions and crazy occurrences transpiring during those times would make this child very special. "The Spirit Child" he would later call her. She was conceived in tumultuous strife and born under an equatorial sun.

CHAPTER 53

EARLY 1993.

GAR LIVED IN a different hotel every night during the last months of 1992. During a subsequent search of his home, the Feds found a half-million dollars buried in a hollow log in the woods behind his house. The money wasn't actually on Gar's property, but they assumed it was his and utilized it to fund the entire investigation. With their investigation now fully financed, the Feds were more determined than ever to bust Gar. They were certain he was the ringleader. Following the discovery of this large cache of currency, they officially seized Gar and Marilyn's home. But this was merely a legal encumbrance. They did not make anyone leave.

In December, Jay took Gar shopping, while keeping him in a secure hotel in San Francisco. Then Jay arranged for a car with a driver to take Gar to Tijuana, where he caught a plane to Acapulco. He assured Gar that he would finish paying everyone their full share, including Gar.

Ha! Fuckin' dopers. They never do as they promise.

But just that quick–in a matter of only a few days–Gar's world changed dramatically. Early one morning he had been in misty San Francisco, and by the middle of the next day he was blinking under the harsh rays of a very hot Acapulco sun.

The twenty-one-year-old lawyer that met Gar at the Acapulco Airport was the son of Tao, one of Jay's long-time associates, a young man named Gilberto. He held a neatly lettered sign displaying the single word, "Gar." The young man was dressed to the nines, and had a wide, friendly-looking grin. Gar would learn that he never dressed any differently, and he never lost the grin.

Gar blinked uncertainly in the bright, mid-day rays outside of the terminal of the Acapulco Airport, and noticed immediately a giant white cross on an adjacent hillside. He had seen this huge thing from the air, and Gilberto, the man who picked him up, explained that it was a Christian cross standing more than 120 feet in height. It was a tribute to two sons who had died, built many years before, and the thing had come to represent Acapulco every bit as much as the Gateway Arch represents the City of Saint Louis in America.

Gilberto was a smart, well-mannered, fairly dark-skinned Mexican who spoke perfect English, with only a slight accent. His new job was to protect Gar, mainly from the police, as well as to set him up in Acapulco. As instructed by Jay, Gar gave him an envelope full of cash as soon as they got to the car. That is, right after Gilberto got the air conditioner fired up. It was a blazing hundred-plus degrees in Acapulco.

Jay had things fairly well organized; the road well paved so to speak. Jay spoke fluent Spanish and evidently had completed many smuggling operations with Tao. Obviously the world-famous *Acapulco Gold* was the product. But weed operations were outdated now. Cocaine had become Mexico's number one industry, after Florida was all but shut down from Colombian cocaine smuggling.

Everything from Central America went through Mexico now, instead of Florida. And a number of things had made the smuggling of weed obsolete. Hydroponics, cloned plants, grow lights, and Yankee ingenuity in general, had made American marijuana far more marketable than Mexican pot. And nowadays it was tremendously more powerful, as well.

So it was the age of cocaine–crack or otherwise–and Tao played that game very well with the corps of Federales he'd fallen in with. And Tao's son, Gilberto with the wide and friendly grin, was an educated apple who had not fallen very far from the tree.

TAO AND HIS dangerous band of Federal Police were extreme characters. They lived all over Mexico in discreet hotels. One night they took Gar partying. It began at Tao's place with mountains of cocaine, and quickly moved to a topless-bottomless strip club that did not allow guns. The arsenal of weapons Tao and his gang checked at the door made Gar's knees buckle.

These men were paid to protect Gar. Since any arrest or extradition warrants would come through their office, it gave Gar an inside track–theoretically. Tao would constantly send *Sky-Tel* messages to Gar, urging him to keep low. Several times he called to say that the American Drug Enforcement Agency was asking about Gar, but did not yet know where he was.

These communiqués had Gar constantly watching over his shoulder, when he was not hunkering down in his hideout. It made life more stressful than he'd ever previously known. He bought a .45 automatic and carried it everywhere he went, even though guns are illegal in Mexico. He figured he'd shoot it out, if it came to that, and die before he'd let them take him to prison for life. The thought that he'd first have to go to a Mexican prison made this fear even worse.

BY JANUARY OF 1993, Marilyn, Amanda, and Justin were living in Acapulco. Gar had a very comfortable villa, which they greatly enjoyed. They had cars, cell phones, and all the essentials of life. Amanda and Justin were enrolled in a good private school. They were all set up. This included an expensive surveillance system of the walled villa, including cameras on the front and monitors throughout the house. And they had a front entryway that only a SWAT team could breach.

ON JUNE ELEVENTH, the Spirit Child was born. Andriana Garyn Walton was a blond-haired, blue-eyed Mexican girl. Born on Mexican soil, Andriana was first a Mexican, until they applied for American citizenship. At that time she became a dual citizen. Upon her eighteenth birthday, she'd have to decide which country to which she belonged.

AFTER ANDRIANA WAS born, Marilyn became disillusioned, more so each day. The not-always-honest way Mexicans do business; the near one-hundred-degree heat every day; the language; the foreign, unique customs; the pressure of impending legal troubles; all of these things worked on her and eventually wore her down.

The holidays not too far away, and with the other kids back in the States calling for her, Marilyn decided to go back north. Gar tried to convince her to leave Andriana for him to raise; but she took all the kids with her. The house on Heacock Lane was still under federal seizure, but they could live there while Gar's lawyers litigated the situation.

FOR A WHILE, everything was okay for Gar because Jasmer and Alison came for a summer visit at the same time that Marilyn was leaving. Cindy dropped Jas and Ali off. She stayed for a few days–long enough to drive Marilyn wild with jealousy–then went back to California. She would come back in a month to pick up the kids. But after this she would not ever come back again, nor would she let the kids come back.

Mexico, despite all its casual splendor, became a prison for Gar that kept him sequestered from his children. He lived under the looming Cross of Acapulco and he suffered. For a time. And then he found a cure.

After the kids left, and after three years of sobriety, Gar began to drink again. Mexico looked much different through rum-infused eyes. As a matter of fact, with several cars, a house, and a reasonable bank account, Mexico became quite appealing. Even the black cloud that resulted from being a fugitive could not detract from this charm. And Gar was a fugitive. Though no indictment had yet been handed down, the police back home were in everyone's business.

The lawyers assured the participants that indictments would be returned any day. There were people cooperating with the authorities in order to lessen their own punishments. So it was suggested that the Feds would likely keep the indictments under seal, and only unseal them as they made the arrests.

It frightened Gar more than he'd ever known on any ocean. He gazed from the courtyard of his villa, drink in hand, at the last of the afternoon's sunlight glinting on the Cross of Acapulco. And he wondered how long it could last. Was there not a reckoning? Didn't the cross represent judgment?

The cross was mute, and Gar had no answers. The tinkle of ice in his glass reminded him of what was really important.

It was time for another drink.

CHAPTER 54

LATE 1993.

"DO ALL GRINGOS have big *Panchos*?" Luz de Gloria asked innocently.

They'd only just arrived back at the villa for a swim. She was ravishing in her French-cut, one-piece suit that had built-in breast enhancement; though she needed no augmentation. For a Mexican girl, for any girl, she was well endowed. Her auburn mane was sun streaked almost blonde, a perfect complement to a light coffee-with-cream skin tone. The dimples in her cheeks and a sculpted nose, though, were what drove Gar wild with desire. Well, faultless curves and a playful nature added fuel to the fire. She was a nineteen-year-old nymph, absolutely oozing sensuality from every one of her perfect pores.

They swam in the hot Acapulco sun, and sipped peach-flavored wine coolers on Gar's patio. Her sense of flirtatiousness wasn't subtle. She swam up to Gar in the shallows on the steps, putting her cleavage against his chin, straddling him and making his shorts bulge.

Then she possessively jerked down his elastic banded swim shorts and began playing hunky-monkey (loosely translated) with Gar's...well, monkey. She asked that question in Spanish. Luz spoke no English. Gar's Spanish was excellent, though, after a year in Mexico. His life was such that he didn't hang around with anyone who spoke English for fear that they might be DEA. Gilberto and his brother Federico were the only ones he knew who spoke English. But they were always busy.

"Yes. Well, I don't look at other men's *Panchos* too often, but I've been told my Pancho is too big for my size body. And if you'll notice, I have a good-sized body." Gar thought he might as well promote himself. No one else was there to do so.

She smiled, grabbed Gar by his "handle," which she of course referred to as *Pancho*, and led him to the bedroom, where she showed Gar a number of new Mexican games. They were mainly versions of the same bedroom amusements Gar already knew; Prisoner's Base, King of the Hill, London Bridge, Simon Says, and of course, Hide the Monkey. After a time she said, "I must go back to the Colonial. We have another show starting at ten."

"Okay, whenever you're ready." The Colonial she mentioned was Tao's restaurant and bar, situated right on the edge of Acapulco Bay. A shielded concrete platform, raised just four or five feet above high water (which, in that latitude of the world is only a few feet different than low water), served as a perfect setting for on-the-water dining where water skiers performed virtually at table side. Luz de Gloria was one of the skiers. It was a great place, and the bevy of female water skiers were wonderful fun; though they often tasted quite salty!

GAR, WHY WAS it so important to you to name your house *Casa Vista del Mar*?" Gilberto was keeping Gar company at his favorite table, while Luz de Gloria skied.

Gilberto's brother Federico was the Master of Ceremonies. Federico, who looked just like Lou Diamond Phillips, was a gregarious announcer. He had an extra long microphone cord that allowed him to table hop while calling the ski show. He always handed the mike to Gar at the start of activities, and Gar would announce with panache, "Iliiittt'ss Shooowwtime!!" and Federico would make much fanfare out of this.

"Well, it has a beautiful view of the ocean...you know Vista del Mar means view of the ocean, Gilberto."

"Yes," Gilberto replied wryly. "I speak Spanish, Gar."

"...but I named it after my favorite fisherman's bar, way up north in Eureka, California." This was a rare moment when Gar could speak English, so he smiled big at being able to explain something personal like this that someone might actually understand. Being a fugitive, he did not talk to anyone about his past, except Gilberto and Federico.

"Okay, I understand. Do you miss California, Gar?" Gilberto could be personable, and he usually was. He was a very nice young man, and he and Gar had spent quite a bit of time together while getting Gar situated. Gar, and Gilberto's younger brother, Federico, were close friends also, but Gar had spent more time with Gilberto.

"Yes, I miss many things, my friend." Gar was melancholic. "You know I changed the address on my house too, remember you helped me to do that. It was actually Casa A-1 on Calle Cumbres. I changed it to A-1-A, because that's my favorite Jimmy Buffett album. You know who he is, don't you? He sings that popular American song, Margaritaville?"

"Oh, yes," Gilberto answered. "I've heard that one."

"You know something else?" Gar continued. "That neighborhood I live in is called Colonia Farallon. And my favorite fishing place in the United States was the

Farallon Islands. As a matter of fact, they used to call me Mr. Farallon. My house represents many things to me. It is very symbolic. Like the sum total of my life. I'll tell you more about it all some time." Gar was well into his cups, and grandiloquent because of this.

"Si, Gar. But I will not call you Señor Farallon. I will call you *Don* Gar." "Don" is a term which expresses deep respect in Mexico. It was the first time Gilberto had used it, and it served to make Gar more sentimental. He thought of his kids. And he wondered what Marilyn was doing. Then he decided that somehow Luz reminded him of Susan. He raised his hand, motioning for another drink.

LUZ FINISHED THE show and came over to the table. She said tonight she had to go home with Jose Luis, her husband, who also skied in the show. It was another bizarre set-up Gar found himself in. Jose Luis, dark with dreadlocks, in excellent shape and somewhat spooky looking, was fully aware that Luz had a thing for Gar, and he seemed to promote it. She'd likely worn him out long ago, Gar thought; she really was a handful. He also suspected that part of his attraction to her was the threat of a dangerous-looking husband.

Luz de Gloria was born on November 21, just like Gar and Marilyn. Though she had been born only nineteen years ago. And that was about three blocks from the Colonial Restaurant. She said, too, that she'd never been much further from home than the Colonial. After Gar learned this, he started polling waitresses and skiers and found that none of them had roamed more than a mile or two from home. Which is where most of them were born: At home.

LUZ WENT HOME. So did Gilberto and the rest of the ski show. The big white Cross of Acapulco caught the enchanting moonlight, and blazed like the second coming high up on the hill. The thing really was an arresting sight. And for an American unused to public displays of religious symbolism, there was no growing accustomed to it. Each time he saw the thing, Gar stopped to consider it. And he saw it twenty times a day.

Gar sat at the table looking out across the bay, the two ski show Master Craft ski boats bobbing at their moorings. Two sport-fishing boats looked inviting parked alongside them. Gar had viewed any number of decent-sized sailfish being maneuvered ashore. They'd pull up right here at the break in the rail where the skiers landed. There was a lower slab just under the waterline for the skiers to take off and land. Gar thought he'd take Luz sailfishing some day. She would like that.

He ordered another margarita. On top of the dozen he had already consumed, he was certainly under the influence. It felt like it was just right.

Gar's drinking was about this: Great spirits have always encountered great opposition from mediocre minds. To that end, drinking licenses a person to do nutty but ingenious things. To exhibit great spirit. To explain all those abstract ideas and observances explorative minds constantly percolate. Gar had such a mind. Indeed, his creed, often directed to others, was that "one has to continue to grow in life." Growth, of course, being learning new things; expanding horizons.

It followed, then, that many people did not understand Gar, drinking or sober. His ideas, his constant questions about often odd subjects, were sometimes not understood. The hilarity, though, that surrounded him while he was drinking, perhaps made his off-the-wall questions and topics more acceptable.

Perhaps he drank to spite Susan, Cindy, and Marilyn. Or to counteract all the emotional letdowns he'd known over the years. Indeed, there were plenty of those.

Or likely it was simply because his parents owned a bar, had always been drinkers, and his image of being a grown up always had a bottle or a glass in the picture.

Whatever. No one had more fun than Garaloney on a tear. At least he thought so. He certainly thought so right now, though he was strangely contemplative. Another of his mottos came from a song–"If there is one thing that I've never done, I've never ever had too much fun?" When stinkoed, though sober just as well, people generally liked Gar's wit and the positive aura that enveloped him.

Deep into his Margarita (with no salt or ice), he thought that the bottom line was that no one had ever prepared him for how tough life really is. Fishing was a difficult and dangerous challenge that he'd survived. But it was nonetheless the acting out of a childhood fantasy. And it was a perfect escape from the pitfalls and demands of married life.

Gar drank so he could continue being a kid. Now, at the age of forty, that was a substantive thing.

CHAPTER 55

1995.

GAR HAD RETAINED a different lawyer before leaving the States; Penny Coopman, of Emeryville, California. She had a nationwide reputation after she had won an acquittal for several Hell's Angels in a very public murder trial. Mike was really Jay's attorney, and Jay had insisted that Gar switch.

Gar called Penny from time to time, and in early 1994 she told him that Mad-Dog Metzger had committed suicide. This was very sad news. Mad Dog and Gar had spent much time together. Gar had lived at his house for several weeks at a time, ducking in and out constantly. He and Mike would stay up and talk for hours. Despite their differences, Gar had admired the outrageous litigator. And he had liked the man himself.

Penny said there was a big investigation and the Feds were into Mike's stuff. She faxed Gar a news article taken from the front page of the Seattle Post-Intelligencer dated March 15, 1995, and entitled, "Of Deceit and Hashish."

And the article said it all. It was a feature article, going on at length about Gar Walton and his sophisticated gang of international drug smugglers.

As the fax machine spat the news article out, Gar sat at his desk reading the thing with growing astonishment and dread. He was stunned. There were two dozen guys involved with the operation, and he liked to think that he was not one of them. Yet they only mentioned Gar Walton in the article.

As he began composing a letter to fax back to Penny Coopman, the front door buzzed. He looked up at the monitor, astounded to see a pickup truck full of Mexican police on the screen.

Gar instantly grabbed his pistol, and ran down one level to the garage where his Gran Marquis was backed in. With key in the ignition, he hit the automatic door opener. When it was almost completely open, he fired the engine, dropped the transmission into gear, and left black rubber across his beautiful tiled floor. He briefly glimpsed the surprised face of the policeman who was pushing the doorbell as he roared past.

He was out the door and headed down Calle Cumbres before the police could draw their guns. These police were actually young soldiers. The same can be seen all over Mexico, riding around with 15 or 20 of them stuffed into a standard-sized pickup truck bed. The policeman–the only one out of the truck–was more than likely a local municipal police officer, operating with federal credentials.

HE FLEW DOWN Calle Cumbres to Avenida Farallon, then took a drifting-skid of a right turn onto Costera Miguel Aleman, and as he was passing through the Circulo Diana Gar hit speed dial on his phone for Tao's house. Miraculously, Tao was home. He said he was just about to call Gar.

It was fortunate that Gar had a hands-free car phone with a microphone in the visor and audio on all six stereo speakers. The police truck was on Gar's ass, and traffic was uncooperative. The cops kept trying to pull alongside him.

Tao said, in Spanish–which then set the language for the entire conversation–"Where are you, Gar?"

"I'm coming down the Costera. I just passed Plaza Bahia, almost to Club del Sol." He was breathing hard as he manipulated the steering wheel. "And I have police with lights...."

"What kind of police?"

"A truck full."

"Can you lose them, Gar?"

"Maybe."

"Do you have your pistol?"

"Yes."

"Don't use it. Only unless you have to."

"I was thinking about shooting over their heads to warn them to back off. I'm driving just like Gilberto taught me, and they're still keeping up."

Tao laughed, "And I taught Gilberto how to drive. Do you have one foot on the brake and one foot on the gas?"

"Yes. And I have both thumbs on the horn and I'm honking at everybody to move."

"Very good, Gar. When you go through the tunnel, turn right after Parque Papagayo and go up to Avenida Cuauhtémoc. Then come up to the Avenida Ejido, and turn to the north on the Calzada de la Cuesta and come to my house. One of the garage doors will be open (Tao had ten garage doors). Pull in and Junior will close it quickly. I will call the police chief, but don't worry if they follow you here. I will send them away."

Tao had that kind of control in Mexico, and it gave Gar comfort. Indeed, he was the *Padrino* in Acapulco. But the police were still on Gar's tail. They seemed to be less concerned now, though. The chase had become more like some of the races he'd had with Gilberto and Federico, driving fast and having fun.

GRADY CALLED HIS brother, Tom. Tom was in Brookings, Oregon, and Grady was a couple hundred miles north in Astoria.

"Hey, little brother," Grady said to him. "I'm coming down there to talk to you."

"Great." Tom laughed. He was the more positive and enthusiastic brother. "I'll tell Teri to cook something good. You'll be here for dinner? Are you coming alone?"

"Naw, don't worry about that. I'm getting a room at the Spindrift Motel. I'll talk to you there. I'll call you when I get there." Grady was being very serious.

Noticing this, Tom said, "You all right, brother? You don't sound good."

"I'll call you when I get there. Yeah, I'm fine. I just need to talk to you alone."

ALMOST AT THAT same time, Gregory and his brother-in-law (and Gar's brother-in-law too) Chuckie, were talking.

The Feds really want to get Gar," Gregory was explaining. "I don't think we owe him anything. He split and went to Mexico, so he's not here to defend himself. We can put it on him, so we can get a good deal. I think we can get out of it with under five years."

Chuckie spit. "Yeah, I don't care," he said. "His sister left me anyway. I don't think we owe him anything. So let's go talk to that Customs agent. What the fuck."

AT THE SPINDRIFT Motel, Tom sat across the tiny motel table from Grady and said, "Okay, what's up?"

"Well, brother, have you thought about helping the police out?"

"No. No, I have not. We're still collecting the money Jay owes us. Why? What the hell is going on?" Tom was reluctant to believe what he was hearing.

"Well, they came to me and they really want to get Gar. And they really want to get that surfer dude, Jay. They figure Gar can lead them to Jay. So I started helping them."

"And you're wired now, aren't you? And I've already said enough to incriminate myself. Are they in the next room, or what?" Tom was nobody's fool. He got quickly to his feet.

Before Grady could answer Tom's question, several federal agents materialized into the room as if they'd been beamed down from the Starship Enterprise. "Yes, we're here. And yes, we've got you. So are you going to help us catch Walton? It will make your future much brighter."

"Yeah, what do you want to know?" Tom, knowing when he was beat, responded reluctantly. He shot a glare of hatred at his brother, Grady, but he began to talk.

"I WANT MY reward!" Dwayne, the pilot, was on the phone with Bruce Falkman, Station Chief for the San Francisco office of the DEA. Mr. Falkman was another client of Dwayne's Air Service (though no one else knew this), and Dwayne was the one who'd told him he overheard Gar and Marilyn talking about money buried behind the house in a hollow log. He heard all this while he was flying them to Tahoe to get married. It was this information, of course, that led to the recovery of the half-million dollars.

"We're working on your reward," Falkman said.

"And I deserve my share of any money you confiscate from Mike Metzger's estate. You would not have gotten that warrant without my testimony."

"Yes, and you're probably the reason Metzger committed suicide. You two were awfully close, weren't you?" Falkman was not happy with this incredibly selfish kid. Granted, he was a good pilot, and an even better snitch. He'd gotten an unbelievable amount of information to them by spying on his clients. But he'd become much too greedy since he learned about the government program to share drug confiscations with snitches.

"Yes, we were close." Dwayne came back in his snooty, rich-kid tone, "But I was just working him, trying to get you more information."

"Okay, listen kid. I don't know where we're at on the Metzger thing. I don't know if there's any drug proceeds we can share with you. I am sure you've got around a hundred and a half coming from that half-mil we took off of Gar Walton. You'll get that in due course. Just be patient."

"All right. But speed it up if you can. I want to buy a new pickup. And my rent is due, and I need to have some work done on the plane...."

GAR WHEELED THE Gran Marquis into Tao's garage just a few hundred yards ahead of the police. He'd gained on them coming up the steep hill that ended at Tao's mansion. The 400 cubic-inch engine in his Gran Marquis didn't slow down for hills.

The door shut behind Gar, and Tao went out the service door. He talked to the police sergeant, handed him a few bills, and that was the end of that. When Gar saw this, it dawned on him that the reason the police kept following, but were lackadaisical the last few miles, was so they could get their payoff. Tao had reached them by phone and warned them off.

"Come upstairs," he told Gar on his way back in.

CHAPTER 56

MID-1994.

THE VIEW FROM Tao's mansion was of the open ocean north of Acapulco. Gar's view was of Acapulco Bay. But both residences were in view of the omnipotent White Cross of Acapulco. Besides having a higher and wider look at the sea, Tao's place was cooler, with ocean breezes blowing in from far out in the Pacific. Gar liked it very much. The horizon was dotted with whitecaps, and he could see small boats working for this night's dinner.

The high-walled compound was huge. There were many types of fruit growing right in the kitchen/terrace/swimming pool area. This was all one big space, with high open arches in the pass ways leading out from the living and kitchen areas. These arches were twenty-feet tall and had no doors. The large, Olympic-sized but kidney-shaped swimming pool actually extended into the living area. This was a classic Acapulco rich person's home. The secret to the architecture was to keep the line between indoors and outdoors too subtle to distinguish. One may sit in the family room watching TV while enjoying the ocean breeze and view, then get up from the couch and dive right into the pool; then swim across to the dining room table, where a mango tree waits, loaded with fruit. Sometimes coconuts will drop nearby during a dinner party, startling everyone. Most of the pool was bathed in the light of the tropical sun; its bottom had tile mosaics of colorful fish.

A watermelon-and-ice blended-cocktail in hand, Tao outlined the situation. "You can't go back to Casa Vista del Mar. It's too hot. I talked to the police captain and they know who you are. The ID you've been using is blown, too. Everyone is talking to the police back in the United States. I think Marilyn is one of them. We've had helicopters flying over my house, and she knows my place...."

"No." Gar was in shorts and thongs with no shirt. He was deeply tanned, but plump as a Poland China pig from doing nothing. "She's not talking, I don't think. I speak with her quite often. I know every pay phone number in my old city in California. I really don't think my friends are, either."

Telephone talk is done only on pay phones in the drug world, so calls can't be traced. Gar was assiduously conscientious about this. He would receive a call on his pager with the number of a pay telephone, and when he called that number Marilyn would answer. In this way, the chances of an intercepted and recorded conversation, should a law enforcement agency be making a clandestine inquiry, is much less likely to occur.

"Well, someone is talking and we have helicopters. Otherwise, I'd let you stay here. I'm going to put you in the Boca Chica Hotel, right now, down in Caleta. Luis Miguel is staying there at this minute. He's hiding too. But not from the police. His fans leave him alone there."

Tao had a funny way of saying everything. He was very serious while at the same time seeming like a mischievous child. He was not a big man, maybe 5'5". And he was dark, like Gilberto and Federico. He was soft spoken, but he had astounding charisma. When he spoke, you listened, and did as he said.

"Really." Gar started to buck when Tao said he couldn't go back to his villa, but the lure of meeting the most famous singer in Mexico stopped him. Luis Miguel was very famous, and Gar's absolute favorite Mexican singer. "Will I get to meet him?" he asked.

"Yes. He's coming here for dinner soon. I've known him since he was a young boy making his first movie with Lucero. They used my fishing boats in the movie. I've helped him with some other problems, too. You'll see. He calls me Godfather." Tao's dark eyes were twinkling with deviltry; he had a silly grin on his face, too. It was the same grin his son, Gilberto, always had.

Gar knew that at some level he was being manipulated. This protection, these favors, would cost money. But he also knew that Tao did these things, did all of his business, because he had a zest for life. There was more than just money involved with his motivation. He liked being a player; and he liked keeping in the game as many other players as possible.

"Okay," Gar responded. "As you wish. We need to get word to my right-hand man, my worker at Casa Vista del Mar, Marcos, that I'm not coming home." And with that statement, Gar relinquished control to Tao.

"Yes," Tao agreed. "We'll tell him, and get you some of your things.

LUIS MIGUEL WAS not really that much fun to be around. He was a horrible drunk; almost childlike after a few drinks. It was embarrassing.

At the Boca Chica over the next several days, they hardly spoke. But Luis Miguel was Mexico's biggest singing star, and Gar was just a fugitive, so that was hardly surprising. Yet one day they swam in the small Boca Chica Bay together. Luis's English was good, and they had a few laughs while the bodyguards scrutinized Gar very closely for who knows what. It couldn't have been weapons, as they were both wearing Speedos. Gar did not want to mention Luis's stardom, and so spoke instead of the beautiful hotel with the tiny ocean inlet that opened into the channel between Caleta and Isla Roqueta, on the northwest tip of Acapulco Bay. They carried on a conversation about the fish they could see swimming in the gin-clear water below, and of the gorgeous women sunning themselves in the hotel chaise lounges.

After an hour of frolicking like kids at a summer swimming hole, something Gar had grown up doing in Pescadero Creek, Luis dove down and retrieved a scallop-edged shell. It was shaped just like the Shell Oil Company sign. He gave it to Gar and said, "You take this home and remember me. Everyone remembers my songs. You remember I can swim and be normal."

"Okay, Luis. But I do love your songs...."

AFTER A WEEK at the Boca Chica, Gar moved to a new place in the Las Americas colony on the other side of Caleta. It was a small studio built right into the cliff. Sliding glass doors shut the terrace off from the bedroom. The covered terrace was where the kitchen and dining room areas were located. A separate room made up the lavatorial on the backside of the bedroom and gave Gar all the amenities he'd need. He planned to work privately and in earnest now, learning how to use his new computer, and how to truly speak the Spanish language.

To one side of the bedroom a huge rock–eight feet high and about fifteen feet long–made up one wall. Gar, using ropes and planks hung from the ceiling, created shelving along the face of the boulder. Under these he placed a long desk. This was his new office. He had his worker, Marcos, bring his computer, fax, copy machine, and all the other office supplies he had accumulated. He carefully installed it all.

He was settled in his new hide out. His view was exactly the opposite of that at his other house. He looked right back across the bay at the Farallon colony. However, he could see the Colonial Restaurant and Ski Show from here. He did not have a view of the ski show at the other house. And the cross up on the hill, like the eyes of the Mona Lisa, seemed to look down on him exactly as it did across town.

The problem was, Tao said he could not go to the Colonial anymore. He had to stop everything he used to do, including seeing Luz de Gloria. He'd known it was only a fling with Luz, but the thought of it ending made him sad. Not for long, though. There are many beautiful women in Acapulco. Cheap too. Marilyn's ex-husband, Dick, had said that "You have to pay for the pleasure of women." And Gar had learned how true this was. But the beauty of Mexico was that the price of pleasure was so much more affordable.

The new place in Las Americas was 147 stair steps up a hill full of small villas. Now that Gar was feeling the gravity of his legal situation (even though he did not yet know that the people back in the States were informing like crazy), he quit drinking. And he started eating healthy foods.

The pounds fell off his body. It also helped that his cars were parked and for sale over at the Casa Vista del Mar. He walked everywhere now. In four months, he lost eighty pounds. He went from 260 to 180 pounds, and from a 44-inch waist to a 30-inch waist.

Gar established a regular circuit of exercise for himself, and several of the many Casas de Citas (House of Dates) helped keep him trim, too. It was a free and easy time in some ways, living outside the Acapulco mainstream. Las Americas and Caleta are exclusively Mexican, and he did not stray from these suburban communities.

Gar never saw other Americans. That is to say not until the day he was sitting on his cliffside terrace, looking across the warren of other terraces, and noticed a blond-haired man with camera in hand. The crew-cut blond, obviously connected somehow with American law enforcement, was taking Gar's photograph with a giant telephoto lens.

A number of things flashed into Gar's mind at this disappointing moment. He regarded this lawman taking his photo from a hundred yards away and considered the white sand beaches with their palm trees, the jet skis and colorful parasailers on the bay, and the newly acquainted assortment of beautiful Acapulco girls. All of this came to mind in a flash. Then the threat Jay made–that if Gar ever made a deal with the police he and his family would die–this thought came briefly to mind. Within a second he knew what was next.

Keep moving.

"Too slow, gotta go." He repeated an old cliché, moving as nonchalantly as possible inside to call Tao.

This phase of things was over. They were on to him now. Acapulco was finished for Gar.

CHAPTER 57

1994 Continues.

TAO WAS NOT home. He did, however, respond immediately to the 9-1-1 emergency Sky-Tel page Gar sent to him.

"What's the problem, Gar?"

"I'm sorry to bother you. I know you are busy. But I was sitting on my terrace working my computer, and I looked up and caught sight of an American policeman taking my picture."

"How do you know he is the police?" A fair question.

"Why else would he take my picture with a gigantic telephoto lens? He was not very far away. And the light was not so good for panoramic photography. It was not a good photograph, at all, unless he wanted my picture." Gar, as Tao well knew, was a shutterbug; he'd taken hundreds and hundreds of pictures in his two years in Mexico.

"Okay, Gar. Hold on a moment." Tao was on another phone now. He always had more than one cellular. At home he had more than twenty phone lines.

After a few minutes of faintly-heard staccato Spanish, Tao came back on the line with Gar. "Put some clothes in your pillow case like you're going to the laundry, or in your beach bag like you're going to the beach, and go down the stairs. Then walk up the street toward the B & B bar. A police car is waiting right now, and he will pick you up as soon as you get to the street. He will get out of the car and open the back door for you. Just get in. The American will not understand what is happening and you will go to the Boca Chica again.

Damn it, Tao was organized.

"How long will I be gone?"

"I don't know. Just take a few things. We can go back and get more for you. I have to make more calls. And don't worry too much. Remember that the Americans can't arrest you. They have to have Mexican police do that for them. And I will not let that happen in Acapulco." Tao was very sure of himself.

"But what if they kidnap me?" Gar asked.

"Well, keep your gun close. And shoot them if they try that. Just keep your eyes open all the time, and don't do anything that will draw attention to yourself if you can help it."

"Okay, Padrone, I have to go pack. I'll talk to you later." Gar started to ring off.

"Very good, Gar. Gilberto or Federico will come to the hotel later. Call me if you need me. Good bye. Oh, wait. Someone wants to talk to you...." The line went silent for a time and Gar strained to hear. When a voice did come, it was a true surprise.

"Hola, Gar. Como estas?" It was Jay.

"Jay?" Gar was unsure, and very surprised. "Is that you?" He stammered for a moment, taken completely aback. "It had been a long time. When are you coming to see me?"

Gar was enormously unsettled by this. And he felt a little bit like he had been conspired against. He had not seen Jay for a long time, and Jay still owed more than half of the money he had promised to pay Gar for getting involved again. And Tao never seemed to know where Jay was. Yet here Jay was with Tao.

The truth of the matter was that Gar did not trust Jay, and he never had. Too much time had gone by now, time during which Jay had not paid Gar but too small a fraction of the money he owed to him, and for Jay to suddenly turn up was decidedly odd.

"As a matter of fact, I was planning to come and see you real soon. I have some papers for you. But you better go take care of business. I'll probably see you later this week." Jay was his usual obscure and aloof self. By papers he meant money. At least that part of his sudden appearance was good.

"Okay. I look forward to seeing you. Lord knows I need *papers*. It's been a long time." Gar tried to be as enthusiastic as he could be.

THE TRUTH WAS that Jay was at work helping Tao establish cocaine sales in the United States. And at that moment, Jay was also entertaining Bubba, who had come down to Mexico for a visit. Bubba was secretly working for the DEA in *Operation Rehash*. *Rehash* was the code name for a controlled delivery.

The reason, in fact, that Jay had money for Gar is that Bubba provided it, instructing Jay to give it to Gar while finding out where he was living. The American cops kept losing Gar. Jay and Tao did not, of course, know Bubba was working for the cops. So Bubba's milking of information from Jay about Gar had to be done surreptitiously and with delicacy.

This was the advanced stage of the controlled delivery. Originally the cops had set it up so that they would sell the hashish in Pakistan, follow it until it was sold in the

U.S., then bust everyone with the money. And in the end they could fill their coffers with the seized money. They had not anticipated that Gar would flee to Mexico, nor stay so well hidden.

All the information they could now gather was very important. Oddly, though, this provided conflicting responsibilities for the agents. There were those that needed to keep looking for a way to arrest Gar and extradite him back to the United States. Then there were other factions that profited by using the pursuit of Gar in order to continue to probe Jay and his cohort, the Tao organization.

Eventually the whole thing would go sour on them while Tao, for reasons of his own, would compromise Gar. But this hadn't happened yet. All this was yet to come....

JAY CAME TO the Boca Chica. "Hola, Gar," he said simply. He greeted Gar by the pool. He plopped into a thickly padded chaise lounge. The pool was built on a balcony overlooking Isla Roqueta and the Pacific Ocean beyond. A riot of red-purple bougainvillea flowers spilled off the balcony's edge. It was a balmy ninety-degree day, with a cool refreshing breeze that took the edge off the heat. The breeze was the reason Gar preferred this place over the hotels around the interior of the bay. Tao liked Gar here because it was safe. None of either country's police kept track of the place like they did with the larger hotels.

"How are you?" Gar responded politely. "Where have you been? I haven't seen you in, well, forever."

"Oh, I've been here and there. Mostly here. Ever since Metzger committed suicide, I've been without a lawyer and out of touch with the case. I just hear from Tao what you tell his boys (Gilberto and Federico). Sounds like the rest of the guys are talking to the cops." Jay had peeled down to just shorts. He produced a bottle of sunscreen from a fanny pack, which he began to apply. He was in pretty good shape, lightly tanned. Gar looked at him and believed he might really be a surfer.

"Yeah, from what I can gather, at least some of the guys have had some contact with the police. I have no idea what they've said, hopefully nothing." Gar sipped a soda water with lime and wiped the sweat from his forehead with a towel.

"I don't know what they're saying either, but I'll tell you, it's not them I'm worried about. It's you." Jay looked at Gar very intently.

"Me? Why are you worried about me?" Gar was surprised at Jay's tone. And slightly offended.

"Oh, I don't mean I'm worried that you're about to run up there and tell the cops everything you know. I'm just worried that someday you might be in that position, and it's you I worry about because you're the only one that knows me and Bubba. And Woody, and a couple of other people real close to me. You're a strong link...." Jay's words trailed off, but he was making a very accusatory point.

"Look, Jay. I have no intention of ever putting myself in a position to talk."

"But they could get to you." Jay pointed out. "You've already had a couple of close calls."

"They're not going to get to me."

"Listen. Many people worry about you, Tao included. You know him and he says you've met many of his associates. Shit, he said that the fucking *Federale* Captain of the whole fucking State of Guerrero, and Mexico City too, not only knows you but calls you to go party with him."

"Oh, yeah. That's true. Jamie. Yeah, he likes me. We went out a couple of times and had some fun. We went to the strip clubs and had a few lap dances. Well, one time we took a couple of girls back to my house. You know...."

"Yes, I know. Tao tells me everything. He says that Jamie did not get to be Captain of not just one state, but two, and two very important ones, by being stupid."

Gar defended himself. "Actually, Tao warned me not to get too close. So I didn't. But the times we went out, he never asked anything about anything. He just wanted to party with someone. And as you know, I'm a companionable partier." Gar smiled.

"Oh, yeah. I know you are. But, anyway. I brought you a small package of papers. About six thousand dollars is all I could come up with. There is too much heat with all your friends talking, and my assets are tied up. I'm not earning much money right now and I can't go up there to find out what's happening. This may be all you get for a while." Gar didn't know that Bubba had actually sent ten thousand.

"Six thousand dollars?" Gar raised his voice indignantly, causing Jay to look nervously around. "That's all?"

"Be careful. Don't draw attention. And listen, just so you know. If something ever does happen, as I've said before, the people I work with are very powerful, and they would be very unhappy if you ever talked about us or made a deal with the police. We know where both of your ex-wives live, and we know where your mother lives in Santa Cruz, too. Just don't forget that. Even prison is no place to hide, because the Mexican Mafia is everywhere." Jay was quite serious.

"Look, my friend, I've never been to prison. But I'll tell you what. I know what a snitch is and what happens to snitches, and you do not have to worry about me being one."

Gar was mad now. He not only didn't like to be threatened, but didn't like being called a snitch. He got to his feet, fists clenched at his sides, and stood over

Jay, glaring down at him. He'd beat the shit out of this dude right here and now if that's the way he wanted it.

"Okay. I know we have nothing to worry about with you; but I just wanted to remind you because, well, a number of people have reminded me to remind you." Jay mellowed significantly at the sight of Gar looming over him with clenched fists.

"All right. I get the point. Now maybe you better leave. And when I see you again, you might want to have a better attitude."

Gar continued to stand by the side of the pool, and he watched as Jay quietly gathered his things and left. No more words were said by the two men.

NO ONE EVER figured out who the man with the camera was. Gar moved anyway. Tao had a friend with a small flat overlooking *La Quebrada*, the cliffs where visitors are thrilled by the divers that plunge a hundred feet from a small platform into the water of a rocky cove. The cove is too shallow for such dives, except when large waves surge in, so the divers must time their fall to hit one of the waves. Proud Mexicans, these divers have their own "La Quebrada" dive that is a basic swan dive, but with the chest stuck out as if daring the ocean to do something about it. They are dauntless and serious men, these divers. They have to be.

The new apartment was in the middle of three similar flats. It was very basic. It had an old reach-in coke box for a refrigerator. The layout was divided lengthwise down the middle, with two small bedrooms and one bathroom on the backside, and the kitchen-living area on the front. The entire front wall of the apartment was glass, with a narrow balcony through the sliding doors offering just enough room to stand and watch the cliff divers.

The apartment had a similar view of the open ocean as that enjoyed by Tao, and a Pacific breeze kept the place naturally cool. The three flats shared a decent size swimming pool. Gar paid to maintain the pool and was pretty much the only one to use it. The other two flat occupants were Mexican and did not spend much time in the sun. Gar asked the single woman from upstairs why she didn't like to enjoy the sun and the pool, and she said that Mexicans, unlike Gringos, want to get lighter, not darker.

And this place, too, lay nestled along the coast under the shadow of the Cross of Acapulco. Nothing escaped the purview of the cross. All communities, both great and small, were within sight of the cross. Men and their pursuits may have been seen as the mere activity of ants by this mute sentinel high amongst the rocks.

Who can say?

CHAPTER 58

THE CLOSE OF 1994.

SHORTLY AFTER MOVING into the new place, Casa Vista del Mar sold. Gar threw everything that was there into the sale, including the cars, and realized a pretty hefty profit from it all. The new flat was furnished and had everything he needed.

Now that the villa was sold, Marcos came to live at the flat. This was none too soon, as Gar liked having Marcos around. He was a good-looking, well-mannered young man who worked hard at making Gar's life easier. He could drive, carry the pistol, clean, and do maintenance. And he could handle all the other things it took to run a house, like waiting in line at the power company, and shopping for supplies at the *mercado*. He was as indispensable as he was versatile.

But he could not cook. And in all honesty, the man was a bit too macho for Gar to ask him to do cleaning or laundry.

One day Marcos mentioned to Gar that they should go to his family home in Atoyac de Alvarez. There Marcos had many cousins from which Gar could pick a cook/housekeeper. After selling the house, Gar had bought a

Volkswagen Jetta. So they loaded the Jetta one morning and left on a safari.

Atoyac is primordial. The Sierra Madre del Sur Mountains, adjacent to the city, is where *Acapulco Gold* is grown. It is also an area where coca plants and opium poppies are cultivated. It is as wild and unruly a place as the Old West was back in the day, almost completely lawless.

Before leaving, Gar called Gilberto and Gilberto told him to be very careful, take the pistol, and not to leave the company of Marcos, because it is an extremely risky city for a Gringo to be alone.

After having been uprooted yet again, and suffering all the emotional strain such a move caused, this safari seemed like a real adventure. Something more important than not. And the intended result was a new girl to brighten the household. What could be more enchanting? It was an easy two-hour drive to get there.

THEY HEADED NORTH in the Jetta, Marcos driving. Gar watched the beautiful tropical scenery slide by: fields of coconut palms planted in neatly maintained rows; banana trees laid out with geometric precision. They traveled up Mexico Highway 200 through the town of Coyuca. They passed through many small, unnamed pueblos. They stopped in one of these unnamed places, and went into a cantina. The bartender served up Coca-Colas, and then, smiling, asked if he could do anything else for them, maybe get them something *special*. Gar caught the tone and considered it briefly.

"Well, we were only going to be here for a few minutes," he said to the man. "But I always have time for a date. Can you arrange that?"

Marcos shot a sidewise look, then began fidgeting on his stool.

"Yes, sir," the bartender said, and he ducked through a curtained doorway. He returned a few minutes later with a striking señorita: dark, with long black hair brushed straight and with a silky shine. She wore a simple pullover cotton dress, burnt orange in color, with a plunging neckline. It hung by loose straps from toasted wheat-colored shoulders.

She was absolutely stunning. So much so that the sight of her took Gar's breath away. She had high cheekbones, an upturned nose, and almond-shaped eyes. But they were large eyes, with dark-hot centers, the whites glistening like pearls, and they exhibited the same brilliant white gleam as her teeth. Her lips were full and red, matching painted toenails. She was barefooted. She had a very slight overbite, her mouth not overly large, her lips pouty. And she had two dimples.

For a Mexican girl, she was of above average height, yet at the same time petite, and with those gorgeous shoulders. Gar stammered a question about cost and the bartender said two-hundred pesos. This was about forty dollars. It was a very acceptable price, but after this long in Mexico Gar felt he must bargain. He started to offer something lower when the libidinous young beauty began flapping the front hem of her skirt.

She was leaned back against the doorjamb as she did this, her feet wedged on the opposite jamb, and when she flapped her skirt high enough Gar caught a strobbing glimpse of ink-black pubic hair. *India* ink black. The way she did that, and the look she gave Gar, was as pure an exhibition of lust as he had ever encountered. She cocked one foot behind her, resting it against the doorjamb. As she did this she gave a slight rock that was pure sex. And when she rocked, a shoulder strap fell, exposing one perfect breast. It was not hefty, but the dark nipple was outsized. The look she fixed on Gar, her smoldering eyes, the whole complete package, was pure animal desire.

The bartender said to Gar, "Sheena likes you, Mister. And don't worry...Gringos always worry so much about loving." Then he started the next sentence with the three words Gar had heard many other Mexicans utter to him, "*Here in Mexico*, we don't worry so much about sex. It is as natural as eating. Our women live for it, just as much as the men. Maybe we live because of it. It is what makes us Mexican, and what we are proud of. I think your American churches tell you it's bad. Our church tells us it's good. You go on and have a good time with Sheena. She wants you. If you wish to leave a tip, help us with our rent, we are very poor people, that would be very good!"

The man smiled, lifting the corner of a drooping *Pancho Villa* moustache. A tired ceiling fan spun so slowly you could see the individual blades. Luis Miguel played on a boom-box somewhere, singing "Eres Tu". This was a favorite song of Gar's.

"What the hell," he muttered to himself. Then he repeated another fisherman's truism. "The Lord hates a coward."

AS GAR APPROACHED Sheena in the doorway, she ducked inside, smiling back at him. There is something about the way Mexican girls smile to one side that is exotic and intriguing; their eyes light as if neon infused.

The room was that of a typical Mexican house, with everything all in one room, except the bathroom. A corner was curtained off for the bed. She led Gar to the bathroom and undressed him; her dress dropped to the floor in one easy move. Her body was breathtaking.

They stepped into the shower, the cold water welcome in the heat. She soaped both of them, washing Gar and herself thoroughly. She dried Gar first, then herself, and she led him to the bed. The room smelled like tortillas and refried beans. The paint was old, but the place was spotless. There were too many things for this small an enclosure, but very soon Gar didn't pay any attention to what was in the room.

On the bed she laid against him, melting her body into his. She was hot. They played for a while, kissing and touching all over. When he entered her, he was almost shocked at how much warmer she was inside. Her lips found his; her tongue wound around his tongue.

She whimpered with pleasure as he moved inside her, raking his back with her nails. And she cried out long and loud as her orgasm came on. It seemed to last for minutes and minutes.

Both depleted, she continued to cling to him like she did not want Gar to go. She was a very sensuous woman. She rubbed Gar's back, asking if she had hurt him and apologizing for her wild scratching. She kissed his eyes and his cheeks and his mouth.

She did not ask where Gar came from, or where he was going. She hadn't said more than a few words. She did say "good bye" and "come back" as Gar dressed and headed for the door.

He left a hundred-dollar bill on her night table, and gave the bartender another one on his way out the door. "Pancho Villa" smiled knowingly, and gave a small bow, saying, "Thank you, senor, please come back any time. Mi casa es su casa."

It was a powerful and liberating experience. Gar pondered that the bartender was right. Gringos did get much too sentimental about sex. Undoubtedly this was caused by a puritanical upbringing. This lovely young girl had showed him how pure and simple it could be. Let God be the judge if this was wrong. Everyone else could bear their own sins.

He wondered, too, if he wasn't getting a little crazier. If maybe the threat of arrest was driving him to live like a condemned man. Indeed, he had likely been the only American that had ever entered the cantina they had just left. And he would bet he was the only one crazy enough to go in the back room and take off his pants.

"All I ever wanted to be was at least as good a salmon fisherman as Michael McHenry," he mused. "And look at me now. Have I done better? Have I gone a step further than Michael? What would Susan say?"

All of these were reasonable questions, but there were no answers. And as he asked them, Marcos looked over, saying, "What? You were talking in English, and I did not understand."

Nothing," he replied. "I was just thinking to myself."

BEFORE THEY LEFT the small village, Gar had Marcos pull up to a tiny store. Giddy still from the liaison, the break in the safari with Sheena, he bought a six-pack of beer. It had been quite a while since he'd drank, and the cold Coronas looked inviting. It was sheer celebration to drink them.

MOST OF THE six-pack was gone when they arrived at the rolling foothills of Atoyac. Marcos wasn't a drinker, and had not consumed any of the beer. Gar had Marcos take them to Atoyac's only shopping center. It was not as organized as an American mall.

The entire city of 40,000 was laid out helter-skelter, as though someone had tossed a handful of immense concrete dice into the jungle. Dense trees and foliage made it look as if there wasn't a city there at all. Only the specks of whitewashed cement glinting through the trees gave it away.

He gave Marcos money and told him to get food for his mother. Meanwhile, he looked through the variety department and found an electric *Casio* piano with a microphone and amplifier. It was a perfect gift for Marcos's three teenage sisters. Marcos, the oldest of six, also had two younger brothers, both right around twenty years old. Gar would slip them a few bills and tell them it was "Haircut" money.

THEY HAD WHAT was to become for Gar a favorite hammock, ready and waiting. Nicholas, Marcos's father, worked in the house next to the Casa Vista del Mar, and had introduced his son to Gar. Marcos had the help of his lovely young sisters to unpack the car. They moved Gar's things into Nicholas and Maria's bedroom. Over Gar's complaints, they insisted he sleep in their bed, and he knew better than to argue too strenuously.

The piano was set up, and the girls provided entertainment that evening. It was more fun than Gar could remember having in a long time. And lingering thoughts of Sheena buoyed his mood. He continued to think about what he had learned at that roadside stop. It was like the stories he had heard about farmers being so hospitable, or hungry for foreign DNA, that they'd insist guests sleep with their daughters. Indeed, Scandinavian people regularly invite strangers to sleep with their daughters. And Europeans in general think nothing of having sex with total strangers, just for the joy of it.

Or so he had heard.

American men, like himself, were much too uptight he decided. He hoped to work on that.

THE NEXT DAY, Marcos invited his cousin Rosa over. She was the most likely candidate for the cook and housekeeper position. She arrived with her older sister, Raquel. Rosa was just eighteen, and Raquel was twenty-one. Raquel had a cute, two-year-old daughter, Brenda Samantha, or Sammy for short.

Rosa reminded Gar of Sheena, but she was not quite that exotic. Nor did she have Sheena's raw animal appeal. And it is a certainty that she didn't have her experience and appetites. But she was a cute girl.

Raquel was a more buxom woman. She was nicely curved like her namesake, Raquel Welch. They were both as dark as Indian clay. Rosey was on the serious side, while Raquel was very chipper and lighthearted, with a quick, infectious laugh.

Gar liked them both, and was pleased when he hired Rosa, who was the one applying for the job, to hear that Raquel would come sometimes, too. She lived close to Gar's new flat, and needed something to do. Her husband had been gone to the United States for several years now.

Gar was so pleased the he impetuously offered a package deal to the two of them: "Instead of paying Rosa only the 250 pesos a week I was offering, I'll put out 400 pesos and pay you each 200 a week."

Both agreed that this was more than fair. Rosa would live at the flat, and Raquel would come in the mornings.

It sounded like Rosa was not entirely adept in the kitchen, anyway, so Raquel would do most of the cooking.

THE SECOND AND last day at Atoyac, Gar said he wanted to go swim in the river. Rosey came to take him. It was more than a mile away. They walked through an overgrown jungle to get there. They walked amongst Elephant's Ear, Monkey Puzzle Trees, and Monterey Cypress. Fuchsia, Frangipani, Gardenia, and Honeysuckle filled the air with their perfumes. The flora and fauna were unbelievable to Gar. He walked amongst brightly colored birds as though in a dream.

Rosey led Gar along an unseen trail that she traveled in bare feet. Her short, pleated, green-and-yellow skirt, and chocolate tube top, were like a carrot to follow. He fell in love, a second time in as many days, watching her move in the rays of sunlight that filtered through the overhead canopy. It was wild. It was the jungle. Birds screeched and his heart thumped.

When they broke out of the woods and onto a dirt street, children began to follow them. Within a few blocks, they were trailed by dozens of small children. Gar asked why they followed, and Rosa, embarrassed, said that they'd never seen a white American before.

Gar found this enormously amusing.

AT THE RIVER there were hundreds of people, and most of them immediately stopped what they were doing. They had been washing clothes and swimming. But they prattled and pointed as Gar pulled off his shirt and dove into the water. He had a strong stroke, and he swam quickly to the center of the torpid river and floated on his back. It was an amazing feeling to be here. He felt a sense of strength. He felt something indescribable, yet unequaled in his memory, and the experience was inexplicable. He felt like, somehow, he was making history.

ON THE WAY back, a band of machete-toting teenage boys fell in behind them. Rosa went back and cursed them in Spanish too rapid for Gar to grasp. He asked her what she had said, and she explained that these boys were sizing Gar up to take his money, maybe kill him and throw his body into the river, but she told them who her father and brothers were. Her father was *Blackie* (el Negro), a very respected cement contractor. The young bandits melted into the undergrowth. They did not want to anger el Negro.

THE FOUR OF them left the scattered and hidden neighborhoods of Atoyac the next morning. Gar thought the safari had gone well. Indeed, he had not one but two bewitching housekeepers, for what turned out to be a very pleasurable trip into the wilds of Guerrero.

He was sad, though, as they passed by Sheena's cantina. Certainly the two new housekeepers would have said nothing if Gar had stopped for an hour. But it would have been inappropriate and sent a signal to them that he did not want to send.

BACK IN ACAPULCO, Gar had a message on his answering machine to call Tao. When he did, Tao related that the indictment had finally come down and Gar and Jay were on it. In fact, theirs were the first two names on it, and it contained quite a list of names.

Gar was stunned. It was finally happening. Now it was no longer a game....

CHAPTER 59

EARLY 1995.

BUT, CURIOUSLY, THE indictment did not really change things. Oh sure, it turned the heat up a notch. But like the frog in a pot of warming water, wherein the gas is turned up slowly, Gar was becoming used to it. Strangely, the most noticeable effect of the indictment, beyond a slight feeling of impending doom, was that he thought more than ever about procreation. The pleasurable aspects of procreation. Maybe he just wanted more offspring before it was too late.

It was the money thing that was the problem. Jay, it was now obvious, would never pay any more money. Gar cursed every time he thought of it. He'd gotten back "in" with a promise of money to retire on, and now he was going to have to look for work, or a business of some sort to open—more exposure.

Acapulco did not have much to offer. It is a city of over two million, and the tourist trade is not what it was during the glory days of the 1950s and 60s. There is much too much competition. The majority of the tourists that vacation there are *Chilangos* (people from Mexico City, almost universally hated by the rest of the citizens of Mexico). As the Acapulcanians say, they come with two or three families and rent one small room for its shower, and eat bread and bologna sandwiches brought with them from home. And Modelo beer. The men of Acapulco scorn Modelo beer. Then when the Chilangos leave, after having spent almost no money, they toss their empty Modelo cans on the beach. In other words, deep-pocket foreigners don't come to Acapulco any more. At least, not nearly in their previous numbers.

Tao knew about the savings Gar had put away from the sale of the house, and sent his sons around with schemes intended to part Gar from some of it (that is the Mexican way). The latest scheme was a rock-solid Mexican ID for $5,000. It included a birth certificate guaranteed to be on file in the Durango public clerk's office, also a military ID, and a driver's license. The birth certificate would be the key to this ID package. Theoretically, an existing certificate of the right vintage (for Gar's age) would be pulled from the clerk's file, and Gar's new certificate, with the proper numbering and stamps, would be inserted in its place. This was 100% foolproof, unequivocal proof of Mexican birth they promised.

Gar went for it. It was a lot of trouble, but when he got the documents he was somewhat impressed. They looked fairly genuine.

Because Gar knew that no more money would be forthcoming from Jay, and that he must find some sort of business to maintain his current lifestyle, Gar told Marcos and Rosey he wanted to get out of Acapulco. He wanted to go on another safari, looking for business opportunities this time. They told him they had cousins in Huautulco, Oaxaca (Wha-Ha-Ca). It was a Pacific port city, and Gar thought there might be business opportunities there. He treated his workers like family, delighting them by doing so. When he said, "We will open a business," they smiled back proudly.

Raquel and Sammy would stay behind to look after the flat. The rest of them set out.

HUAUTULCO IS SMALL and does not have much in the way of burgeoning commerce. So they didn't stay long. Gar told them he could not smell money there. But if they wanted to know what money smelled like, then Cancun was the place to go. Gar had been to Cancun on vacation with Jasmer and Alison.

In Huautulco, Gar learned something. In Mexico, female cousins hold a particular attraction to male cousins. Since all of the Huautulco cousins were young men, Rosey was inundated with attention. When it proved to be too much for her, she began taking Gar's arm everywhere they went, sitting very close to him whenever possible. Because they were always bare-legged, her thighs brushing constantly against his own left him feeling warm, fuzzy, and horny. He spent a lot of extra money taking everyone to eat, just so he could feel Rosey's thighs again. They had that soft, downy, peach-fuzz-like hair that tickled like a feather.

THERE WERE SEVERAL cross-country routes to get to the Caribbean. One would take them to San Cristobal, Chiapas, where there is a famous grand cathedral. However, Marcos and Rosey's cousins convinced Gar that *that* route was much too dangerous for foreigners, or anyone else: "You will come upon stones across the road, and before you can back up, there will be stones behind you. Then you will be shot through your car window."

So they took a less exciting road cross-country. This would allow them to deviate from the well-traveled road in Tabasco, and visit the waterfalls of Blue Water at Palenque in the State of Chiapas. Gar liked this idea, as he just *had* to be able to say he'd been to Chiapas. And the Blue Waters of Palenque is very famous, and said to be blessed (or haunted) by Maya spirits.

THEY CROSSED TO Tabasco in one day. The scenery going across the country was not nearly as lush as that on the coast. There were unfenced cow fields, rocks and straggly trees, and long stretches of road with only tiny, insignificant rivers occasionally emerging. And the few small towns they did pass through did not have the same attraction, the same allure, as the coastal cities. On the coast, it seemed locals understood and liked Gringos. Inland, they just stared, slack-jawed, as if a multi-headed burro had wandered down the dusty highway.

They stayed in *Villahermosa*, the capital city of Tabasco. The girls of Tabasco are credited with a unique distinction: every single one of them is said to be a prostitute. The legend insinuates that prostitution is akin to a religion to them. Gar had grown rather fond of prostitutes; it was such a natural and straight-forward way to deal with a man's yearnings. He left Marcos and Rosey at the hotel and went for a drive. Out in the middle of nowhere, a lovely girl materialized on the side of the road.

Thinking of Sheena, he pulled up and said hello. She said, what would you like? And he said, how much? They agreed on a price and she hopped in. She pulled at Gar's clothes even before they were completely off the public highway.

It was a wild and crazy romp. But she somehow managed to rob him. He had hidden his money in his shoe, and she got it out of the shoe–without taking the shoe off! It was amazing. It wasn't too much, maybe a couple hundred dollars. But he'd still have to explain to Rosey why they had to change the morning departure time until Gar could go to the bank, when he had just gone to the bank that evening as they arrived in town.

GAR WASN'T SLEEPING with Rosey. But he sure wanted to. She got more attractive to him every day. He did not want her to know about other women. And he was still resolving the age difference in his mind. She was ready, though, or so it seemed.

One day, when they were back at the flat, he was talking to her about going across town. "I have to drive to the hardware store. Do you want to go?" Gar smiled at her.

Rosey smiled back, her full white teeth had a slight gap between the top two. "Yes. I would like to stop at the store, if possible, and pick up vegetables. And you can buy me an ice cream if you want." Her eyes twinkled.

"That would be fine with me. But I have to shave and shower first. It will only take a few minutes." Gar said this over his shoulder as he walked to the bathroom.

Rosey followed, continuing to talk about vegetables. Then she changed the subject. "I watched my father shave when I was young. He would use an old-fashioned straight razor. Not one of the new ones, like you use. What does this mean?" She was tracing his original initials tattooed on his shoulder with her dark brown finger. He noticed the squared off cut to her nail.

"Oh, that was an old girlfriend's initials. I don't even remember her name. This was not true. These were Gar's initials. But he went by a different name now, and did not wish to mention this.

"Did you have many girlfriends before?" She had a sly smile.

"No. Not really. I don't know what many would be. And do we count the ones when we are little? And do wives count?"

"Did you have more than five? Wives count. Young ones don't?" She was playing now.

"Yes."

"More than ten?"

"Yes."

"More than twenty?"

"Probably not. Actual real girlfriends, I don't think more than ten." He said this as he turned on the water in the shower, and then turned to look at her as she hugged the door, swinging on it.

"Rosa, when you watched your father shave, did you watch him take a shower, too?"

"She blushed, smiled, lingered a moment longer, and said nothing. Then she left, closing the door softly behind herself.

And not only that. She would often run around the flat, after her shower, bundled only in a towel; talking to him, sitting down and exposing fleeting glimpses of the *waterfront*, procrastinating before putting on her clothes. Even going so far as to perch on the edge of his bed while he was under the covers, touching his face, arms, and hands as they chatted, dragging out her time in his company. It was a tense time with her, as her cousin Marcos was irreplaceable and Gar did not want to make an advance towards Rosey if it would anger or alienate Marcos, and he had a feeling it would.

But she sure had a way of keeping the blood pressure boiling.

Wow!

PALENQUE AND THE Blue Water held some kind of witchery for Gar. He was drawn to it in fascination. It had just rained, and the water wasn't blue when they got there. It was just a medium-sized river running over a twenty-foot drop. The water turned a spectacular turquoise blue when it wasn't muddy; it held Gar in a hexing spell.

Determined to see the Blue Water, they waited several days for the river to calm down after jungle rains. In that time Gar climbed the falls and felt the ancients talking, or so he imagined. As he sat on a rock within the falls, he could hear voices. Maybe a tone such as two frogs might use. But it was not frogs; of that he was sure. It was coming from two rocks. Later, someone knowledgeable in Mayan lore would explain that the Maya believe they reincarnate as rocks. The experience never left him. He would ponder for years exactly what it was that he had heard.

On one afternoon when Gar was tramping alone alongside the river and taking in the sights, he was startled when an elderly but spry man stepped smartly out of the jungle and snapped off a salute. He introduced himself to Gar with great vigor.

"My name is Jim Harper," he said, extending a hand and shaking firmly. He was dressed in khaki bush fatigues, neatly pressed, with a matching pith helmet shading friendly eyes. He was every bit an American, and Gar was taken aback at seeing him here. "And it's good to see another American, if only for a moment."

"Yes," Gar mumbled, a bit too surprised to speak. "Pleased to meet you."

"I've just come up from Argentina," Jim Harper said. "And I know I must be getting close to the United States when I meet a bloke like you, an American I mean."

"Argentina?" Gar stammered, incredulous. "You mean, like, the Argentina in South America?"

"Too right. Been a bit of a walk." The man named Jim Harper had a well-worn but functional walking staff and looked extremely fit. He grinned at Gar's surprise.

"You have walked here from Argentina? Why, shoot, that is more than two-thousand miles!"

"Indeed it is, young man, and I'll have to be off. It's been nice meeting you." The man grasped Gar's hand and shook once again. And with that he disappeared back into the jungle.

Gar didn't know what to make of this encounter, but he certainly found it interesting. After a short period he put it from his mind. There were other things to think about.

During the wait, Gar took his little entourage out in the evenings for dinner. One night, Rosa ordered a drink. She dared Marcos to drink. And he did it. She continued to taunt him to drink with her, cocktail for cocktail, while Gar looked on in amusement.

Marcos fell out after a short time, but Rosey stayed and wanted to dance. They danced the fast ones until a slow one came. She accepted Gar's invitation, even as she was already in his arms. They moved around the floor while she held her body fast against his. It aroused him beyond comparison. Her smell was of roses and violets. Her nose and breath were as velvet against his neck.

Was she blowing in his ear on purpose?

The pressure was now escalating dangerously high. At the end of the evening Gar took her back to her room. He left her at the door with cheek kisses and a hug.

He cursed his own modesty as he went to his own room for a cold shower.

Cooled off, he wondered if what kept him from Rosey was blue-nosed priggishness, her cousin Marcos, or the fact that an escalation in a sleeping-together relationship would be akin to marriage.

Hmmm. He thought about something a Mexican man once told him: "Gar, here in Mexico, your housekeepers expect you to sleep with them. If you don't, they will think that you are not a man." Was this true? he wondered. Is this what this young, romantic, and very spunky girl was thinking? Or was it deeper than that? From what he'd learned about Mexican women so far, it's usually not overly complicated like it is with American girls. Most señoritas just want love, marriage and children.

"It's as *easey, peasey, japoneasy* as that!" Gar decided. "It's simple: It's all about love, marriage, and family...Rosa wants a husband."

But is marriage what he wanted? He certainly could imagine a life with Rosey, all right, except for his legal problems. Marilyn had already, a year earlier, found a young guy and divorced Gar. And being married to a Mexican would make extradition more difficult, should it come to that. And that might just be a deciding factor in the big picture.

But she would not wait forever. Of that he was sure. If he didn't answer one of her signals soon, she'd beckon elsewhere.

CHAPTER 60

LATE 1995.

WHEN JASMER AND Alison had visited Acapulco two years earlier, Gar took them to Cancun for a week. During that week they took a tour south one day to Xcaret (Esh-Car-Ette), a beautiful and natural tourist attraction featuring cenotes (water filled, limestone sinkholes) and underground rivers. They visited a natural Caribbean cove where one can swim with dolphins. Centuries earlier the Maya used the cove to prepare to swim out to the island of Cozumel, about two miles distant, where they gained fertility for the coming year.

It was that previous trip with his kids that prompted Gar to stop short of Cancun on the present safari with Marcos and Rosey. He wanted to show them Xcaret. They stayed in *Playa del Carmen*, about four miles from Xcaret. Like Palenque, the weather would again hold them up for a few days. But only two days spent in Playa del Carmen, with its white sand beaches and uniquely blue sea, was sufficient for Gar to get a good, serious whiff of money. The place was the first town south of Cancun, about thirty miles, where one caught the ferry to Cozumel, and it was growing fast. Cancun was now saturated with every conceivable business venture. Playa del Carmen was not. Not yet.

Gar announced that they would not go to Cancun to search for business. They would settle in right here. Rosey liked it too, and Marcos didn't care. He knew that he'd always work for a wage, thus his job was the same wherever they settled. Rosa, on the other hand, knew she might become a 50% partner one day. She viewed things in a completely different light.

GAR AND ROSEY flew back to Acapulco to pack the house and ship it. Marcos stayed to look for a new place in Playa del Carmen. He continued to stay at the Blue Parrot hotel, where they had all stayed. In this way, Gar could call Marcos every night to check on progress. As it turned out, it only took Marcos a few days to locate a fairly new, three-bedroom duplex in a small development called *Tohucu* (Toe-Who-Coo).

Rosa had never flown, and was atingle with excitement by the time the *Aero Mexico* jet was in the air. Gar gave her the window seat. She gawked at the flat, Yucatan jungle as the plane banked to the northwest. And she gasped at the sight of the luminous blue-green waters of the Caribbean, stark against the white sands of the beaches below. The sight was captivating. The island of Cozumel appeared clearly in the distance, with a tiny ferryboat making its way back to Playa del Carmen.

When she noticed Gar's hand on the armrest between them, Rosey put her hand on his, and then locked in her fingers. The sideways look she gave him lit the white of her eyes in such a way that she had never looked lovelier.

Gar told her so.

She became serious, wiping an errant curl of hair from her forehead. "Gar, what do you think we will do?"

"Oh, we will pack all our personal things at the flat, and hire a moving company to take it to Playa del Carmen. Hopefully Marcos will find us a nice place to live."

"Yes, I know that," she smiled as if being patient with a child. "But what will we do?"

"Oh. You mean you and I. Ahhh..."

"Yes. What is going to happen with you and I? Marcos is very jealous. He sees us flirt back and forth, and it bothers him. It would be easier for him if he knew, for sure, what we were doing."

She really was quite a girl. Gar lamented over her because of their age difference. But it did not bother her. And maybe they were equal emotionally. Certainly women mature faster than men.

"Well, why don't we get married? I would like to spend my life with you. Would you like to be my wife? Give me children?" Gar could hardly believe what he'd just asked. And, then again, it felt perfectly natural to ask her this.

"Of course," she said in her simple, perky voice. And they kissed, long and tenderly, to seal the deal. The Yucatan Peninsula disappeared behind them and below, and they did not notice its passing.

They discussed logistics. She said she'd need to tell her parents first, and that she'd like an Atoyac wedding. Gar told her that he would help her parents with the cost, and it would be a good wedding.

CLOSING UP SHOP in Acapulco was not that difficult. The furniture belonged to the flat's owner. There were probably only two or three pickup loads of stuff. They contracted with a *Mayflower*-type moving company to package and deliver their possessions.

"No problemo," the truck driver said. With this method of transport, Gar felt a little more confident when he locked his trusty .45 in the safe. He prayed it would make it there undetected, as guns are strictly forbidden in Mexico. He did not want to get arrested. But he did want his pistol.

The biggest problem in Acapulco was not related to moving. After they arrived, Rosa said she needed to go alone to Atoyac to talk to her parents. Meanwhile, Raquel and Gar would help the movers. Helping load the truck took only a single afternoon. After that, the flat was virtually barren. There was no need for Raquel to come around anymore.

Gar stayed there for two more days, without hearing a peep from Rosey. He still had a telephone and an answering machine that she knew how to call, and he had given her plenty of money. Something was wrong. It made him feel like maybe it was too good to be true. His heart had soared when she had responded to his proposal with the words "of course."

When she finally returned–a ball of fire, ready to head back across the country–she did not mention one word about marriage. In fact, she never did again. And neither did Gar. It remained unspoken that something had gone wrong, that parental approval had not been granted. A part of Gar was not surprised by this, for in his heart he knew he was too old for her. And he respected her too much to ask about it, afraid of hurting her feelings or putting her on the spot. This is the way in Mexico; many good ideas are simply abandoned, and once that happens, it is wasted effort to mention them again. Mexicans do not waste effort, Gar had learned this and abided by it.

THEIR NEW HOME was bisected from front to back, with a hallway down the middle. To the right side of the hallway there were two bedrooms sharing a bathroom in the middle. On the left side was first a living room, then a kitchenette with a bar. The kitchen table in the dining area encroached a little way into the living room. And at the back of the hallway to the left was Gar's master bedroom. He had his own bathroom, and with ingenuity he squeezed in his desk, bookshelves, TV and VCR. And a mountain of clothes. For all the clothing he drilled through two walls on opposite sides and stuck a twenty-foot piece of one-inch pipe through the holes. Then he bought the store out of hangers and hung all his garments neatly.

Early evening, as they all prepared to go out somewhere, Rosa would treat Gar to a *Victoria's Secret* display of various colored undergarments. She wasn't completely uninhibited. She'd mostly stay in her room. But she would open her door and ask someone something, and a flicker of leg and hip, a flash of brassiere, would wink in the partially opened door. Occasionally she'd neglect to close it entirely, and a scintillating peep show would then unfold. Gar's bedroom door, three feet across the hall from hers, was usually open. This was where he spent most of his time. And the peep shows were quite a distraction.

THE MARIACHI MUSIC drifted across the Playa del Carmen town square. It was a roving band that went from restaurant to restaurant, playing for tips. Gar sat with Rosa on a bench watching some kids trying to Roller Blade on the uneven cobblestones. It was a pleasant eighty degrees, and Frangipanis were abloom nearby. They were only a hundred yards from the beach, and the small surf could be heard in between songs.

The mariachis, at least fifteen of them in the group, came toward them. "Would you like to hear a song?" Gar asked Rosa. They'd just had a nice seafood dinner.

"Oh, yes," she said, excited. She had an abounding energy, and loved everything.

"What would you like to hear?" Gar asked her. He waved the musicians over.

She looked at the handsome leader, who stood out front of the group now in formation before them. His uniform was tight fitting with many brass buttons, white in color with black and gold trim. The man was absolutely resplendent, as only the musicians in Mexico can be. She told him in her high, sweet voice, "Amor Eterno, please. Do you know that one?"

"Oh yes, Missus, we will play that better than Juan Gabriel. For you and your husband, we will play our best." Rosa gave Gar a secret look when the man said this.

They started to play. The horns come in first, then the strings join in, and a very strong voice narrates a sad, moving story. It tells a story about a boy singing to his mother about eternal love. Rosa grabbed Gar's hand. With her other hand she turned his face, and traced his jaw line with one delicate finger. She did this while she whispered all the words of the song to him.

It made Gar cry. This song was so tragic, so tender, yet so pure with love, that one did not need to understand all the words. Knowing it is about eternal love, while listening to the potency of the music, is heartrending.

Rosa's tenderness had its affect as well.

When the mariachi finished playing several more songs–Guadalajara, Si Nos Dejan, and Cielito Lindo–Rosa said, "You're very sentimental, aren't you?"

"Yes."

"I like that about you. You care about Mexico and Mexicans."

"Yes, I love Mexico. It is my home now." Gar still felt the music. The mariachi had continued on to the other side of the square.

"Excuse me." A man and a woman were sitting on a bench close by. The woman was speaking to them. "Thank you very much for calling the mariachi over. We are from Guerrero. But now we live here. In Acapulco there are many mariachi, but we don't hear them so much here."

"Oh, really?" Gar answered. "We are from Acapulco, too."

"Very good. We are Pisanos." The man spoke this time. They were older than Rosa, but not quite as old as Gar. Maybe in their thirties.

Gar was feeling good about his Spanish. "Yes, yes. And what are you doing way over here? Why did you leave Acapulco?"

The husband responded. "My uncle lives in Playa, and he convinced us there is much opportunity here, much more than in Acapulco. So we moved our two children here, and now we have a restaurant. We are happy we moved.

"Very good. Do you make *Mole'* (Moe-Lay)?" Gar was excited. He loved Mole' and could not find it in Playa. Mole' is a spicy peanut sauce, enriched with chocolate, and commonly served over chicken. It is mouth-watering delicious.

Now the woman responded. "Yes. I will make Mole' for you any time. You just tell me when you are coming."

"How about tomorrow for lunch? We will bring my right hand man, who is her cousin (he nodded at Rosa), for *comida* at two o'clock. If that is okay with you? Gar was smiling. This was an event in what had otherwise been a slow search for a prospective business. These hard-working people with their ideas would be able to help him find answers.

"Yes, two o'clock will be fine. Oh, here's my son, Jose Junior. Say hello to our new friends from Acapulco." Junior was about fourteen, and had just skated up on Roller Blades. They all took the opportunity to exchange names and other greetings. Junior had one of those engaging and enthusiastic smiles; Gar liked him right away.

He asked Junior, "Isn't it difficult skating on these bricks in the plaza? There are too many big cracks, no?"

"Yes, sir," Junior said. "But this is the best place. Really, it's the only place to skate. All the streets in Playa are dirt, mostly, and the ones that aren't are too small with too much traffic."

"Really?" Gar was suddenly intrigued. "Do you know of other kids that would like to skate, but can't?"

"Oh yes, señior Gar. Roller Blades are very popular, and everyone at my school wants to Roller Blade. But there's nowhere to go here. Sometimes we go to Cancun with my mother, but it's hard with the restaurant...." He trailed off, somewhat sad.

Gar looked thoughtfully at junior for a moment, thinking about how to pose the next question. "If I opened a place for you to skate, would you come there and give me business?"

Without hesitation and with a beaming grin, Junior exploded with excitement. "Mister Gar, if you open a Roller Skating Rink, every kid in Playa will come there and pay you money to use it!"

Gar smiled. This was exactly the right answer.

Rosa switched her hand to his leg and gave it a squeeze. She knew a connection had been made, that this was exactly the type of thing Gar had been looking for.

THAT NIGHT, WHEN they got back to the duplex in Tohucu, as they tiptoed in quietly so as not to wake up Marcos, she followed him to his bedroom instead of turning into her own.

As they kissed and fumbled with clothing, she said, "I haven't done this before."

"Don't worry. I will go very slowly. Just tell me what you like. And tell me what you don't like, too." His breathing was very heavy.

"I like you," she whispered with conviction.

A street light seeped through one window, leaving a sort of square spotlight to one side of the room. He maneuvered Rosa into the light. He wanted to see which color lingerie she'd chosen for tonight. It was the wine-red with black lace. It was an excellent choice, one of his favorites. But the black bra didn't quite match, so he took that off.

God, she was gorgeous!

THE NEXT MORNING, however, he woke up to find that Rosa was not in his bed. He could hear her and Marcos in the front of the house, chattering like always. Listening in, it wasn't about Gar. Nor was it about Rosa and Gar.

Hmmm....

Gar went out to the kitchen. Marcos was seated at the breakfast bar and Rosa was behind it. She gave Gar a slight shake of the head and a certain look. It instantly discouraged his plan to put his arms around her and thank her for the wonderful evening.

"Good morning, Mr. Gar," the both sang to him.

"We've got a plan now." He grinned and poured himself a cup of coffee. "We're going into the roller skating business. Marcos, we need a lawyer. Rosa, we need a place for kids to roller skate, with a big flat cement floor. Those are your jobs for the day. Go find 'em." Gar, despite Rosa's cold shoulder, felt pretty good. He'd sort this out with her later. But the fact remained that they had made very sweet love the night before, and this thought pleased him enormously.

"I don't know anything about lawyers," Marcos questioned. "What do I say? What do I look for?"

"Well, first, we want a lawyer who speaks good English, so I can be sure I understand everything. And we want one who can help us to open a Mexican Cooperation." Gar had already done some of his homework. Every business in Mexico is a federal cooperation. "I already have the name for our cooperation, too. Would you like to hear it?"

They both smiled and said, "Yes."

"We will call it *ROSMARKGAR* (he pronounced it Rose-Mark-Gar)," Gar said proudly. Of course he had arrived at this name using the same method Marilyn and Amanda used to figure out Andriana's name. His little Spirit Child was the inspiration. He explained it all to them. He also told Marcos that the lawyer should be well versed in criminal law. Just as a precaution....

THIS IS HOW it began in Playa del Carmen. Rosa would only *sneak* in to be with Gar. She was adamant about not telling Marcos. This made Gar sure that he would never understand, or be able to predict, women. He had been so sure she wanted love and marriage.

When he one day noticed birth control pills in her bag, he knew for sure it was only about the sex.

And that was about the same time he kept bumping into Victoria. He met her at the El Faro Hotel in town, where she was a waitress at the hotel's restaurant. El Faro in English means "The Lighthouse," and the hotel sported an actual signature lighthouse adjacent to the hotel proper. The lighthouse was a functional miniature of a real lighthouse, complete with winding staircase up the center of its thirty-foot tower and with a bona fide revolving light at the top. It was this charming architectural oddity that lured Gar to the hotel. And when he ate in the restaurant and was served by Vicky, he was very glad that he had discovered the place.

Vicky was tall, slim, and dark. She had long, thick, wavy black hair that hung like a lion's mane. She was an older version of Rosa, age twenty-seven, with three beautiful daughters (as she loved to refer to them). The daughters were two, seven and ten years of age. She spoke perfect English, which she had picked up through hard study. She was actually better suited to Gar's needs. And she was dramatic and fiery, just like the Mexican women stereotypically portrayed in movies.

And she was *Jaroucha* (Ha-Roach-Ah), a girl from Vera Cruz. The Jaroucha are said to be Mexico's greatest lovers. Gar found that fact to be very intriguing. But he did not know how she felt about him. That is, until he was visiting the friend that had introduced them, and she invited him to see her small apartment. As soon as he sat down she switched the floor fan from its revolving mode to stationary, and pointed it directly at him.

It is also said in Mexico, when a girl points the home's only fan at a single man, she is in love with that man.

CHAPTER 61

1996.

THEY LOCATED AN ideal site for the roller rink. It was an old cantina the owner had built with ample floor space so he could put on wedding dances and other large parties. Doubtless numerous *Quincineras* had been hosted here. Quincineras are fifteenth-birthday parties for girls and they are very special. They are an important coming-of-age ritual in Mexican society, and this place was the perfect site to hold one.

It was an eight-thousand square foot cement slab with twenty foot high walls surrounding it. Good bathrooms were situated on each of the far corners. A large stage had been erected across the back wall between the bathrooms. And perhaps its most important commercial recommendation was that it was kitty-corner to Playa's only movie theatre. Both of these buildings being perfectly located in the small, downtown area. Location, location, location!

On the frontage wall there was an office, the size of a small trailer house, erected twenty feet in the air. The windows across the front of the office looked down at the street. Across the back they looked out over the large future skating rink.

It was absolutely perfect. It would drain the rest of Gar's savings, but it was a worthwhile investment. They had located an attorney, Joel, who had the paperwork for the Cooperation completed, a lease option on the building filed, all the ducks lined neatly in a row. Gar was now the proud owner of Playa del Carmen's first and only Skating Palace.

THE FIRST THING Gar did after taking possession of The Palace was arrange for Rosa's father and brother to come over from Atoyac to resurface the floor; they were excellent concrete finishers. Once there, they also built several concrete jumps and ramps for the skaters. These were a work of art. Between Gar's imagination and el Negro's ingenuity, the jumps were user friendly and safe.

They brought Raquel with them, and she moved in and took over the house. Which was fine, because Rosa was working exclusively at *The Palace* now. Rosa had quit sneaking into Gar's bedroom. Apparently she had fallen for a flautist in a *Jethro Tull*-style Mexican Salsa band.

Again, Gar quit trying to figure women out.

That was the bad news. The good news was, Raquel and Gar were alone at the duplex much of the time. Sammy, Raquel's young daughter, often went with Marcos, or Rosey, or Grandpa to the Palace. She was a cute little cut-up and everyone wanted to take her. That was when Raquel started the running-around-in-just-a-towel-after-<u>her</u>-shower thing.

Usually they'd get ready, at the same time, to go out in the early evenings. Gar too would be wearing just a towel wrapping. The towel thing actually made it easy to cool off after a long hot day, and before going out into the muggy night. Someday somebody is going to do a sociological study about this towel thing in equatorial climates and discover some most compelling results.

One night Raquel asked him to brush a snarl out of her hair. She sat on the edge of his bed, where he was watching the news. He turned, straddling her from behind. He brushed at the snarl, his free hand groping for purchase to keep them balanced. Several times he may have lightly touched one or both of her breasts—they were large targets—but only slightly, and perhaps with a stray finger. When he did this she turned, slightly smiling, and there was that sideways thing that turned on her Mexican eyes as if they were lit from within by lamps.

Finishing with the brushing, Gar said, "Hey, you want to play catch-me-fuck-me?"

She crinkled her nose and asked, "What's that?"

"You run, I give you a fair head start, and if I catch you within, say, five minutes, I get to fuck you."

She took off squealing with delight.

For as long as she was there, which was only a few months, they played together like this. And she was a wild one. Married and a mother, with a husband who had been gone for several years, she was experienced and wanting. And her quick laugh made her exquisite fun.

THE PALACE ROLLER-RINK was the talk of the town. Playa del Carmen was not a big town, with about ten thousand people on a good day, so word spread fast. Gar was still preparing the place. He had located a Roller Blade rental business in Cancun, and he bought it out. He hauled the seventy-five pair of skates, also fifteen bicycles, back to Playa. And with that, things were beginning to take form.

A plan to open a separate bicycle rental, down at the ferry dock where there was heavy foot traffic, was being devised. The bicycles themselves, as well as the rental location, would be plastered with, "Skate at The Palace" advertisements.

THEN VICTORIA AND Gar fell into the sack together one night, and life took off abruptly and precipitously. It started out at the restaurant where Vicky was a waitress, the El Faro Hotel. Gar was just finishing a late lunch and flirting with Vicky over coffee, as he had been doing for weeks, when he suddenly asked whether she would like to have a drink when she got off work. He was thinking about her turning the fan on him previously when he had briefly visited her apartment.

"Si?" She batted beautiful eyes at him. "A drink. A drink of what?" She was bustling about, cleaning adjacent tables.

"I don't know." Gar hesitated. Perhaps he had gone too far. "A margarita or something. Whatever you want."

"When I get off work?"

"Yes."

"So!" Vicky snatched off her apron and flung it into a tray of dishes. "No more work. It is time for the drink!"

Within five minutes they were seated in the dark hotel bar. Within an hour they were in the small room with the revolving light at the top of the hotel's lighthouse, clothing strewn all over the floor, and they were both giggling.

Vicky was a passionate, impetuous lover; she made her presence unmistakably known. Much to the chagrin of Raquel and Rosey.

Rosa, who had not been staying there much, came back to do her peep show thing. And Raquel put on her shortest shorts, skimpiest blouses, and found dozens of things down low to bend over and clean. They were very jealous.

And Vicky was returning home with Gar most nights. She was a vociferous and passionate screamer when making love. This woke the other girls.

It became tangled for a time. In the end, Raquel returned with her father to Acapulco, Rosa stayed permanently with her flautist, and Vicky, along with her three beautiful daughters, moved in.

The young girls—Meche, age ten; Alejandra, age seven; and Angelina, only two—were very sweet and well-mannered children. Mom was strict. They had lost their father a year earlier, which made it easy for them to adopt Gar, right away, as Papa. This put Gar's planets back into alignment. The playboy life had been a wonderful diversion, but it was nice to be a part of a family again. Especially one where Papa was always the center of attention—another "here in Mexico" tradition.

Indeed, now, besides Vicky, he had three beautiful girls who would point the fan at him and give him attention.

IT WAS THE summer of 1996. Hurricane *Rachel* had just passed through the week before. Vicky teased that the name in Spanish was actually "Raquel," who was trying to get even because Vicky had stolen Gar. Gar swore he was not sleeping with either sister, but Victoria is clever and intuitive. She has dreams that tell her things.

Rainstorms continued even after *Rachel* was long gone. It was that time of year. They come in from the east, between Puerto Rico and Venezuela. Then they usually bump against Cuba, where the storm intensifies, before it then screams across the Yucatan Peninsula and into the Gulf of Mexico. Normally, these tropical storms do not change the temperature noticeably. Although now and again it will drop into the seventies, and *serape* salesmen make a killing as people think they're freezing to death. The average temperature in the town of Playa is somewhere in the mid-eighties. It is slightly cooler than Acapulco.

When it did not rain, Gar and Vicky took walks on the beach, strolling along the edge of the surf like the two young lovers they had become. Hand in hand they walked, her head on his shoulder. And in the evenings they would sometimes take a blanket and walk the north beach, where there was only jungle and no people except the occasional turtle poacher. When far enough up the beach, they'd spread the blanket and make love. It was portentous and powerful sex, with the essence of Maya apparitions looking on. Palenque aside, Gar had never felt a stronger spectral presence than he did on the north beach of Playa, especially removed from town and hemmed by jungle.

"You're different than others, Gar. Different than I imagined American men." Vicky said one night after they'd made love on the blanket. They were lying on their backs, looking up at the stars. They milky way, this far removed from city lights, was a sheet of white paint splashed across the sky. The jungle smelled fecund, green and complicated. A faint necklace of colorful buoy lights encircled the Island of Cozumel in the distance. The lights twinkled and winked like a faraway lighthouse.

"Am I so different?"

"Yes, very much so. I like having chaca-chaca with you." She was smiling Gar could tell, though it was dark.

"Chaca-chaca?" Gar chuckled a bit.

"Yes." She said yes like "Jes," with a deep, husky voice. "That is my name I use with my daughters."

"You mean your three <u>beautiful</u> daughters...."

"Jes."

"You are much less inhibited than lovers I have known." Gar prompted, picking up on her original train of thought. "Less shy."

"What is shy? Is that like afraid?" They were speaking English, and though hers was very good, it was not all-inclusive.

"Yes, shy is like afraid, but I should say it is when you lack confidence. Bashful or timid are two other words," he explained.

"Okay. I understand. No, I am not shy," she laughed. "I was maybe a little bit when I was younger; before I learned more about my vagina (she pronounced it Bah-He-Na). I think Mexican girls know more about their vaginas than American girls."

"Oh, really?" Gar asked. "Why is that?"

"First, we do not cover our vaginas until we are maybe five or eight years old. It is so hot, here in Mexico, we do not like to wear clothes. I remember when I was young, maybe five, me and other girls would sit in the yard, in the dirt, and look at our vaginas; opening them and talking about them. We didn't care. Sometimes our mothers would tell us to come in for dinner, to wash our hands first, and wash your vagina, too, they'd say. 'You've been sitting in the dirt, and you've got your vagina all dirty.'"

"Ha! That's funny. Yes, I don't think American girls are like that. I built a house in my old city, and I put a bidet in the master bathroom. Do you know what a bidet is?"

"Of course. We have them in the rooms in my hotel." She was speaking of the El Faro Hotel, where she worked.

"Well, when the house was finished, many people came to see it. I would give them a tour. And most of the girls that saw my bidet did not know what it was. And when I told them, most thought it was strange. Some said it was sick and dirty. I wanted to tell them: 'Not as sick as a dirty vagina.'"

Now she laughed. "Having children makes women less worried about their vaginas. I think girls worry about the pain, when they are still virgins, about something like a penis entering and hurting them. Then when they see a child pass through that same canal, when they feel that pain, they know that no penis can hurt them."

"Interesting." Gar became thoughtful. "So, do you look at your vagina? Do you inspect it?"

"All the time," she answered matter of factly. "And I keep it very clean. I wash it as much as I can. It is my soap, and my vagina, so I will wash it all that I want." She laughed a low, husky laugh.

"Yes, I do that to my *Pancho*, too, and it feels so good." He was laughing. Then he got serious. "You know, I think I am falling in love with you.

"Me too," she said simply, and they hugged each other tight. A small breaker crashed. A noise in the brush line of the jungle turned their heads the opposite way, and Gar reached for the fanny pack where his pistol was squirreled. The fanny pack was right by his head where he had left it, but when he hefted it he knew immediately that there was no longer a pistol inside.

Further inspection revealed the pistol, and Vicky's pack of cigarettes, were gone. The money, incredibly, was still there. How could that have happened? The pack was right at their heads. They had not slept, they had only made love. And the pack was zipped closed, with the money still inside. It was astounding. Maybe unexplainable.

Welcome to the jungle, baby.

CHAPTER 62

SUMMER, 1996.

THEY GOT THE Palace Roller rink open around the first of July. Kids were clamoring to get there first, before the skates were all checked out, and the line for admission stretched around the block. The seventy-five pair of skates were of various sizes, and the kids didn't care if they got the right size or not. This was an event, and they wanted to be a part of it.

Gar charged the least he could for them to get in. With the door fee they got free skates, subject to availability. On busy nights, kids would take turns, sharing skates with friends. Gar tried to make his profit on the concession stand, using the same formula he had figured out some years earlier when he did his *GAR WALTON PRESENTS* shows. Let the door pay the rent; put the concession money in your pocket. In this way, one does not gouge those that cannot afford it—those that just want to be there—and those that have money will spend it at the snack bar.

It was a marvelous thing, this roller rink. Gar taught a hundred kids how to skate. He'd walk along with then, holding their hands, helping with their balance until they'd take off. Which was usually within the first ten minutes. The laughing and shouting was well worth the money and effort he had put forth to get the place open.

And he had become a Playa celebrity. Everywhere he went, people would smile and wave, "Hello *Don* Gar. How are you today? Thank you very much for the wonderful thing you are doing for our children." With the kids he was like a rock star, they'd follow him like the Pied Piper of Hamlin. At times he felt like they wanted to ask for his autograph, but were a little too shy to do so.

When he first began pondering business ideas, Gar thought that he would not try to do something touristy, as tourism is a seasonal thing. He had already decided, before he met Junior on the Plaza that night, that whatever he would do would become an established local business, targeting Mexican locals and not vacationers.

The first idea that he entertained was a roasted chicken business. The kind where whole chickens are rotisseried on a spit. These eateries are very popular in Mexico. He thought they'd raise the chickens, too. A small farm would give them a place to live; the rotisserie would only take a very small and inexpensive downtown location for their business. It was a good plan, but the roller rink was a great one.

From the very first day Gar had set foot in Playa, he roved the town at night, checking out the local music scene. He listened to Reggae, Salsa, Meringue, and a little bit of Rock & Roll. In fact he bought an assortment of used instruments from musicians leaving town. And his pride and joy was a new *Pearl* drum set, which he played every day. He very soon had enough instruments for a band.

When Gar was twenty, he had set two goals for himself: since he liked diving, he vowed to make a living on the ocean; and, because he loved Rock & Roll and dancing, he'd become involved somehow in the music business.

The first goal he had accomplished; the second he was still working on. His familiarity with the local music scene, and now a venue, The Palace, would be the springboard he needed to promote bands. Maybe, he dreamed, one day he'd get his old friend, Luis Miguel, to come sing at The Palace.

There was a large, alcoved entrance in the middle of the front wall of The Palace, but off to one side was a regular size metal door. They cut it halfway up and made it a Dutch door for the service of food to the street. And inside, in that same corner, they set up a few tables. It was here that Vicky sold Mexican food: tostadas, tacos, and Mexican desserts to both the customers and passersby on the street.

Gar also had a cart inside where he put block ice. Shaved off, put into paper cones with flavored syrup poured over the top, the ice made fine snow-cones. That was his baby, the snow-cone wagon. He even made his own syrups. They sell the concentrate in most Mexican markets, small bottles of super-concentrate flavoring, but there is an art to mixing in just the right amount of sugar, and Gar was an expert at this. It took masses of sugar.

AN ODD THING happened one afternoon. Gar was alone at the Tohucu duplex. The front door and all the windows in the house stood wide open. This was their air conditioning.

He was back in his bedroom, at the desk, working out something on the computer, when he heard Tao call out, "Hola, Gar!"

He went to the front door, and there was Tao. He stood outside, waiting, with another Mexican man. The other man, a bit older, was obviously along for the ride. There was a red Nissan at the curb, so he probably *was* the ride. Tao introduced the man as his cousin, Abel.

They talked. Tao explained he was there to "work." Playa is very far from Acapulco. But as Tao pointed out, it is very near to Colombia, which, of course, is the source of a great deal of the world's cocaine.

Then Tao produced a hand held GPS receiver and he asked Gar to show him how to work it. It just happened that Gar had NOAA charts of the Mexican oceans. With these, he was able to teach Tao how to equate the GPS readings to positions on the charts. And he showed him how to use the waypoint functions to navigate from one position to another.

After a few hours, Tao and Abel followed Gar to The Palace so Tao could check it out.

Then they said good-bye. Tao said he'd be around for "a while," and would come again to visit with Gar. But he never did.

Yet Gar noticed Abel, in his conspicuous red Nissan, several times parked by The Palace. He seemed to be watching. And he saw him driving by the duplex more than once. It was very peculiar. And it was unnerving.

CHAPTER 63

AUGUST, 1996.

ANOTHER RAINSTORM HAD just passed through the Yucatan. It killed a spell of late-August heat, and replaced it with the first signs of Autumn, which in Mexico is the mild-weather time of the year. The rain left Playa del Carmen dark and somber looking.

Gar opened The Palace at five in the afternoon, the appointed time to open the gates. Kids were backed up around the corner in line. As usual, Gar let Junior in first–he had a free lifetime pass. Gar had made him a celebrity, although Junior, with his winning smile, didn't do too badly on his own: Junior was the best skater in town. Aside from the occasional adult, that is, who'd bring custom Roller Blades in and show off an ability they learned somewhere more urbane than Playa del Carmen.

The theme song that signaled the opening was "Welcome to the Jungle" by Guns 'n Roses. An artist, a very good one, had come in and painted the entire inside walls with jungle scenes: lions, and tigers, and bears. Oh, my! Welcome to the Jungle signaled closing time, too. The rest of the night, disco played. It was perfect skating music. And it was very popular with the kids. No one likes to dance more than the youth of Mexico.

There had been a *Palapa*-type thatched roof on the building, at one time, but three-fourths of that was missing due to another hurricane; the one before Rachel. So when Junior came in, he'd get his crew of boys together and they'd skate the floor in perfect formation, squeegees skimming the floor before them. This impressed the girls. They'd do the same thing a time or two at night with dust mops. Gar would get on the PA, clearing the floor, making as much fanfare out of it as he could.

The PA was used to promote contests and skate competitions, and also as a preview of coming attractions. They had two-for-one nights, lady's nights, and one night they weighed everyone and charged them by the kilo in order to determine the price of admission. All of these stratagems spelled bargain, and served to keep the bodies coming in the door where they might buy goodies from the concession stand.

ON THE TWENTY-EIGHTH of August, Gar had to run back to the house to make more syrup for his snow-cones. It was a process that took an hour or two, and involved boiling a large pot of water to dissolve several big sacks of sugar. Then the concentrate had to be added, followed by a cooling period, and finally the bottling.

Meche was at the house. Gar played Chutes and Ladders with her while the syrup cooled. She said she did not want to go back to The Palace with him, so with the syrup finally bottled he would go alone.

He spent a few minutes on the computer, before he left, making a new flyer for an up-and-coming skate competition. He produced a number of these on his Xerox copier. He'd get Junior and his gang to hang them around the small town.

IT WAS DUSK when just out of the Tohucu entrance, headed down the main drag, a car came up fast on the tail of Gar's pickup. It was identical to the scene he had with the Highway Patrol when they'd confiscated his truck in Northern California: They were without headlights and stayed tight on his bumper, and when he eased over, they would not pass. He felt an ominous sense of *déjà vu*.

Then they put a small, flashing light on their roof, which lit up red, and the situation became clear.

"Dammit!" He no longer had his pistol. He had carried it for these last years, not hoping to kill anyone, but to have it to brandish about in an effort to buy time to get away. And here was a time when he needed it but didn't have it. Gar pounded the dashboard in frustration.

That was not going to happen here. Not tonight. He pulled over and got out. He had his "rock-solid" ID he had bought from Tao. And he was sure he could bribe his way out of just about anything with cash. He just needed to take the lead, and in the right direction.

As he walked back to the unmarked Oldsmobile coupe, he saw that there were four stern-looking men in the car. For some reason, he thought Tao was one of them. But he turned out to be mistaken. Still, he couldn't shake the feeling that Tao was nearby.

Watching....

Part Four

EL PRISIONERO

CHAPTER 64

AUGUST 28, 1996.

"LET ME SEE your identification, please." The stocky, well-dressed Mexican driver of the Oldsmobile spoke politely but commanding. He was clearly accustomed to domination, and expected to be obeyed. He met Gar at the front of the Olds. The other three passengers fanned in a circle around Gar. This was all obvious cop stuff, basic police tactics employed all over the world.

"Was I driving too fast?" Gar tried to lighten the mood. He had not been driving too fast.

"No, sir. We would like to check something. May I please see your right shoulder? Just pull up your tee-shirt." Uh, oh! These guys wanted to see his tattoo. Fortunately, Gar had planned for this and covered his initials with roses.

The men crowded around, pointing and poking at the roses, saying that they looked like they might be covering initials. One mentioned that the tattoo looked pretty fresh. Then the stocky driver spoke again.

"Would you please show us your upper teeth, in the back, if you don't mind?" He was polite enough about it. But, shit. They were looking for bridges. And Gar had permanent upper bridges. However, the spokesman then said, "Would you please take out your false teeth?" Maybe a break. They couldn't confirm the initials under the tattoo depicting roses. And he did not have removable false teeth.

"I'm sorry," Gar said, grabbing and tugging on his bridges. "I do not have false teeth."

But then they pointed at the bridges. They determined that the teeth were not real, although they were glued in permanently. Based on this, they decided they had the right man.

"You must come with us."

"Wait!" Gar interrupted. "I can give you money for gas, or refreshments, or whatever you wish, so that you can go back to your office and recheck your records before you do anything irrational."

"You must come with us," the man insisted. "We will take you to our station and there we will talk. There is an extradition warrant to the United States for you."

"Where is your station?"

"It is on Sixth and G Streets, just a few blocks from here. My partner will drive your truck there."

"Okay." Gar was trying to be pleasant. He still hoped to offer them money again, although this was clearly not working. And these appeared to be the dreaded *PGR* police. The Mexican Feds. They might not take money.

WEHN THEY PULLED up at the PGR station, Gar tried again.

"Oh, there's my lawyer's office right across the street!" he exclaimed. "Let me get him. He can help fix this." Experience had taught Gar that it is often better to have a third party do the bribing.

But when Gar said this, the driver stepped on the gas, throwing a rooster tail of gravel into the air behind them.

They went to the Municipal Police Station, but only to drop off Gar's pickup truck.

"Did you leave the keys in it?" The spokesman asked the driver of the pickup when he got back into the car.

"Yes, my Captain."

"All right, then. We're off." And he accelerated rapidly onto the highway, pointing the vehicle towards Cancun and clearly out of town.

Gar dropped Tao's name, Jamie's name, every name he could think of. But his words were ignored. They were not going to Sixth and G Street, a few blocks away. They were going to Cancun. This was serious indeed.

THEY PULLED UP in front of a small concrete building in Cancun some time later. The windows on the front of the building had bars. The sign affixed discretely to the building filled Gar with dread:

PROCURADOR GENERAL de REPUBLICO
Cancun, Quintana Roo, Mexico

The PGR station. Mexican jail. The worst possible thing had just happened. This was it then. Gar's mouth was suddenly incredibly dry, and he felt sick.

INSIDE, GAR SPENT his first night in jail. He did not know how many more there would be. He was alone in a small cell. They brought him restaurant food, Saran-wrapped on Styrofoam plates. They came around once an hour, asking if everything was okay. They would not answer any questions.

Nor would they respond to Gar's requests to call Joel, Gar's lawyer.

It was a long first night. Sleep was fitful.

The next morning they brought Gar out to the office for booking. They never used handcuffs. And they never had less than ten policemen around him during the entire procedure.

The office was open and sunny, with lots of windows. Gar sat in a chair talking to a friendly woman secretary while she typed on a form. She reiterated that this was about an extradition warrant initiated by the United States. It had something to do with federal drug charges.

On the wall was an official display board listing the PGR hierarchy: Jamie Nunoz, Gar's old drinking buddy in Acapulco, was listed at the very top. He was the sole commander of the hundred names listed below him.

Gar, though, seemed to be the only one who knew him. Everyone shrugged at mention of his name. It was hopeless.

THE SAME DAY, they flew him to Mexico City on a chartered jet. The airport is located on the east side of the capital city. It is a two-hour drive from one side of the city to the other. And that's by freeway.

The largest city in the world with a population over twenty million, Mexico City is so enormous that it almost defies description. According to legend, the city was founded in 1325. The city rests in an endorheic (characterized by interior draining) basin, and it is walled in by the Sierra Madre Mountains. It lies in a huge bowl. To the southeast, the city ends in a plain that meets the Sierra Nevada, dominated by a smoking volcano. This was Mt. Popocatepetl. And it was generally in this direction that they drove. The volcano got larger as they neared, until it absolutely dominated the horizon.

Approaching the south side of the city, Gar recognized signs pointing the way toward Acapulco. He asked, again, if these guys knew Tao of Acapulco. They shrugged.

When the freeway sign said, "Last Mexico City Exit" before entering the toll road to Acapulco, Gar perked up. He was thinking that Tao had the fix in, and they were going to Acapulco. He held his breath as the off ramp approached.

But they took the last exit. That dream was dashed. The pain of this was exquisite to Gar. To have one's hopes built up, however foolishly, and then dashed in this manner was emotionally painful almost beyond tolerance.

The Suburban wound up a small hill. At the top was an obvious prison: high walls, guard towers, razor wire, parking lot dotted with police cars. And over it all, brooding in the distance, sat Mt. Popocatepetl. Black smoke trailed from the top of the volcano, torn sideways by high-altitude winds, and it cast a gloomy pall over the countryside. The entire scene was one of abject torment. Hieronymus Bosch could have created nothing more dismal and foreboding than this.

"Don't worry, Gringo," one of the police said. "There are other Americans here." He was perhaps trying to be kind. The other policemen nonetheless chuckled at Gar's discomfort.

Gar had presented his "rock solid" identification to them to inspect. "But I'm not American," he insisted. "I'm Mexican...."

"Okay, Gringo. Whatever you say." They laughed.

IT WAS MID-AFTERNOON when Gar arrived at the Mexican prison, and it was only about six in the evening when he was turned loose in a building full of other prisoners. He had been interviewed by the Captain of the prison, a man named Mr. Paniagua. Someone had alerted Mike, another American prisoner, that Gar was being processed in. As it would turn out, Mike was Gar's age, a fisherman wanted in the United States for smuggling, and he was lodged in the prison pending extradition. Gar's circumstances exactly.

Mike's most noticeable characteristic was a large mouth that was perpetually cocked in a lopsided grin. His buckteeth were like seven miles of picket fence. You could see every tooth when he opened his mouth to grin. Sandy haired, gangly, tall, angular, and boney, a person looking at Mike did not have to imagine what he looked like as a kid. He could not have changed much since. He was a very open and engaging person. People seemed to like him on sight.

"Where ya'll coming from?" Mike asked.

"Oh, I was over in Quintana Roo." It was nice to see a friendly face and speak English for a moment. "Near Cancun, in a small town called Playa del Carmen."

"I don't know it. I was living in Vera Cruz–Tuxpan. I was running a sword-fish boat."

"Really? You're a fisherman? So am I. A salmon fisherman." Then Gar quit speaking, as he suddenly remembered he had an alternate ID that said he was someone else entirely.

"Don't worry too much about this place. It's fine if you've got money. Do you have any?"

"Oh, some. I just opened a business in Playa del Carmen. It left me pretty well tapped. I don't know how much I can put my hands on. Hey, is there any way I can make a phone call?" Gar asked.

"Yeah, that front desk where you came in; there's a phone on the wall right there. You can call local or collect. You just have to get one of the guards to open that gate right there by the desk. We can run all over this building, but going out there by the phone is different." Mike was still smiling. He was the fidgety type, scratching and shifting from foot to foot, but he was certainly helpful. He appeared to be pleased to have a fellow American to talk to.

"Can you show me how to get there?"

"Follow me," Mike said, waving one arm in a big, dramatic circle, the stupid grin plastered from ear to ear.

GAR CALLED SKY-TEL. He left the same message on Tao, Gilberto, Federico, and even their sister Erica's Sky-Pagers: "9-1-1. PLEASE HELP! I'M IN RECLUSORIO SUR IN MEXICO CITY. THEY'RE CALLING ME GAR WALTON HERE!!!"

Two days later, when he hadn't heard anything, he tried again. He found that those Sky-Tel Sky-Pager numbers had all been disconnected.

THAT FIRST NIGHT, when he saw he wouldn't be gang raped, or beat up or killed, Gar decided this was doable. Maybe it was even possible to consider it a challenge. After all, the place was just another community, albeit one with cement walls around it and armed guards on patrol. He'd been living in various types of Mexican communities for the last four years. He'd show these people just how Mexican he had become.

The building and area he found himself in was called *Ingresso* (Admissions), and it was painted lime green with gray trim–both inside and out. It was a three-story, rectangular, flat-roofed building measuring perhaps 500 feet by 300 feet. The only entrances to the building–one from the front desk, the other out to an exercise and courtyard–are at the middle of the long walls. The doors open onto a central landing, and cell ranges branch off of those in wings. There are caged rooms on these landings, some of which serve as commissaries. The landings are the same on all three floors, though the cages are used differently. One bottom-floor wing is a large, open dining room; the other is comprised of bathrooms, showers, and isolated rooms for storage.

The top floors have four ranges of cells. They spread down each side of each wing and look out across a small hallway through windows to the outside. The cells are standard steel-bar fronted cells. There are twelve of these cells down each of the four ranges on each of the two upper floors.

Many people like Ingresso, as it is protected and removed from the general population. Gar thought it smelled like circus sawdust and corn chips. Renting a room there costs a monthly fee of $1,000NP (New Pesos) or about $200USC (U.S. Currency). And even more than smelling like a circus, it looked like a circus and sounded like a loony bin.

Walking into Ingresso for the first time was like walking into a colorful bedlam. The smell of frying foods filled the air and children scampered about underfoot. The commissaries in the central landing offered every possible amenity for sale, from toilet paper and toothpaste to ice cream cones and icy bottles of beer. Fat guards dandied infants on bouncing knees. Teenaged lovers necked in the corners. Old men played checkers, and groups of women sat knitting in a circle. Men, women, and children mixed together in a happy party atmosphere. It was as unlike what Gar thought prison would be as it could get. He found it astonishing.

Gar came in with several thousand pesos, but Captain Paniagua locked it in his safe. He told Gar he'd give it to him after a day or so.

"It's going to take you a few days to get situated," he explained. "And I'll have your money for you when you need it."

Strangely, Gar believed him. And Paniagua explained the extradition process. If Gar agreed to be extradited, it would take exactly 120 days for him to get out of there. If he fought it, it could take years.

ON THAT FIRST night, at 8:30 p.m., the guards came around locking everybody up–somewhere. It was time for them to do their "List" (the evening count). Gar had nowhere to go, so he was locked in one of the small cages on the second-floor landing. It was cramped. There were about sixty other hombres in there with him. A few had sleeping pads. Most didn't. You were expected to tip the guards at least three pesos every night at List Time. And if you didn't, this is where you stayed for the rest of the night.

Gar got seated in a corner. There was no room to stretch out, let alone lay down. And it was cold. Xochimilco was the name of the colony in which the prison was sited, and it is about 8,000 feet in elevation and rather cold at night.

Mike brought a chunky, rosey-cheeked Mexican by the iron bars of the door, and introduced him as "Manzanas." Apples, in English, which was what his cheeks looked like. "Do you want a better place to sleep, Mr. Gar?" Manzanas asked. "I can let you stay with Mike for two-hundred pesos ($40USC)."

"I don't have any money," Gar said simply. He was very weary. It had been a long and eventful day, and he didn't feel capable of making decisions. He would have to go along with Mike's judgment for now. And Mike had brought this Manzanas man to him.

"But you have money with Paniagua, no? I can wait until tomorrow. He'll give it to you then." Manzanas spoke with a big, magnanimous grin: a "don't worry, be happy" grin.

"How can I get out of here?" Gar didn't understand how all of this worked.

"Rambo," Manzanas called to the guard. "I will pay Mr. Gar's list tonight. Please let him out." Manzanas paid Rambo five pesos. And now Gar owed Manzanas 200 pesos.

AT MIKE'S CELL, Mike disclosed he was getting nothing out of the deal. "Don't get comfortable," he admonished. Mike was a helluva nice guy, but not that nice. "So, you do have money with the Captain?" The front of Mike's cell was covered with plywood. The cubicle was about 8' × 12'. It had a toilet and a shower, a bunk against one wall, and not much else.

"Yes. Paniagua said I'd get it back. I've got two or three thousand pesos I left with him."

"Shit, for a thousand of that, you can rent cell-two, right next to me. It's empty. The guy just left."

"Yeah, if he gives me the money. I've been around a lot of Mexican cops, and I just don't trust them." Gar was shaking his head. He was on the floor with an extra sleeping mat and blanket Mike had provided for him. Next to Mike's bunk, the cell was just wide enough for one person to stretch out.

"Paniagua's a pretty good guy. Oh, he'll charge you for all sorts of things: cell phones, televisions, having your girl spend the night, or if you want drugs. But he's usually square. If he told you he's giving you back your money, he will." Mike sounded very sure.

"All right, then. I'll rent the place next door: *Room Two With A View*, my favorite room number. And did you say wives can spend the night?"

"Oh yeah. Mine used to all the time. Costs usually a hundred pesos–twenty bucks. Same as a gram of coke. You like coke?" Mike's voice perked up when he asked that. It was pitch black in the cell; Mikes' boom box played softly on an American oldies station.

"Nah. I've had my times where I fooled with it, but I'm mainly a drinker. I only do coke, the times I've done it, so I can drink longer." Gar yawned.

"Oh, we got booze here, too. And I do coke so I can do everything longer." Mike laughed. "Okay, I'll talk to you in the morning," he said. And he rolled over toward the wall.

"Thanks, Mike. I really mean that." And Gar, surprisingly, went right to sleep.

CHAPTER 65

AUGUST 29, 1996.

STEPPING OUTSIDE MIKE'S cell, the morning was sunshiny. Sunlight bathed the half-wall of windows on the outside of the hallway. There was a little bit of smog, but not enough to block the view of the volcano. Popocatepetl, known by everyone as simply "Popo," had its ever-present column of steam rising in the distance. It was beautiful to look at, truly. The smog, in this area, was usually minimal. Gar was to learn a great deal about this smoking volcano, piecing the information together from a number of sources. The volcano was primordial, having been noted for its occasional eruptions since the 1300s. Aztecs who lived nearby had named the volcano Popocatepetl, which means smoking mountain. During the 1520s, soldiers in the army of Spanish conqueror Hernando Cortes entered the crater of Popo to obtain sulfur to make gunpowder. It was a moody, smoking, brooding giant, capable of raining down death and destruction as it had done many times in the past, and Gar grew to view the volcano with uneasy distrust. Yet this morning it looked picturesque and benign.

Gar went to see the Captain. Paniagua was his usual jovial self. He got Gar's money, and had him sign a receipt.

Everything was official and neat. Gar gave him a 300-peso tip, which he accepted graciously.

Gar had always carried his cash in a small silk pouch, which Paniagua also returned to him. The pouch came as a carry bag for Oakley sunglasses, and had a drawstring. He simply tied that drawstring through a hole in the elastic in the front of his Jockey shorts. Then he tucked the bag down inside the front of his pants. No one knew it was there, and he dared them to try to get it, should they learn that it was.

MONEY DOWN AROUND his testicles, Gar went to the store; he was starved. He bought a sandwich and Coke, and stood by the floor-to-ceiling glass on the bottom floor landing. The view was out into the exercise area and courtyard. It had basketball nets, small soccer goals, and picnic tables. There was a little bit of grass, and a few small trees. The wall around the 300' by 500' yard was topped with razor wire. Fifty men strolled around in the area, hands clasped behind, talking in the morning sunshine.

A henchman of Manzanas came up to Gar and said, "Hey, let's go back in that bathroom and talk. I think you owe me money." Word was out that Gar had seen the Captain. But Gar didn't owe this guy a thing.

Gar laughed and took a bite from his sandwich, then passed the sandwich to his left hand, freeing his right. The entire courtyard stopped to stare back through the glass wall. Everyone knew that something was up.

"I'm sorry," Gar said to the man. "Did you say I owe you money? You know what? Fuck your mother!" Gar turned slightly, his left side now facing the man.

The henchman, known as "Flaco," started a slow-motion swing, without any more talk. It was not deserving of a block or evasion, it was coming so slowly. Before it landed, Gar hit

Flaco so hard on the chin that he was lifted into the air and thrown back against the glass. Gar didn't spill his Coke; he made sure of that. Seeing everybody look at each other, nodding in approval, he thought he'd be real cool. So he took a bite of his sandwich, then a long drink of the Coke, and he walked away. He walked away like Dirty Harry, without even a backwards glance at the man lying in a heap.

It was a power move, and perhaps Gar's first valuable jailhouse discovery. He intuitively knew that in a new jail, or neighborhood of the lower sort, you always need to hit someone as soon as possible, preferably a bully. What he discovered, though, was something he'd later learn is called building your "Personal Power Base." By whipping the pain-in-the-ass vulture, who no one really liked anyway, all those people that watched were now part of Gar's Personal Power Base. They shared something in common. They would all nod and say hello to him from that moment forward.

He made sure everyone knew who he was, and went right out after the whipping and walked among them, finishing his breakfast and admiring the view of Popo off in the distance.

MIKE CAME DOWN from his second-story room to find Gar talking with one of the prisoners who was an incarcerated Federale. There are a number of federal police locked up at Reclusorio Sur. Oddly, they are the ones that normally have the illicit drug concessions. Or maybe not so odd since they control the drug trade throughout Mexico.

"I heard you had to knock out Flaco a little while ago," Mike said. "Good job! He's a pain in the ass. He works for Manzanas. Manzanas would normally be pissed, but he's looking for you. He wants to rent you room two right next to me." Mike was excited about the fight.

"Ahh, yes. *Room Two With A View*. And, hey, we can see the volcano from our rooms." Gar was smiling about his new room. The room-two-with-a-view thing was actually started by his stepfather, Jack. Jack would always rent room two at the Half Moon Bay Inn in order to watch the annual *Chamarita* Parade. It also reminded Gar of waterfront hotels in Eureka, California, and Charleston, Oregon, where he always rented room two. The fact that his new lodgings would be room number two was auspicious. "Let's go find Apple Cheeks," Gar suggested, not at all displeased with the way the morning was going.

Mike said, "All right. You know, that mountain in front of the volcano is called the sleepy woman. Can you see her?" He pointed into the distance.

"Oh, yeah. Real clearly. Yeah, her hair; nose and chin; a breast; there's even an eye. I'll be dipped." Gar spoke admiringly, then they headed for the building.

HE GOT THE room. And, for an extra $200NP, he got plywood that bolted right on the bars to make it a wall; including a door covering. Privacy and security. And Mike gave him a padlock for his door.

Then he went to call home. Since he had rented the room, tipped the Captain, and knocked out Flaco, doors were opening effortlessly for him. The locked gate to the front desk, where the telephone was accessed, opened right up for him too.

"Hello, my love," Vicky came on the line. "We got your truck from the police station. Marcos saw it there. Different people saw the PGR taking you away. I took Joel and

Marcos, and we went to the PGR station in Cancun. But they wouldn't let us see you." She was crying now.

"I know, my love. They were in a hurry. I'm in Mexico City, at Reclusorio Sur. Can you come here and bring my lawyer?"

"We don't have money."

"Listen, I have about seven-thousand dollars left in my safe. Can you open a safe?"

"Jes."

"Okay. Write this down. The combination is 1-14-56. Do you have that?"

"Jes. Uno-Catorce-Cincuenta y Seis." She said it so cutely, Gar wanted to climb right through the phone.

"Okay. You got it. I'm fine. I miss you. I have a room of my own. When you come here, you can come right to my room. We can make Chaca-Chaca." Gar announced this proudly.

"Crazy Gringo!" She laughed through the tears. It was involuntary.

Maybe things would be okay.

CHAPTER 66

SEPTEMBER, 1996

"THE MEXICAN JUDICIAL system is Napoleonic," Joel began. He and Vicky were sitting at the card-table-turned-dining-table Gar had set up outside Room Two. They were, of course, enjoying the view. Besides a clear view of the volcano, there was another building across on the other side of the courtyard called "COC" (Center for Observation and Classification). They could watch guys hanging out of the broken windows of the COC building, tossing things at people below–presumably people they knew, but who could say? Mike had said that COC was the ugliest place in the prison. "Only people that cannot pay anything to the guards for *List* go there," he explained.

"What does that mean, Napoleonic?" Gar inquired of Joel, raising his eyebrows and paying close attention to the man. He had one arm around Vicky, but he was very intent upon what the lawyer was telling him.

"Well, it's an old French system. It basically means that once you have been arrested, you are guilty. And I don't mean guilty until proven innocent. I mean you are guilty once they arrest you and take you to jail." Joel, a professional-looking, very light-skinned Maya, originally from the City of Merida, was shaking his head.

"So what are my chances of getting out?" Gar asked.

"You have to prove that they arrested the wrong man, mistaken identity as it were. That is the only defense a Mexican court, under our constitution, can entertain. And there is no trial. Just written proofs (evidence)."

"I keep telling them I am Jose Gar Ledesma, and they keep saying I am Gar Walton."

"Yes."

"What can I do? They have my ID."

"And I have your Gar Walton passport." Joel smiled.

"Oh, yeah. It was in my safe."

"Jes. I got it out when I got the money," Vicky said.

"Okay. Let's keep it close by. I'm not sure if I want it here. Did you bring me more clothes, my love?"

"Yes I did. I have more blankets for your bed, too. I do not want you to get cold on these nights without me."

Mexican women can be extremely dedicated. And Gar liked that.

"Will you help me make my bed, later? Where are the blankets?" Gar realized she'd only brought in a bag of food. This was another nice thing about Ingresso. Visitors came and went at will. They could bring you clothing and bedding and food, and they could hang out in your cell, or anywhere else. Outside there were picnic tables, and swings for kids. Mexican jails are very family oriented; conjugal visiting is allowed and encouraged.

"Yes, your things are out in the rental car. I will get them, and help you, but I have to leave at five." It was around noon.

"I'm told, like I was saying on the phone, that you can spend the night if we tip the Captain a hundred pesos. Would you like to spend the night? Would you mind, Joel?" Gar spoke to both of them.

"Of course," Vicky piped up.

"No, not at all," Joel said. "I have some friends I'd like to look up when I leave here, anyway."

"All right. So what you're saying to me is, if my ID is "rock solid," like my friends in Acapulco guaranteed, I will have no problem."

"That is correct. They have 45 days to give you an answer. And it has already been almost 30 days...."

"But if the ID is not good, I'm fucked," Gar finished.

Vicky smiled and whispered that he'd be fucked anyway.

"That's about the size of it," Joel said with finality, turning his palms into the air.

Vicky put her head on his shoulder, squeezed his arm into hers, and wiped a tear on his shirt. "I will marry you if it will help," she said.

"I will marry you anyway," Gar countered.

"There is really nothing I can do right now, Señor Gar. We must wait to see what the court says. Then you have some time to put in your evidence. Then they decide again. Then there are *Amparos*."

"What are Amparos?" Gar closed one eye, and raised the other eyebrow.

"Oh, in the United States they are called a writ of habeas corpus." Joel explained.

"Oh, yeah. I've heard of them."

"What you must do with an Amparo is make a claim, or several claims, that you are being restrained from your liberty either unlawfully, unconstitutionally, or both. If the judge agrees with you, they work very well. Sometimes a judge will let you out instanter. Immediately. There are some that say the Amparo is the reason for corruption in our judicial system; that is because they give a judge unlimited power to let you out, and for access to that power, they will sometimes take money." Joel explained. He was a bit more animated now.

Mike, Gar's new friend and neighbor, was looking on. Mike had a profile like Mr. Ed, the television horse of years past, and he hopped from foot to foot as he listened.

Gar's attention drifted from Mike's humorous continence to the volcano in the distance. At the moment, Popo was belching out great bellows of ominous ashen-white smoke. Gar tried to make sense of all this Mexican legal business, but was agitated by the threatening volcano.

"I understand. I think. Have you written many Amparos?"

"No. I have never written any outside of law school. I've never had a client like this. Like you. Remember, I am a business lawyer. If you need an Amparo, you must hire someone else."

Mike jumped in. This was the chance he was waiting for. "Hey!" he shouted. "I've got a damned good fuckin' lawyer from Vera Cruz!"

"Are you from Vera Cruz?" Vicky interjected.

"Yes, I am. I lived there for five years, until these assholes arrested me the first time. That's what I wanted to say. My lawyer, Caesar, got me out, the first time, with a damned good fuckin' Amparo. Then I went, like an idiot, right back home to Tuxpan. And sixty days later, which is how many days they have to wait, they arrested me again." Mike was angry. He was stomping from foot to foot now, with hands in both of his trouser pockets.

"You've done this twice? Been here twice, fighting extradition?" Gar was incredulous.

"Yeah, I been meaning to tell you that." Mike had this peculiar way of saying things. He was one of those guys you could not help but like, and there was no way you could ever get angry at him.

Vicky said, "I, too, am from Vera Cruz."

Mike said, "I been thinkin' you was Jarocha." And everyone laughed at the way he said it, because of his Texas accent.

Joel, the lawyer, said, "Maybe you should get his lawyer's name and phone number. Do you have that now? I will call him if you do, and if you want me to, Mr. Gar?" He was looking at Mike but speaking to Gar.

Gar nodded assent.

"Hang on," Mike said. "I've got it right here." He ducked into his room, and then came out thumbing an address book. "There it is, right there. He's in Poza Rica, Vera Cruz. Caesar Contreras. That's one good son-of-a-bitch, right there. If there's any way to get you out, he'll by God do 'er!"

Joel copied the information into his day planner, gave the book back to Mike, and said, "Thank you. I'll go call him this very day. Gar, would there be anything more, at this moment?"

"No. I guess you will stay for a few days?"

"I will stay for as long as I can assist. You know, as I said, this is really not my area of law. I can only help you find someone with the proper expertise." Joel spoke formally and he started collecting his things. Gar had learned that Joel always spoke formally.

"Very good, my friend," Gar replied, as he stood and shook hands with Joel. They shook the Mexican businessman style, which is like the old soul-brother handshake. Both men draw their arms back, then smack palms together, locking thumbs. "Please help Victoria with the Captain, if you don't mind."

"No problem, sir. I will take care of that. Good day, Mr. Gar. And good day to you, too, Mr. Mike. I am Joel Escalante, at your service." And Joel and Mike shook hands.

"By God, you seem like a pretty good sum-bitch, too." Mike spoke to him with a smile. Gar remembered Mike is a Texan. It seemed like the Texas accent came out more in a group; perhaps when his guard dropped it snuck out.

VICKY RETURNED AN hour later with a Mexican kid following her, carrying and dragging a ton of stuff. She had even brought his old bible from beside his bed–the one Dad gave him, thirty years earlier, when he was fourteen. She tipped the kid, sending him off smiling.

Gar didn't yet have a hot plate, so they cooked dinner at Mike's. Actually, Mike cooked, while they sat at the table between the two cells and watched him put on a show. He was a funny guy. Vicky and Mike were instant friends. Of course, Mike seemed to become instant friends with everyone. They joked about his cooking, Vera Cruz, and the Jarocha girl Mike used to have come to visit him, but did not any longer. He was wistful when he spoke of her.

AFTER DINNER, BACK in Room Two, Vicky explained that Paniagua liked her, and that dealing with him would be no problem. "He said he would not charge us tonight because I came so far," she illustrated.

"You know, my love, it does not sound very good. I don't think I am going to come back to Playa or my Palace. I really miss my Palace and all the kids...."

"I know, and they missed you too. Some of them were crying when they found out."

"Maybe you should move here. Rent a moving truck and bring everything, including Marcos and Rosey, and come here and make a roller rink right here close to the prison.

We have everything. You could live right here and visit all the time."

"I have a cousin here that I could stay with," she answered thoughtfully. "I'm going to call her tomorrow. We could come here. You know Marcos is babysitting my children right now. We could move here if you want us to. Do you want us?" She could be so sweet.

"Yes, of course I do. And I want to marry you. Although I thought we were already married," Gar said.

"Well, as you know, here in Mexico," she paused and smiled and emphasized the words, as she knew Gar thought them funny. "...when a man and a woman move in together, and say they are husband and wife, that means they are married. But maybe for you, and your case, we will need to get them proof; get an Act of Matrimony Certificate."

"Let's pretend that we just got one and tonight is our wedding night." Gar pulled her close. They were already cuddled together in the tiny bunk, and the lights were out and the door was locked.

"Crazy Gringos," she murmured.

Mike's stereo played next door. Jim Morrison and The Doors singing, "Come on baby light my fire; Try to set the night on fire...."

Gar smiled. *Mexican prison, under the right circumstances, could be charming*, he thought.

CHAPTER 67

JANUARY, 1997.

"TODAY'S MY FAVORITE girl's birthday." Gar was sitting at the hallway card-dining table talking to Mike over morning coffee. Popo was shooting steam about three miles up into the crisp and very blue, morning air. Though the volcano was thirty miles away, a smell of sulfur was wafting their way.

"Susan is her name," he continued. And I've never been able to shake her. Well, her memory, that is. We broke up almost twenty years ago. She's happily married now, and has almost forgotten me. I've called her every six months or so since I've been here in Mexico. I keep seeing her everywhere. She's like, this small blonde, but she's Spanish, and I keep seeing her same Spanish features, the eyes maybe, or the Spanish jaw line, in different Mexican girls. Especially the Mexico City girls that come in here to visit, like Vicente's sister."

"The good looking one?" Mike asked.

"Yeah, the older of the two. The real light one. Susan looks a whole lot like her. You know, the largest Spanish influence in the country is right here in Mexico City. Back in the 1500s, the Spaniards came and landed at Vera Cruz, and...."

Mike was nodding. He got easily bored when Gar started in with the history. "Yeah. So. Why in the hell did she leave you?" Mike was always brutally to the point.

"I don't know."

"She knows you're here?"

"No."

"Got her number?"

"No."

"And Vicky won't call to get it for you?" He smiled five miles of picket fence on that one. And the pickets needed painting.

"No. Some things you can't ask. Vicky can be a little jealous."

"She can sure let everyone know when you're doing a good job, too." This time he laughed.

"You can hear her?" Gar asked.

"Does a sea lion have a watertight asshole?" Mike looked smug.

"Probably not after you're through with it," Gar said.

"Vicky coming today?" Mike demurred.

"Supposed to."

GAR AND THE Captain of the prison, Mr. Paniagua, sat on soft-leather chairs in the Captain's office, contentedly puffing on Cuban cigars. Three months after arriving at the prison, Gar and the Captain were friends, of sorts, though Gar knew the friendship would last only as long as his money lasted. The men puffed their cigars, and brooding Mt. Popo puffed sulphurous smoke and steam into the atmosphere in the distance. Both men had their feet up on the captain's desk.

"So how much would it cost me to quietly get out of this place?" Gar asked the Captain.

"I keep telling you, Señor, eees impossible." The Captain's English was not the best, but he had a glint in his eye and he clearly enjoyed these cigar sessions with Gar. This was not their first one. "There is...*que es la pinche lingua*," he muttered then said, "not enough money in the world for this thing."

"Every man has his price," Gar noted quietly, puffing and looking off at the volcano. Popo chose this moment to eject a great burst of dark exhaust, doubtless accompanied by flying cinders, and Gar could actually feel the earth's tremor through his feet on the desk. The towering column of smoke grew to the size of an anvil-shaped thunderhead, and a low rumble could be faintly heard through the distance.

The Captain quickly dropped his feet to the floor and stood up, looking concernedly at the volcano. Gar scrambled to his feet as well, and both men noted the sudden silence in the prison around them. Usually a raucous clanging Bedlam of sound, the entire prison had fallen silent, and hundreds of men gazed, motionless and silent, at the distant volcano. The low rumbling grew perceptibly louder. Great blasts of steam, smoke and ash were being hurtled from the mouth of the volcano. It was a spectacle of immense proportions.

"No, senor," said the Captain, his eyes still on distant Mt. Popo. "It has been tried. I can take your money and promise your freedom, but you will be killed. I cannot control my men. The story will be that you were killed while trying to escape, and the money will never be mentioned.

"Even if you were personally in charge of the operation?" Gar, too continued to stare at the volcano.

"Especially if I order it." The Captain's English suddenly improved dramatically. "There are men who want my job. I would not be allowed to live either; at best I would be arrested and thrown in my own jail. The thing is impossible." Paniagua turned his head to Gar and looked at him with an unusually serious expression on his face. "Do you understand?"

"Yes," Gar said, looking at him. "I guess I do. But it is hard. One always hopes."

"I know." The Captain turned away, looking again at Mt. Popo. "But we are alive, you and I, and able to enjoy some conversation and a good cigar." The volcano blasted and thundered on the horizon, and his final words were almost lost in the sound of the explosions. "And life is short enough, my friend. Life is short enough."

"YOUR MOTHER CALLED me. She said she sent the money to Caesar for your Amparo." They were in the room. Vicky was now living in Mexico City. She'd moved all their possessions to her cousin, Elizabet's house; it was all stuffed into one bedroom.

"Oh, good. I talked to him on the phone the other day. The money hadn't gotten there yet. Caesar told me, though, that he had started work anyway and discovered a few things. The reason the court ruled I must be extradited is all my identification was false."

"But you knew it was, my love."

"Yes, but Tao and his associates told me that the way they do the birth certificate is they pay someone who works in the clerk's office to pull out an old certificate–they are numbered–and put that number on my new one and put it in the right order in the files. That way when they go to check the original file number, my copy matches the original. And then, of course, all the other ID is based on that name. But Caesar told me when they checked the clerk's office in Durango, there was no such number, no such name, nothing. When I bought the ID from Tao, I paid five-thousand dollars for a piece of paper that any kid could make on a computer. It was nothing. It had green ink, and that was all."

"I have not trusted those people since the first day I met them," Vicky said loyally.

"What makes me really angry is that when I moved to Playa, I called them and told them, please, please tell me–is this ID one hundred percent good? I am going to establish a business based on this ID. I have to go through PGR checkpoints every time I go to Cancun. I have to know, for sure, that I can trust this identification one hundred percent. And they told me, don't worry, it is guaranteed one hundred percent rock solid. And now I find out they were really full of shit. And I helped them a lot, too. I helped them with many things, financially. And I tried hard to be a good friend to them. It makes me very upset." Gar shook his head in disgust, clenching his fists.

"You know they came to my house after you were arrested, Federico and his father Tao, and they wanted your American passport."

"Probably so they could sell it. Did you remember that Tao came by the duplex in Tohucu, just a week or two before I was arrested?"

"Jes."

"I think.... I didn't tell you this." Gar paused a moment, thinking. "Tao has a Commandant associate in the PGR. I met him, partied with him, and I know him real well. Jamie Nunoz is his name, and he is in charge of Mexico City, Guerrero and Quintana Roo. I think those guys set me up. Tao was there to 'work' he said. I think they had a load coming from Columbia, and when they offered the police somewhere along the way money to let them pass their coca, the police said he needs more. So Tao offered his big-fish Gringo friend, telling the police he would also get a good bust out of it. It would make good propaganda for the American DEA, while they slipped a couple of tons of cocaine under their noses."

"I think you're right," Vicky said.

"He might have even used me as a diversion. You know, maybe the Mexican police he was working with waited until the day the boat with the coca was coming, and that was the day they told the DEA about me, and where I was, so they would come down to Playa to watch me for a few days, while Tao brought in his load." Gar was really steaming now.

"You know you are right. Maybe not exactly, but you have the right idea. He sold you, that we know for sure. These men are not nice men. Tao told me that since I speak such good English, I must make sure you understand that you are not to talk to the American police if you go back." She rubbed Gar's temples. They were snuggling on the bunk. It was their couch as well as bed.

"Yeah, they sent Miguel Angel. You remember the young lawyer of theirs? He was a messenger one day for Jay...Jay was my boss, and he was waiting close by in a hotel while Miguel Angel delivered the message. He said Jay told him to remind me that they know all of my family, including you and your daughters, and that I better keep my mouth shut. 'No deals,' he said. 'Or else.'"

"You cannot go back, my lover. If you go back and make a deal, you'll be dead in two days. If you don't make a deal, you will stay too long in prison."

"I know. I will just stay here for as long as I can....with you."

"And your three beautiful daughters." She smiled sadly.

"Aren't they my step-daughters?"

"*Here in Mexico*, we don't have such a word. If you say they are your daughters, then they are your daughters. They call you Papa, and that's all that matters."

"They are my daughters, then. And I love them very much." Gar was absolutely serious. He didn't know if he had ever before felt so sad. The prospect of losing these people who loved him was almost more than he could bear.

The mountain continued to rumble in the distance.

CHAPTER 68

EARLY 1997.

VICKY HAD A *fire sale* of Gar's stuff going on so she and the girls could continue to live in Mexico city. And when the stuff was gone, she got a job. It was a difficult period, as her cousin lived on the other side of the city. It took two hours by train for Vicky to come visit Gar. Then two hours for her to return home. It was a strain on everyone. Her job did not pay much, despite the superior clerical skills she possessed, because she did not know anyone in Mexico City. And Mexico is founded upon nepotism and patronage.

ON A BRIGHTER note, Gar's name was called out one day by the guards. The guard calling for him was at the gate at the top of the cell range. The inmates kept their own lock on the range gate, and the guard didn't have a key. Gar went to the gate.

"You're wanted at court," the guard said. "Courtroom number twelve. You have to go right now."

"Hot damn!" Gar shouted. "They ruled on my Amparo. Maybe I'm going home! Let me grab my shoes and shirt."

THE SET UP in Mexico City Reclusorios (there are three of them) is amazingly efficient. The courtrooms are just beyond the prison walls. There are tunnels from the prison, underneath the walls, that go up into the courtrooms. Hearings are held with the prisoners standing on the prison side of a bulletproof window with a mouth-level speaking hole in its middle. There is a chute underneath to pass papers. A prisoner does not need a guard to escort him through the tunnels to court.

Gar was let into the tunnel system by the same guard who had come to get him. He went down the stairs, then found the right tunnel for Courtroom Twelve. Walking along, he noticed mattresses lying in different areas along the tunnel. Until recently, there had been a women's prison right alongside the men's prison, and the two prisons shared the same tunnel system. Of course, here in the land of perpetual enterprise, men and women prisoners could tip the guards to go into the tunnels in order to visit with one another in the evenings. Though it was likely that the men did most of the tipping. The women were bait. Some nights there were hundreds of couples, or so it was said, camped on the handy mattresses.

Gar kept a sharp eye out, as the lighting in the tunnels was not that good. There were also stories of robberies in the warren of passageways. It was a bit spooky walking along unsupervised. At least, though, they had evidently run out of the pukish lime-green paint used in the rest of the prison. By the time they painted the tunnels, they were using a nice fuchsia with coffee trim. Very Mexican.

At the other end he went up the stairs, down a hall, and found the Courtroom Twelve window. Papers and trash littered the floor on Gar's side of the window. His lawyer, Caesar Contreras, was there on the business side of the window. Caesar spoke perfect English.

"We won," he said without preamble. The bailiff passed papers through the chute while Caesar continued: "Your charges in the United States accuse you of importing hashish–but they never recovered any of this drug. They never did a laboratory examination to prove it was hashish, or any other contraband. In Mexico, this is not acceptable. The United States calls your charges Conspiracy. We have no such laws here in Mexico. Those laws are not about what you did. Conspiracy is concerned with what you thought about doing. We have no thought crimes here. We base our laws on facts only. That is why the court has denied your extradition. Under the treaty, the crime you are extradited for must be a crime in Mexico. In this case, it is not."

"Wow!" I'm flabbergasted." Gar wanted to repeat Mike's words and shout, "You're a good fuckin' sum-bitch of a lawyer!" Instead, he said, "Thank you Caesar. Thank you for myself, and for my family. My mother will be very happy, and so will my wife, Victoria. When can I hope to get out of here?"

"Well, we are not through yet. This is only round one. Now the prosecutor will appeal. His appeal will take three to five months. But then we will win." Caesar was a man of few words. He didn't laugh or joke. He didn't waste time on talk.

"And then I can go out of here?"

"No. They will take you to Immigration from here. I don't believe you had a valid Visa when you came in, but even if you did, it is no longer valid. Thus, they will take you there and try to deport you. We will fight that, and win, but it will take $10,000 in American currency: five for me, and five for Immigration. I will have to bribe them. This Amparo I won based upon the law. Over at Immigration it is different." He was a full-service lawyer, anyway.

"Okay. I will have to see what I can do." Gar was happy about the win; he could see some light at the end of the proverbial tunnel. But the $10,000 was a deflating thought. He didn't have any more money. Jay still owed Gar oceans of money, but getting a hold of him was beginning to seem like a hopeless task.

He was broke. He had been moved to COC, the armpit of the prison, because he could no longer pay rent. He was surviving because Vicky was bringing Gar's collection of CDs to Jamie Rodriguez, the Director of COC, to pay the rent. This month it had cost him the Eric Clapton boxed set.

"Call me. I have to go. I have another client waiting," Caesar said. Then he turned, in his perfectly-tailored white suit, and he left.

Gar called out, "Thanks again," through the speaking hole, but his words may have been lost.

He stood looking through the window for a while longer. No one seemed to mind. No one noticed, nor did they care. He could see a judge way back in an office, maybe a hundred and fifty feet away. That is how the judges preside. The never talk to the parties. They simply look at papers, handed them by bailiffs, make notations, or sign, then go back to shuffling through the files. Through the half-glass wall in the judge's offices, the judges can see the litigants and lawyers. But just barely.

It was a weird system. But it was the only one Gar had...for this moment. Walking back to his housing unit, Gar glanced up at the brooding, smoking volcano, which dominated the southeastern landscape. It looked malignant today, powerful and somehow angry, and Gar was suddenly and inexplicably frightened. It was like living as a cringing creature at the feet of a gigantic beast, he decided, where he could be crushed and destroyed without warning. Plumes of dark gray smoke were being torn from the lofty crater by the winds aloft and smeared ominously across the sky. He could smell the sharp bite of sulfur in the air.

"WELL, WHAT HAPPENED?" Mike asked as Gar returned from court. Mike had been moved to COC, too. Both of the fishermen had depleted almost all of their resources. Thanks to Vicky's powers of persuasion, and Gar's CD collection, Gar lived in the only good range of cells in COC. He lived alone, the range was gated and they had their lock on it, and visitors could come to the room. Mike was completely broke, but he was living with Vicente. Vicente paid the rent, and Mike did the cleaning and cooking. Vicente also derived a fair amount of entertainment from Mike's antics.

"Well, the good news is that I won my Amparo." Gar gave him a big grin. He felt like dancing. Thoughts of the volcano were lost in Mike's optimistic presence.

"No fuckin' shit! I told you. I told you that Caesar is one good sum bitch of a lawyer!"

"You did, Mike. I know you did. And I owe you for getting me setup with him."

"But. I know there's a but in there somewhere," Mike said. "You gotta wait, don't you?" Mike knew the process. He'd been through the whole thing once before, and was months ahead of Gar on this go-around.

Gar thought a minute. He looked out the window of the COC building. He was two floors higher than he'd been in Ingresso, and he had a reverse view looking back at his old cell. It was fairly smoggy today. The sun was an obscure brown ball in the midday sky. "Yes," he finally said. "I have to wait while the prosecutor appeals."

"Another three to five months, right?" Mike said.

"But Caesar says I'll win...."

"And he needs ten thousand to get you through Immigration. Am I right?" Mike chuckled knowingly. The mossy picket fence appeared, all seventeen miles of it. "Hey, if you get him the money, he'll get you through that with a good Visa. The DEA will be all over you, and the Immigration people, trying to get you deported. But you'll get a good Visa, and it will be good for sixty days. They can't bring extradition proceedings against you for that sixty days. But you better be gone somewhere before that time is up."

"Okay. The other problem, though, as you might have noticed, is that I'm broke. I don't know where I'll get that kind of money. Mom went way out on a limb to pay Caesar for the Amparo. No one else answers the phone. I'm sort of bottomed out at low tide here, Mike."

They sat in silence for a few minutes. COC was a much bigger building than Ingresso. Four stories, with an extra two ranges per floor, it was the prison's tallest building. It looked out over the walls at the parking lot and Mexico City beyond.

Ingresso had 96 single-man cells. COC had 216 much larger cells, only twelve of which were rented for sole occupancy. The other 204 cells had two to five men per cell. A few of those were "The Hole". All tallied, there were normally more than five hundred men living in COC. Mike and Gar sat in companionable silence at the card-dining table listening to the cacophony their five-hundred neighbors were making: singing, whistling, cursing, laughing, fighting; TVs, and boom boxes turned up way too loud.

"Watch." Mike broke the silence in their cell. "Tomorrow, or maybe the next day, someone from the Mexican State Department, the Secretaria de Relaciones Exteriores, will come here and read Mexico's official extradition agreement in your case. They'll tell you that they will only extradite you on about half of the charges. When they do that, the United States cannot prosecute you on those charges. It makes a guy want to go back, instead of fighting extradition. And you know what? Now that you've won, if you get released to Immigration and get deported rather than extradited, you will not get the advantage of that agreement. The United States will be able to prosecute you on all of the charges."

"Really. Then they will have, in a sense, started the plea bargaining process even before I get back. Do you believe the offer to knock charges off to get you to agree to go back is influenced by the United States prosecutors?"

"I know fuckin' well it is. You saw President Clinton come down here to personally certify Mexico as a partner in the drug war?"

"Yeah."

"Well, that was the first time an American president has ever visited Mexico. Ever. You can believe they're sucking each other off, I'll tell you that.

"You think they are actually sucking, Mike? Or are they back scratching while they bugger each other?" Gar laughed.

"You know what the fuck I'm talking about." Mike's pickets blazed with fury, but then he began to laugh too.

It was hopeless. But men laugh in the face of hopelessness all the time. Sometimes it is the only thing they can do.

CHAPTER 69

LATE 1997.

CRACK COCAINE WAS very much a part of the prisoner's lives in Mexico. Gar did not participate. Mike, Vicente, and a number of the others that he knew used the stuff though. Very few survive it intact. Gar watched many guys go from being well situated, to living like a street person in a very short period of time. Crack was the reason Mike's girlfriend quit coming. It was also why his fellow Vera Cruz fishermen quit helping him financially. It was rather sad.

Even though mostly broke, Gar still had a decent television set and his room was fixed up comfortably. The TV reception in COC was the best in the prison because the building is two stories above the rest, and it faces the city. Gar was able to cook in his kitchenette, work at his desk, or kick back on an extra-wide mattress and watch the tube. Life was as comfortable as it could get.

The kitchenette consisted of a full sheet of plywood wall-mounted three feet above a fixed cement bunk. The bunk served as a substantial shelf for cooking supplies. It also worked well as a bunk for the three little girls on the nights they stayed over. Those nights were almost nonexistent these days.

The nights they did come, they would cook, play Chutes and Ladders, watch television, and laugh like a normal family. It was a good time, and a fine example of how human beings can adapt to almost any situation.

The American Embassy visited every few months. They dropped off paperback books and multiple vitamins. And they asked about prison conditions. When Americans complained, they went to the prison director. This was a fair amount of leverage, but not Thor's almighty hammer by any means. The Mexican guards were not anxious to get their names mentioned to the Embassy. However, they had been running the prison the same way for decades, and they were not about to change too much. Corruption and graft, in a Mexican prison, is certainly every bit as dominant as it is on the Mexican streets.

After having read one of the books brought by the Embassy, Gar decided his situation was not that bad. The book was written by a Jewish man who had survived Auschwitz during the holocaust. This man spoke of prison conditions so horrible, it was impossible for Gar to imagine them. After reading this book, he did not complain about Mexico's not-so-pristine prison: the poor and intermittent supply of water; lighting and plumbing haphazardly installed in cells; the lack of basic hygiene provisions.

The Embassy had arranged for a box of food to be delivered to the cell each day. Fresh vegetables, some coffee and sugar, a small amount of meat, a kilo of tortillas and, of course, plenty of rice and beans. There was no shortage of food to eat.

The *Dieta* box offered an abundance of food. Enough variety, as well, to give Gar various cooking options. So he spent several hours each day cooking. Meche, now twelve, had a running joke with Gar. She would come and check what leftovers were around and say, "*Uh, oh*! Here's another one of Papa's *experiments*." They both found this immensely funny.

ONE DAY MECHE went downstairs alone to the small commissary on the ground floor. Gar, Vicky, and the other two girls worked at preparing the afternoon meal.

All at once, a friend ran up to the cell door and said, "You had better go. You better hurry. Something's happening with your daughter. On the second floor landing."

Gar dropped everything and ran out the door, Vicky close on his heels. At the landing, Meche was standing with Jamie Rodriguez, the COC Director. One of the guards was leading a twenty-year-old Mexican boy away.

"Mr. Gar, you cannot let your daughter walk through this building unescorted. That boy was trying to molest her." Jamie said.

Gar was shocked. "She's only twelve!" he plainted.

"I kicked him in the balls!" Meche blurted proudly.

"Meche!" Vicky shrieked.

Jamie cut everyone off. "Yes, but that boy is in prison and age does not matter to him. You know that almost everyone respects visitors here. But there are some who do not. There are some bad people here, Mr. Gar. Watch your daughter very carefully from now on." The Director admonished.

"Yes, sir. I will." Then to Meche. "Come here!" He put his arms around her. "Are you okay?"

She smiled up at Gar and looked smug. She was enjoying the attention. "I'm fine. I had it handled. I kicked that fucker in the balls."

"Meche, watch your language!" Vicky scolded.

"Atta girl," Gar praised her. "But from now on, you must be more careful. Mr. Rodriguez is right. There are some bad men here." Now Gar used the fatherly tone. It worked well with Meche.

AND BAD MEN there were. The sale of crack, weed, alcohol, and Ruhypnol sleeping pills did not help matters. Crack was the worst. Some are totally addicted on the very first puff. And that is a fact, not an old wives tale. It is the truth.

One of the guards, "Big Foot" (*Pie Grande*), once told Gar that there are more than fifty murders at Reclusorio Sur every year–approximately one per week.

Gar witnessed numerous bodies being wheeled out to the front gate on food carts. The same serving carts with which they moved the large pots of food to the dormitories would go by the opposite way, draped with a corpse. He hoped they went to the front gate, or so the macabre standing joke amongst the inmates went, rather than to the kitchen for tomorrow's stew.

ONE DAY GAR headed toward dorm nine–there are ten dorms besides COC and Ingresso. Just outside the range gate, there was a fair amount of blood globed about on the floor. As Gar walked down the stairs, and out the front of the COC, the blood trail grew larger and wider. There were whole footprints of blood now. The man had been stabbed–as most are–in that artery at the top front of where the leg joins the body, in the groin area. Dorm nine is the same direction as the prison hospital, and halfway there the victim lay in an eight-foot circle of blood. The man was dead. It was Gar's next-door neighbor; he was a happy-go-lucky kid and a good friend.

It was obscene. The ghastly specter of this man dead, in a pool of what constituted his entire blood reserve, would haunt Gar for a long time.

The bodies on carts, the fist and knife fights every day, the thievery, the rat packing in cells, Gar had managed to avoid all of this through his size, bearing, and a fair amount of luck. But this grisly murder–which was over an unpaid crack bill he was later to find out–hit too close to home.

It depressed him, and he couldn't stop thinking about it. And Gar desperately missed Marcos and Rosey. His relationship aside, they had become good friends. And now they were gone, not to be heard from again. All of these unhappy things added up. It wasn't good.

VICKY CAME TO visit one day in a smart-looking work suit. It was a workday and an unplanned visit.

Something was up.

She was overly attentive, and said she'd paid the Captain, on her way in, to stay the night.

They made clinging love for what seemed like most of the day.

That night she said, "I'm bringing the girls on Saturday." It was a Wednesday.

"Oh, really?"

"Jes. They need to see you."

"Good. I always want to see them. They make me happy."

"You know they love you very much, my love. You are their father."

"I know that. I wish I could be there more for them."

"They are going to Vera Cruz, to my family home with my sister, Lupita, in two weeks," she said.

"Okay. How long will they stay with Lupita?" Gar asked.

"Well, I am going there too. Maybe in one month. We have to go there to live. We cannot stay here any longer. Please understand it is too expensive, and in Minatitlan I have a house. It is my house. We can live there, in our own home, with my sister Lupita next door, for nothing." She was crying now.

"Yes, I know. I remember you've talked about your home before. I thought this might happen one day. I just hoped it would be later, not sooner," Gar said, his lips turned down in sadness.

"So, they were going to go last week, but they said they could not go without saying goodbye to their Papa."

"That's very sweet. We'll have a small party. I'll make some *experiments* for Meche, and we'll play Chutes and Ladders."

"Jes. We will have fun. I will bring you your favorites: roasted chicken and bar-ba-coa (Mexican lamb)." Vicky was perking up because Gar was taking the bad news stoically and calm.

"Okay, my love. Life will go on. I will keep fighting my case. Maybe I will win and come to Vera Cruz to stay with you." Gar said.

"We will wait there for you." She cupped his chin in one chocolate hand; her black globes stared intently into Gar's baby blues.

THEY HAD THEIR going-back-to-Vera-Cruz party, and the three girls hugged Gar very nearly to death before they went away. It left him lonely and sad.

Vicky visited another couple of times before she left. Then she came over twice more, a three-day journey across country on a bus, after she had moved. It was nonetheless very lonely now.

Nine months passed since winning the Amparo. Gar spent much of this time gazing at Popo, a small, still figure contemplating the brooding rocky mass of the smoking volcano. The thing was frightening in its enormity, and Gar finally concluded that it could not be understood.

Caesar had assured Gar, after winning his Amparo, it would not take more than five months for the prosecutor's appeal, but still he waited. Mike had cancelled his Amparo and formally agreed to be extradited. He, too, had won his Amparo, but then there was the long wait during the prosecutor's appeal. Eventually Mike had run out of patience. They had had long talks, agreeing that the United States was likely influencing the process.

Gar went, one day, one particularly bad day, to the judicial services office in the prison. Many lonely months had passed without a visitor. He felt a stillness in his soul, an emptiness, that had to do with lonesomeness and memories. Gar had reached a decision. He told them he wanted to withdraw his Amparo, and he agreed to be extradited. They looked up his case number, typed the letter in formal Spanish, and after Gar signed it they took it to the court clerk and filed it.

That was at the end of 1997.

ON FEBRUARY THIRD, 1998, the Interpol Police came, unannounced one morning, and took Gar out of Reclusorio Sur. He had been there seventeen-and-a-half months. Long enough to become institutionalized, as well as emotionally reproached. The ride to the airport, to meet the U.S. Marshals, was utterly surreal. He was so shocked he did not think of bolting. He thought only of getting on the plane and in a few hours being back in the United States. He had long imagined that he would never see his country again;

never eat American food; never laugh at American humor; never see a pink nipple again.

The last thing he saw of Mexico City, the jet climbing to altitude and leaving this phase of his life behind, was the smoking, wind-torn peak of Mt. Popocatepetl. The airliner carefully avoided the volcano, so Gar was unable to gaze into its crater, yet shimmering waves of heat were eerily visible beneath the clouds of emerging black smoke.

Part Five

THE DEFENDANT

CHAPTER 70

1998.

THE MARSHALS TOOK possession of Gar at the Benito Juarez International Airport. No ceremony. No TV, newspapers, or inquisitive reporters. The Marshals put their handcuffs on Gar, and the Mexican Interpol took their handcuffs off. Some reciprocal signing of papers went on, and they were on their way to the gate. An American Airlines 747 waited. They were the first to board. The Marshals led Gar to the back of the plane. There they sat in the only three-seat row without a window. They didn't want Gar to gnaw a hole through the window and leap out to freedom at 25,000 feet.

The Ann and Andy Marshall team introduced themselves as Linda and Ed. They were nice enough. They cuffed Gar, hands in front, and checked often to see if the cuffs had become too tight. Linda put her jacket over the cuffs as they were walking through the airport. This wasn't so bad. With the cuffs in front, Gar was able to enjoy an in-flight shrimp scampi dinner.

There was a layover in Houston for an hour or two, then a flight up to SeaTac, arriving at midnight local time. SeaTac is an appropriate abbreviation indicating that the airport lies midway between and serves both the City of Seattle and the City of Tacoma, Washington. At Houston, Gar sat in a chair at the departure gate. Linda and Ed stood close by, chatting with a Houston Marshal. An attractive twenty-something girl came and sat next to Gar, though every other seat at the gate was empty. She was likely thinking to solicit something. She looked at Gar, smiled, then glanced down at his hands cuffed in front of him. Upon seeing the handcuffs, she leaped to her feet, and as if shot from a gun she bolted away.

LINDA AND ED took Gar to a small county jail in the State of Washington that night. The next morning at five, the county guard woke him to catch the van to Seattle for arraignment: the "Court Chain."

Gar had phoned his American attorney from Mexico, Penny Coopman, and told her he would be coming back. She had said that the Feds always work fast, and they'd likely have him arraigned before she could make the trip from the Bay Area to Seattle.

She had that right.

She also instructed him to postpone everything in court, including a plea, until she could make the trip up there to be with him.

AT THE COURT, a court-appointed attorney named Joe Quiver introduced himself and said he would provide Gar with representation for today. Joe came off as a very personable individual and Gar liked him. However, Joe said he could not represent Gar for more than this single appearance, as there was a conflict. There is a rule in legal circles that the same lawyer, or even two lawyers from the same office, cannot represent co-defendants that may have potentially differing interests. To do so is called a conflict of interests. Gar would find out that after more than twenty codefendants had preceded him in the Seattle area, many local attorneys were conflicted. Nonetheless, he explained to Joe that he already had a lawyer, and that Penny had instructed him not to do anything until she could make the trip. Joe so moved the court, and the court granted a one-week postponement until February 11th.

AFTER COURT, GAR got booked into SeaTac Federal Detention Center. This consisted of seven hours of sitting in a holding cell with a half dozen other new "fish." He spent that seven hours watching the slow, ticking passage of time on a clock high on the wall. The Feds were big on clocks. They were everywhere. Gar thought it might be portentous, this federal obsession with clocks, and it might not bode well for his future to be faced with a plethora of ticking clocks the minute he got into federal custody. The detention center administrative staff filled out the required papers, which took all of fifteen minutes. The rest of the time Gar spent getting used to English conversation again, and staring at those damnable clocks.

He couldn't help but notice that everything was beige. The walls were light beige, and the clothing worn by the prisoners was a darker shade of the same beige. It was a beige world. And the place smelled of Simple Green disinfectant, which smells like the *Ipana* brand of toothpaste so ubiquitous in Mexico.

UPSTAIRS ON THE fourth floor he was ushered into Unit 4-A, Gar's new home. It was a triangle-shaped high-ceilinged room, a large open area in the center and surrounded by sixty inmate rooms. Each of these rooms measured exactly eight by twelve feet, and contained a bunk bed, two lockers, sink and toilet. Community showers were scattered handily around the perimeter of the unit. The large open area contained tables for eating as well as playing games. The unit is two tiered. There are four television rooms, two on each tier. Gar went for the first week to the one designated as the Spanish TV room. He was going to need deprogramming.

The maiden night, he was assigned to a cell with a black Muslim. "Cowboy" was a nice enough guy. He explained to Gar that *here in the United States*, different races don't usually cell together.

"Okay. So what do I do?" Gar asked.

"I'll talk to the counselor in the morning. I'm the head orderly. I'll get you moved," Cowboy said.

THE NEXT MORNING, Gar was up early. The first thing on his mind was to take a long hot shower. This was a luxury he had not been able to experience for a long time. At Reclusorio Sur it had mainly been sponge baths from a five-gallon bucket, or cold showers. He had freshly laundered clothes now too. And there were help-yourself bins of soap, shampoo, deodorant, shaving cream, and razors available for the asking from the Correctional Officer (CO). This was wild. He'd gone from a no-star to a five-star hotel almost overnight.

And then they started passing out the breakfast trays. Bacon, eggs, pancakes with syrup, plenty of milk, and a big box of fresh Washington-State apples.

"Madre de Dios!" He exclaimed aloud. "I'm at the Ritz!"

IN THE MIDDLE of the triangle of cells there are twenty or so tables. Gar sat at one of the tables with a White guy and an Asian. He said to them, "Good food, huh?" with a full mouth.

"Umm, err."

"Mmmm."

"Hey, is there a law library here? The Marshals told me to just ask anyone." Gar swallowed his bite of pancakes and reached for a strip of bacon, then chomped a biscuit with the other. The flavor of the food was heavenly; he had butter and jelly lathered on everything.

"There's one downstairs, but we don't get to go there. They have a small one over in that room." The Asian guy pointed off to one corner.

"Is it open now?" Gar asked.

"It's open all day, as far as I've seen. We get out of our cells at five thirty in the morning, and it's open then. And when they lock us down at ten tonight, it will still be open." White guy said.

"Okay. Thank you." Now Gar had a mission. He'd long planned, while laying around his cell in Mexico, to become a so-called jailhouse lawyer should he ever make it back to the United States. Now was the time to start.

"How do I make a phone call to my lawyer?" Gar asked the guys.

"Those two phones over there," the Asian pointed, "ring straight through to the Public Defender's Office. Otherwise, if you need to call a private lawyer, you have to get the counselor to do it. Put in a *cop-out*, that's what they call a request form. They're right there in that rack." The man pointed again, at another wall this time.

"Okay, and what do I do with the cop-out?" Gar asked.

"Come on. I'll help you. Let's take our trays up to the kitchen cart first." The helpful middle-aged white guy stood up, and Gar could see he was quite tall. "I'm John, by the way," he said, offering his hand to shake.

"I'm Señor Gar. Or I guess I should just say Gar." He took the proffered hand and shook it solemnly.

GAR SLID A cop-out under the counselor's office door, and with a new pad of paper and pencil obtained from the guard in hand, he headed for the small law library in the far corner. He was full of breakfast and determined to do what was required to get a grasp on the law.

Inside, the room was remarkably small. It was not more than ten by twenty feet square. There was one small worktable fitted into one corner and four chairs, two of them now occupied. And there were several racks of law books ranged about the walls.

Gar started browsing the bookshelves, with no clue as to what he was looking at. One of the men, an older man who looked exactly like Gar's father, spoke to him in a kindly manner.

"We spend a lot of time in here," he said after introductions were made. "We know our way around. Is there something I can help you find?"

"Well...." Gar spoke slowly, with really no idea of what to say. "I just got extradited from Mexico. It's a fairly serious drug case. They say I smuggled twenty-five tons of hashish. And I have no choice but to fight the charge." He was speaking very tentatively. Not knowing these guys, he did not want to say that the threat of the Mexican Mafia was following him like a dark cloud of death.

"You know, those drug cases are easy to beat." The older man spoke knowledgeably. "Hell, they don't have jurisdiction anymore to prosecute them. Not since them guys down in California started whipping them on federal jurisdiction."

"What?" Gar was astonished by what he had just heard. He was coming back to face a nightmare. He could not make a deal, and if convicted he would probably get a long sentence. What was this guy saying? These charges were easy to beat?

"I'm Veryle, and this is Tim. If you'll notice his size, you'll see why we call him Big Tim." They all shook hands.

"I'm pleased to make your acquaintances. What do you mean by what you just said? I have no experience with this legal stuff at all. I worked on my extradition case in Mexico a little bit, and got divorced once. But that's it."

"Okay. Let me show you," Veryle said. "Sit down here with me, and I'll try to explain it real simply. Here is the United States constitution. At Article One, Section Eight, Clause Seventeen, it says that, and this is referring to the power of congress: *To exercise exclusive legislation in all cases whatsoever, over such district....*" He stopped for a second, pointing.

"All right," Gar said.

"And now," Veryle continued. "Here at these parentheses, what it says inside, <u>not exceeding ten miles square</u>. They're talking about Washington, D.C. They do not have constitutional jurisdiction outside of that ten-mile square. Only on federal enclaves, and a few islands like Guam and Puerto Rico. They can't prosecute for a crime committed anywhere else. Where was your hashish operation supposed to be?" Veryle was on a roll, and sounded very knowledgeable and sure of himself.

"The say over here on the Washington coast."

"See there? They ain't got no business even having you here. That's a State crime." Gar couldn't get over how much Veryle looked like his father. Nor could he believe what he was hearing. He didn't know much about the law, but from what little he had learned in his years before going to Mexico, it seemed like things had sure changed.

"So what do I do?" Gar asked.

"When did you get back from Mexico?"

"I just got back yesterday. Or at midnight the night before, rather."

"Did you go to your arraignment hearing yet?" Veryle was still talking. Big Tim seemed supportive, but so far expressed his approval through nods and grumbles.

"Well, I went yesterday, but they postponed it until next week so my lawyer could get here. She's down in the Bay Area." Gar was still shocked about what he was hearing.

"Perfect" Veryle said. "If you can derail these guys early—you're the one that has to give them jurisdiction–you can stop this thing before it even starts." Veryle was almost triumphant.

"Ummm."

"You have to ask them questions," Big Tim finally spoke. "And not answer any of theirs. If you answer their questions, if you tell them who you are, you're dead."

"What do you mean, who I am?"

"Well, we've been going over arraignment transcripts," Tim explained. "And asking guys when they come back from court. And in every case, at the arraignment proceeding, the magistrate will use various tricks to get you to identify yourself. In my case, for example, I went into court, the magistrate sat down, and the first thing he said was: 'Okay, this is the case of the United States versus Timothy Clement. Have I got your name right, Mr. Clement?' And he didn't. My last name is Clagett. So I correct him and say, 'No, your honor, I'm Timothy Clagett.' And right there they had me. I gave him jurisdiction over me by doing that. And I did it because I didn't know, and they tricked me. But you!, you are going to go in there knowing."

"Really?" Gar was most intrigued. "And what will I say?"

"I think you might have the best chance of all of us." Veryle cut in. "There's more of us here that are fighting jurisdiction. But we have a guru, his name is Charlie Millwright. I think we better get you with Charlie."

"Sounds good. Hey, I need to write to my girl in Mexico. How can I get that done?" Gar needed to change the subject in order to digest what he had heard. This was all coming hard and fast.

Tim said, "Oh, I can help you there. I have a girl in the Philippines I write to. Here's an already-stamped Air Mail envelope. Just limit yourself to one page and you'll be fine. Mexico is closer, so the postage should be enough. When you're done, drop it in that mailbox next to the CO's little square cubicle."

"Oh, yeah. I know where you mean. Thank you . I'll get you back when I can." Gar shook Tim's hand. It was the size of a catcher's mitt.

"Ahh, don't sweat it. We're going to get you out, and then you can send me some money." Tim had a fox-eatin'-the-hen grin on his face when he said this.

FRANCIS DISKMAN, THE Assistant United States Attorney (AUSA) assigned to Gar's case, did not like the way arraignment had gone. Or not gone. Why was this Walton postponing the hearing? It was only an arraignment, for Christ's sake. Enter a not-guilty plea, set a trial date, and be done with it. Why would he need to talk to his California lawyer? Freakin' defense lawyers are bad enough, but these California lawyers are the worst. And Penny Coopman was a freakin' dyke from Berkeley. She had been held in contempt of court the last time she appeared in Seattle and sanctioned a fine for her courtroom antics. "I smell trouble," Diskman said to himself. "I'm going to call over to the FDC."

"YES, THIS IS Counselor Davis. How may I help you?"

"This is Jerry Diskman over at the U.S. Attorney's Office. Are you, or do you have a Gar Walton on your case load?"

"Yes, I do. I believe. Let me look at my list. Yes, he just came in. I haven't talked to him yet," Ms. Davis said. She was an average-looking Indian woman, maybe forty years old.

Diskman was a plump, fifty-year-old, all-white Republican; what the term WASP refers to when used in its most pejorative sense. Except Diskman wore a bad hairpiece. "Has Mr. Walton tried to contact his California attorney yet?" Mr. Diskman asked her.

"Well, as a matter of fact, I just got his cop-out, requesting a legal call to a Ms. Penny Coopman in Emeryville, California. Why do you ask?"

"Well, quite frankly Ms. Davis, I have to ask if there is any way you can stall that telephone call. Walton presents a real problem to this office. This is an ongoing case, part of a longstanding investigation conducted since 1992. Six years. We do not want to deny him counsel. He has a local, court-appointed attorney, Joe Quiver, a member in good standing of the local bar. But we need to get Walton arraigned. He's pulling typical prisoner tricks, stalling us, saying he needs to get his lawyer up here. And we don't even know for sure that Ms. Coopman is his lawyer. Ms. Davis, would you please hold off until next Wednesday on that lawyer call? It would sure help this office, and I would personally owe you one." Diskman's ooze was as smooth as honeydew vine water.

"You know, I'm actually leaving in a few hours, and will be gone until Tuesday. So, essentially, if I don't look at Walton's request today, I would only be putting it off one day if I wait until next Wednesday to process it." She was pleased with herself, and always willing to toady to her superiors.

"Okay, Ms. Davis. You have helped us very much. Thank you. Please call me if there is anything you need from this office. Good day to you." Diskman had been sure, at all turns of the conversation, to keep the full weight of the United States pressed on Counselor Davis. But not much weight was needed. She, too, worked for the same employer.

GAR SETTLED INTO the confines of his imprisonment as comfortably as he could, and tried to do constructive things. He got his letter written to Vicky. He met and talked with Charlie Millwright, the jurisdictional guru. He called mom. He met some more of the *constitutionalists*, as he'd heard other guys call Veryle and the others.

The week passed and he composed a list of questions to ask the magistrate at the arraignment. It seemed sort of silly at first, but Charlie said that if Gar asked these questions, and refused to answer any of theirs, it would "Pop him right out." Just like that. They would have to release him. He could go back to Crescent City, see Andriana, and pick up the pieces of his life. Go down to Santa Rosa and visit Jasmer and Alison.

This shouldn't be too hard. He should have agreed to extradition a long time ago. This shouldn't be too hard at all.

Gar desperately wanted to believe.

CHAPTER 71

EARLY 1999.

FEBRUARY ELEVENTH CAME, and Gar was on the court chain. This time he was taken to Tacoma. He had his list of questions. He had not been able to call Penny. He didn't know if she would be waiting at court, or not. Charlie and Veryle had said that there was no way she would be there. "She's part of the conspiracy, man," they had said.

Hmmm?

But sure enough, Penny was not there. A different court-appointed attorney was waiting for him, a man named Tom Pena. Pena met Gar just before court, in a small room with a wire screen between them. The lighting was poor. As they talked, Gar had a startling hallucination (not a normal occurrence, by any means) and thought he saw devil's horns poking through Tom Pena's bushy black hair. It freaked him out.

He told Tom he did not need him, and to please go away.

Tom said he had to be there. The court would not let Gar stand alone, unrepresented. But Tom agreed to stand silent.

IN THE COURTROOM, Jerry Diskman was smiling at Gar. Gar had no idea that the man had blocked his attorney call to Penny. Or even, really, who Diskman was. The way he was smiling, though, and the arrangement of the two sets of tables, made it obvious that this was the prosecutor.

Yet even that title held little significance for Gar. After six years in Mexico, the line between police and criminals, defense and prosecutorial lawyers, had become either blurred or non-existent.

Diskman was wearing a teal-colored suit of decent material over a crisp white shirt, with a hand-painted red, white and blue necktie. He said, "Mr. Walton, I just heard from your lawyer, Penny Coopman, this morning. She said she'd be up to see you very soon. She has some pressing engagements early this week, or she would be here today.

"Hmmm," Gar thought. But he said nothing.

"Thank you, Jerry," Tom Pena said.

Then: "All rise!" the bailiff cried out.

As Gar got to his feet he noticed the large and standard government clock high on the wall where everyone in the courtroom could see it, and noted that the clock read 9:02. They live by the clock, he idly thought, all of these people, just as I used to do. That was perhaps the most fundamental difference between the cultures of Mexico and the United States—an obsession with time in the nation to the north.

Magistrate Ronald sat down and announced the case. "This is case number C-R-9-4 dash 5-0-7-4-R-J-B. The United States of America versus Gar Charles Wallman...Am I saying your name right, sir?"

Ha! Until that moment, Gar had been skeptical about Veryle and Charlie's teachings over at SeaTac. But he could see that this man was really trying to trick him into saying his real name, Walton. Into giving the court jurisdiction over him.

"May I see your oath of office, please?" Gar responded. "The oath you took to uphold the constitution of the United States–may I see that please?" Gar did as he was told. Answer their questions with questions of your own. Don't give them jurisdiction (And they have to pop you right out, Charlie had said.).

"What?" Magistrate Ronald was incredulous.

"Under what clause of the constitution do you hold me here, your honor? May I please see your authority to hold me here? Is this not a court of admiralty? The name you are using for the adversary and accuser in these documents is depicted in all capital letters, my name is in upper and lower case letters. May I see the man you refer to in all capital letters? Will you produce that fictitious man before me in court today?" Gar kept asking questions because he was scared shitless. Magistrate Ronald's jaw had dropped so far, and eyes bugged so wide, it gave him a deer-in-the-headlights look.

"Mr. Walton," the Magistrate finally managed (pronouncing Gar's name perfectly, though he'd had no help from anyone). Gar could not help but notice this. "We are just here to read your charges and get your plea. I'm going to read the charges now..."

"Excuse me, your honor. I have a constitutional right to make my record. I'd like to make my record. Would you please tell me by what authority in the constitution you hold me here?"

"By the constitution itself I have authority."

"Article One, Section Eight, Clause Seventeen says you have jurisdiction only over ten miles square in Washington, D.C., as well as a few federal enclaves. Is this courthouse on federal property? May I please know by what constitutional authority you refer, specifically by Article, Section, and Clause, to hold me?"

Gar was persistent.

"I'm going to read the charges now, Mr. Walton (he said it right again), and then you can make your record. Mr. Pena, is there anything you wish to say on behalf of your client?"

"He doesn't represent me," Gar blurted out.

"Your honor, Mr. Walton has asked me to defer to himself at this hearing. He does not want my assistance," Pena said.

"If I may offer some help," Diskman, with fears of his own, now entered the fray, but he did so in an uncertain manner. He appeared to be nervous, almost frightened. "I suggest we postpone this arraignment, much as I would prefer otherwise, until Mr. Walton's regular counsel can get here. She called me and said she could be here next week. Maybe Mr. Walton will let her speak for him.

"I just want to know: By what constitutional authority–Article, Section, and Clause–does this court continue to hold me. May I leave now?"

Magistrate Ronald intervened, ignoring Gar. "Clerk, have you heard from Ms. Coopman?"

The Clerk: "Yes I have. She called and said she could be here later this week, or next week."

"Well, I'm going to finish this arraignment." Ronald was pissed now. "I'm going to read the charges."

THE MAGISTRATE READ the charges, then asked Gar to enter a plea. Gar asked another jurisdictional question involving the suspension of the writ of habeas corpus, and Ronald entered a plea of *Not Guilty* on Gar's behalf.

On the way back to SeaTac, Linda–the nice Marshal lady that brought Gar back from Mexico–was driving. She'd been friendly on the way to court. On the way back, she wouldn't speak to him at all.

Hmmm?

Back at SeaTac, Gar couldn't wait to get to the unit so he could discuss what happened with Veryle and Charlie and the rest of the guys. But he didn't go there. They took Gar straight to the eighth floor. The hole–solitary confinement.

There was no way the FDC staff did this on their own. It had to have been ordered by the court, the prosecutor, or both.

Why? If those questions Gar had asked were innocuous, why had they reacted this way?

FOR SEVEN DAYS, Gar sat in his solitary confinement cell writing cop-outs. He sent them to the warden, the captain, counselors, everyone he could think of. He accused them of depriving him of his ability to defend himself. He spoke of collusion in separating Gar from his study group: collusion with Prosecutor Diskman when the prison staff are supposed to be neutral.

And there was, quite naturally, a large government timepiece for Gar to watch the entire time he spent in this close and solitary confinement; this one was a red-charactered digital. He found himself watching it, enrapt, and his thoughts would fly far away from him. It was when this happened several times, and he jerked back to an awareness of his circumstances only to discover that several hours had elapsed without his knowing it, that he began to feel a strange mistrust for these clocks themselves. He knew this to be irrational. They were only clocks. But he began to fear them.

The seven days of sitting alone convinced Gar that the court had a real problem with the questions he had asked. They had answered none of them. They did everything he had been told that they would do. The tricking him into saying his name thing was as obvious as a child trying to wheedle cookies out of an adult. It was so simplistic; it was puerile.

AFTER A HUNDRED cop-outs and letters, they let Gar out of solitary confinement. He was sent back to Unit 4-A. No staff member could explain why he had been sent to the hole. They promised to check on it and get back to him, but none of them ever did.

Charlie had now taken over the main thrust of Gar's questions. Veryle had explained all he knew. Charlie next convinced Gar that he must go *pro se* (i.e., represent himself, instead of having a lawyer represent him).

When Gar asked why, Charlie told him so that he could present a jurisdictional defense. "That's the only way you can win," Charlie convinced him.

PENNY CAME UP to visit. She said she needed another $200,000 to represent Gar at trial. However, she did have an offer of seventeen years from Diskman. Gar declined, saying he could not accept any offers. He did not explain the death threats. How could he? Who could he trust at this point? He'd given Penny close to a hundred-thousand dollars, and now she couldn't get rid of him fast enough. Was she really working for the prosecutor? In 1992, she'd only agreed to take Gar's case if he signed a paper saying that they would never pursue a cooperation agreement.

She said she absolutely did not do pleas like that. Now she was there to present him with an offer and then leave.

She's working with Diskman, Gar decided. She's a successful lawyer, and Gar had once heard: "Not all lawyers are successful, just the dishonest ones." The honest ones are all poor. Or something like that.

He told Penny, "I don't have $200,000. I don't have any money. What are you going to do for me for the balance of the fee I've already paid you?"

"I'll have to discuss that with my partners," she said.

A FEW WEEKS later, she sent him a check for a thousand dollars. Penny was history. Gar was all on his own.

CHAPTER 72

LATE 1999.

THERE IS AN inherently derogatory question within contemporary jurisprudence, a question that cannot be ignored because of its growing applicability to the profession, and the question is simply this: If law school is so hard, why are there so many lawyers? Gar asked himself this question over and over again, and could not come up with a satisfactory answer. So he decided to act as his own lawyer.

After a *Faretta* hearing, wherein Gar waived his right to a lawyer, Judge Bryan granted Gar's motion to proceed *pro se*. This was a bone-headed move on Gar's part. He would eventually wind up turning things over to Attorney Pena, who was still on the case as "stand-by" counsel. The last-minute turnover would be after the entire time for valuable pretrial motions was gone.

Gar insisted on a speedy trial. He filed nothing but worthless motions questioning the court's jurisdiction. And he did nothing about developing a trial strategy. The April thirteenth trial date came very quickly. Nor did Tom Pena prepare for trial. He took Gar's word for it that he would conduct the trial himself.

When the time for trial arrived, Gar did not have a clue about what he was supposed to do. He gave it his best though, objecting to what sounded wrong (though normally not in proper fashion), and speaking to the court using sentences beginning with legal-type colloquialisms like: "If you will," or, "If it pleases the court."

When he got to *voir dire* (the winnowing of jurors), he got completely lost. Tom Pena began helping more and more. The court, and the prosecutor, did not help him. Just the opposite. They sped right along in an obvious and conscious effort to confuse Gar. And it worked.

Back at SeaTac, it would take hours to get processed with the other returning prisoners, and back up to the unit after court. Law library time was almost nonexistent. The amount of discovery material to be studied, and Charlie and Veryle explaining their crazy last-minute legal theories, had Gar right up against the wall. He got precious little sleep.

The morning that trial was to begin, he gave up. He hauled as much of the discovery material as he could to court. It was no easy task, hauling boxes while in handcuffs. And the Marshal escort would not help.

No. Once a person enters the legal system, he is considered by practitioners of the system, and everyone associated with it, to be guilty scum. Only the judges maintain a pretense that the reality is otherwise, and this pretense is a thin one. The jailers work for the Department of Justice, and so do the Marshals. The prosecutors *are* the Justice Department.

And for a prisoner to elect to represent himself is suicide. It is an uneven playing field to begin with. Prosecutors regularly write *Final Orders* for judges. For a person to go *pro se* in that environment is tantamount to presenting no defense at all. Prosecutors joke amongst themselves that pitting their skills against a *pro se* defendant is like whipping out a rapier against an unarmed child.

Judge Reinhardt, an esteemed jurist of the Ninth Circuit United States Court of Appeals, once said he thought that allowing a defendant to proceed *pro se* was such a travesty, it should be deemed a denial of due process of law.

JUST BEFORE TRIAL, Prosecutor Diskman offered a plea bargain of seven years. It must be acknowledged that attendant upon offers such as these is a provision that the defendant sit down with law enforcement officials and prosecutors and tell them everything he knows. The defendant is also required to testify against those he has told on. During this same time, Gar also received a reminder from Vicky. Her answer to his previous letter finally arrived. It takes a month for mail to go to Mexico, and a month to get back.

In her letter she said: "I don't know what to say about your case, but if you make a deal YOU WILL BE DEAD IN TWO DAYS!!"

Was she saying something beyond what they'd already discussed numerous times. Was she reiterating this because she had received new threats? What was it? There was no way to ask and get an answer in time.

Whatever the answers to these questions, it hardened Gar's resolve. He could not accept any deal. He had no choice but to throw himself to the lions.

THE MORNING OF the trial, Gar stood up and said, "Your honor, if it pleases the court, I wish to turn over my defense to my standby attorney, Tom Pena."

"Motion granted. I assume that was a motion. If not, Notice taken and accepted. You're doing the right thing, Mr. Walton," Judge Bryan said. Though at times he came off as harsh to Gar, he was an interesting guy. He looked exactly like Grady Harris, the brother of Tom Harris–the same two brothers that carried the meat of the workload in getting the hashish ashore. And it was interesting that Judge Bryan owned a commercial salmon boat himself, and spent all of his spare time salmon fishing. He was a fellow salmon fisherman. He'd talk about it, during breaks in the trial, with various fisherman witnesses. This made Gar feel lonely and left out. He wanted to talk about salmon fishing too. But, of course, the judge couldn't sit and idly chat with a defendant.

TRIAL BEGAN SUDDENLY, with Tom Pena reading Grand Jury testimony on the fly. He needed to go through the testimony of witnesses that were about to testify. Pena would do this on breaks, during lunchtime, and at night. Occasionally, Judge Bryan would recess for an hour or so, allowing Pena to go to the library and study.

Under normal circumstances, it would appear this was horribly inadequate, a shoddy way to run a trial. But the circumstances were not normal. Witness after witness continued to come to the stand, pointing a finger at Gar saying, "He did it. He's your man. That guy right there."

Of that entire list of prosecution witnesses, including other codefendants, none of them received a sentence of more than five years in jail. The average sentence was 35 months–just under three years. Several men received a sentence of only a single day in jail. Their plea agreements, to a man, dictated that they must say what they were saying against

Gar, or go back to court for a full sentence of ten years or more.

GAR'S DEFENSE RELIED solely on cross-examinations. After each witness painted a dismal picture of Gar, Tom Pena would bring their plea agreement to the witness box and go over it with them. The intent was to convey to the jury that the witnesses had an enormous incentive to lie. Therefore, it logically followed that a reasonable doubt existed concerning their testimony.

Several witnesses admitted they had served their short sentences and were now out on probation, and they were told by their probation officers that they must testify or go back to jail.

Diskman would recross, and ask, "Have you told the truth here today? Has anyone asked you to lie?"

"No way," they would answer. And that would be enough for the jury to forego any reasonable suspicion of doubt about the testimony.

After a week of the prosecution presenting witnesses saying that Gar did it, the prosecution rested. Judge Bryan turned immediately to Tom Pena and said, "Mr. Pena, when does the defense wish to begin presenting its case?"

And Tom Pena said, "Your honor, the defense rests."

Bam! Just like that, the trial was over. No rebuttals. No anything. Gar was watching the jury when Pena said this, and they were stunned. They had watched a Christian fighting a coliseum full of big cats for a week now, and they were ready for the Christian to turn the tide. They expected to see him raise his sword and smite those that would destroy him. Or at least try.

But what they got was nothing: "The defense rests." And it was not said with any vigor or persuasion. It did not resonate around the courtroom as it might have done if F. Lee Bailey or Clarence Darrow had pronounced it. No. It was a squeak, like a church mouse may have emitted in the pale moonlight of a midnight parish. It was wholly inadequate, an admission of defeat. And the jury took that to the jury room to deliberate on.

They deliberated for a day and a half, but only about some of the ancillary charges. Gar was ultimately tried on eleven counts; Conspiracy to Import Hashish; Conspiracy to Distribute Hashish; Actually Importing Hashish; Actually Distributing Hashish; and seven counts of Interstate Travel in Aid of Racketeering. The racketeering is like when someone calls someone in another State and says, "Hey, come to my state and help me with a crime." These seven counts were based, mostly, on seven telephone calls. After arguing over these seven counts, the jury voted to acquit on only one of them.

Thus, though it was only one pile of hashish Gar was convicted of importing, there were nonetheless a number of separate crimes committed in doing so. As it would turn out, the jury would convict on ten of the eleven counts. In so doing, they determined Gar committed ten different crimes. This made Diskman happy, because if Gar managed to overturn one of the charges on appeal, there were still nine more counts to hold him in prison. Prosecutors are thrilled by long sentences and multiple convictions.

It might strike the average citizen as strange, a counterfeit duplication of counts for one crime. But this is the way business is transacted in today's courtrooms. A man who kills another human being is convicted not just of murder, but of hate too, because the victim was of another race or creed. But doesn't everyone who murders someone hate that person, at least at the moment?

Multiple crimes deserve multiple sentences. John Q. Citizen understands that. He appreciates it moreover. This is the nature of contemporary American society. It is a society which reacts to fear, carefully locks the front door, and peers uncertainly through the curtains.

FUNDAMENTALLY, THE TRIAL, although a slam-dunk, was flawed. A jury's conviction is only as exact as the instructions they receive from the judge.

In Gar's case, Judge Bryan instructed the jury, on the drug charges, "You must determine if Mr. Walton imported hashish, and if he did...."

The same basic instruction on all charges. There was no mention of the quantity of hashish. Therefore, the jury convicted Gar only of importing and distributing hashish–an undetermined quantity of hashish. Nor was there an instruction on whether Gar was a leader/organizer in the affair, as he was subsequently found to be.

And these were mistakes.

AT THE AUGUST 1998 sentencing hearing, Gar would object to the constitutionality of the guidelines used to sentence him, and he did it five times. His lawyer objected, as well, to the judge sentencing Gar based upon actual amounts of hashish when the jury did not determine any amounts. And there were zero amounts of hashish recovered. This was actually a similar argument to that presented by Gar's lawyer in Mexico: no drugs, no lab reports, no tangible evidence, no certain facts.

And the prosecution was asking for an enhanced sentence based on Gar's role in the crime. They said that Gar was the ringleader of the operation, and they wanted an extra ten years for that. Gar's lawyer objected to that, too.

Judge Bryan sentenced Gar to twenty years based on drug quantity, and ten more for his role as a leader. Thirty years total!

When the judge passed sentence, Gar felt a sense of coldness pass over him and everything became fantastic and dreamlike. He stood before the judge with his lawyer standing beside him and listened to the judge's words as though they were spoken very slowly and from a great distance. He glanced up at the big government clock hung high on the courthouse wall, and he could no longer see the ticking of the second hand. The sweeping second hand he had so tediously watched a hundred times before was inexplicably gone. And the clock hung frozen and unmoving.

Thirty years. That couldn't be right, could it? When everyone else had been sentenced to three? Maybe part of that sentence would be suspended or something. Gar struggled to listen to the judge's words, but he could make no sense of them. And then it was over. The judge was gone, and Gar's lawyer was saying how sorry he was:

Thirty years? Yes. I'm so terribly sorry. We'll appeal, of course. Thirty years....

These factors, the ones that were objected to at the sentencing proceeding, would become the substance of many a forthcoming appeal. Every court in the land, including the United States Supreme Court, would eventually agree with Gar. They'd hold thousands of sentences just like Gar's to be unconstitutional. But soliciting sympathy was not the same thing as overturning a conviction. The sentence had been passed. And any sort of relief, even if it could be gained, was to be years and years in the future, if it were to be realized at all.

Thirty years.

CHAPTER 73

1999-2000.

A RUSSIAN POET named Yertushenko once noted that justice is like a train that's nearly always late. Gar thought about this observation a lot as the millennium approached. And then he thought about how Italian trains were notoriously late, until Benito Mussolini came along to get the nation organized.

The thoughts were not entirely dissimilar. Maybe the price you paid for justice negated the possibility of the existence of justice in the end. It was a conundrum.

THE BIG HOUSE, the original *Big House*, is the Bureau of Prisons (BOP) United States Penitentiary at Leavenworth, Kansas. It was built in the late 1880s, and it was designed to look just like *the* White House. Big House–White House, another American play on words. USP Leavenworth was to be the prison to end all prisons. The worst of the worst would be sent there, and through hard work and clean living they'd leave completely rehabilitated. If they ever left. And many of them, nowadays, don't.

The Marshals moved Gar to Leavenworth in May of 1999. He had been languishing at SeaTac for over fifteen months. When the bus pulled up in front of the hundred-year-old prison–huge and imposing, a terrifying sight–Gar said a prayer. He sensed that this was a new low in his life, and he wondered if he would survive it.

Once inside though, he quickly got into a groove. He met a few legal-beagles in the law library with new and better ideas. He'd wake up, though, sometimes in the middle of the night and exclaim with wonder, "Holy fucking balls! I'm in Leavenworth!" This is a statement that carries so much weight, no one could possibly comprehend the burden without actually going there. Very few men can make the claim. Living in the same building that Al Capone and John Dillinger once lived in caused considerable trepidation for Gar.

There probably aren't as many murders at Leavenworth as there are in Mexican prisons, but there are certainly more fights and stabbings. The whole environment is "off the hook," as youngsters like to say. Gar stepped carefully around the place, wearing a forged grin. He found himself saying "excuse me" to anyone he came within three feet of. It was a fearful, depressing time. The old prison was ice cold in the winter, and as hot as sin in the summer. It stank of bad plumbing, sweat, and fear. The windows were glazed so no one could see out of them, and the prison perimeter was a twenty-five foot high brick wall that one could not see over. The only view of the outside a Leavenworth prisoner has is limited to what he sees on the television.

And, of course, there are clocks. Many, many clocks. Clocks everywhere you go. You cannot go anywhere in Leavenworth without being confronted by a timepiece. It's as though they are placed there to remind the inmates of exactly what they are doing.

They are doing time. In Gar's case, thirty years. There must be two thousand clocks in Leavenworth, averaging about two for every man imprisoned there. There are six of them visible in the chow hall alone. And the curious thing about these clocks is that every single one of them reports a different time. None of them are synchronized. So amidst all of these clocks, no one really knows what time it is.

It is like a Twilight Zone episode where you expect Jack Nicholson to appear with wildly unkempt hair and begin screaming. In Leavenworth, no one knows what time it is.

WHILE THERE, GAR met an ex-CIA-turned-spy who actually knew about Gar's case. Gar would question this at first, as there are so many swindles in prison. But this man knew details of Gar's case that hadn't come out in court, things he shouldn't have known. And with this information emerged a sordid tale of government complicity.

The spy, a man named Harvey, said Gar's case was known as *Operation Rehash*. This was the first time Gar ever heard the term. He explained that Gar's whole scenario was known as a "controlled delivery." The load of hashish was observed and at times escorted by several government agencies, all the way from Pakistan to the United States, where it entered the country at Gar's Fish Company. It was clandestinely observed as it was trucked to New York for distribution. The agents waited until it was all sold before moving in and seizing the money. And the money was what it was all about. The money was actually a bonus to domestic law enforcement for their willingness to look the other way. It was an exercise, a profitable one, for law enforcement and security agencies of the government.

The mission statement of *Operation Rehash* was: "To provide and assist Afghanistan Taliban toward mutual endeavors." Gar filed requests under the Freedom of Information Act to numerous agencies, and learned that his case was indeed called *Operation Rehash*. The irony of such a mission statement did not escape Gar years later, when an Afghanistan-trained Mujahedeen-turned-Taliban named Osama bin Laden organized the terrorist strike that brought down the twin towers of the World Trade Center. Through a history of malfeasance, the United States had inadvertently engineered a piece of its own destruction.

FORTUNATELY, AFTER TEN months, they transferred Gar out of Leavenworth. The BOP performed an adjustment of how they classify inmates, a security-point system, and Gar's total number of points dropped. Leavenworth is a "high" security prison. Gar was now classified as a "medium" security inmate. He asked to go to Sheridan, Oregon, where there is a medium-level FCI (Federal Correctional Institution) near to Andriana and Marilyn. Instead, they sent him to Pekin, Illinois. This was the wrong way, but at least it was a less dangerous prison. The increase in distance from home, though, added to Gar's unhappiness.

At Pekin, Gar put together his Supreme Court appeal. This was after the Ninth circuit Court of Appeals denied him counsel to assist with its preparation. He had continued to act as his own lawyer for his regular appeal. But when that was denied, several of the Leavenworth jailhouse lawyers convinced him to apply for counsel for the Supreme Court appeal. "That expression, Gar, about having a fool for a client if you represent yourself is dead on," they had said to him. They also got him off the jurisdictional bandwagon and steered down a more conventional legal road concerning sentencing issues.

So he applied for a lawyer and the Ninth Circuit took five long months to issue a one-sentence Order: "Your motion for counsel is denied." That was in May, 2000. Gar became so depressed over this denial he asked to see the prison psychiatrist. The psychiatrist would call him in every afternoon for a one-hour session. After a week, the man convinced Gar to try Prozac.

The Prozac helped, but it was not an answer to all of his problems. The weight of a thirty-year sentence was bearing down on Gar's shoulders. Dispirited, he began to believe that his luck had run completely out. The knowledge that his case was a small piece of a much larger government black-op conspiracy was the last straw. He almost gave up.

But he kept working on his petition for a writ of certiorari to the U.S. Supreme Court until June, 2000. On that day, on the 19th, he mailed his petition. Under the rules, "Once placed in the prison mailbox, the petition is deemed filed in the court."

On June 26, 2000, the United States Supreme Court handed down their ruling in *Apprendi v. New Jersey*. *Apprendi* would turn courts on their heads, and prosecutors completely upside down. *Apprendi* declared: "Any fact, other than a prior conviction, that increases a defendant's statutory penalty for a crime, must be submitted to a jury and proved beyond a reasonable doubt." In other words, judges could no longer find facts that would increase sentences.

Gar had insisted upon this very point at sentencing. Indeed, he had objected to the court enhancing his sentence from the basic five-year maximum for an undetermined amount of hashish, to the lifetime maximum for allegedly leading and organizing an operation involving more than 6,000 pounds. His sentence was enhanced on points never proved to the jury. And now the Supreme Court was saying this was wrong....

A NEW PRISON came online in Victorville, California. They were looking for bodies to fill it. They preferred to initially have mature inmates with no history of problems. Gar mentioned to his Pekin counselor that he would like to be on the west coast of the United States. "I was born there, and I don't know anyone east of the Rocky Mountains. And I'm not problematic," he told the counselor. His name was submitted for transfer, and two weeks later they told him to pack his personal stuff.

"You're going to Victorville," they said. He prayed a move would change his attitude, bring him hope again.

The same day he packed his stuff to leave, news of the *Apprendi* case reached the prison. Prisoners don't have the luxury of daily, or even weekly, case law reviews. New cases normally take a month to reach the prisons. He would have to wait until he reached Victorville before he could put together the required supplement to his Supreme Court petition.

IT TOOK ONE week to get to the brand new prison at Victorville. They laid over at the transfer center in Oklahoma.

At Victorville, there were a number of things that immediately caught Gar's attention. As the bus pulled up in front, fifty BOP employees lined the sidewalk staring in total disbelief; as if they'd never seen prisoners. It was as hot stepping off that bus as it had been when he'd disembarked from the plane the first time in Acapulco. And the prison yard was stark, barren sand, presenting a rocky, desert landscape. It looked like a scene from purgatory.

On the way inside, Gar asked how many people the prison held, and they said eighteen hundred. He asked how many were there now, and they said, with this bus, right around 250.

It was a brand new, almost empty prison, and they were the first "fish" there. For weeks, the staff continued to stare at them as if they'd been dropped from a flying disk. The weather continued in the 100s throughout the summer (he arrived on July fifteenth). Dust devils were the only break in the desert monotony.

THE LAW LIBRARY in Victorville was small compared to Leavenworth and Pekin. It was not much bigger than the satellite library they had at SeaTac.

Gar needed to put together a supplemental argument to present to the Supreme Court in light of this new *Apprendi* decision. And he tried to do his best work. But the Supreme court did not even vote to hear Gar's case, because his appeal to them could only be based on an error by the Ninth Circuit, and the Ninth Circuit had not made any errors.

Now his judgment, as the law reads, was indeed final. The only legal consolation was that his judgment had not become final until after *Apprendi v. New Jersey* was decided. In theory, he should be entitled to the application of *Apprendi* to his case in an up-and-coming *habeas corpus* petition. Maybe.

But his chances were running out. Worry began to etch Gar's face; physically he felt old and tired. He looked old, and felt like the ghost of Christmas past, laden with chains.

He quit looking in the mirror, frightened by the grim face looking back at him. Stuck in the high desert, the ocean felt like it was a million miles away. And Susan was even further away than that.

It was about this time that Gar stopped seeing clocks. They were there, all right, but he no longer saw them. There was no point to them, so he dismissed them from his mind and became impervious to their influence.

If only became Gar's mantra: "If only the judge would finally see things my way, and grant this up-and-coming *habeas corpus*."

It was the only hope he had left.

CHAPTER 74

2001.

THERE IS AN old Hebrew proverb that translates wonderfully to modern times. "The court is most merciful," the proverb goes, "when the accused are most rich." The people in America's prisons were not at all surprised when O.J. Simpson walked out of the courthouse a free man. They expected this. The only thing that truly surprised them was that there was such a large and naive segment of the population that thought the result would be otherwise. By now Gar had become quite cynical, but he had become very pragmatic about money.

MOM, OF COURSE, had stayed in the fight all along–spiritually, emotionally and financially. When Gar began discussing his Section 2255 (*habeas corpus*) with her, she asked what she could do to help him.

"Well, this is my last, best shot, Mom. I believe that under this new *Apprendi* ruling I have action. I can put together a pretty fair petition myself, but it would look much better with a lawyer's name on the signature line. Especially after I represented myself so abysmally during trial and appeal."

"Honey, I just sold my little piece of property up in Westwood. It's only around fifteen thousand, and I need some of that money for some other things, but what do you have in mind?" Gar knew she was amenable to helping him financially as soon as she called him "Honey." If she used her favorite pet name, "Sam," then it was a sure thing.

"Mom, if you could spare $5,000 of that, I have several lawyer's addresses I will write to, asking them what they can do for that amount of money. And we'll go with the best response."

"Oh, Sam...."

Gar smiled with delight.

"I can do that. No problem. Just let me know who you decide on."

"Yes!" Gar pumped his right fist in the air.

JOE QUIVER HAD impressed Gar. Joe represented him on that first day back from Mexico. So when Joe said he could do the job for $5,000, Gar happily called Mom with the address. She sent Joe a check straight away.

It was the first time since his return to the United States that Gar had an unconflicted relationship with his lawyer.

He started sleeping better at night, and this enabled him to do sharper work on the first draft of his petition by day.

Gar even began to fantasize that one day before he reached the age of seventy he might be released. He would be able to call Susan again. Maybe patch things up with his kids. Things were not going well with them. Jasmer was at a disciplinary type of school; Alison refused to speak to him; and catching up with Marilyn, in order to talk with Andriana, was difficult without the resources of the free world: Internet directory assistance, a car, ability to go out at night, and so on.

WORKING WITH JOE was easy. He was a smart attorney. He wasn't a public defender; he'd only been doing a cycle of what is called "panel work" when he represented Gar that first day back from Mexico. He did that to pick up experience he wouldn't have otherwise received in his private practice.

This was to be Joe's first *habeas corpus* motion. However, Gar had done six or eight of them for other prisoners and had a better than fair understanding of the process. Together they'd make their claims persuasive for Judge Bryan. The sentencing judge is the one who decides these petitions.

IN MAY OF 2001, they filed Gar's *habeas corpus*. The court ordered the government to respond and show cause why the writ of *habeas corpus* should not be granted. The thrust of the prosecutor's response was that Gar was not entitled to <u>any</u> consideration of his three claims because the motion was filed late.

"There is a one-year time limit on the filing of a *habeas corpus*," Joe Quiver said to Gar on the telephone. "That is, one year after a defendant's judgment becomes final. The prosecutor is now arguing that your judgment became final in March, 2000, right in the middle of that five-month waiting period you were forced to endure by the Ninth Circuit while they were deciding on your motion for appointment of counsel to assist with your appeal to the Supreme Court."

"What kind of argument is that?" Gar demanded. "That doesn't speak to sentencing issues."

"I know. The prosecutor is now saying you should have done your Supreme Court appeal while you were waiting for appointment of a lawyer to assist you with that very same thing. Either that, or you should have filed your *habeas corpus* motion while your appeal was being considered by the Supreme Court." Both of these were ridiculous propositions, not at all in accordance with the pertinent rules that govern such matters. Joe at least had the decency to sound embarrassed when he explained all of this to Gar.

It was so ridiculous it smacked of connivance (this was Gar's old nemesis, Prosecutor Diskman, making the government's argument). It worried Gar. Every available hour he studied, researching the issue, finding that there was no case law dealing specifically with the circumstances he faced. And this is why Prosecutor Diskman so cleverly crafted this argument. When the law is sketchy, the court will always rule for the prosecution.

What law existed concerning Gar's unique situation (unique because he represented himself, then later asked for a lawyer), supported the premise that after the Supreme Court denied Gar in November of 2000, his judgment was final. And on that same November, 2000 day his one-year time clock began to run on his *habeas corpus* motion. Accordingly, his May, 2001 filing was within the allowed year. Attorney Quiver agreed that there was no other way the law could be interpreted.

Judge Bryan, however, disagreed. He denied the *habeas corpus* as being time barred. It was as nonsensical as it was ludicrous. It convinced Gar that the court was not, for whatever reason, yet ready to lean his way. The law favored Gar, though not explicitly enough. What made the decision so utterly disturbing was not only that Gar lost his one best shot at a reversal of his sentence, but he had lost when using an experienced lawyer. Everything before this time had been at best, homemade or frivolous.

The day following the denial, Gar went to the psychiatrist for an increase in his Prozac. Weight continued to fall off his body. His remaining hair grayed considerably that year.

And the irony of the rationale used to deny him relief did not escape him. It all came back to the freakin' clocks. American jurisprudence is rife with mention of the tolling of clocks. It is mentioned in the famous Black's Law Dictionary. It suffuses the extensive and lawyerly American Jurisprudence editions. The federal supplements depicting noteworthy case law are replete with talk of tolling of clocks. And it is even mentioned in the federal Rules of Criminal Procedure.

The clocks mocked him now for his previous distain. The clocks had become his enemy. He had only to gaze at his aging countenance in a mirror to confirm this.

CHAPTER 75

2002–2005.

THE FACT OF Gar's conviction, that he had a role in the hashish smuggling operation, was never in dispute. That is to say, not after the jury rendered its verdict. Although Gar had never admitted guilt, he'd never appealed it either. Once a jury finds guilt, it is nearly impossible to overturn that decision.

It was the degree of his culpability that was subject to interpretation. He was not convicted by a jury of any specific drug amount, nor of whether he supervised five or more people (the requirement for the leader/organizer sentencing enhancement he received). Those were Gar's facts, and now the law was actually on his side too. The problem was that Judge Bryan's ruling that his writ was late negated his entitlement to the benefit of the new *Apprendi* ruling.

The *Apprendi* ruling confirmed that two constitutional amendments were violated at Gar's sentencing. But now this did not matter. Another dreadful set of circumstances unfolded in just the right (or wrong) sequence to deny Gar justice. A law professor named McHugh once wryly noted that, "A short glass of facts is worth a tub of law." Perhaps Gar's circumstances were an example of this idea.

THE RULE FOR appeal of a *habeas corpus* denial is strange. One must get permission from the same judge that denied the thing in order to appeal. Therefore, the judge must admit that he may have been wrong. They rarely, if ever, do that. It didn't happen this time either.

His last, best chance for relief had been shot down. It was horribly depressing. If any prisoner in this situation says that suicide is not a thought, he would be lying. Every prisoner considers it, some more seriously than others.

Gar certainly did, but he fortunately came to his senses. Mainly because of the message it would send to his children.

IT WAS APRIL of 2002, when Judge Bryan denied the *habeas corpus* motion. The consensus of the legal community, at that time, was that after 9/11 judges were profoundly affected. The courts clamped down tighter than a pair of handcuffs.

Prison really began to drag. Medical care is almost nonexistent in federal prisons. And dental is worse. An aging prisoner, like Gar, cannot get regular care from a prison physician. This fact, together with the court's decisions, began to take its toll on Gar. Life became very dark for him. The days and the months began to drag by. And then for the first time in his life, he felt his health begin to fail.

"THAT'S A PICTURE of my daughter," Gar said to his Unit Manager, as he laid a photo gently on the desk.

Mr. Merlak said, "Well, she's quite pretty. Thank you for sharing this."

"I have a letter here from her too. I won't burden you with my personal letter, how much she loves and misses me, but I wanted you to notice the return address; She lives in Oregon. Not all that far from Sheridan, Oregon." Gar raised his eyebrows and he smiled at Merlak.

"Oh, I see. You're trying to tell me you'd like a transfer to Sheridan. How long have you been here?"

"Twenty-four months. The last twenty with clear conduct. If I'm ever going to get to see my little girl, that's where I need to go. Victorville is just too far away for her Mom to drive."

"Okay."

"Her name is Andriana. She was born in Mexico while I was down there and indictments were coming out up here; it was a crazy time. She's never really had much of a chance to know me. She's...."

"I get your point, Walton. We can put you in for Sheridan. I can't promise what the Region Office will do."

"Thank you, Mr. Merlak. You just made my day. My little girl's, too." Gar left the office smiling for the first time in a long while.

A LONG HOT summer and fall passed. On December fifteenth, 2002, Gar hit the prison yard at FCI Sheridan with a new head of steam. This was a much different prison, at least in appearance. For one thing, everything was green. Birds flitted from tree to tree within the confines, and a luxurious carpet of grass covered the ground. This abundance of life affected Gar. It filled him with a renewed sense of determination.

He'd taken a computer training course at Victorville. Based on that, he convinced the teacher at the Sheridan Computer Lab to hire him as the assistant tutor in the Microsoft Word and Excel classes. However, as soon as the regular tutor heard Gar was hired, he quit himself. Within a few days of arrival at Sheridan, Gar went from being a new fish to being the only tutor in the Sheridan computer program–a fairly prestigious job. This was the best job Gar could have hoped for. He was totally fascinated with computers.

He was also placed on the list to be hired at the UNICOR furniture factory. UNICOR pays the most of any job in federal prison. It is by far the best place to work. He was soon to be a part of this.

AS 2003 CAME on, so did a new plan for the defense. Gar refused to admit defeat. He had over seven years in prison now, and twenty more to go (that is, with the fourteen percent off which he was entitled to for good behavior).

The new attack on his sentence was based on a letter from Vicky. Specifically, the one line of her letter that read, *If you make a deal, you'll be dead in two days.*

Gar argued now that the prosecution did not fairly represent a plea bargain. They did not explain that protection was available. In principle, this was true. Practically, though, it was arguable. How, for example, could they protect Vicky in Mexico? How many other relatives would be in jeopardy, whether or not they agreed to protection? The main problem was getting back into court. The judge denied this attempt, and it was denied all the way to the Supreme Court.

THEN A NEW Supreme Court ruling came along in 2004, *Blakely v. Washington*, and this case changed everything.

The essence of this case as it applied to Gar was that the sentencing enhancements that the judge applied and Gar had contested were now clearly unconstitutional. The Supreme Court had finally agreed with what Gar had been saying all along.

He filed another petition based on those facts, and in light of the new *Blakely* interpretation of those facts.

Judge Bryan again denied, saying Gar should have raised this issue in his first *habeas corpus* motion. Gar wanted to call Judge Bryan and shout, "I RAISED THESE VERY SAME ISSUES IN MY FIRST MOTION! REMEMBER? THE ONE YOU DENIED AS TIME-BARRED BEFORE EVEN LOOKING AT MY CLAIMS?"

But he didn't, of course. He waited patiently, certain that the Supreme Court would eventually issue further rulings that would benefit him. And he was right. One year later the *Booker* case came out, and Gar was ready to try again. But this time he did it differently.

Gar put together another creative petition. This time he would accompany his new submission with a creative strategy: *The Human Factor*.

His good friend and confidant at Sheridan, Randy Wynn, introduced Gar to John Timothy. John Timothy, or "JT," is an accomplished writer and a published author with a legal background. He's also wonderfully creative, and worked writing briefs for a number of Arizona defense attorneys in the past. JT would tell Gar about time he had spent with a small group of Arizona judges over breakfasts. He related that those judges, during coffee, frequently agonized over the prison sentences they'd been forced to hand out, and often searched for a case where they could do something different for a change. It was JT who introduced Gar to the concept of the human factor, and enlightened Gar on the merits of appealing to a judge on a personal level.

Gar had already sent several letters to Judge Bryan, apologizing for the extra work he caused the court defending himself with far-out jurisdictional theories. Now he wrote the judge about salmon fishing, and the fact that all Gar ever really wanted in life was to be a great salmon fisherman (or at least as good as Michael McHenry). He also gave the judge a synopsis of what he thought were the "secrets to being a better salmon fisherman."

The new concept was infused into a petition for writ of *audita querela*. The parallel strategy to accompany this new approach was that Gar would prompt family and friends to write to Judge Bryan, telling him how sorry Gar was, and that they would help Gar to get back on his feet if the judge were to let him out early. The idea was to tell the judge who Gar really was, who his friends were, and why he was entitled to careful consideration.

It evidently got the judge's attention, because he responded by sending Gar a *Minute Order* saying: "You didn't ask for appointment of counsel, but I think you should."

Everything in court is done by motion. Gar had his motion for appointment of counsel done and mailed within an hour of receiving the judge's *Minute Order*.

This was a good sign. A very, *very* good sign.

He couldn't wait to tell everyone: Randy Wynn and JT; Mom; Andriana and Marilyn; his friends in Crescent City; Jasmer–all those who had written support letters to Judge Bryan. And this list also included Susan. He was back in touch with Susan again.

Gar still didn't look at clocks. He still mistrusted them. But he acknowledged, now, that they were there. They still represented the auspices of the adversary, and maybe they were a necessary yin to the yang of life. Maybe, if they could not be defeated, they could, with adaptation, be borne.

Either way, they continued to tick. And the judge had suggested that he request counsel....

CHAPTER 76

2005.

IT DOESN'T TAKE much for a prisoner to find encouragement. Even as little as the belief that he is being *listened to* can be enough. Judge Wapner, of The People's Court, said that the ability of the judge to put himself into the shoes of the men before him is the heart of being a decent judge. And maybe now Gar was being listened to. That is all he had been asking for. A chance to be heard.

But in prison, it doesn't pay to wear your heart on your sleeve, and you don't put your business on the street, as the saying goes. There are too many ways for things to go wrong through sharing information, so you learn to keep things to yourself. Guys in American prisons tend to take themselves much too seriously. That's why you hear about so many bizarre things going on behind the walls. They're acting out images of themselves. No matter that they're not really like that. Oh, there are a number of psychos. But by and large prisoners are mostly good people who made bad decision.

RANDY WYNN WAS one of the good ones. Randy had become Gar's best friend at Sheridan. He was the only one he had confided in, about all the ups and downs he experienced with Susan and other heartfelt matters. Randy was ten years younger than Gar. He had also been at Sheridan for more than ten years. Gar first saw Randy out on the baseball field pitching softball. He was Sheridan's number one lobber. Athletically built, because he spends hours each day working out, Randy became Gar's personal trainer, pulling him out of the law library and making him walk the track on a daily basis. This was the time they used for giving each other advice on a range of subjects: women, kids, other family, legal affairs, and so on. And a fair amount of good-natured ribbing went on.

It was Randy that had prompted Gar to search harder for Susan's address. "If you love her that much, I don't understand why you don't try harder to get her address," Randy had scolded. Gar finally got the address through some old friends from Half Moon Bay who now lived close by. After Gar and Susan wrote for a while, they decided to make weekly phone calls. The weekly calls Gar would make to Susan, Mom, and Andriana were the highlights of his week; a balm for his emotional wounds.

The calls to Susan were to her place of employment. She was still happily married. "My husband would likely not understand," she had told him. She was now 49 and Gar was 52. Time had not changed their feelings for one another. Susan was very excited about Gar's latest defense. And she was anxious to know everything.

"WHAT'S GOING ON now?" Susan was her usual enthusiastic self.

"Well, it's complicated," Gar gathered his thoughts.

"Try me."

They were on their weekly call. They had fifteen minutes for Gar to hear about Susan's business and family, and for Susan to hear about Gar's latest activities. It was the summer of 2005.

"Okay, the judge denied my petition."

"Oh, FUCK!" she shouted. He loved it when she swore. One would never expect cuss words to come from those cute lips.

"But. And this is a big but. Judge Bryan said some real amazing things. It took him sixteen pages to do so, too. First, he said my sentence is unconstitutional. However, he also said that there was no provision in the law that would allow him to correct my sentence. He complained that the law was plain bad."

"Okay. And?"

"Well, there's a new case out. It's called *United states v. Crawford*. In that case, the Ninth Circuit defined under what circumstances they could recall their original mandate. In other words, this finality of judgment situation, that I continue to tell you is my biggest obstacle, has maybe one way that might allow me to get around it. And my judge has zeroed in on that way, asking the court of appeal to recall my mandate so he can resentence me. It's the only way to reopen a closed case."

"So, all right. Let's get them to do that." She has this unique way of seeing only the positive things in life, and nothing is impossible to Susan.

Gar cautioned, "The circumstance for recall of the mandate must be extraordinary, and Judge Bryan held that I meet that criteria, that my circumstance is indeed extraordinary. It's almost as if he has motioned the court of appeal on my behalf. But we will have to go through a normal briefing process. We will have to explain why my case is extraordinary. My lawyer feels good about it, though."

"I understand. You've been telling me all along how different your case is, how unique."

"The appeals court in *Crawford* actually laid out a two-pronged scenario that is identical to mine. I'm feeling better about this than any other appeal I've had in court. It really looks good. I told you a while ago about the status hearing we had, where Judge Bryan, via his speaker phone, began telling me about his salmon boat, with the prosecutor there listening to us bullshit like old buddies?"

"Yes, you told me that. REALLY," she squealed with excitement, "you might have a chance. Far out! I can't believe it. That is so fantastic! You really might get out." She was bellowing into the phone.

"He even quoted Gerry Spence, that famous defense lawyer from Wyoming. He said, 'Sometimes a judge just wants to do justice and can't...and he gets sad and angry.' I'm paraphrasing, but the Judge Bryan said he's angry and just wants to do justice. I'll send you a copy of his order." Gar took a deep breath, and let it out real slowly.

"But what?" Susan was still excited. "What will happen now? What's next? What do you think is going to happen?"

"Okay. Trying to keep it simple, here's what I think. We will go to the Ninth Circuit with four different arguments. But it will all boil down to that final page of Judge Bryan's sixteen-page order. Will the court of appeal respect him, and the conclusions he makes on that page? It really comes down to the human factor again. Judge Bryan decided to consider my human side, and now we pray that the court of appeals will respect him, as a human being and as a long-time fellow jurist."

"They don't have to agree with his findings?"

"No. They will be inclined not to; courts don't like to let prisoners out. But he's a senior judge, and I think he is well respected. They'll give him some deference, all right. Maybe a lot. I've yet to find a case where he's been overturned. It is all about whether or not they want to do this for <u>him</u>."

"Oh, Gar. I'm praying for you. What if you win, what will you do?" Susan asked.

"I don't know. Smile a lot, I guess."

"What do you want to do?"

"See my kids. Have lunch with you. Beyond that, I'm pretty open."

"You want to go fishing?" Her voice sounded mischievous.

"You fuckin' A!" he shouted. He didn't hesitate.

"If you had your wish, what kind of boat would you want?"

"Well, you know Michael has always been my hero."

"You and every other Half Moon Bay fisherman for the last forty-some years."

"So, if I had that one wish, you know, like the fabled leprechaun granted me a single wish, I'd like to have a boat just like the *Merva W.* A sixty foot, nine inch, *Edmund Monk*-designed traditional troller, just like Michael's."

"Really? Painted sky blue like his?"

"I always called it Z-Squad blue."

"You mean you still want to be a Z-Squader? And fish, and chase women, and drink?"

"Why not? Maybe not the drinking part any more, but the rest sure sounds fun."

"Oh, Gar," she snapped in mock irritation. But he could tell she was pleased. "You'll never grow up, will you?"

"No. I don't know," he admitted. "Maybe not."

"Shit," she said. "There goes the warning click. And we just started talking. We have to hang up now, don't we? I'm so excited for you. I love you. Please get out of there."

"I'm trying. I love you, too. Bye, talk to you some time next week." He hung up, and glanced up at the ubiquitous government wall clock. Fifteen minutes had never passed so quickly. Time was playing with him still.

CHAPTER 77

2006.

THE BRIEFS WERE submitted by both sides in April of 2006. Gar, now 53 years old, was approaching his tenth anniversary in jail. Jasmer, 23, worked repairing refrigeration units. Alison, 21, was finishing her senior year at NYU. Andriana was 13, and the apple of Gar's eye. She continued to make the honor roll at her school in Medford, Oregon. This, among many things, got her half off on any size pizza at Papa John's. Gar was so proud of her for that!

Cindy and Marilyn, both entirely friendly with Gar, were single. Victoria, and her two beautiful daughters (Meche got married), were now living back in Playa del Carmen. Vicky was single, too. She said she wished Gar would hurry up and win his case and come down to stay with her. "We're still waiting for you," she said to him.

"Do you still love me?" Gar asked on the phone.

"Jes," she responded as only she could. "Of course I do."

The fact that all his ex-loves remained single was perplexing to Gar. Was he a hard act to follow? Or was he so bad that women were forever afterwards soured on relationships with men? He honestly didn't know.

GAR HAD REACHED a pinnacle at the Sheridan furniture factory (UNICOR). He was the factory manager's clerk, and spent all day on the computer. Evenings and weekends he worked in the law library. In a place where satisfying jobs were hard to come by, Gar had two of them. He waited patiently to hear an answer to his latest appeal.

And he continued walking the track with Randy Wynn.

"What's up, Gar Walton? You ready to do five miles?" Randy asked as they fell into step together. Randy lived in another unit and was always out in the yard before Gar. The track extended around the baseball field, as well as another area about equal in size. All the way around was a quarter of a mile.

"You bet. Although I have to get to work in exactly 27 minutes."

"Oh, you always have to go to work."

"Hey, you know something? I've always wondered, how come everyone calls you Randy Wynn? You know, like it's one name. Never just Randy, or just Wynn. But I think I've figured it out. You always call everyone else by both names. You don't always, but most of the time you call me Gar Walton. So, I naturally answer back with Randy Wynn."

"Oh, you think you're so smart. That's not it. They do it because they think that's my name. People here have been doing it for years. Somebody else started it a long time ago and it just stuck."

"No, really. Why don't they call you anything else, like, say..."

"Handsome?" Randy filled in.

"Well, I wasn't going to say exactly that. But, okay, handsome."

"Thank you."

"I think I'm onto something. You're the only one I know who uses both Gar and Walton, and you're the only guy

I know that everyone calls by both names." Gar wouldn't let it go because he had made a big discovery and was proud of it. That it was meaningless didn't matter.

"You know, you're an amazing guy, Gar Walton," Randy said dryly.

"And it is very intelligent of you to notice that." Gar smirked back at him.

"So what's up with your appeal?" Randy asked, half over his shoulder. He was always about a step ahead of Gar, trying to force him to walk faster.

"Well, it's September already. We filed all our briefs in April, so it's been about five months. My lawyer said three to five months. I should hear something any day."

"I wish you'd hurry and win and get out of here so you can send me money. Or at least come and visit me."

"Ha! Like if I got out of here, either one of those things would happen." Gar jested with him.

"You mean," Randy complained, "If you win your appeal, you're not going to remember your old friend, Randy Wynn?"

"See? You even call yourself Randy Wynn."

"Fuck you, Gar Walton!" Randy said, laughing.

And on they walked in companionable silence for a while, until the public address system barked, "UNICOR Work Call." Gar said he'd see Randy at the lunch break.

"I'm going to walk your legs off for teasing me, and for not sending me any money or visiting me when you get out," Randy threatened.

"I knew I shouldn't have said what I said as soon as I said it." Gar grinned, and he walked off toward the furniture factory.

It was still the summer weather pattern. Today was one of those rare mornings Gar loved. A low overhead ceiling before the sun burned through, and the wind off the ocean coming from just the perfect direction, allowed the smell of the ocean to permeate across the twenty-mile distance between the coast and the prison yard. The halogens–iodine and bromine–were pungent when the wind was blowing just right. And the smell of decaying vegetation, seaweed and sea life, came faint but clear across the intervening distance to the coast. It was the smell of the sea. A smell that, years before, Gar thought, smelled just like shrimp taste. At Sheridan, this only happened perhaps once a year, and it was always the harbinger of something good.

MIDMORNING THE DOOR control officer at the furniture factory called Gar's name over the PA. He told Gar to log off his computer and get his jacket, because there was something going on back in the unit.

"Don't worry, though. It doesn't sound bad," the door officer said. "I think your lawyer's on the phone. They want you for a legal call."

"I've been waiting for an answer to my appeal. Maybe it's finally decided. Thank you," Gar said, barely containing his excitement.

BACK IN THE unit, Gar's counselor told him, "Your lawyer and your judge are waiting for you. Sit down here and we'll call them back." Counselor Perona was mysteriously smiling. He was a naturally friendly guy anyway, but today he had an exceptionally wide grin.

Hmmm, Gar thought. What the hell?

"MISTER WALTON, THIS is Judge Bryan. We're here at my table in my law library. We have you here by speakerphone. Also present is the lawyer this court has appointed to represent you for this hearing, Russell Leonard, and representing the government for this hearing at my request is Assistant U. S. Attorney Helen Brunner. Do you hear me all right?"

"Yes, loud and clear. Good morning to everybody."

Mumbled good mornings could be heard over the telephone speaker on Gar's end.

"Now, Mr. Walton, I need to ask you a couple of questions. The Ninth Circuit has recalled the mandate in your case. They've sent it back to me for me to consider your sentence in light of the Supreme Court's holding in *Booker* versus the United States. The first thing I need to ask you is, do you understand that I could increase your sentence?"

"Yes, I understand that your honor." Gar was very excited. They had recalled the mandate! Judge Bryan now had the power to sentence Gar to a constitutional and hopefully lower sentence. After more than ten years of standing in endless lines, of regularly wearing ear plugs to dull the constant noise, of practically living in the law library researching and writing brief after brief. Ten years of hiding from clocks. Ten years of slowly dying hope. This couldn't be real.

An old adage briefly and inexplicably flashed into Gar's mind. It was that judges are like parents. You have to give them good reason to do what you want. But it was too late for that now. All the reasons had been given. He just hoped that the reasons he had given would be good enough.

"On the other end of the spectrum" the judge continued, "if you were released tomorrow, do you have a place to go? A family member you could go live with? Someone who can help you get a job?"

"Yes, I certainly do. During the pendency of this appeal I've discussed this possibility, at length, with my family. We decided that while I have several options, I should go stay with my mother, Annabel Alongi, in the Sacramento area." Gar was so excited his voice was cracking a bit.

"Yes, I thought you had that covered, Mr. Walton. I've received quite a bit of correspondence from your family and friends. You have an admirable and substantial support group. I believe, based on their correspondence, also my conversation with your counselor at the prison, Mr. Perona, that you're a hard worker and an honest man. I still remember, and want to reference for the record, several letters you wrote to me in which you apologize for the trouble you've caused the court, and for the drugs you've helped to put on the streets of the country. I believe your apology to be heartfelt and genuine. I also appreciate your advice on salmon fishing. And I'll have you know I took it to heart and it helped me." He stopped for a moment.

Gar waited.

No one said anything.

"Okay then. I've been accused of sometimes being long-winded. My clerk, Jean tells me that. I guess I should read the transcripts of my hearings and see for myself if they're right. Are you ready, then, Mr. Walton, for me to revise your sentence in light of *Booker*? Knowing I may give you a longer sentence than I originally imposed?"

"Yes, I am," Gar said simply. It was all he could manage.

"I'm sentencing you, Mr. Walton, to one hundred months in custody, followed by three years of supervised release." The judge paused as though for effect, and Gar took it as an invitation to speak.

"But I've already served more than a hundred...."

"Just wait," the judge said. He was clearly tickled with himself. "Now your attorney has submitted a motion for early termination of supervised release." Another dramatic pause.

Gar was close to bursting. He didn't entirely comprehend all of this.

"Mr. Walton, as I said, I am sentencing you to one-hundred months in custody with thirty-six months of mandatory supervised release. The Bureau of Prisons has informed me you are entitled to about fourteen months good time credit. It's not exactly that, but close enough. Thus, your time in custody, on a hundred-month sentence, would actually be eighty-six months. Plus thirty-six months of mandatory supervised release, which makes a total of one hundred and twenty-two months. As of this moment, you have served one hundred and twenty-one months. I am granting your motion to terminate supervised release one month early. In other words, you have actually done your supervised release while in custody. Not the first time that's happened. Your counselor tells me the prison can have your release papers, and bus ticket, ready by tomorrow morning. Therefore, sentence passed, you can go home tomorrow morning."

Gratified and teary-eyed, Gar choked out, "Thank you, your honor."

"You won't have," the judge continued, "any probation to contend with. Do you think you can manage without a probation officer?"

"Oh, yes, sir. That won't be a problem. I can't wait to go to work out in the real world. There's a million things I want to do."

"I trust smuggling drugs is not one of them?" The judge showed his best paternal manner.

"No sir. This experience has retired me from that profession. I'm done." Gar's answer was clear cut and emphatic. It left no room for doubt.

"Very well. You can put this behind you and go take care of your mother and your children. It sounds like they could use your help. You can go salmon fishin', too, Mr. Walton. And I wish you luck. As a matter of fact, I sincerely hope I see you, one day, on the fishing grounds. We'll work out a code." This was living proof that the judge was a *bona fide* salmon fisherman. Salmon fishermen speak in cryptic codes on the radio. All of them.

"If you're as prolific a fisherman as you are a *writ* writer," the judge continued, "I want to know you." Judge Bryan sounded happy.

Gar spoke very animated now. "If I call you on the radio and mention *audita querela*, you better steer my direction. If I say, *recall the mandate*, you better stack your lines on the boat and come runnin' full steam ahead." Gar was giddy beyond any time in the last decade. This was almost as good as those days on which his three kids had been born.

The clock was nice to him again. Enough time had apparently passed. The clock was his friend. One of the first things Gar vowed to do upon his release in the morning was to buy a watch.

THE NEXT MORNING Gar was up well before dawn. He had his photo album and address book in a mesh bag slung over one shoulder; after all these years, this was all he needed to take home. Dressed in grey sweats and tennis shoes, he walked one last time up the sidewalk that led to the door, the one door that he'd come in, but never walked back through. The red door. It was painted red because it was out-of-bounds unless you were called to pack your stuff to go home.

Gar, strong and virile from years of exercise and clean living, shook firm hands with a group of friends that were waiting in front of the law library. They were as excited as he was, and hugs were generous.

"Don't look back," Randy Wynn warned.

"I know, Randy Wynn, I won't," Gar said, then spun away to walk the last fifty yards.

He was just a few steps from the door, and someone behind started clapping, then another, then there was chorus of clapping that grew with each second. It was more than the group of friends, and became so loud it was impossible to tell how many men were behind him applauding...then whistling.

Gar pulled open the door, focusing hard ahead, fighting the urge to look back.

As the door was swinging closed, above the roar, Gar heard the unmistakable tone of his personal trainer and good friend, Randy Wynn, say: "We love you Gar Walton. You fuckin' did the impossible. You give everyone hope..."

The door swung closed, the bolt clicked hard in its slot; Gar was officially on the way out, locked out of the prison now.

But the bellowing and clapping could still be heard.

CHAPTER 78

DECEMBER, 2006.

"GAR-A-LONE-IIEEE, IIIIITTTSSS SUUUSSSAN," Mom called out in a sing-song voice. She could be so funny. Seventy-six years old: Mom still likes her tight jeans, and swimming every day in her bikini. She believes in having merry fun, but while still working hard. A forever-young kind of fun, like teasing Gar because there was a girl on the phone. It was entertaining staying with her in her Sacramento home, especially when the weather kept him on shore.

"Okay. I've got it in my bedroom."

"YOU'VE GOT TO come down here. And I mean right now, or tomorrow at the latest." Susan was animated, more dramatic than she usually was. She was calling from her office in Santa Cruz.

"What's up? Do you miss me?" This was an out-of-character telephone call. Gar had met with Susan exactly twice since coming home from his ten-year sabbatical. But everything had been very platonic. They simply hugged "Hello" and "Goodbye", and enjoyed a pleasant lunch-time conversation.

"No. Well, okay, I missed you. But that's not why I called. I have a customer for you. He has two Italian-style seafood restaurants and he's opening a brand new restaurant down on the wharf that will include a seafood stand. He'll have a steaming crab cooker going out front. He says he will pay you three dollars a pound for all the crab you can deliver. More later, as the price goes up." She paused for a second. "And you know him. Or, at least, he knows you."

"Three dollars a pound?" Gar considered this for a moment. He considered a lot of things very quickly. The crabbing season was going very well. He was getting two dollars a pound at the dock in Crescent City, running 400 pots. And he needed every dime he could lay his hands on. Storming winds were blowing all week in Crescent City, so he'd come to Mom's house in Sacramento. He had crab live-tanked on the boat. He could run up and get the crab he had in the tank, run the load down to Santa Cruz. He'd been pumping fresh seawater into the live tank for days, hoping to get a better price because of the storm.

"How much crab?" He blurted into the telephone, mind computing. "And is it a one-time deal, or will he buy through the season?"

"Yes. That's the thing, he said he was sure he could buy at least 4,000 pounds a week." Susan said excitedly. "You have to talk to him. His name is Leo. He's Rudy's nephew. Remember Rudy Rossi? The artichoke farm, and his ranch, and Bootlegger's Cove...."

"Of course. How could I forget my godfather? Four thousand pounds a <u>week</u>?" Gar shouted into the telephone, his mind really whirling now. Good Lord! that was a hefty boat payment, and then some. Mom had mortgaged everything to come up with the $330,000 needed to buy the ***Annabel Lee***. All he could think about these days was making money and paying that loan down. Now he began to get excited. Rudy Rossi's nephew? Imagine that!

"I can make the trip up to the boat, then back down there, in about eighteen hours, if I hurry. I will drive all night. I just need to make sure Mom's okay, and put a few things in an overnight bag, my toothbrush at least. I hope I don't need fancy clothes. I haven't stocked my wardrobe yet." Gar was picking up Susan's excitement. He was babbling.

"Come as soon as you can. Go straight to the old *Dream Inn*, you know where that is I'm sure—you took me there one time.... There will be a room reserved there, in your name, for tomorrow and the next day. Leo's paying for everything because he asked you to come down. He will meet you on the wharf with your load of crab. I'll call him and tell him what to expect. How much are you bringing?" She was so serious. It was almost like his drug smuggling days. Some of the guys he knew could be so clandestine, saying everything in a life-and-death manner and always in a whisper. Like she was doing now.

"I'll bring him 4,000 pounds. That's almost exactly what I have on the boat. Will I see you there?"

"No. I have to be at work, and I don't know when you'll get there, or I would go with you. But I'll tell him to expect you late tomorrow morning. Call <u>me</u> when you get to town. Okay, Garaloney?" She was acting strange.

"Okay. Is that it?"

"Love you, bye." She rang off.

"Love you too. And thanks, I think," he squeezed in before she hung up.

GAR MADE THE drive up to Crescent City to pick up the crab. Ruminating all the way about the serendipities of his new life: No longer waiting in lines; not having to live in a tiny cell–essentially a bathroom–with another (and usually strange) man; going to bed at will; having a remote control and TV all to himself; no more high-drama with all the young gangsters trying to play tough; no longer having someone half his age constantly telling him to tuck his shirt in.

He reflected on the day, just a few months ago, he walked out the prison door, head and eyes rigidly forward, not wanting to break the superstition of "Don't look back." As he walked across the parking lot and up the street to the 7-11, where he had a Western Union MoneyGram waiting, the first thing he noticed was how quiet it was. No more yelling and hollering and whistling, domino slamming, nor PA announcements of who needs to do what–and where. It was silent, and when Gar mumbled this to himself, the cars on the street slipping almost silently by, he realized that much of the noise that had disappeared was the din inside his head. He found peace walking up that street. A bird chirped nearby and another answered. The Oregon sky was overcast, but bright and promising. There were geese migrating south, a cacophony of scattered and earnest tootles. Maybe the people in those cars going by knew his feelings, saw the serene countenance, the watery eyes. Or perhaps they were too involved with tribulations. But Gar, as he walked, was not a part of any of it anymore, he was no longer a number, or grouped by his color, age or politics, he was a free soul, with the power to make autonomous decisions, walking forward with vivid prospects. He was a bud coming abloom, or more probably a planted acorn taking root, soon to become a grand oak.

In the front seat of his truck, Gar began to weep: "I'm free, and I'm driving up this highway to pick up crab, my crab that I caught on my boat. Going to load that crab and take it to sell. And I might be going to see Susan." With a shirtsleeve, Gar wiped tears from his eyes, sniffed hard, and spoke softly, eyes looking cautiously to the sky: "Thank you Lord. I'm an undeserving soul, I know, but thank you for this chance. I swear to you I'll do well!" He slammed one balled fist on the dashboard, fed the truck more throttle, and drove on in his ever-dogged resolve.

DRIVING THE CRAB back to the south, Gar missed most of the major Bay Area traffic because he went through after the morning rush hour. He got to Santa Cruz at noon and checked into the motel. He was on the phone to the number Susan had given him right away.

"My name is Gar Walton. Susan..."

"Gar Walton, Mr. Farallon, I am Leo Rossi. I am glad you called. I am the great nephew of Rudy Rossi. I met you years ago, with my father, Vince Rossi, and Rudy. You probably don't remember me. I was only around 12 or 13 years old." He actually sounded a little bit like Rudy. He used the same endearing, formal tone Rudy had used when speaking with Gar so many years ago.

Gar told him that. "You sound a lot like your Uncle Rudy. I don't know what to say. This is like having an incarnation of my Godfather right here on the phone. I sure have missed my old friend, over the years. He was a great man. I'm, I, I can't believe it. Susan called and told me to come down...." He found himself at a loss for words. "She said you wanted to buy some crab."

"Yes. Indeed, I do. Bring them right out here so we can take care of them. I know they've been out of the water for eight or nine hours, so let's get them into my chiller." Leo had a smooth, typically Italian way of speaking.

"Okay, I'll be right out. See you in a few minutes."

LEO WAS DEFINITELY an incarnation of his great uncle; albeit a fancier version. He met Gar at the door of a large new restaurant situated prominently on the wharf in Santa Cruz. He'd obviously seen a picture Susan had, or maybe Gar had changed less than he thought, but the man recognized him. Leo looked like a cross between Michael Corleone and the Don's hired killer, Luca Brazzi. He was tall and heavy. His girth was equal to that of Rudy. He was dressed expensively–charcoal slacks, pullover burgundy cardigan, and tasseled *Gucci* loafers. He was a presence. An enormous man, dressed to the nines. He looked fresh as a daisy though he'd been up since daybreak. He had a head as big as a water buffalo.

"Garaloney," he boomed, shaking Gar's hand. He had obviously been talking to Susan.

He led Gar inside to a quiet corner looking out at the Santa Cruz Lighthouse and *Steamer's Lane*, where all the kids surf. The restaurant was all but deserted at this hour. It didn't open until dinner time. Two burly seafarer-dressed waiters, beckoned by Leo, disappeared out the door and began unloading the crab.

"MY FATHER TOOK me to see Uncle Rudy, sometimes," Leo began, his look melancholy, eyes watery. "It was never often enough. It was only as a reward, when I'd done well in school. It was a special treat, to go to Rudy's ranch for lunch. Sometimes, we had seafood, which Rudy cooked for us in his cookhouse kitchen. I loved watching him cook, and I'm sure that is why I went into this business."

"Yeah, I loved eating there with Rudy." Gar felt nostalgic as the memory of the man flooded back. The memory, really, of where it had all began.

"So one day," Leo continued. "My father asks Uncle Rudy, he says, 'Hey Uncle, how the hell you get such fresh seafood way the hell out here in the middle of nowhere? I know you don't catch it yourself. What is going on?' And Rudy, he says, 'It's real easy. I got Mr. Farallon. He brings it to me. He goes out into the deep sea by the Farallon Islands and brings me nothin' but the best of the best.' He told us who you were," Leo's eyes narrowed at Gar, "and I'll tell you, he loved you. He loved you like a son."

"Yeah, I used to bring him stuff every chance I got. I loved him like he was my own father, or Godfather, I'd call him sometimes."

"Yeah, he loved you too, I'll tell you. He'd go on and on about you. But, anyway, one day we had lunch–I don't remember what–it wasn't fish. And we were disappointed. But then we decided to go up to the Beach House; what the hell, it's only a couple of miles from the Cascade up there. We wanted to go up there so Dad and Rudy could have a couple Coffee Royals. And there you were. You were stacking mountains of fresh-cooked crab legs all down the bar. I don't know, it looked like you'd cooked up a million pounds to me. I was still pretty young. You told everyone to throw the shells on the floor. That's how you wanted it, like they were peanut shells. And I have never forgotten that." He paused for a moment, as though considering, and then emphatically added, "Never!"

"Really? Yes, I remember that. And I remember your father, and you too. Vince was your dad's name, right?"

"That's right."

"Yeah. I was thinking about the old Peanut Farm, a bar over in Woodside where we used to go drink, way before we were twenty-one, back when I was a kid. They threw the peanut shells on the floor." Gar smiled at the memory.

"So I figured we could do them one better and do the same with crab shells."

"And something else I remember about that day," Leo looked Gar in the eye. "You talked to me like a man. When Rudy introduced Dad and me, you shook my hand and paid as much attention to me as you did my Dad. You were like a God to me for that. And you told me that you could tell by my handshake, by my looks, that I'd go far one day. I never forgot that.

"I remember you," Gar told him. "You were an impressive kid."

"So. You're fishing again, and now you're out." Leo's eyes narrowed and he leaned in close to Gar. "I hear you got a nice boat."

"Yeah. I got a nice debt, is what I got."

"Maybe I can help with that. Matter of fact, I would like nothing more in this life than to help out Mr. Farallon. From now on, we will get you top dollar for your seafood. And if you need something, more gear, crab pots or something, anything, you just ask. Uncle Rudy and me are at your service."

SO IT WAS with these pleasing words still echoing faintly in Gar's ears, and a check for $12,000 in his pocket, that Gar found himself waiting for Susan on the open tailgate of his now empty truck.

The sun was going down into the sea, a great red ball, and gulls cried overhead on the deserted end of the wharf. Susan stepped around the tailgate and silently gave Gar a hug. She peeled a Coors Light from the plastic of a six-pack and sat companionably beside him. She had changed out of her dressy work clothes. She was the same blue-jeaned girl she had always been to Gar.

"So you gotta get back, huh?" she asked him.

"Yeah," he replied, his eyes drawn to the sinking ball of the sun. It was about to enter the water on the far horizon.

"Sold your crab?"

"Yep. Truck's empty, as you can see."

"Isn't Leo great?"

"Yeah. He's a nice guy. I'll probably be able to see you every week, long as the season's running and he's buying."

"What about Vickie?"

"What about her?"

"Have you seen her since you got out?"

"Naw. I've been too busy. I called her a couple of times."

"And?"

"She wants me to come down there. To Playa del Carmen." Gar laughed, thinking about it. "I think she wants to open another roller skating rink." Gar laughed again, his voice pealing into the evening air. It wasn't such a bad thought. A roller rink, and laughing kids, and snow-cones. Legitimately this time.

"Are you going to go?" Susan didn't laugh. She kept her eyes on the red sun, half-eaten now by the sea, and sipped from her can of beer.

"Yeah, I am," he admitted. "For a week, to see where we stand. I've got to pay Mom back for the boat though. As soon as the crabbing season's done, the salmon season starts. You know that."

"Yes."

"And then there's albacore. I don't know how I can commute to Mexico though..." Gar let his voice trail away. The sun was almost gone. They both watched it sink out of sight.

"But I wouldn't mind opening a roller rink for kids again. Maybe I can do both. But the fishing comes first."

The lighthouse on the point suddenly became visible with the absence of the sun, flashing its silent message into the gathering gloom, and Gar and Susan's eyes were drawn there as though mesmerized. A lone pelican stood forlornly on a piling just next to them on the wharf. And the cries of the gulls grew fainter as they found their nearby roosts.

Susan tossed her empty beer can into the bed of the truck and pulled another one from the plastic. Gar tossed his empty and grabbed another one too.

"I heard Cindy is still single all these years later," Susan said out of the blue, perhaps a tinge of jealousy in her tone. And she spoke rather loudly in the darkening gloom. "She's an old maid now, and she lives on Prozac."

Gar laughed at this unexpected pronouncement, spraying beer from his mouth and nose, and coughing as he attempted to control his mirth.

"And Marilyn's on her seventh husband," Susan declared. "At least that's what I heard. Maybe it's ten, though! She was always so secretive and sneaky."

Gar completely lost it at this point, falling to his back in the pickup bed, and kicking his legs in the air. He laughed until tears flowed from his eyes. The beer spilled all over the place.

Susan joined in, and by the time they were through laughing, the sun was completely gone and they found each other in one another's arms. Susan looked into Gar's eyes, and he looked into hers, and they sobered at the proximity and what each of them saw there.

"Gar," she said, holding him a few inches away so she could look at him. She saw the flash of the Santa Cruz Lighthouse reflected in his eyes, and felt the surge of the sea in his arms, and she became mute. She knew what she wanted to say, about missed chances, and starting again, and the years passing too quickly now, yet she couldn't utter a word. There were a million things to say. But they were things that couldn't be said.

"I know," he whispered quietly to her, as though she had spoken all of her thoughts aloud. "You don't have to say a thing. I know."

"You come see me," she said. "Every week. And we'll have a beer. Or maybe coffee next time. You know I can't drink.

"Yeah, me either. And I'll try."

"Every week. I need to know the sea hasn't gotten you." She was whispering too. But it was as though he was very far away from her and couldn't hear her any more. He was listening intently to the soft suspiration of the surf. And the occasional strobe of the lighthouse beacon showed a strangely distant look in his eyes.

CHAPTER 79

SALMON SEASON, 2007.

GAR WAS FISHING at his favorite opening-day-of-the-season spot, the old "Pa's Canyon," just south of the main Farallon Island. The crabbing season had been good and he had paid off nearly half the note on the ***Annabel Lee***. Leo helped a lot. He could have had a cheaper boat, or a used one, but Mom had insisted that he get what he wanted. And a spanking new sixty-one foot nine-inch *Edmund Monk* design was the best of the best.

He had enjoyed a brief, surprising radio communication from Angus, his old nemesis, who had called over the Mouse and welcomed him back. For a moment he was too surprised to respond. Goose had actually sounded sincere. When Gar had finally answered, concluding a conversation that was probably a little stilted and assuredly too brief, he nonetheless felt grateful. Old Goose. Still out here fishing. Gar felt strangely good about it, buoyed with a new-found sense of optimism and belonging.

The breeze freshened out of the west and Gar went to join Jasmer on the back deck. This was the best part of all. His son was a sturdy, likely lad, and the ***Annabel Lee*** was eventually going to be his boat. With a little luck, it could be paid off in two more seasons. Gar watched his son from his side of the stern trolling pit.

As the downrigger wound the thin trolling wire up, Jasmer leaned over the side, anticipating the first leader. The wire was pumping wildly with a fish. They were in 'em.

As the leader broke the water's calm surface, and he could see a nice sized salmon at the other end, Jasmer began to sing in perfect iambic pentameter (five beats to the line), to a tune sort of like *Someone's in the Kitchen with Dinah*:

"I like salmon fishin'
(boom, boom, boom)
Salmon fishin's alright
And I like Salmon Fishin'
Cause the beach is in sight."

Gar smiled. He had crooned this same song into his son's glowing face when Jas was only three weeks old. Now it was being sung back to him. He had come full circle. He was back on the ocean where he belonged and the replacement generation he had sired was right there with him in the stern; catching salmon.

The sun beamed down, gulls wheeled overhead, and Gar steered a course just parallel to the green and brown tidal rip streaming past his port bow. He was into the customary flotsam of the rip almost before his son sang out to take a look.

THE ***ANNABEL LEE*** was the only boat fishing Pa's Canyon, the only boat in sight, and here, bobbing merrily down the rip, came ten small bales. Sea weed maybe, or more likely cocaine. All well wrapped in neoprene and riding securely in the water, and each of them floating in an evenly-spaced row, as though plunked down by fate.

Gar eyed the bales with astonishment, thinking immediately and involuntarily that the hold was virtually empty, and that the ten packages would pay off the boat. Completely. Free and clear. Just these ten, and they were not very big. Maybe a couple of kilos each. And here they were floating fortuitously into his path.

Jasmer's voice came to him, breaking his astonished reverie. The boy had seen them and knew exactly what they were.

"DAD?" he exclaimed...

EPILOGUE

EPILOGUE

KARACHI, PAKISTAN.

BUBBA WAS AN old hand at this now. He eyed the Australian-skippered tug in the harbor, a vessel only Liberian registration officials knew that Bubba owned, and he crumbled some of the black hashish between his fingers. He raised the stuff to his nose for a sniff. It was good. It was the best in the world.

Hash, man. Operation Rehash, and it was time to roll with it again. Bubba flicked the sticky, crumbling stuff off his fingers and shouted to the attentive officials standing quayside.

"Load the shit up," he said. "Same terms as last time."

The sun beat down on the Karachi docks and the redolent and pungent odor of hashish filled the morning air. Emerald-green and white clad Pakistani navy men began loading muslin-wrapped bricks into bobbing lighters for transport out to the ocean-going tug in the harbor.

It was business as usual. Bubba flipped a cell phone from a tunic pocket and pressed speed dial. Seconds later a telephone rang on a desk in Langley, Virginia. The connection was made but no human voice answered.

"It's on its way," Bubba said simply, then snapped his phone shut.

His part was done.

The author, a Salmon Fisherman.

Made in the USA